Bruce E

CW00822577

Murder on the Moor

Detective Inspector Skelgill
Investigates

LUCiUS

1

Text copyright 2020 Bruce Beckham

Kindle edition first published by Lucius 2020

Paperback edition first published by Lucius 2020

For more details and Rights enquiries contact:
Lucius-ebooks@live.com

Cover design by Moira Kay Nicol
United States editor Janet Colter

EDITOR'S NOTE

Murder on the Moor is a stand-alone crime mystery, the fifteenth in the series 'Detective Inspector Skelgill Investigates'. It is set in the vicinity of Over Water, a peaceful corner of the English Lake District – a National Park of 885 square miles that lies in the rugged northern county of Cumbria.

THE DI SKELGILL SERIES

Murder in Adland
Murder in School
Murder on the Edge
Murder on the Lake
Murder by Magic
Murder in the Mind
Murder at the Wake
Murder in the Woods
Murder at the Flood
Murder at Dead Crags
Murder Mystery Weekend
Murder on the Run
Murder at Shake Holes
Murder at the Meet
Murder on the Moor
Murder Unseen
Murder in our Midst

Glossary

Some of the Cumbrian dialect words, British slang and local usage appearing in *Murder on the Moor* are as follows:

Alreet – all right (often a greeting)
Arl – old
Bait – packed lunch/sandwiches
Beck – mountain stream
Birl – spin (Scots)
Bob Graham (the) – a fell-running challenge
Butcher's – look ('butcher's hook' – Cockney)
Caw canny – take care, be wary (Scots)
Chin music – bouncers aimed at the batter's head (cricket)
Crack – chat, gossip
Cuddy wifter – left-handed
Cushat – woodpigeon
Daein' – doing (Scots)
Dander – temper
Deek – look/look at
Do one – go away (London)
Donnat – idiot
Early doors – early on
Gadgee – bloke
Gannin' yam – going home
Grouse butt – stone shelter for game shooter
Guddle – fish with the hands in shallow water
Happen – maybe, looks like
Hissen – himself
Howay – come on
In-bye – walled pasture near the farmstead
Int' – in the
Jam eater – nickname for urban resident of West Cumbria
Kaylied – inebriated
Ken – know
Kent – knew
Lug – ear

Marra – mate (friend)
Mash – brew tea
Mere – lake (Old English)
Midden – waste heap
Mither – bother
Mind – remember
Misper – missing person (police slang)
Napper – head
Nail – rattletrap of a car
Nowt – nothing
Off've – from
Ont' – on the
Oor – our
Ower – over
Owt – anything
Pattie – deep-fried mashed potato mixed with, for example, fish or cheese
Pereth – Penrith
Policy woodland/policies – plantations around a stately home
Porch – small shelter around external door, sometimes open-sided
Reet – right
Reiver – rustler of livestock
RSPB – Royal Society for the Protection of Birds
Scop – throw
Sledging – offensive taunts (cricket)
Sneck – lock fastener
Tarn – small mountain lake, usually in a corrie
T' – the (often silent)
Tek – take
Thee/thou – you
Theesen – yourself
Twa birds wi' oan stane – two birds with one stone
Twat – to hit
Us – me
Virga gloriam – shoot for glory (Latin)
Water – lake (Old Norse)

While – until
Wyke – inlet where a boat may be landed
Yon – that/those
Yonks – ages

PREFACE

A wing and a prayer

There can be few birds that have been the subject of a whodunit – a national hue and cry, no less – but *Circus cyaneus*, or hen harrier by its common name, hit the headlines in 2007 when a pair of these elegant raptors were blasted out of the Norfolk sky, watched in horror by a Natural England warden and other reliable observers. And there was a twist in the tale, for the nature reserve adjoined the royal estate of Sandringham. Shooting together that day were Prince Harry, a friend, and a gamekeeper.

The warden notified the police; there ensued an investigation. No feathered bodies were recovered. No witnesses came forward. Nobody knew anything.

The Guardian newspaper succinctly reported:

"Two hen harriers dead, one prince questioned, no charges."

Why the hullaballoo? It is not as if Britain is unaccustomed to losing its wildlife: there are 44 million fewer birds since 1966, according to the RSPB. But certain endangered species are 'red-listed' – and the hen harrier is so classified. It clings by the tips of its talons to a precipice marked "extinction". Under the watchful eyes of conservation organisations and their dedicated volunteers, only fifteen pairs breed in the whole of England.

PROLOGUE

The Lakes

"There's only *one* lake in the Lake District." That Skelgill relentlessly trots out this aphorism is a source of discomfort to his long-suffering colleagues, obliged to stand and simper until the punch line is delivered. A more fair-minded inflection would be that there is only one *lake* in the Lake District, since the solution to the conundrum is that, with a single exception, the main freshwater bodies, the glacial ribbon lakes that endow this rugged part of England with its unique character are called either 'mere' or 'water'. Thus Windermere, for example – and here another opportunity for pedantry, when the innocent visitor refers to "Lake Windermere" and Skelgill hoots that this is akin to saying "Lake Winder Lake".

The one and only lake is Bassenthwaite Lake, "Bass Lake" in Skelgill's parlance, lying in the north of the National Park and, though bordered by the busy A66 trunk road, largely inaccessible and accordingly his favoured haunt. To nose his rowing boat out from the secluded harbour of Peel Wyke offers an escape into solitude with which even the surrounding fells cannot compete. And there are big pike to be hunted.

But there is another pool that has long intrigued him, just three miles to the northeast, no larger than a mountain tarn and probably the least frequently visited of all those in the county. That is Over Water. Designated a Site of Special Scientific Interest, it is protected by law. It is not only a wildlife haven, but also an oasis in more than appearance, being entirely surrounded by the great sporting estate of Shuteham Hall.

Knowledge of the flora and fauna of Over Water is incomplete. Moreover, following the recent discovery in

10

Bassenthwaite Lake of a rare species called the vendace – a kind of freshwater herring – the conservation authorities have become alert to the possibility of its presence in Over Water; that would be a further and powerful reason to justify the continued legal status of the site. But the vendace is a fish of peculiar habits, and foremost among them is its elusiveness. To winkle a specimen out of its water world of waving weed would require an angler of considerable prowess and exceptional local knowledge.

1. OVER WATER

"Happen it's a red herring."
So went Skelgill's disavowal upon being assailed by fellow officer (and angler), George Appleby, whom word of Skelgill's quest had reached. The desk sergeant had shared his scepticism. The appearance of the vendace in Bassenthwaite Lake could be explained by migration via the River Derwent, from its last known surviving population in Derwentwater. But Over Water has no such tributary; an entirely separate watershed feeds it.

"Fish might fly," had been George's contribution, an equally apposite reworking of the well-known proverb.

Skelgill at this juncture had excused himself on the grounds that a silhouette resembling their superior officer had appeared at the far end of the corridor.

"Let us know what they taste like, lad!"

The departing Skelgill had raised a hand – and unseen his eyebrows, for such an experiment would not be something to which he could ever admit. Though, truth be told, it is intriguing, if not exactly mouth-watering; for so dedicated an angler, he eats precious little fish. Recalling this aspect of the conversation, he is reminded of the Cumberland sausages stowed with the cooking contraptions in the bow of his boat.

But it is too early yet. First he must pay more than lip service to his commission. There is his reputation to think about. Though this gilded invitation to fish Over Water is attributable in part to his connections, there is some obligation to deliver the goods. The holder of a string of local records, he is also one of a select coterie of anglers actually to have caught a vendace; apparently he knows what to do.

As befits his outwardly restless nature much of Skelgill's fishing is of the active type: fly fishing for trout involves continual casting and movement around the lake in pursuit of the feeding shoal; plugging for pike entails long energy-sapping retrieves, jiggling and jerking the lure to imitate a wounded minnow. The vendace, however, is not fooled by such methods, and Skelgill has resorted to float fishing with maggots. Other than occasionally refreshing the bait, therefore, first warming up the wrigglers in his mouth, it is a sedentary occupation, his boat at anchor, his body relaxed, his gaze transfixed by the fluorescent orange quill that stands proud from the taut mercury-like meniscus of the still water.

It is a glorious May morning, the sky a crystal dome of cyan. As the rising sun breaches the ridge at his back, pouring its first rays down the brindled fell, the mist on the water glows golden, as if ignited prior to dispersal. Also illuminated is the fresh spring green foliage of Bullmire Wood, the extensive policy woodland that cloaks the western shore. Resonant in the charged air a dozen species of songsters combine in delicious harmony, their dawn chorus punctuated by the irregular *kirruk* of a moorhen, its jarring intervention a rebellious triangle to the greater orchestral manoeuvre.

A zephyr, conjured by the sudden warmth causes Skelgill's boat gently to rotate. As yet he has needed neither hat nor sunglasses, and he is forced to squint as he is turned to face the east; it is a contrasting landscape, though its detail hard to discern through the slanting sunbeams, a palette of browns; the lake is fringed by reed bed, extending first into fen and then rising moorland, a great wild expanse of heather and bilberry, *bleaberry* in the local vernacular. The immediate fell is Great Cockup, an outrider of the immense Skiddaw massif; Cumbria's last wilderness before the landscape sinks northwards as farmland and merges into the Solway marshes. In the foreground, half-hidden at the edge of the reeds is a wooden hide, of the sort frequented by birdwatchers, a basic shed with horizontal window-slits for all-round observation; unobtrusive, it is reached by a shielded pontoon.

The wind genie was transient, but Skelgill's craft has sufficient momentum to bring him full circle. The sun again at his back, his eye is drawn by the glint of a buzzard that lifts off from Bullmire Wood, picking up the day's first thermal, an effortless spiral; an invisible staircase to heaven. The bird begins to mew, a plaintive entreaty; there is a reply, but perhaps its mate is on duty on a nest somewhere in the canopy. Skelgill might be hypnotised, for all the movement he makes.

Then a gunshot rings out. A twelve-bore, from within the wood. Still Skelgill does not flinch. There is nothing unusual about that; the sound of a shotgun on a Sunday morning is as familiar as the peal of church bells. True, it is not the game season but this is probably a keeper, licensed to shoot crows that predate pheasant chicks, and woodpigeons that scavenge the grain put down for them. Though foliage muffled the report, its origin was close; the reverberation was almost instantaneous.

Meanwhile the buzzard has entered into a slow descent, rather disjointedly – Skelgill waits for it to organise itself, to tuck in its wings and plummet like a peregrine upon some unsuspecting prey, or perhaps just to impress its partner. But it does not. The wings trail loosely above the body. The bird has shed its natural buoyancy. It falls in a series of untidy curves, like an autumn leaf, or a butterfly stunned by a passing car. Silently, it sinks into the canopy.

Transitioning from musing to consciousness, Skelgill's mind conflates the sight with the sound of a few seconds earlier. *The bird has been shot.*

He stares grimly at the empty sky. The buzzard is a protected species. Before his very eyes, a wildlife crime has just been committed.

And now, Sod's law kicks in; his float begins to twitch. It is his first bite since he began fishing an hour and a half ago.

Peremptorily, he lifts his rod and reels in. Glaring in the direction from which the gunshot emanated, hand over hand he hauls the anchor. Then he snatches up his oars, backs down, and pulls hard for the woodland shore.

14

It takes him under a minute, but that is the easy part. There is no gently shelving bottom on this side of the lake, only a vertical bank guarded by alders, their roots spilling out where erosion has depleted the soil. Skelgill ties the painter in a double half hitch and swings himself ashore by means of an overhanging branch. The ground is marshy, the vegetation a mixture of sedge and rush and stitchwort, and he curses as his left boot is topped by black peaty sludge. He could do with a staff to speed his progress; he casts about but nothing suitable comes to hand. He throws caution to the wind and ploughs on, driven by his anger and determination to right the injustice. The terrain begins to rise gently, becoming less boggy but affording thicker growth of the shrub layer. He comes up against impenetrable stands of blackthorn, and bristling coppiced hazel that oblige him to zigzag and even backtrack, and it is not long before he is losing the bearing that had imprinted itself upon his mental map. Only the occasional flicker of sunlight over his shoulder helps him to stay roughly on course.

Overhead, the mainly oak canopy is dense, almost entire; there are only occasional glimpses of blue. He doubts that anyone could have shot at a moving target unless they were standing in a glade. As he pushes on a magnificent coppery cock pheasant explodes from almost under his feet, shocking him with its violent *hiccup* and simultaneous whirr of wings. As if he needed reminding: the wood is a factory farm for pheasants, and somewhere nearby will be an enclosure, and possibly the clearing he seeks. He decides to trust that the bird's instinct is one of homing, and follows its line of flight.

Sure enough, before long the undergrowth abruptly thins out. Bushes have been systematically cleared, leaving only the trees, several of which have been felled. Skelgill sees a high fence of green mesh – it is a section of the perimeter of an open-top release pen. Fox wires run around at shin-height, and at intervals there are one-way pop holes inspired by the lobster fisherman's creel to allow stray birds to return to safety. Inside, much of the undergrowth is worn away and bare ground exposed. Pheasant poults will be transferred here in July or August, in time to acclimatise themselves for the start of the shooting season on 1st October.

Skelgill has moved as covertly as comes naturally – but against that was his desire for speed; complete silence has been impossible. He is breathing heavily, having taken no respite since rowing. Now he becomes conscious of the need for greater stealth. He is in the vicinity of somebody with a shotgun – and they won't know who or what is approaching.

It is ten minutes since the shot was fired.

But now comes a banging of another sort, a hammering, an ascending scale of notes about two seconds apart. He rounds a curve in the fence to see a man of about his own age – or maybe early thirties – about six feet, a strong frame, swinging a sledgehammer, shirtsleeves rolled up to reveal muscular forearms. Skelgill can see that he is building a simple frame designed to suspend a quill drinker – he is knocking in a round post – lying ready is a second and a cross member, and the triangular feeder itself. The man is unaware of his approach, but a black cocker spaniel has got wind of him, and trots up to the wire; it seems eager to get at him, but there is no immediate way through. For his part, Skelgill realises that he does not have a plan to deal with the opening of this encounter. Any second now, the interest of the dog will betray his presence. Before he knows it, he hails the man.

'Hey up!'

There are cordial nuances of "ahoy there" and "good morning" in his salutation – but it fails to elicit a commensurate reaction. Instead the man pivots aggressively, weighing the sledgehammer two-handed as if readying himself to take a sideways swipe – though Skelgill is a good ten feet away on the other side of the fence. The man freezes in his action pose, and Skelgill senses he is very quickly summing him up, in the way of what threat he poses.

Skelgill finds himself mulling over whether a convivial "Excuse me?" might have been more suitable (but he dismisses the idea as too submissive). On the other hand, "Oi!" would have been overstepping the mark, given the practical balance of power. Realistically, he cannot simply march up and deliver a bald accusation.

He is unacquainted with the landowner, but it strikes him that this man seems less like a gamekeeper than he would anticipate. His attire is of good quality, county-style moleskin breeches, a tattersall shirt and a tweed cap. He has short red hair, and a trimmed ginger beard on a strong jawline, and piercing blue eyes; there is something of the naval officer in his demeanour.

'Whit are ye daein'?'

The dialect, however, dispels the impression; it is Scots Borders, in Skelgill's estimation. He suspects the man has held back a more forthright version of his question.

'I heard a shot.'

The man glances involuntarily to his side. Three or four yards away a shotgun is propped against the stump of an ash; boasting an intricately engraved stock, to Skelgill's eye it is a pricey model. On top of the stump lies a hessian sack that looks decidedly lumpy.

Skelgill has a feeling of déjà vu – of confrontations played out many times in his youth; his standing role being that of the interloper. He has to remind himself he is a policeman. But then he also has to remind himself he is off duty, carries no ID – and is technically trespassing. The man replies tersely.

'This is a sporting estate.'

His answer is apparently a logical rebuttal of Skelgill's challenge. Although his tone is not particularly forgiving, there is again a hint of restraint in his words. It may be due to his inability to fathom Skelgill's status. But Skelgill too is battling with doubts. He is not blessed with the ability to conjure up quips off the cuff – unlike the silvery-tongued DI Smart, or even DS Leyton, with his self-deprecating one-liners. But his boyhood adventurism has at least equipped him with a stock of rehearsed excuses that he can call upon in such circumstances.

'You might have been injured.' He pauses before he adds a rider. 'There was just one shot – that's unusual.'

The man fleetingly looks tempted to say it was all he needed – but he forces a scowl, perhaps realising it would amount to an admission of sorts. And Skelgill's point is disarming – this somewhat dishevelled stranger could have been coming to his aid. As if it is listening in on the conversation, and satisfied with the explanation, the dog darts away at an angle and disappears into a clump of elders. The man watches it indifferently, before turning back and offering a somewhat grudging reply.

'We've had a problem wi' poachers lately.'

His response is curiously ambiguous; now he scrutinises Skelgill more carefully through the mesh of the release pen. Skelgill's own attire might just fit the bill – certainly he could not be mistaken for a walker who has wandered off course – he looks more like a commando separated from his unit – and the one item that would categorically identify him as an angler – a vest jangling with chrome instruments and colourful lures lies discarded in the boat. When Skelgill does not respond the man speaks again, more assertively now.

'There's nae right of way here.'

He seems to be saying that it would be reasonable to suspect Skelgill of being up to no good. It probably irks him that he has not already sent him packing. Skelgill is prompted to state his semi-official business.

'I'm surveying Over Water – on special licence from the Centre for Ecology and Hydrology.' Skelgill makes no show of producing any such licence, though he sounds convincing. 'I launched at the wyke beyond where the birdwatchers park.'

The man stares broodingly at Skelgill, though mention of the ornithologists elicits a hardening of his features. But it seems Skelgill's unflappable artlessness has held sufficient sway. Skelgill assumes the initiative.

'I'd better get back on the job. The fish I'm after don't feed readily once the sun's up.'

'Aye.'

The man relaxes his grip on the sledgehammer and rests it at his side. But he stands watching Skelgill as he casually raises a palm in lieu of an adieu. Skelgill glances at the spaniel, which is now back close to the wire, and makes a double-clicking sound with his tongue against the roof of his mouth. He turns and

takes a step away, but stoops to pick up something in his stride –
and continues, holding the item out of sight. He twists his head
over his shoulder, and calls back.

'Like I say – you might have shot yourself in the foot.'

Anyone knowing him would detect just a hint of triumph
creeping into his tone.

He heads for the sun and in half a minute is gone from sight
of the release pen. Beneath his own controlled façade his pulse
has not quietened. It was a tense exchange, crowded with hidden
inferences. He reproaches himself for his rashness – it was a
hopelessly risky mission. Yet though he was thwarted he has
collected some intelligence. Plainly the man is the only person
shooting this morning. He looks reflectively at the object he has
picked up. For the purposes of fishing he often salvages quills to
fashion into floats; the woods abound with cast-off pheasant
plumes. But he brushes across his cheek the broad, barred
feather; there is no mistaking the super-soft touch that affords a
bird of prey its silent approach.

2. CONSERVATION

'Cor, flippin' heck, Guvnor – there's a queer old couple at the desk asking for you by name – insisting on seeing you. They look like climate change protestors.' DS Leyton has entered his superior's office bearing a tray and three mugs. Skelgill seems more interested in the larger one, and his eyes track its progress to his desk. DS Leyton hands a second mug to the seated DS Jones, at whom he winks, and then settles in his regular spot in the chair beside Skelgill's filing cabinet; though grey in colour, it has properties more akin to a black hole.

'What do they want?'

'Something about a bird being shot.' DS Leyton makes a reproving cluck. 'Imagine – if everyone wanted to speak to a DI every time there was a bird shot round here, we'd never get a scrap of work done. All these trigger-happy farmers.'

Skelgill scowls over his steaming tea.

'It's not farmers that are trigger-happy, Leyton – it's toffs from your neck of the woods.'

This is rather disingenuous of Skelgill, and DS Leyton recognises it. He raises an admonishing index finger.

'You should see my neck of the woods one day, Guv. Shooting, yeah – I'll give you that – but not the sort you're thinking of.'

Skelgill shrugs indifferently; but his sergeant has fought his corner, he has to concede a draw.

'What species of bird?'

DS Leyton looks surprised – that his superior is apparently interested.

'What? I dunno. No – actually, the geezer said it was a buzzard, now you mention it. Is that an actual species – or is it just like sparrow or crow or seagull?'

DS Jones is nodding, as if she knows the answer, but Skelgill glares at DS Leyton.

'When was this?'

'Just now, Guv. Well – I mean, I don't know when it was shot.' He looks baffled and a little flustered. 'I told 'em to file a complaint with George, but they won't budge. They're probably supergluing themselves to the coffee machine as we speak.'

Skelgill rises and pushes back his chair. He glances cursorily at his two colleagues and then more studiously at his mug – which he picks up and carries away without further explanation.

In the reception area Skelgill has no difficulty in identifying the "queer old couple" to whom his sergeant has referred, although it being a Monday morning there is competition for queerness as the flotsam and jetsam washed up by the weekend's societal storms bring their accrued problems to the police. However, the pair evidently have retained faith in his coming, for they are watching keenly and, seeming to know it is he, rise as one upon his arrival. In their early fifties, Skelgill would guess, most striking is that they are unusually tall. As he approaches, Skelgill realises the woman must be his own height, and the man several inches taller. Smartly clad in matching olive-green waxed-cotton jackets, hiking trousers of the same cut but different hues of khaki, and walking boots unsullied by mud, they look like they have just kitted themselves out at one of the district's many outdoor gear shops.

The man reaches forward. It is not Skelgill's custom to shake hands in these circumstances – at this juncture he never knows which side of the law the person he is meeting might be on.

'Inspector Skelgill? We are the Vholes. Neil and Christine.'

It is an educated northern accent. They strike Skelgill as the sort who have retired early to the Lakes from somewhere in Yorkshire, having been regular weekenders for many years; it is quite a common type. He is obliged to shake hands with the

21

man, and the woman is queued up to do the same. She has their next line ready.

'Professor Hartley of Braithwaite said we should ask for you.'

There is a polite note of inquiry in her intonation. Perhaps now that they have him in their sights they have shed the belligerence reported by DS Leyton. Besides, if mention of the shot buzzard were not enough, the woman's name-dropping has achieved a critical mass. And he has no grounds at this moment to contest their claim of acquaintanceship.

'Ah – Jim.' He inhales to buy a second or two. 'How can I help?'

The couple look at one another meaningfully. And then they glance around as though disturbed by the presence of fellow complainants. The man, Neil Vholes, lowers his voice.

'We have some footage we would like to show to you.' He pats a leather satchel slung over his shoulder.

Skelgill hesitates. He glances across at DS George Appleby to see he is leering wryly. Skelgill indicates with jerk of the head that he will use one of the interview rooms. He leads them along a corridor via a plate-glass electronic security door released by the desk sergeant and into the first room on their right where there is a table and four plastic chairs. He gestures for them to be seated but does not wait. He has his tea still and takes a slurp. They look on a little longingly, but Skelgill does not appear to notice. He addresses Neil Vholes.

'You say you have a video, sir.'

The man was obviously waiting for the invitation. Now he begins fastidiously to unpack a laptop from his bag and fire it up. Skelgill notes that it is a pricey model, and the protective case is customised with a pixelated image that might be a murmuration of starlings. The woman is watching the procedure anxiously, as if in dread that some technological malfunction will thwart their mission. While he waits Skelgill contemplates the similarity that extends from their matching clothing to their physiognomy. Christine Vholes has straight shoulder-length brown hair with a fringe, and Neil Vholes an almost identical hairdo, merely cut shorter, to just below the ears. They also share the characteristics of a long head, prominent cheekbones, a narrow thin-lipped mouth, a rather pasty complexion and narrow set greyish blue eyes beneath faint brows. They must surely be brother and sister; perhaps twins.

'Here we are, Inspector.'

The man rotates the laptop and positions it at the head of the table so they can all see. The full-screen image is of a dark bird against a blue sky. He clicks the 'play' icon and the frozen bird comes to life, circling in a tight spiral. There now ensues a short sequence – spine-tinglingly familiar to Skelgill, his second déjà vu in as many days – although this of course is not a déjà vu in the accepted sense; it is real, accompanied by an unfamiliar commentary provided by the voices of the Vholes; Neil Vholes closest to the microphone, loudest, evidently operating the camera, and Christine Vholes in the background:

"It's hunting."

"No, Christine – this is display flight – over its territory."

"Do you think it's the male, Neil?"

"It looks smaller – but you really need to see them together."

"The female could be incubating."

"Yes – it's about the right time."

Then the distinct sound of the muffled shotgun report.

The female voice:

"Ooh." It is tentative, and worried.

The camera loses the bird momentarily when it does not follow the expected trajectory and the picture zooms out a little before homing back in on the now descending raptor. It is exactly as Skelgill remembers. There is a hiatus in the narration until the corpse falls into the canopy, when the man hisses – "Disgraceful" – there is repressed anger in his voice, like that of a schoolmaster many times defied and now disobeyed once again, a certain helplessness yet an underlying determination to do something about it. More steadily now, the camera zooms out again – showing clearly what is Bullmire Wood and the bright silvery expanse of Over Water (Skelgill catches a brief glimpse of himself in his boat) – and pans around until it is revealed to be recording from inside the shadowy birdwatching hide. And there is Christine Vholes, hunched on a bench beside the camera operator, staring rather manically into the lens.

"A cold-blooded killing, Neil."

The man is more composed.

"State the location – and the date and time, please Christine – for evidence purposes, just in case it is incorrectly programmed on the camera."

The woman does as she is bid, and then the film ends. In unison, like a pair of perched owls, the Vholes lean expectantly towards Skelgill.

For his part Skelgill is experiencing a curious conflict of emotions. While on Sunday he was all set to drag to justice the perpetrator by the scruff of the neck, he has since undergone an inexplicable loss of will, and is ready to consign the matter to history, as one of those things that make his blood boil – like gratuitous littering at beauty spots – but which he can somehow shrug off, knowing that otherwise he would go around with an accumulating tonnage upon his shoulders, when it is not his burden to bear. But, beneath the predatory gaze of the Vholes he reminds himself that wildlife crime is a serious matter and, while animals may live by the laws of the jungle, humans may not. There is also Professor Jim Hartley – his friend might have a vested concern.

Skelgill finds himself asking a necessary question but one he immediately regrets.

'Were there any more witnesses?'

The Vholes glance at one another as though there is some issue of which they have not spoken. Neil Vholes inhales as if he is about to respond – but then, as if through telepathy, they appear to agree to let it pass.

Instead, it is Christine Vholes that pipes up; it seems she will make a subsidiary point.

'There was a fisherman.' She extracts a notebook from her coat pocket and tears out a page. 'This is his car registration – no doubt you will be able to track him down should you require corroboration. He must have seen it – he rowed towards the shore immediately after the bird was murdered.'

Her inflammatory language is eclipsed in Skelgill's mind by a flash of alarm, that they took his plate number. He is thinking – what other footage do they have? The zoom on the man's camera is phenomenal. They could probably have recorded him picking his nose. He is thankful he wasn't on the water long enough to have been faced with the dilemma of a call of nature.

He rises decisively.

'Okay – we can look into that. I'm going to send someone along who can take a copy of that file – assuming you're willing?'

The woman now produces a memory stick. They have come prepared.

'We can't accept a stick, I'm afraid, madam. Anti-virus protocol. It has to be burnt onto a disc. My colleague will also take written statements.'

Neil Vholes rises as though wishing to shake hands again. Skelgill takes evasive action, stepping away, cradling his mug.

'You will treat this as a serious matter, Inspector?'

'Sir, *serious* is my middle name.'

As Skelgill returns through reception he passes the entrance to the canteen. At the waft of fried bacon his stride falters. "Two-dinners" more like, is Skelgill's middle name. The desk sergeant hails him.

'Get owt, Skelly lad?'

DS George Appleby means vendace – but Skelgill answers more cryptically.

'Dead buzzard.'

*

When there is no answer to his knock at the Braithwaite cottage of Professor Jim Hartley – but a familiar tuneful whistle just audible – Skelgill employs his outdoor skills to defeat the natural hawthorn hedge that borders the quaint slate property. He infiltrates the sloping back garden from behind a potting shed. Sure enough, at the top of a narrow lawn that runs down to Coledale Beck, facing away from him and apparently fly fishing at an improbable distance from the little stream is his erstwhile angling mentor. In fact, he is practising, false casting with a tiny fragment of white cloth tied where the point fly would be, for maximum visibility. He wears a panama hat upon his shock of white hair, the only clue to his age; for in his effortless casting action he seems to have rolled back the years; it has Skelgill watching with admiration, and reminding himself that he forces it too much: he always wants the rise that is just out of reach, when a perfect cast is better than spooking all the fish in the lake.

'Still got it, Jim.'

The elderly man starts, and allows the line to crumple upon the lawn. However, he immediately recognises the voice of the interloper.

'Ah – but evidently neither the hearing nor the peripheral vision I once possessed.'

'I sneaked through the hedge. Plus you were probably miles away.'

Jim Hartley grins sympathetically.

'Well – Derwentwater, maybe.'

He seems pleased to see Skelgill. In typical northern fashion they do not exchange handshakes or man-hugs (heaven forbid), or enter into physical contact. Though in standing a little awkwardly apart there is something missing in this regard. The professor suddenly looks alarmed.

'Or did you mean the rod? Don't worry – I haven't forgotten it is earmarked for you.'

Skelgill reddens.

'I meant your casting, Jim. The rod – aye, it's a beauty alright.'

He seems to understand it would offend his friend to say any different, disconcerting though he finds the interaction. Then, to his relief, he notices something, and reaches to take hold of the end of the venerable split-cane artefact.

'Looks like your tip ring's lost its lining.' He squints critically, angling his head back to focus. 'I can sort this – I've got stuff in the car. It's a five-minute job. What's the diameter of the blank – about an eighth?'

The professor chuckles approvingly.

'A man after my own heart!' He refers to Skelgill's use of the imperial measurement. 'In that case, I shall see to elevenses. Come hither – through the house – it is more forgiving than the hedgerow.'

When Skelgill returns from his shooting brake grasping a small kit comprising pliers, lock knife, hot-melt glue, a cigarette lighter and a replacement rod tip guide he finds his friend seated at a garden bench in the dappled shade of a gnarled though profusely blossoming apple tree. The professor is pouring steaming tea into mugs and there is a large plate of small peculiar-looking cakes, and a stack of textbooks and papers. Skelgill, not unnaturally, finds his eye drawn by the former.

'Rum nickies, Daniel.' The professor pats the uppermost book of his pile. 'I have been doing some research in the library – not food, but by happy coincidence I chanced across the recipe whilst browsing aimlessly. It seems baked like this they have been a local delicacy but a well-kept secret for some generations.' He offers the plate. 'What do you think?'

Skelgill needs no further encouragement; he is familiar with Cumberland rum nicky as a dish-sized pie or tart, but not as convenient bite-sized morsels. After a few moments' work, and nods of approval, he swallows and reaches for his mug.

'Spot on, Jim – I take it you can drive on a couple of these?'

He speaks half in jest, but refers to the alcoholic content. The professor grins wryly.

'Oh – I think half a dozen and you should be safe – two tablespoons of Old Vatted Demerara went into this whole lot. Help yourself.'

Skelgill makes a sign that he shall, but reaches now for the fishing rod, propped carefully against an overhanging branch, and draws it down across his lap. He inclines his head towards the heap of books, the uppermost of which is entitled 'British Birds of Prey and their Haunts'.

'Looks like we're on the same page, Jim.'

The professor inhales, a little sombrely.

'Ah – I believe you refer to the Vholes.' (Skelgill, taking his knife to the tip of the rod, glances up in accord.) 'They did not waste any time. I hope you didn't mind my referring them to you?'

'Jim – I was *there* – on Over Water – I saw it. I went to investigate – unofficially, like – but came up against a dead end.'

The professor raises his bushy white brows – mention of Over Water plainly has piqued his curiosity – but he resists any temptation to digress.

'I rather felt with your country credentials you are uniquely placed to deal with this kind of issue. But I had no idea you were a supplementary witness.'

Skelgill is now using the cigarette lighter to heat up the metal shaft of the rod tip guide. He concentrates as he counts under his breath and then snatches up his pliers and with a jerk removes the damaged end-piece.

'Bingo. That doesn't always come off so easy.'

'Nice work.'

'Brute force, really, Jim.'

The professor sighs.

'It must be so satisfying to mend as one goes. It is one thing to be defeated by the fish – but always a frustration when one's equipment is the reason to call it a day.'

Skelgill shrugs unassumingly; praise from his old mentor elicits an altogether different reaction than everyday situations, when such modesty might be more than a tad affected. He deflects the compliment with a question.

'So what's with the Vholes – Vholeses – whatever they call themselves?'

The professor chuckles again.

'I think it is the former. The extended plural does not quite have the same ring as Joneses.'

There is a flicker of a reaction from Skelgill at what is a coincidental mention of his female colleague's surname. A falling apple petal drifts past his line of sight, but he remains head bowed over his little project.

'They are academics. Brother and sister. It seems they are relative newcomers to the area. They both have positions at the agricultural college at Caldbeck. I believe he is an environmental scientist and she is an administrator. I met them through the Nats.'

'The gnats?'

That Skelgill is asking an altogether different question is not apparent to the professor; however, in any event his response carries the appropriate clarification.

'Allerdale Natural History Society. "The Nats" is what the members call themselves. Of course, they are all abuzz with the harriers.'

'Harriers? The bird?'

'You don't know?'

Skelgill is now concentrating hard, melting indirectly the strip of glue he has inserted into the hollow replacement tip. He deftly fits the new piece onto the end of the blank and leans back to align it by looking one-eyed down the length of rod. He grimaces as he presses and holds it in place while the glue sets.

'No idea.'

'Ah – we have a pair of our very own. Hen harriers. Quite a coup. Only fifteen pairs bred in England last year. They are nesting on Over Moor. By good fortune the nest site is visible from the public hide beside Over Water. That's why the Vholes were there at such an ungodly hour. The Nats have mounted a round-the-clock watch. The Vholes were putting in a shift before church.'

There had been two cars when he arrived. A battered Ford Consul, steamed up within and externally coated in dew; without investigating Skelgill had concluded an overnight camper had found the secluded spot. There was also a nearly new Volvo; probably it belonged to the Vholes.

'So are you involved in this?'

'Well – I am a member, of course – but I have pleaded age and infirmity. We have plenty of robust volunteers. There is a young couple who are hardly ever out of there. However, the committee have engaged me to write an article for their newsletter, about raptor persecution. It is for press and publicity purposes – to foster public support and, not least, exert maximum pressure on the landowners.'

At this juncture he reaches to extract an old hardback from the pile. He displays the front briefly to Skelgill. Rather oddly it is entitled 'Pesticides and Persecution'; the illustration is of a farmer astride an open-top tractor ploughing against a backdrop of chimneys and industrial smog.

'I came across a fascinating piece of research.' He opens the book and checks the title pages and begins to leaf through. 'This was published in 1967 – and – let me see – yes here we are – this study was conducted in the mid 1950s.'

He holds open a page that shows, printed in black on yellowing stock, juxtaposed, two maps of Great Britain. There is detailed text below, but Skelgill stares at the images. The twin outlines of the island of GB are shaded in various degrees from light hatch to black. He realises he is expected to comment.

'They're a mirror image.'

'Precisely!' The professor sounds positively triumphant. 'Now hear this. The map on the left represents the population density of the common buzzard per square mile.' He looks meaningfully at his student. 'On the right, a most unusual parameter – we have the density of *gamekeepers* per square mile.'

He lays the book spread out and leans back, as though he rests his case.

Skelgill, having completed his task has reverted to the rum nickies; munching, he raises his eyebrows. It is literally a graphic illustration of the point.

'It's going back a bit, though, Jim – the Fifties.'

'Daniel, we might live in the age of enlightenment – but old habits die hard.'

Skelgill can hardly gainsay this point. And, notwithstanding yesterday's incident – as his friend has alluded to – he knows more than enough of the ways of country folk and gamekeepers to appreciate that there is an entirely different prism through which the environment may be viewed. And, bluntly, it is the one he has grown up with. It is not hard to empathise with farmers and land workers, often scraping a tenuous living, who are supposed to stand by while their livelihood is pillaged by predators protected by lawmakers elected by urban voters who share little in common and have a simplistic understanding of rural life. They have seen neither a fox steal a newborn lamb or slay an entire coop of chickens, nor a buzzard devour the crimson breast meat of a live pheasant poult. *Nature, red in tooth and claw.*

The professor evidently detects Skelgill's pensive weighing of the situation.

'Frankly, Daniel, the death of a buzzard is hardly to be mourned.' (Skelgill looks up in surprise.) 'I have a copy in that pile of a recent study which calculated that only one in four makes it to adulthood. They are thriving to the extent that there simply aren't sufficient territories. The majority of immature birds starve. Next time you see one on a post by the verge – remind yourself it has been driven off by its parents and is forlornly waiting for roadkill. It is the rather ironic corollary of successful conservation.'

He sees that Skelgill is still looking unconvinced.

'Sad though it is – anthropomorphically speaking – when one of a breeding pair is killed. In the case of Bullmire Wood, the brood is unlikely to survive.'

Skelgill nods slowly.

'But, harriers – ?'

'Another kettle of fish entirely, Daniel. There is a widespread belief in ornithological circles that they are the victims of relentless persecution. Proof is hard to obtain, but the circumstantial evidence is compelling. In contrast to the overpopulated buzzard, a mere five per cent of suitable hen harrier territories in England are occupied.'

'Why the difference?'

'Well – put simply, they are a perceived threat to the red grouse.'

Skelgill nods pensively. There is serious money in grouse shooting.

The professor makes an expansive gesture with both hands.

'Daniel, you appreciate the irony of hen harriers taking up residence on Over Moor?'

Skelgill shrugs.

'It's a sporting estate.' He finds himself repeating the words of the man in Bullmire Wood.

'Well – that, too, of course – though I suppose in that case you could call it foolhardiness, if only the birds knew it. But, forgive me; I am being obtuse. Over Moor – Over Water – Overthwaite – you know the name origin?'

Skelgill frowns. Now he thinks about it, he does not.

'It is a derivation of the Old Norse, the word 'Orri' – meaning grouse. And, of course, Great Cockup, onto which the moor extends – has its etymology in the Old English – *cock* being the blackcock. Over Moor has been prime grouse country since the Dark Ages.'

'There's grouse butts up there, right enough.'

He refers to the lines of stone shooting shelters that cross the fellsides.

'I believe it is one of the most productive estates this side of the border.'

'You said the hen harrier's *perceived* to eat grouse.'

'Therein lies the rub – in reality ninety-five per cent of the diet is small mammals – mice, voles, shrews – next come the likes of meadow pipits. True, grouse chicks would be on the menu, and even the occasional adult – but a minor component. And in eliminating rodents, the harriers remove competition for heather shoots, the primary food source for grouse. But they hunt ostentatiously over open moorland – they look all the time like they are seeking what the gamekeeper strives to protect.'

Skelgill occasionally flushes grouse while out on the fells – notably the Skiddaw range in question. And he knows that, since grouse cannot be captive-bred, the bird is a scarce commodity. It is clear that harriers would not be welcomed.

'So, you're saying they couldn't have picked a much tougher spot.'

'Well – it is certainly rather double-edged. There is no shooting in the breeding season, and the land is private so there are few walkers or dogs – one could be excused for choosing it as a nest site if one were ignorant of the Glorious Twelfth. So now you see why the Nats have set up their surveillance. And we come full circle to the Vholes' complaint. While a single buzzard may not merit the attention of Cumbria Constabulary, given the precarious situation in which our harriers find themselves – a shot across the bows might be timely, wouldn't you agree?'

Skelgill makes a face that signals reluctant solidarity. The professor gives a little "ahem" cough.

'Daniel, have another rum nicky. Take two.'

3. SHUTEHAM HALL

Monday afternoon

'It's like a fairy glen.'

DS Jones sounds wistful as she surveys their surroundings while Skelgill's car makes more hasty progress than the narrow winding track can comfortably accommodate. She refers to the atmospheric effect created by an unusual blend of native and non-native vegetation, at eye level exotic large-leaved shrubs and ferns and, glimpsed between them, the massive hirsute trunks of sequoias that lurk like grizzly bears and steeple skywards as if escape the vertiginous wooded ravine in which they travel.

On their left the little valley begins to open out as they approach their destination, and the policies become more varied. A small artificial lake that has an ornate two-storey log-cabin-style boathouse, with what looks like accommodation in the upper floor, a balcony and glass doors, catches Skelgill's eye. Down a steep rise overlooking the lake tumbles a thin waterfall; above, on a grassy plateau, a belvedere is strategically positioned, garden chairs are arranged in the shade of its domed canopy around an outdoor stove. Rather bizarrely, beyond that, gleaming like a beacon in the bright sunshine is an old red telephone box.

'More like *Alice in Wonderland*. Look at that lot!'

It is DS Leyton who exclaims from the rear seat. An expanse of lawn unfolds, haphazardly populated by a fantastical array of topiary – a good two score of yews ornately sculpted, standing between ten and twenty feet high and spaced apart like they are the pieces on a giant crazy chessboard.

'I'm expecting to see a white rabbit any minute, Guv.'

But Skelgill's attention is drawn away, beyond the topiary garden, to the castle, which now heaves into sight. That Skelgill thinks of it as a castle, when it is called Shuteham Hall is due to its austere facade. An angular construction of uneven chequered sandstone in a range of hues from deep brick red to pale puce, with the occasional lump of charcoal, its distinguishing feature is a near absence of windows on the ground floor, and only mean apertures on the two storeys above, with occasional arrow-slits where there may be a staircase, or in a high gable. This ancient edifice was clearly erected in troubled times; a 'hall' one would expect to boast great windows, admitting precious daylight upon luxuriant tapestries and affording views over the grounds, designed for friendly fellow gentry, to be welcomed and impressed, rather than foes to be doused in latrine contents and sent homeward with a spear between their legs.

Skelgill draws his car to a halt on the gravel before what appears to be the main entrance. Set in a jutting tower, it is not a grand portico, but beneath a weathered crest that might incorporate a stag and an eagle, and a stone lintel carved with the motto *VIRGA GLORIAM*, just a heavy door of old wood ribbed with iron bands. Now he hesitates, screwing up his features in indecision. That he is accompanied by his colleagues is not due to a sudden escalation in their taking seriously the shooting incident, but to the fact that the three are en route to attend a hearing at West Cumbria Magistrates Court in Workington; a case of burglary in which DS Jones is due to give evidence. He spies a sign affixed to a stake beside the door; it denotes "Estate Office" and points to the right. There is the suggestion that new arrivals should not trouble the main house. Skelgill acts on this deduction.

'You pair mosey along to the office – see what you can find out. I don't reckon his lordship will be cooperative if we barge in mob-handed.'

His subordinates seem a little crestfallen, and glance at one another – as if suspecting Skelgill of some ulterior motive; an assessment that would be correct, in as much as, by going alone, he retains maximum latitude for diplomacy, as envisaged by the professor. DS Jones is quick to perk up, however.

'Sure, Guv. Maybe the factor will be more forthcoming than the landowner.'

They exit the car. Skelgill waits for his colleagues to round the corner of the building. The spot on which he stands, in the angle of the tower and the main frontage is quite a suntrap, and the heat of the day has accumulated in the old walls; a couple of white butterflies, one with striking carroty tips to its wings tumble in their aerial courtship dance, before settling together somewhere in a bed of yellow tulips and pale violet *Camassia*. Skelgill steps forward and hauls on a bell-pull; it feels connected, but he hears nothing from within. While he waits he is visited by the thought that he has not planned what he intends to say; but it is fleeting, for it is not his style. Where he might have preferred to be better prepared, however, is in knowing his adversary; in the hurry to get organised a junior officer was delegated to make an appointment – all Skelgill knows is that the landowner goes by the grand-sounding epithet of Lord Edward Bullingdon; accordingly, with the sudden clunk of a latch, he anticipates a stony-faced butler in traditional formal garb.

Not so. A woman who does not seem to be expecting him opens the door. She regards him with surprise but without hostility. She must be of about his age, a little above medium height, slim, with dark hair held in a band; dark irises and regular features with clear, fair skin. She wears flat black pumps, black tracksuit bottoms and a black vest top that exposes her bare shoulders and arms, sculpted without being muscle bound. In one rubber-gloved hand she holds a yellow cloth daubed with honey-coloured polish. If her general appearance is somewhat unexpected – though it seems she must be a cleaner – more extraordinary is that she has a black eye.

Skelgill displays his police credentials.

'DI Skelgill. One of my colleagues telephoned to arrange for me to meet Lord Bullingdon at two o'clock. I'm a few minutes early.'

The woman smiles pleasantly, and in sliding back to admit him he notices she casually looks him over.

'Teddy normally sees visitors in the library. If you'd like to come in, I'll take you through.'

Her accent is local, though fairly mild, and Skelgill cannot immediately place it on his county map. He duly steps past her and waits while she heaves the heavy door to. They are in a darkened vestibule which he realises is a kind of defensive gate keep, in which it would be possible to entrap an intruder. The walls are of bare stone; there are spears and shields and other medieval paraphernalia, including an ancient cast iron mantrap with horrible rusted jaws, and ahead on the right in a niche a suit of armour with its gauntlets clasped around the hilt of a sword in the pose of a sentry.

'This way, please.'

The woman walks lightly with distinctly good balance. She takes him around a corner and up three worn steps into the atrium of the central bastion of the original castle; overhead, two concentric balconies run around the rectangular tower house, and above a beamed ceiling from somewhere admits shafts of sunlight. The ground-floor walls are all of bare stone, though decorated here and there with ancestral portraits. But the woman attracts Skelgill's attention now. On the back of her singlet where the garment curves out at the base of her spine is the single word, "Karen", and between her shoulder blades, a second transfer reads, "Karate North".

'Does that explain the shiner?'

The woman keeps moving but turns to look over her shoulder, her ironic raising of her eyebrows telling him she understands and that his detective work is accurate. She does not, however, offer any elaboration, but Skelgill is sufficiently encouraged.

'You should see the other lass, eh?'

'I was fighting a man.'

They have reached a further oak door, which is open, and she leads him through. It is an internal room, windowless, lit poorly though cosily by shaded wall lights. Ahead is a massive stone hearth, swept clean. All other wall space is lined with shelves of books of uniform antiquity, en masse giving an impression of rich binding and gilt, though on closer examination many are in need of repair. At either side of the hearth sits a heavy cracked leather armchair, but otherwise a massive oak table takes up the centre of the room with Regency chairs ranged around it. On the table, with its lid off, stands a trade-sized tin of traditional furniture polish. Evidently the woman has been working here. She turns to face Skelgill, and he looks with some concern at her wound; he feels so entitled now that the ice is broken. That she admits it was perpetrated by a male has set ringing a little policeman's alarm bell; and he is reminded of the weird and wonderful excuses that women come up with to protect their underserving partners; an accident with the hoover, the hairdryer, the hamster – "I head-butted his fist" – they have all been pressed into service to explain 'self-inflicted' injuries. He notices she wears no rings – although that might be a function of her job, or indeed her hobby. He questions her with a note of reproach in his voice.

'I thought in karate you weren't supposed to hit your opponent.'

She regards him evenly.

'You don't have to make contact to score – but if you do you're not meant to injure. In the heat of the moment it doesn't always work out.'

She continues to hold his gaze; he gets the feeling she is being straight with him. His demeanour softens.

'Do you represent the North?'

She shakes her head.

'I used to – I just coach and train with them now. Do some sparring. It's my son Kieran that competes. I spend most of my spare time ferrying him around to competitions. We were in Glasgow yesterday.'

Skelgill wonders: now that he sees her more clearly he would be surprised if in fact she is over thirty.

'What age is your lad?'

'Eight.'

'Eight! He must be good – what'll he be like when he's bigger?'

She looks pleased; not just in her renewed smile, but in the proud glint in her lanceolate eyes. She moistens her lips with the tip of her tongue and slides both hands behind her back and makes a movement like she is flexing her spine. Skelgill finds himself wanting to straighten his hair, or do something to it, and has to resist the involuntary urge. For a moment they both seem lost for what to say next. But then a casement clock that is hung just behind the door strikes two; its notes hang chidingly in the ether, and the woman gestures with the gloved hand that holds the duster.

'I'd better let Teddy know you're here. He's got a habit of disappearing.'

She lowers her gaze and brushes past Skelgill; he inhales a waft of polish and perfume and perspiration that he doesn't mind.

'Thanks – Karen.'

She glances back, rotating easily at the hips at the sound of her name, and flashes him what is this time a more enigmatic smile.

Left alone, he stands pensively. The ticking of the clock seems loud now, when he had not noticed it before, and the pungency of turpentine from the open tin of polish gains ascendency in the still air. He feels watched; there is a period portrait over the fireplace. It could be a woman, although on reflection beneath a cape the subject is clad in armour, and the big hair is probably a fashionable wig. He tries the experiment of moving across the room to see if the eyes follow him, and they do. Or, at least, that is how it seems. He finds himself standing beside an exhibit case, positioned upon an antique sideboard, about three feet high and a little more in width. The glass is sparkling and the oak frame in tip-top order, qualities that he attributes to the just-departed Karen. Inside, however, the collection of avian taxidermy does not reach the same high standards, and has deteriorated badly. The case has been infiltrated by dust; colours are faded, plumage moth-eaten;

artificial eyes bulge unnaturally. There are predominantly game birds ranged upon a rising foreground of rock draped in desiccated moss and heather. He recognises most of them: pheasant, woodcock, golden plover, and both species of grouse, red and black. On lichen-covered branches are some smaller passerines, rather jauntily posed – meadow pipit, stonechat and wheatear, characteristic of the local moor – and behind these, perched ominously upon sturdier logs, are the predators, raven, buzzard, merlin – and he is wondering if there is what could be a hen harrier. He is just about to slip his phone from his pocket to steal a clandestine photo when he is jolted by a voice.

'Grandfather took every specimen single-handedly. Those were the days, my man!'

Bringing his empty hands out by his sides Skelgill wheels around to see framed in the doorway a broad if crooked silhouette. Immediately any doubt about the person he encountered in Bullmire Wood being the laird is dispelled. Besides, the accent is that of the upper classes. Moreover, as he comes forward with a slightly shambling gait Skelgill sees that the man must be in his seventies. He wears brogues and shapeless maroon corduroys, and a green jersey beneath which a college tie is loosely knotted and from which one dog-eared collar of a shirt protrudes. His features are in the Churchillian mould, those of the bulldog, seemingly crowded into a round countenance and displeased for it; the mouth is downturned at one side as though in special protest. He has a head of tousled sandy-grey hair, and bushy brows, and his lop-sidedness extends right through to a kind of one-eyed bearing, as though he has long favoured a dominant side and his bones have become calcified in the pose. Skelgill thinks he would probably be his own height were he to straighten.

'You're not from the Forestry?'

Skelgill is questioning what sort of message has reached the man about his appointment.

'No, sir.'

'Ministry of Agriculture?'

'No – I'm not, sir.'

Skelgill wonders if he is testing him out, or putting him in his place in the scheme of things. He takes the bull by the horns.

'What I am, sir – is that, firstly, I'm from Buttermere – where I grew up – and, secondly, I'm from Cumbria CID. Detective Inspector Skelgill.'

It is an unconventional introduction and the man – Lord Edward Bullingdon, or "Teddy" – regards him penetratingly, staring through his leading eye, the right; the left half-closed as though he might be squinting along the barrel of a shotgun.

'They've been trying to confound me with red tape all morning. But if I hear you correctly I think what you're telling me is that you're pretty darned good at sitting on the fence.'

Beneath the avuncular delivery Skelgill detects an undertone of entitled coercion.

'I never sit on the fence, sir. But I've got a clear view of both sides.'

The man hesitates, and then shrugs. Thwarted in part, he adopts a more equivocal manner.

'Well – if that's the best you can do, I'll take it. CID, you say? Has there been a murder?'

It appears there is going to be no suggestion of sitting down for a leisurely meeting, as the man now stands his ground. It suits Skelgill to come to the point.

'I didn't think you'd want a patrol car parked in your driveway, sir. Besides, it's something that's come across my desk – and I was passing this way with a couple of my colleagues.'

'*It* being?'

'A buzzard shot above Bullmire Wood was filmed by some birdwatchers early on Sunday morning.'

Lord Bullingdon slaps his protruding hip like he might be whipping a steed.

'*Pah* – nonsense! Half the idiots don't know what they're talking about. They've been trying to tell me there are harriers on Over Moor – utter poppycock! Sent up a deputation a few weeks ago. Interfering blighters.'

'So you know about the hen harriers, sir?'

The landowner leans towards Skelgill, now screwing up even his good eye.

'Don't tell me you're in on it, too? The deputation failed, so they've cooked up a reason to send in the police.'

He is not so far from hitting the nail on the head. Skelgill realises he must 'caw canny' as his Scots friend and erstwhile colleague DS Cameron Findlay would counsel. He opts to deal with the less contentious aspect of Lord Bullingdon's complaint.

'I'm no bird expert – but I've had it on good authority. It seems you've got the only pair in Cumbria. I should have thought that's a feather in your cap, sir?'

As he speaks these words he immediately wonders if it is an unfortunate turn of phrase. Realising his fears, the man half turns away and flaps an arm in the air, and harrumphs something approaching, "It'll be that, alright".

Skelgill recognises the potential quagmire and backtracks to firmer ground.

'Regarding the buzzard, sir – if an alleged wildlife crime – like any other – is reported, we're duty-bound to investigate it. I've seen the evidence myself, and there doesn't seem to be much doubt that it was shot from your property.'

The man hems and haws for a moment or two. Skelgill notices he makes no attempt to deny that it could happen on his estate. But he has shown himself to be sharper than the impression he gives, and perhaps he is cognisant of the get-out clause that is implicit in Skelgill's charge. Anyone could have fired the shot.

'Pah – you'll need to speak with Daphne – she makes all the sporting arrangements these days.'

Skelgill waits for clarification, but to no avail.

'And where might I find Daphne, sir?'

His question is answered not by the man but instead by a soprano voice that carries from the hallway. Rapid footsteps are accompanied by a shrill cry.

'Daddy!'

Into the library bustles a short, stout woman – Skelgill guesses in her mid-thirties – breathless, and clad in a two-piece suit of checked wool tweed, matching olive stockings and sensible shoes. In contrast to the venerable peer she has a tight helmet of glossy chestnut hair – but there can be no doubt of her pedigree, for facially she bears an extraordinarily close resemblance to her pater; indeed Skelgill realises the crooked, one-eyed expression is not merely an acquired characteristic, but a hereditary trait, and an ascendant one at that. Somehow it is more disconcerting in the much younger, female member of the family. She ignores Skelgill altogether, such is her focus upon her mission (or, he reflects, maybe she simply considers him unimportant).

'Apparently a bird of prey has been shot!'

Edward Bullingdon waves a dismissive hand.

'My dear – the earth is not about to open up and swallow us.'

'Daddy – we have the police here!'

He gestures at Skelgill.

'Quite right – this fellow's a Chief Superintendent – something like that.'

Now she seems to register Skelgill's presence. She gawps at him, rendered speechless. Her father steps into the breach.

'Daphne. In poor light a darned buzzard's no different in profile to a crow. Common mistake to make. Probably potted a good couple of dozen in my time. Can't be helped.'

The young woman looks aghast.'

'Daddy – we have our reputation to think of. It will feed the clamour for licensing.'

Now Lord Bullingdon scoffs dismissively.

'Daphne, my dear – this good chap's on our side – we were just discussing – you know, sweeping and carpets and all that.'

The young woman glances sharply at Skelgill to see his reaction does not remotely correspond to her father's claim. At this she seems to pull herself together.

'Daddy – it appears Miranda is leaving shortly – she telephoned asking for the Aston to be brought round to the stables. Meanwhile I have radioed for Lawrence to come up. Let me reunite the Chief Superintendent with his colleagues at the office and I can deal with this matter.'

Upon mention of "Miranda" Edward Bullingdon looks suddenly vexed, and positively distracted.

'Dammit.'

Muttering under his breath he hobbles away without word of explanation or farewell. Skelgill is left alone with the man's daughter.

'Chief Superintendent – I must apologise – Daddy can be rather abstruse – I should take what he says with a substantial pinch of salt.'

Skelgill shuffles rather self-consciously from one foot to the other.

'It's just plain Inspector, madam. DI Skelgill. Based out of Penrith.'

In her congenitally lopsided manner, she fronts up and offers a firm hand, which Skelgill is obliged to shake.

'Daphne Bullingdon. I run the estate office and all affairs of a sporting nature. I have ordered some tea for your colleagues. Come this way, please – we can go through the kitchen garden.'

She leads him from the library and across the atrium and through a stone passage that, from a kind of scullery gives on to a half-courtyard, flanked on their left by a somewhat less ancient wing of the property. The kitchen garden appears neglected, its beds dominated by leggy clumps of low-maintenance lavender, rosemary and sage. Their path merges with the gravel driveway that skirts the castle and runs directly towards a succession of buildings, some of the same old reddish sandstone, and others of a more utilitarian farming type. As they pass one of the former, vertical iron bars on its windows attract Skelgill's eye.

'In there is our gunroom – attached is a malt whisky bar, a humidor and a billiards room with a championship-size table.'

Skelgill nods comprehendingly, but does not remark. Now they approach a more modern construction, steel-framed and clad in green-painted aluminium.

'These are our rearing sheds. We have brooder huts with free-range runs at the back. Our birds are organically nurtured in full compliance with the code of practice issued by DEFRA – the Department for Environment, Food and Rural Affairs. We export most of our meat to Belgium and France. It provides winter employment for three of our hands and contributes directly to the local economy.'

Skelgill senses that he is hearing an excerpt from a well-practised monologue; as her father had intimated, no doubt they receive probing visits from the authorities, such as those responsible for animal welfare. At the side of the building to which the woman refers he notices a commercial incinerator.

'All waste is disposed of according to the highest standards of hygiene. That is a DEFRA-approved model.'

Such an insider view as this casts the game shooting industry in a different light from the popular notion of a bucolic pastime in which a few old birds are downed for the pot. Skelgill has heard it said that more pheasants are reared in Britain than sheep, which is a mind-boggling statistic to anyone who frequents the fells.

Ahead of them an older property stretches along on the right of the track, which is walled-in on the left; arching above and uniting the two sides is a glazed canopy that runs the length of the building. It reminds Skelgill of a traditional country railway station. The canopy is in need of repair, and his gaze is drawn to a shattered pane that looks like it has been holed by an impact. He is thinking twelve bore.

'That was a pheasant.' Clearly she is alert to wherever his scrutiny falls. 'It was shot from the bank beyond. It crashed right through the glass.'

Skelgill looks afresh. There are apocryphal tales of hunters knocked out by the birds they have winged – it is said that red grouse can reach eighty miles an hour downwind. It would be quite a clip round the ear.

Beneath the hole, by ironic coincidence, there is a row of rusted iron hooks driven into the crumbling brickwork, no doubt for hanging game – for beneath stands an old table (rather incongruously ornate in its style and probably a valuable antique if restored), pressed into use as a plucking bench; beside it a rough timber and plywood hopper; strewn about in the dust are stray feathers. Close at hand are a tree-trunk chopping block, an axe upon it, and a manually operated guillotine. This is evidently the meat-processing end of the operation; it is practical, if primitive.

It seems Daphne Bullingdon would willingly continue her commentary. Further along there appear to be stables, but they have reached the office; indeed this section of the building has a glass frontage, rather like a retail outlet – and Skelgill can see his colleagues seated at a coffee table. DS Jones is pouring tea from a china service. DS Leyton surreptitiously palms a finger of shortbread to an overweight chocolate Labrador. They look up expectantly at Skelgill as he enters; he seems to give a curt shake of his head; he might be refusing tea, but it is hard to be sure. Daphne Bullingdon makes as though to offer him a seat, but he saunters across to a reception counter; on the wall beside it is a noticeboard displaying photographs, some of them captioned. The subjects include tweed-clad 'guns' taking aim in the heather; the 'guns' shooting high overhead in a forest ride, the 'guns' posed at ease around the tailgate of a Range Rover, raising celebratory nips of whisky; and a crate of dead pheasants from which the head of a springer spaniel sticks out like that of a child submerged in a soft-play ball pit. There is nothing especially new to Skelgill, but he is reminded this is a pastime for the well heeled and probably even more well connected.

Daphne Bullingdon breaks the silence.

'I have summoned Lawrence Melling – he is our head keeper. He may be able to shed light on the unfortunate matter of the buzzard. Indeed, I should like to know what his explanation will be.' She hesitates, and cocks an ear towards the entrance. 'In fact, that sounds like him now.'

Indeed there comes the popping of an engine as it is throttled back and a quad bike slews to a halt outside, throwing up a cloud of dust, and a black working cocker bounds from the dog box and darts across to inspect the vicinity of the plucking bench. The rider cuts the motor and hauls off his full-face helmet and Skelgill immediately recognises him as the red-bearded man he encountered in Bullmire Wood. So he is a gamekeeper, after all.

46

The spaniel is a marvel of perpetual motion and is back across the yard in the twinkling of an eye, nosing through the gap the second the man unlatches the door. It makes a rapid round of the occupants, effusive and fawning in its greetings.

In contrast Lawrence Melling enters with the calm, self-confident bearing of an admiral summoned to the bridge to deal with a crisis beyond the wit of his underlings. Preceded by the tang of cologne, he wears a freshly pressed version of the countryman's ensemble Skelgill had observed yesterday. If Daphne Bullingdon had led them to expect a forelock-tugging scapegoat resigned to an unfavourable hearing before their kangaroo court, they could not have been much wider of the mark.

Skelgill remains standing at the back of the room. His immediate impression is of a mutual aversion between the landowner's daughter and the newcomer. They exchange no words of salutation and instead Daphne Bullingdon makes a collective introduction as Skelgill's two sergeants rise. There ensue nods rather than handshakes – it is apparent to all this is not the kind of amicable meeting in which potential sporting clients are wooed.

Skelgill notices the man's narrowed eyes linger appraisingly on DS Jones – but this changes to a flash of apprehension when he senses he has not taken in Skelgill's presence – and now does so. The look of alarm becomes one of recognition, but he makes no acknowledgement. Instead he turns pointedly to Daphne Bullingdon as she requests, for his benefit, a replay of the video on DS Jones's electronic tablet.

The group still on their feet, the man watches implacably. He shows no flicker of emotion, despite that he is being presented with something of a smoking gun. He responds only when the recording ends.

'Like I say, we've had problems with poachers of late.' He is looking at Daphne Bullingdon, though his words might be directed at Skelgill, as if by reference to their previous exchange. 'Nor would I put it past the sabs.'

'Lawrence, what on earth do you mean?' Daphne Bullingdon's tone is incredulous. 'That this is some kind of subterfuge?'

'It's well known they plant pole traps and poisoned hawks – Ma'am.'

The delayed "Ma'am" conveys a note of defiance. Daphne Bullingdon inhales between gritted teeth.

'Are you suggesting the buzzard was shot in a deliberate attempt to blacken our reputation?'

Skelgill seems content to let her do their job for them, in interrogating the man. Of course, they are not to know what words were exchanged by prior radio contact. He must allow for the small possibility that this is a choreographed exchange – but if so it is proficiently acted. The gamekeeper raises a hand and rubs a thumb and forefinger against his neatly groomed beard.

'Convenient, how they filmed it. There could have been an accomplice in the wood who did the shooting. Have they produced a carcass?'

It is a challenge issued for the ears of officialdom, knowing that, without this evidence, the police would be batting on a very sticky wicket. Daphne Bullingdon looks questioningly at Skelgill. Now he is obliged to speak for the first time. He responds in an offhand manner.

'We'll have a scout round for that – with your permission, of course, madam.' He senses that Lawrence Melling is regarding him with a glint of triumph in his eyes. The woman nods cooperatively, but Skelgill moves quickly on. 'As for the authenticity of the footage, I understand the couple are members of Allerdale Natural History Society. I believe you know they're monitoring the hen harriers that are breeding on your land.'

'We take our conservation responsibilities very seriously, Inspector.' She casts a censorious glance at the gamekeeper, but he merely regards her unsympathetically. 'We are fully compliant with the strictures of the Wildlife and Countryside Act.'

Skelgill is no birder, as the modern parlance goes, but of the species that haunt the fells, lakes and forests he has acquired a working knowledge. Yet it has always struck him as curious that townsfolk, dedicated urbanites – wealthy hedge fund managers that wouldn't even know a hedge if they fell into one – are handed a gun and a hip flask and encouraged to blast away at whatever flies in their direction. He has seen dedicated ornithologists, trained observers armed with state-of-the-art optical equipment, struggle to make the kind of split-second decision that distinguishes fair game from a protected hawk. But along such lines he finds an avenue reasonably to emphasise his point. He looks squarely at Daphne Bullingdon.

'As Lord Bullingdon pointed out, in the heat of the moment it's an easy misjudgement to make. Inexperienced guns told there's pheasant or grouse being driven towards them. But it could be a costly case of mistaken identity.'

Daphne Bullingdon reacts somewhat plaintively.

'But we have no shooting until at the earliest the twelfth of August.'

'Aye – but by then this pair of harriers you've got breeding could have three or four youngsters flying about their territory. They won't know the date. One trigger-happy client could put you in the national newspapers.'

Daphne Bullingdon shudders with revulsion; but she seems lost for words. Skelgill continues.

'I suggest you meet with the Allerdale Nats to come up with a plan. Better you work together than be at loggerheads.'

Lawrence Melling visibly sneers – it is plain he has disdain for the conservationists, and he makes no pretence at interest in reaching some accommodation. Now he tosses a small hand grenade into the midst of the discussion.

'There's nae guarantee the nest will be successful.'

Daphne Bullingdon glares with indignation – yet Skelgill senses there is some impediment to her pulling rank and insisting upon the proposed compromise. It might be she lacks the authority, but it seems closer to a failure of self-confidence in the face of a mutiny. The simmering standoff is defused, however, when Lawrence Melling plainly becomes distracted – for he is first to recognise what, in a sudden crescendo, becomes a clatter of hooves in the yard.

A rider arrives at a canter and, spying the party in the estate office, reins their steed around with aplomb. Skelgill finds himself staring with all the others; the glistening bay stallion is a handsome beast, but the aristocratic equestrienne in the saddle comfortably eclipses it. Immaculately clad, she slips off her riding hat and shakes out a cascade of raven tresses; it is something of a Lady Godiva moment. Her gaze penetrates the glass, and she beckons with her crop.

Lawrence Melling responds to the summons with no word of excusing himself from present company. Skelgill sees that Daphne Bullingdon literally stamps her foot, though she attempts to conceal her petulance by marching across to the counter and picking out a leaflet from a plastic dispenser. She brings it back and opens it out before him, demanding his attention.

'This is a map of the estate. It is designed as an orientation guide for our guests. It shows the locations for driven shooting, along with a recommended safe walking route. I am sure that with carefully considered planning we can designate an area of Over Moor as a wildlife refuge.'

The map is accurately drawn, with some quaint local detail. It is the sort of illustration that would ordinarily engross Skelgill, but he has half an eye on the window. He sees that the woman on horseback makes no effort to dismount and instead waits for the gamekeeper. When he takes hold of the bridle and offers up a hand, she leans upon him and brings her face close to his ear. She must whisper some confidence, for the hint of a smile reveals itself at the corners of his hitherto inscrutable mouth. A few more words then pass between them. He leads the horse away, out of sight. The woman nonchalantly enters the office, ignoring the dogs that crowd her. She similarly disregards Daphne Bullingdon and DS Leyton. Though she casts an interested glance upon DS Jones, she makes directly for Skelgill.

He sees now that she might be in her early forties, but she is a woman that knows she commands the male eye; indeed he finds himself fighting such an instinct. She is tall, and slim yet shapely, her figure delineated by slick black riding boots, skin-tight white jodhpurs and a white short-sleeved nylon show shirt with diamond buttons and a choker collar. Such snug tailoring does not leave a great deal to the imagination. And her centre parting frames an equally striking countenance; sultry Mediterranean features that are pursued by photographers the world over.

'To what do we owe the pleasure of your visit?'

Her voice is husky and her accent refined. And while the gamekeeper had brought with him a brashness that extended to his intrusive aftershave, the woman at close quarters exudes a subtle, floral scent, jasmine with undertones of sandalwood. Her question intimates some knowledge of who they are.

'A sporting matter, Miranda – there is no need for you to concern yourself.' It is an irate Daphne Bullingdon that interjects, as though now she fears being doubly usurped.

The woman turns to her.

'Darling – why would I be concerned?' She uses 'darling' in the non-familial sense, the platitude of the celebrity classes. 'Your father tells me you are just beginning to make a fist of things.'

Stung by the backhanded compliment, Daphne Bullingdon bristles; her prominent nostrils flare. Her habit of becoming lost for words under stress is something with which Skelgill can identify; in his youth a swift left hook always enabled him to let off steam. But any such resolution is circumvented: the door bangs open and Lord Bullingdon shambles wheezily into the office. He has donned a threadbare wide-brimmed waxed-cotton hat and a cape of similar fabric and vintage, and leans heavily upon an antler-topped thumbstick. Ignoring the rest he approaches close to the tall woman, who regards him rather pityingly.

'Miranda – what's all this about taking the Aston?'

Miranda Bullingdon waves a careless hand.

'Teddy Bear – you know I don't like driving the Defender – it's such a big awkward beast – and so slow to overtake.'

Edward Bullingdon shows no embarrassment at this public revelation of his pet name, though Skelgill sees his subordinates exchange a look of mild wonder. Neither the epithet, nor her soothing tone, however, appears to allay his disquiet, and he glares lopsidedly at his wife.

'Besides, where are you off to in such a hurry?'

She pouts forgivingly, rather as a mother over the forgetful antics of a child.

'I'm sure I told you – there's a fashion show this afternoon at the Sharrow Bay.'

Lord Bullingdon shakes his staff at her.

'What – dressed like that?'

'Teddy Bear – it doesn't matter what I wear – I shall be modelling. Besides, it is a private function, exclusively hunt wives – in advance of the May Ball.'

Before he can muster a reply there comes a further distraction; outside a gleaming midnight blue Aston Martin slides into view. Lawrence Melling rises athletically from the driver's seat and walks around to stand beside the passenger door. It seems to Skelgill he makes eye contact with Lord Bullingdon and gives a faint nod. In the landowner's shoes he would be tempted to interpret it as a sign of insubordination. Lord Bullingdon clears his throat somewhat ominously.

'What's he doing?'

'Oh, Teddy Bear – I offered Lawrence a lift. He has some business with the gunsmith in Cockermouth.' The woman reaches forward and places a calming hand on her husband's shoulder. 'But I must dash. The county await my presence. *Mwah – mwah.*' She ducks in with rapid air kisses, and he sways belatedly. She steps lightly away, but pauses before Skelgill and meets his gaze. With a shrewd smile she glides from the office.

Amidst a stilted silence Skelgill watches as she approaches Lawrence Melling. The man reaches to open the car door, but she evidently says something; he clearly adjusts his intention and climbs into the passenger seat himself. She takes the driver's side and a moment later the car surges away.

'I should never have put her on the darned insurance, dammit!'

But now Lord Bullingdon seems to become aware of those around him – and he looks distinctly like he wishes he were not there. He turns brusquely to Daphne Bullingdon.

'Where the hell's Julian got to? I haven't seen him since breakfast. He was complaining about there being a surfeit of devilled kidneys and a dearth of mushrooms.'

Daphne Bullingdon visibly steels herself in order to answer.

'He's working on his entomological survey, Daddy. He says there's only a short window of opportunity – at this time of year – for the orange tip butterfly.'

'*Pah* – darned fool.' He glares at Skelgill and then his colleagues, as if wondering who they are. 'If a man doesn't want to shoot, he could at least get a proper job in the City. Tantamount to treason. Leaving a woman to fill his shoes. *Pah!*'

He storms out, waving a dismissive hand, which may be aimed at his daughter. By clear inference the circumstances of succession are not working out to his satisfaction. DS Jones manages to attract Skelgill's eye, and gestures to her wrist. He nods, and addresses the preoccupied Daphne Bullingdon, her soured expression ironically a virtual carbon copy of her father's.

'Madam – we've got about twenty minutes before we need to leave. My colleagues will take some details from you.' He brandishes the leaflet, still opened out to display the map of the estate. 'I'll just have a quick wander, if you don't object.'

His inflection does not in fact invite opposition, and he makes for the exit, but in any event the young woman is obliging.

'Be my guest, Inspector.' She scuttles ahead of him, to hold open the door. 'And be assured that I shall conduct a thorough investigation into this matter. I shall not rest until I get to the bottom of it.'

Skelgill conjectures that behind the lopsided Bullingdon countenance resides a dogged resolve that could one day prove to be the nemesis of some antagonist. He nods befittingly and takes his leave.

When his colleagues return to his car, parked before the old hall they are a little surprised to find him apparently napping in the driver's seat, the window rolled down. DS Leyton slaps a hand on the roof – a little more rudely than he perhaps intends – and Skelgill's eyes jerk open.

'Forty winks, Guv?'

'I was thinking, Leyton.'

His superior is plainly irked, but DS Leyton continues as though it is of no concern to him.

'I could do with a spot of Bo Peep myself, Guv – the littlun had us up in the middle of the night, teething the missus reckons.'

Skelgill looks like he has little concept of what his sergeant might be talking about, and still in something of a stupor he starts up the engine and, his colleagues on board, he pulls away without offering a rejoinder. As they skirt the expanse of lawn with its great topiary chess set they spy a youngish dark-haired man upon a high stepladder, clipping with garden shears at the limits of his reach.

'That don't look very – '

Before DS Leyton can complete his analysis – presumably with "safe" or "stable" or other such adjective – the ladder begins to wobble and the man, making an early decision to take charge of his fate jettisons the shears and leaps backwards into mid air. It must be a good six-foot drop from the level of his boots to the ground, and he sprawls face down upon the closely mown turf. However, what at first seems like a successful escape manoeuvre – as he begins to raise himself up on all fours – is summarily thwarted when the stepladder, having rocked towards the yew, now rebounds and topples completely, flooring him with a blow to the base of his skull.

'Aargh ya!'

It is DS Leyton's sound effect – though he gives the distinct impression of being thrilled by such good fortune as to witness the comedy moment. DS Jones reacts with a more sympathetic intake of breath. Skelgill, who has drawn the car to a halt, takes the middle ground.

'They're pretty lightweight, those aluminium steps.'

And, sure enough, the man is not permanently down. He shakes his head as if to dispel the stars he sees, and then seems to realise he has an audience. He scrambles to his feet and performs a little Chaplinesque mime – a staggering dance which may owe more to genuine concussion than his sense of humour – but he indicates with a rap of his knuckles upon his crown and a broad grin that he is fit to continue, and he goes about the business of restoring the ladder to its position and retrieving his shears from the bush. Skelgill takes his foot off the clutch and they move on.

'Just as well we're not from Health & Safety, Guv.'

'I reckon we've given them enough to think about, Leyton. They've not liked having their cage rattled.'

DS Leyton nods phlegmatically.

'I take it you had no joy with finding the dead bird, Guv?'

Skelgill muffles a curse such that it sounds like a gasp of exasperation. While this was something they had discussed beforehand – that a search of the woods for the corpse of the buzzard would be a requisite were they to launch a formal investigation, it was not something that Skelgill in his own mind had taken seriously. On Sunday morning the gamekeeper's dog would have made short work of sniffing out a kill, and there was the jute sack that looked like it contained the very same. Seeing the commercial incinerator beside the rearing sheds had confirmed Skelgill's expectations. Likely the only surviving remnant of the buzzard is the feather he had picked up beside the release pen – and, of course, any old buzzard could have shed it. His intimation to Daphne Bullingdon and her keeper of a 'scout round' was a hollow threat, and it was plain the keeper knew it, if she didn't. If Skelgill's subordinates now assume that was what he went off to do – despite that there was inadequate time even to reach the right area of Bullmire Wood – a little detective work on their part would reveal the sandy mud caking his boots to match that of the shoreline of the artificial lake. Drawn by instinct, he had found himself awed by the pipe dream of owning a private fishery, with its two-storey boathouse that one could camp in. He had stood, eyes closed, while voracious rainbow trout ripped mayflies from the calm surface; it is a sound, a visceral *splosh* that spikes his pulse like very few things in life.

He is about to put DS Leyton right about the futility of his enquiry, simultaneously craning his neck to get a last glimpse of the little lake, when DS Jones cries aloud.

'Look out!'

A figure breaks from the trees and dashes across the track, oblivious to the onrushing shooting brake. Skelgill deems there is no need to decelerate, though it is a close shave. In a whirring blur of legs and arms the vision disappears into the shrubbery opposite.

'There's your white rabbit, Leyton.'

Skelgill's assessment has limited merit, other than in the more general surrealist sense. The fellow – for it surely was a fellow, despite that he appeared to wear over baggy trousers a long pale dress (although it may have been an agrarian smock-frock of the kind sported by eighteenth century peasants) – was distinctive for his skinny frame and angular movements, strained aquiline features, trailing fair hair and sockless sandals. On a short handle he wielded a wide-mouthed butterfly net like a lepidopterist of yesteryear.

'Mad hatter, more like, Guv.'

Skelgill tilts his head from side to side.

'Second thoughts, I'd go mad professor.'

It falls to DS Jones to provide clarification.

'That must be Julian Bullingdon. Daphne Bullingdon explained that she is the child of Edward Bullingdon's first wife. Julian is the son of the second – apparently she was some kind of artist – she put in place these creative touches around the grounds – the topiary, the phone box, the Swiss-chalet-style boathouse.'

'Was?'

Skelgill's question is lazy but she understands.

'Miranda is wife number three. She is a former model.'

His features are immobile, indicative of some re-evaluation of matters in this new light. Eventually he comments.

'Still a model, by the look of it.'

56

He snatches a sideways glance at DS Jones, as if to check her reaction, for his choice of words is a little provocative, but she simply nods in agreement. However, a silence descends until DS Leyton, who has a nose for all things 'soap opera', voices the gist of what his colleagues may be subconsciously mulling over.

'Seems to me Lady Miranda's taken a bit of a shine to the gamekeeper. I reckon that's put the cat among the pigeons, Guv.'

Skelgill sets his jaw and renews his grip upon the steering wheel.

'Why would someone in her shoes go for him? Looks to me like he's getting above his station. Arrogant type.'

DS Jones inhales as if to speak, but then seems to think the better of it. But Skelgill prompts her.

'What?'

'Oh – just that – well, sometimes that 'type' can have its own appeal – for some women.'

Skelgill does not immediately reply. For a moment his female colleague's response diverts him. Certainly it had not escaped him that various antipathies (and otherwise) were played out during their visit, and little if any of it for the benefit of the three detectives. But his primary focus has been upon their stated mission, and the reaction of Lawrence Melling in this regard.

'Remember we're here for the birds. Get things in proportion. We've done what we came for. We can wash our hands of the lot of them.'

4. MISSING

Monday, noon – two weeks later

'Y ou spoke too soon, Guv.'
DS Leyton has arrived at his superior's office wielding a sheaf of papers. Skelgill responds by looking irked; he does not appreciate the cryptic reproach. Or perhaps it is the lack of tea.

'Remember we were over at that queer old place – Toad Hall, whatever it's called? The hawk that was shot – those chicken harriers.'

'It's hen harrier, Leyton, not chicken.'

DS Leyton looks like he thinks Skelgill is gratuitously splitting hairs. He contrives a face like a schoolboy unfairly ticked off and now going on strike. Skelgill is obliged to make amends.

'Why did I speak too soon?'

His sergeant immediately perks up, no grudge borne.

'All those wacky characters – you said we could forget about them – except now there's been a burglary.'

Skelgill glowers indignantly.

'What's it to us?'

He is questioning why CID would be called upon for a petty crime. DS Leyton raises the documents and declaims in the pompous manner of a master of ceremonies.

'Lady Bullingdon's jewellery stolen to an estimated value of a quarter of a million.'

Skelgill splutters. That someone can own trinkets worth more than the average house conjures all manner of largely unreasonable reactions in the average police officer. What do they expect? Why do folk need to flaunt their wealth? Why were the valuables not kept in a safe deposit?

In the absence of a coherent rejoinder from his superior, DS Leyton continues.

'We've had a couple of uniforms up there, doing interviews. Seems they've drawn a blank. Main problem being, Lady Bullingdon can't say when the theft occurred. Could have been any time in the last few days – and they've got no CCTV.' He reads at arm's length. 'No signs of a break-in. No reports of intruders or strangers. And there's no forensics to speak of. Seems the jewellery was kept in an unlocked drawer of a dressing table. We sent a fingerprint officer but the furniture's all been cleaned and polished.' He looks up at Skelgill. 'Reading between the lines, Guv – I'd say it's an inside job.'

'Not necessarily, Leyton.'

Skelgill is thinking of Karen, the cloth-wielding karate cleaner. He has witnessed first hand her dedication to duty. She would be every burglar's best friend. Unless she caught them in the act, in which case they might have something to regret. He consults his watch and scowls, as if there was something he wanted to do but is now thwarted.

'Like we've got some special powers of mindreading.'

Though he uses a rather fatuous analogy he makes an incisive point. A crime of unknown occasion destroys the mainstay of detective work – the capacity to ascertain the whereabouts of, and therefore eliminate, suspects. It is the next worst kind of investigation to that of a murder without a body.

'Anything from the statements?'

'Not really, Guv – I didn't print them off – just brought you this top line summary and some photos.'

He hands over the materials but Skelgill immediately lays them upon his desk.

'What's Jones up to?'

'I think she's running a training session for the DCs. I caught sight of her in one of the seminar rooms.'

'Get her to go through them – she can give us a rundown on the way – I need to duck into Penrith – we'll leave in half an hour.'

'Righto, Guv – anything you want me to do?'

Skelgill shrugs, but then begins to delve impatiently into his in-tray. At length he extracts the brochure given to him by Daphne Bullingdon. He squints at the small print on the reverse side.

'See what you can find out about their finances. Here – they've got a trading company, Shuteham Hall Limited.'

'Should be "unlimited" – *hah!*'

But Skelgill either does not approve of or does not see the joke. DS Leyton swiftly retrenches.

'You thinking it's an insurance job, Guv?'

Skelgill turns down his mouth.

'That amount of money, Leyton – brings into play quite a few possible motives.'

DS Leyton mirrors his boss's somewhat pessimistic expression.

'From what I've seen so far it's not clear how organised they were. You'd want valuation certificates and proper photographs. I suppose if they've just taken out a brand new policy it's a little alarm bell. All we've got at the moment are paparazzi shots of Lady Bullingdon in some of the gear.' Skelgill's gaze drifts over the papers. 'I'll get one of the gofers onto Companies House – see what's been filed by way of accounts.'

When his sergeant has gone Skelgill gathers up the printout and takes it over to the light of the window. He ignores the top page of type and turns to the photographs. Miranda Bullingdon poses casually yet provocatively, engaging with other socialites at some event – prestigious, judging by the lavish outfits. Her shimmering dress leaves plenty of space to showcase the jewellery against her smooth honeyed skin. He is reminded of the subtle fragrance when she approached.

*

Chanel N°5. Now he sees it on the dresser. She has moved half a step closer than would be normal, intruding upon his personal space. Is it from her or the uncorked bottle that fragrant tentacles coil into his nostrils? The effect is heady; the woman seems to exude some exotic wavelength; there is a kind of immaculate perfection about her, despite today's informal attire.

Miranda Bullingdon breaks his trance – she presses the moulding that forms the rim of the cabinet and a drawer that is not apparent slides open. It is shallow and lined with black velvet and still contains a substantial trove of gemstones and precious metals.

'They didn't take everything?'

'It seems they had good taste. Just a diamond tiara from Tiffany's – a duty-free gift in lieu of salary after a New York photoshoot. A De Beers diamond tennis bracelet with matching earrings and necklace. And a Rolex that was given to me by Versace.' She sighs wistfully. 'Well – Gianni.'

Skelgill endeavours not to show he is in over his head – but he sees her scrutinising his reaction in the mirrors. Quickly, she shifts her gaze to her own reflection, and makes a considered adjustment to her hair. Skelgill concentrates upon the glittering array of valuables; those remaining would not take much space in a bag or large pocket. Why not just snatch the lot?

'Did they think you wouldn't notice?'

She seems to understand his point.

'Well, the fact is, I didn't.'

Against a tide of reluctant inertia Skelgill finds strength in protocol and shifts sideways towards the room's only window, undersized but cut deep into the thick stonework. He glances out momentarily before turning to face her.

'Could you tell me about that, madam?'

She seems amused that he feels the need to establish a respectable distance between them.

'Before I went out for coffee this morning – I thought I might just wear the bracelet. It was missing – along with the other items. I last wore them at the Hunt Ball, on Saturday.'

Though Skelgill more or less knows the answer from the photographs he has perused, he asks for clarification.

'So it was just what you wore to the ball, nothing else?'

'That is correct, Inspector.'

'Is it possible you took them off somewhere else? Put them safe, automatically. Folk do it with their reading glasses all the time.'

She looks further entertained – there is a challenging glint in her eye.

'And where would I have taken them off, do you think?'

Her tone is entirely warm, as if she revels in the notion of having her movements interrogated. Skelgill is finding her mood difficult to fathom – after all, would not most women be distraught, beside themselves with woe at such a catastrophic loss? He deflects her question with a nod towards the dressing table.

'Madam, is it likely you left them on top?'

'I think I should have noticed in the morning.'

A little self-consciously Skelgill casts about the room. The centrepiece is a four-poster bed and the décor is traditional in its style; it is not easy to establish the status of this domain. The woman seems intuitively to know what he is trying to work out.

'I sleep alone, Inspector – it's more satisfying, don't you think?'

Skelgill feels blood rising to his cheeks. He turns his head towards one of two internal doors.

'Where does this lead to?'

'To Teddy's room – the other is the bathroom.'

Skelgill unaccountably is finding his questions sticking in his throat.

'Do you keep your doors locked?'

'Oh – why would I?' She purrs throatily. 'After all the years changing without underwear, beneath prying eyes – it is not something I think about.'

She has moved to face him – although he has crossed to contemplate the interconnecting door. It has a mortise lock; the key is on her side. He senses she is willing him to look at her, and that the comment about underwear was given special emphasis. She is barefooted, and clad in a close-fitting nude velour tracksuit, the top unzipped to her breastbone.

The distraction might just be in his head. He determines to concentrate upon what is surely a straightforward crime. He steps over to the window once more and, looking out properly now, sees the black shadows of the topiary cast by the sun, and the pale gravel driveway winding around the verdant lawn. He becomes conscious of the aroma of citrus – beneath him on the sill there is an expensive-looking candle in a branded glass container. He speaks with his back to her.

'After the ball – how did you get home?'

'Teddy drove. He doesn't drink these days. Alcohol disagrees with his medication.'

Her answer would seem to rule out an opportunistic taxi driver – although frankly it strikes Skelgill as improbable that a complete outsider could have found their way with such precision through the castle grounds and corridors and stairs to home in on this tiny drawer. He turns, and fixes a stare decisively upon the languid pools of her dark eyes.

'How about at the ball – do you recall anyone admiring your jewellery?'

She averts her gaze. It could be an act of reflection – or, judged more cynically, of affected modesty.

'Oh – I suppose I did attract some attention. But I don't believe a jealous wife would have wreaked her revenge upon *me*, do you, Inspector?'

She is quick to join up the dots – a little too swift for comfort.

'What about serving staff?'

'There must have been thirty or more.'

Skelgill knows she makes a good point.

'Who took the photographs?'

'Oh – she's a local snapper – I've seen her around. She syndicates her work. Country Life sometimes uses her material. But there were no renegade paps, if that's what you are thinking.'

Skelgill is trying not to think too hard. For him, detective work is like fishing – though he would not openly characterise it as such. But he knows he would never tackle an unfamiliar water by rowing to the centre and flailing about in all directions. He

63

would walk the perimeter, taking in the topography and habitat, watching for signs of bird and insect life. Then he would begin somewhere promising – a small bay perhaps, or the mouth of a beck; at the very least a wind lane – places where food collects, for all creatures obey their basic instincts. Literally clueless at the moment, he is in the middle of the metaphorical lake. Sure, he can pick a direction and spin out a plausible theory – a rogue photographer has a buyer waiting online, follows her home, watches for her bedroom light to go out, knowing she will sleep soundly after all the champagne; the security at the castle is almost non-existent. *Tch* – he can invent a dozen plausible lines of inquiry that would radiate like endless ripples. Better to stick to the shore, work from outside to in. Ask questions, and don't mither himself too much over the answers.

'The photos that we received were uploaded on the Gazette website yesterday morning. Are you aware of any visitors since then – or even of who might have entered this room?'

Miranda Bullingdon has picked up a gold chain from the drawer; she pours it absently from one hand to the other, apparently enjoying the sensation.

'Almost anybody could have entered this room – but I am sure they would have been able to explain themselves.'

He realises she means an authorised person.

'But you wouldn't expect to find one of the gardeners in here – a stable hand – or the gamekeeper?'

Though he says it offhandedly he detects a flash of animation in her eyes – but it quickly turns to amusement as though she suspects he is provoking her.

'As I understand it, most of our workers are what you might call Jacks of all trades.' She cocks her head towards the bathroom. 'One day a plumber, the next a pheasant plucker.'

She chuckles and Skelgill's response is by comparison stilted.

'We've interviewed most of the staff here. Nobody has knowledge of an intruder – by that I mean an outsider.'

'Are there not poachers who skulk under the cover of darkness?'

Skelgill regards her quizzically.

'Are there poachers – this time of year?'

There is a certain technical aspect to this question, it being the breeding season, with few full-grown birds to be found. Miranda Bullingdon is unperturbed, albeit her answer is a little oblique.

'Lawrence likes to keep us on our toes.'

Her tone is decidedly sardonic.

'Are you saying there aren't poachers?'

She waves a hand beside her head – that she can't be bothered.

'Oh – probably there are. It gives him an excuse to prowl about at night, I suppose. Playing at soldiers.'

Skelgill wonders why she is saying this. She seems to be just loosening her colours from Lawrence Melling's mast. But then maybe he would be misguided to think they were attached in the first place. Or should he suspect there is a feint at play? He tries not to show his doubting thoughts – and in doing so finds himself rushing to a point he might prefer to have reached with greater subtlety.

'If you don't mind my saying – madam – you don't seem too upset.'

'Where would that get me?'

Skelgill senses that to raise the financial aspect would be undiplomatic.

'It sounds like these pieces have sentimental value.'

She looks down at the gold chain cupped in her palm and, weighing it abstractedly, closes her eyes momentarily.

'I try to avoid having regrets. It is better to live.'

Without warning she starts towards him and begins simultaneously to feed the chain beneath her hair and around her neck.

'Would you do this – it is too short for me to see.'

Notwithstanding the adjacent dressing table with its ample mirrors, before he can react she is toe to toe, turning up her chin, making her demand impossible for him to resist. He feels the silky skin of her fingers as she transfers the ends of the chain; his must be like sandpaper – but they are at least trained to deal with tiny fishhooks and near-invisible knots and thus, conscious of her gaze upon his, and holding his breath, he successfully fastens the clasp. He releases it and lets his arms fall to his sides; there is a moment when nothing happens – but the instant he meets her eyes she smiles sweetly.

'Thank you.'

Beside them, close to the window, there is a Victorian mahogany chaise longue and without warning or explanation she half swoons upon it, in a manner that in most women would be seen as theatrical, yet she carries it off as though it is an entirely natural thing to do – like a movie star arriving for a session with her longstanding therapist. Skelgill hears himself forming a sentence that is only vaguely relevant.

'Lord Bullingdon must be concerned for you.'

'I gather Teddy is at the office – being interviewed concurrently. Divide and conquer, no, Inspector?'

Her eyes have many expressions; now it is one of insouciance – that she understands their modus operandi, but quite relishes the idea. Skelgill, however, feels the need to apologise.

'It's just so we can be time efficient, madam.'

She shakes her long black tresses, as if experimentally, just to see how they will fall after the fitting of the chain. She regards him with a look of surprise, that he has not pursued some obvious advantage.

'I am at your mercy, Inspector.'

Skelgill is experiencing a kind of out-of-body dreamlike state, the sensation of floating above the scene and looking down at himself in the boudoir together with its alluring occupant. And also like in a dream he is able to have a little conversation with himself: a discourse in objectivity, and that this is a game of cat and mouse – and further, that now would be a good time for him to make a dash for the skirting board.

If he employed a notebook and pen their deliberate folding away would serve to mark that he considers the interview to be complete. But these are anathema to Skelgill – why write things down and make them all equal on the page, when hunches semi-digested do not lie in one's gut with equal weight? (At least, it is a plausible excuse to his colleagues for his blatant aversion to the written word.) In lieu of such accessories Skelgill ostentatiously consults his wristwatch, and further signals his imminent departure by edging backwards towards the door to the landing.

'I'll bear that in mind, madam. Obviously it's early stages – but as soon as there is any significant progress I'll update you personally.'

The woman turns a pout of disappointment into an accepting smile. She curls her feet beneath her thighs and reaches for an old paperback novel from an occasional table beside the chaise longue. She settles back, and raises the book, displaying the cover. Skelgill sees it is entitled *The Maltese Falcon*. Now she smiles more winningly, as if in solidarity.

'I prefer the classics. There's nothing like a detective with a gun in his pocket.'

*

Making his way down the sequence of stairs and landings, his ears inexplicably burning, Skelgill finds himself arrested by a ghostly apparition: ahead is his own shadowy image captured by a full-length antique mirror; though its powers are waning and it is heavily desilvered. He checks overhead and around to ensure he is unobserved, and then addresses the glass, standing to attention. This is not a regular habit – the reflection he is most familiar with is his face half covered with shaving cream, and blood beginning to ooze – but now, scowling, he makes a more general appraisal. Immediately he seems to experience a flash of enlightenment and delves into his left-hand trouser pocket. With difficulty he pulls out a small polythene bag containing an assortment of coloured feathers so striking that they must surely be dyed. Indeed, these are the fly-tying materials he purchased during an abridged lunchtime visit to his favourite tackle shop in Penrith, prior to rendezvousing with his colleagues. He regards the packet as if he is surprised to see it in his possession. Then he replaces it, and scrutinises the mirror once more. At length, emitting a subdued growl, he seemingly dismisses the source of conjecture and moves purposefully off.

Without reflecting specifically upon the encounter with Miranda Bullingdon, he recognises that she did hit the nail on the head as far as the detectives' modus operandi is concerned. There was more to it than time efficiency – if not exactly "divide and conquer" as she had suggested. Having previously met several of the household, his subordinates had speculated about who should conduct which interviews. While DS Jones had been surprisingly vehement in voicing her opinion, DS Leyton, treating the matter as academic, had suggested 'rock paper scissors'. Skelgill at this point had become distracted by obduracy: how can paper ever beat rock? His objection must have something to do with the fellsman in him. By the time he had tuned back in, DS Jones was putting forward the proposal that he should interview Miranda Bullingdon and the housekeeper, Karen Williamson; that DS Leyton should interview Lord Bullingdon and Daphne Bullingdon; and that she should interview Julian Bullingdon and Lawrence Melling. She had been rather coy in her reasoning, other than to suggest that the interviewees would be most communicative when pitted accordingly against the respective strengths of the individual officers. Ordinarily this would be a subject upon which Skelgill would rule without consultation. But, having thrown it open to the floor he felt a certain obligation to go along with the outcome. Moreover, rather like at a formal dinner where places are dictated by place cards, he was pleased with the hand he was dealt, and not inclined to jeopardise his position. This despite a certain disquiet regarding the prospect of DS Jones being paired with Lawrence Melling. However, if truth be told, he was likely to get nowhere with the man; for there was already a smouldering antagonism between them. He had wondered if this lay at the root of DS Jones's logic.

Members of the wider household – domestic and estate workers, contractors (some of the latter yet to be identified), along with other possible 'visitors' (postie, couriers, salespeople) – are to be tackled in due course, when more is understood about both the theft and the nature of the daily routine at Shuteham Hall.

Now Skelgill finds Karen Williamson precisely where he has been told she will be available. Not, as might reasonably be expected, innocently erasing fingerprints from antique furniture, but in a largely fallow walled garden that is located behind ivy-clad brickwork reached in a southwesterly direction across the topiary lawn. Standing in a raised bed of healthy looking lettuce plants, she has swapped her karate casuals for a loose-fitting navy boiler suit, though perhaps to give her face and neck some protection from the early afternoon sun she has let loose her dark hair, of which there is a surprising amount. Hoeing patiently, she reminds Skelgill of a worker in an oriental paddy field.

'You could do with one of those conical hats.'

She looks up in surprise. Then she smiles broadly in recognition, revealing even white teeth. Skelgill is struck by the contrast: here is an expression that asks for nothing. She even seems pleased to see him.

'You're probably right – I believe you can dip them in water to help you cool off.'

Skelgill nods approvingly at the prospect. Inside the walled garden the air is stilled by its high red brick enclosure, and the sun has emerged above a magnificent white cumulus cloud and quickly makes known its proximity to these latitudes. Perhaps he licks his lips, because the woman responds with a welcome suggestion.

'Fancy a mash?'

Skelgill frowns dubiously.

'You know what they say about the bear and the woods. But, where?'

She gestures past him, roughly in the direction from which he has entered between tall wooden gates that were sufficiently ajar for him to slip through unannounced. Against the south-facing wall runs a succession of conjoined greenhouses, a glinting shanty of uneven lean-tos; there must be a thousand panes, and a good many of them fractured. The paintwork of the uprights is flaking almost beyond redemption, and cast iron gutters are askew and downpipes have tumbled away. Within, all Skelgill can make out through the hazy, algae-stained windows are swathes of trailing brown stems of what once perhaps were beds of tomatoes and cucumbers and squashes, trained upon wires, but now looking like a blighted crop, desiccated and preserved for posterity. He voices a further doubt.

'Won't it be too hot?'

She shakes her head and then has to part the strands of hair that cover her face; he sees she has caught the sun on her cheekbones and the bridge of her nose, the beginnings of war paint. He realises all traces of her former black eye have gone.

'I have a secret shady spot – beneath a grapevine – and most of the glass is missing. This way.'

She spears the hoe into the tilled earth of the bed and hops nimbly over the three-course brickwork surround. Skelgill falls into step alongside her, just beyond arm's reach. She leads him towards the opposite corner from that of the gates. Conscious of her masculine attire, he is reminded of Miranda Bullingdon's remark about Jacks of all trades.

'I thought you were the housekeeper, not the head gardener.'

She chuckles, perhaps a little ironically.

'I can use all the overtime I can get – the price at the pumps these days.'

Skelgill is moved to question further this point – but he becomes distracted as she disappears into a little corner section of hothouse that is overwhelmed by a vine that is contorted like some captive prehistoric octopus, filling the interior with shoots, suckers and tendrils, vigorous growth that absconds through the many broken panes. He ducks into the cool green light of the interior, brushing aside the cascading vegetation, disturbing tiny flying insects that are illuminated by narrow shafts of sunlight. Against the whitewashed back wall is a dried out hardwood bench, on it a hessian bag from which a vacuum flask protrudes; an upturned orange crate serves as a handy table.

'This is the sort of thing I do.'

'What do you mean?'

70

'I've been making camps since I were a bairn. Even now – bivvy spots – for night fishing, that sort of thing.'

The woman takes a seat at one end of the bench and he settles beside the opposite armrest.

'Cosy I suppose.'

Skelgill appraises their surroundings.

'Aye – but it's more than that. It's like your own little world – of wilderness, adventure, jeopardy – even if it's in the back garden.'

'Is that why you got into the police?'

Skelgill in a way is stunned by her question. How rare it is for someone to ask him about himself, about his motives. Rarer still to ask about his feelings – though she has not quite got that far. Is it his job – or is it just him? What is the provenance of a belligerence that folk can read a mile off, that warns of the recalcitrant riposte such an inquiry will elicit? Well into his second decade of serving the Crown, has the relentless pressure to perform, to see justice done presided over the imperceptible deposition, layer upon layer of a defensive shield? They would not know there are chinks all over – not know he would welcome such probing – not know he is imprisoned like a crab that has outgrown its exoskeleton and is desperate for the next instar, yet afraid to make the transition, should it leave him formless and floundering. He feels a curious sense of release, here in this little den, this leafy arbour with its dusty green light, an attractive woman at his side who shows no trace of purveying her own agenda, free of Machiavellian intent. *Ach!* What an extreme reaction to such an innocent question! It is what normal folk ask one another every day. He'll probably ask her the same thing any minute. But his procrastination is such that she takes over.

'A long story, eh?'

He gives a forced laugh, meant to rebut her solicitude; though of course she is right. She hands him a tin mug of tea, and he leans forward, resting his forearms on his thighs, dangling the cup between his knees. The hardened earth at his feet is criss-crossed with the crystalline patterns of glistening slug trails. He exhales resignedly. Much as he would like to sit here chatting all afternoon, even now he can't escape the professional suspicion that this could just be yet another variation on a theme. The theme being – hotfoot from Miranda Bullingdon's boudoir – that of how to manipulate a situation for one's own benefit. Of course, he encounters it on an almost daily basis – often so blatantly as to be laughable; some suspects brought in for questioning should be despatched not to the cells but to stage school, such are the heights of their thespian talents. But Karen Williamson – she cannot possibly have pulled off a massive jewel heist.

Before he can fulfil his prediction and turn the question about vocation around upon her, she does it for him.

'I'm a qualified physiotherapist.'

'Do you do backs?'

It is a knee-jerk response that he instantly wishes he had not voiced. But though there is a slight pause the young woman takes no offence, when some reasonably might.

'Of course, why?'

Now it is awkward for Skelgill. But he sits upright and flexes his spine and groans contritely, as if to authenticate the sincerity of his remark.

'For my sins I'm in the mountain rescue. I did my back in, years ago. I should have had it seen to. Now it flares up if I'm not careful – like if I lug my boat onto shingle without thinking about it.'

'It sounds like a herniated disc.'

'That sounds like something I'd rather not hear.'

For a moment there is a silence: she does not volunteer anything more; he is rather tongue- tied. Yet there is a sense that each willingly awaits the other. Eventually Skelgill finds an exit strategy.

'Why aren't you being a physio?'

She responds immediately.

'Well – I am – for the district karate squad. But that's just a voluntary role. It keeps my hand in, so to speak.' She raises her eyebrows at the hackneyed pun. 'When I had Kieran I went part time. But with the cuts to local authority services the part-time posts were the first to go. Then Kieran's dad and I split up. That was when I saw this job advertised. It didn't pay as well but it came with a cottage – that made all the difference.'

'Where were you living?'

'Workington – then for a few months with a friend in Cockermouth. I managed to get Kieran moved to the local primary. The school bus picks him up from the bottom of the drive.'

'So where's your cottage?'

'Not far. You came down from the hall?' (He nods.) 'If you follow the track past the gates of the walled garden and round the corner, it's less than a hundred yards. It was the gardener's cottage at one time. They've got five properties on the estate. The only condition is that I sometimes have to do B&B for shooting guests, if there's a big party – if there's an overflow. Usually they fit them into one or more of the empty cottages – or close friends of Teddy's they put up in the hall.

Skelgill is interested to hear this. He takes the opportunity to navigate back towards the course he ought to be following, though there is some way to go.

'Has anyone stayed over the weekend?'

Drinking, she shakes her head.

'No – it's just during the shooting season. There's a peak in August when they start the grouse. Then in October for the pheasants. They'll generally have a house party for Christmas, with a big shoot on Boxing Day. It ticks over the rest of the time. They're busiest at weekends – but obviously my cleaning job's fine to do during the week, and it's pretty flexible – dust is a patient client.'

Skelgill is nodding amenably.

'How long have you been here?'

'Coming up for three years.'

'What about the other staff?'

'Well – Cook – she's called Pru – she's the longest serving. She's been with Teddy's family for generations. She lives in. There's a kind of maid's room above the kitchen that's been extended over the scullery to make a little bedsit. She has a girl – Janice, from Overthwaite – who comes in evenings to help her with dinners – prep and serving and clearing up – she's been here longer than me, as well.'

Now the woman seems to need to be prompted – although it might just be Skelgill's imagination.

'How about the gamekeeper?'

'Lawrence?'

'Is there more than one?'

'Er – no. He came last September, I think it was.'

'What's the story there, then?'

Karen Williamson seems a little unnerved.

'I believe the bags had been falling for a number of years – last August was the worst on record. So Teddy replaced his old keeper – I think he was more or less due to retire, anyway.'

'And has he made a difference?'

'They say there's been an improvement in the organisation. I suppose with the birds it's too soon to judge – until nature runs its course. And there are others involved – four estate workers. They're all Eastern Europeans – a really nice crowd – turn their hand to all manner of jobs – although their English isn't always that good.'

'Folk say that about me.'

She simpers tactfully – but for his part he has noticed she did not dwell on the subject of Lawrence Melling. As for the remaining staff, those employees whom 'inside information' places in a category of being necessary targets for inquisition, for some reason Skelgill feels little compunction to pursue them at this juncture. It could be said there is the disconcerting ability of foreigners to switch into impenetrable mode, their smattering of English dropping away like autumn leaves after a heavy frost – but his personal experience of scores of émigré workers from the old Soviet Bloc is of industrious, honest, cheerful types – who have swapped their homes and families for the company of strangers, poor quarters and workman's wages; faithfully to remit the latter to their loved ones. If he harbours any resentment, it is against those who would exploit them by paying rates the locals will not get out of bed for.

'So what do you reckon, Karen?'

'What about?'

For the first time there might just be a slight tremor in her voice – perhaps she detects a change in tenor brought on by his use of her name and the open-ended question.

'Who should I put in thumbscrews?'

As she stares at the dusty ground in front of her the sun is suddenly obscured, and she widens her eyes as if she is trying to readjust to the inferior light.

'Aren't I the prime suspect?'

Skelgill does not answer for a moment, and as he turns his head to look at her she reciprocates. To his relief her gaze is fiercely interrogative. He makes a face that perhaps goes some way to being reassuring.

'I'd like proof they're stolen.'

She looks shocked by his statement.

'Oh – but surely they are?'

Skelgill shrugs and casts about the cramped space. Lying on its side he notices a rusty zinc watering can that has a screw thread on its spout, and it reminds him how he is always losing the push-on rose from his own plastic version. He ought to obtain one like this. It looks discarded. Maybe it is available?

'It wouldn't be the first theft I've been called to that never was. Sometimes things disappear and then magically reappear.'

Karen Williamson frowns pensively.

'Cook said she heard Teddy telling Daphne that Miranda didn't want to report the loss.'

Skelgill is reminded of an incident from his childhood. At the age of five at infant school he 'borrowed' a desirable miniature toy car from a classroom display. But it was soon burning a hole in his pocket – and his cheeks were burning even hotter when the teacher lined up the class and made them turn out said pockets. Miraculously, by some instinctive sleight of hand he was not caught. The pupils were then conscripted to scour the classroom – and by the same magic to which he has just referred, by the end of the search the model car was back in its place! It was the last thing he ever stole – or, at least, the last thing that wasn't a fish – but a fish is a wild animal, and no human can own a wild animal.

'Happen she thought they'd turn up – like I say.'

'That the thief would have second thoughts?'

Skelgill produces a wry grin – she might have read his mind – but he is interested in her use of the word *thief.* If any one thing she has said would convince him of her innocence, it is this. Almost certainly if she were self-referencing she would have said *person.* But he reminds himself to retain a small percentage of doubt. It would be too easy to fall for her unaffected candour when it is so starkly juxtaposed to Miranda Bullingdon's seduction technique.

'But isn't it most likely just to be an actual burglary? At night – when there was no one around and everyone was sleeping?'

Skelgill nods slowly, though he does not quite agree with her assessment of probability.

'There were no signs of a break in.'

She regards him uncertainly.

'I'm not sure they always lock up properly. I mean – I believe Teddy does it when he goes to bed – at around ten. You can't get through the main door from the outside once it's locked. But the scullery door to the kitchen garden, that's got a Yale lock on it so people can get in with their key. Cook normally opens that at seven. I have a spare key in case I need to start any earlier.'

'Doesn't a Yale automatically lock itself?'

'There's been some mornings – not often – when I've gone up early and it's not been locked. Of course, it could be someone's already come out and left it on the latch – like Julian, doing his nature study.' She hesitates for a moment, as if she might believe otherwise – but then she shrugs lightly. 'But there are also French windows in the Georgian wing that could be left open. You could get through into the old part of the hall that way.'

Skelgill nods noncommittally. It is true, a confident cat burglar would have few qualms in creeping about while folk were asleep, but in a place the size of Shuteham Hall – there must be fifty rooms – it would surely require more than random chance to home in on Miranda Bullingdon's jewels? It doesn't yet quite stack up.

'Was she in the habit of leaving her valuables lying out?'

The young woman furrows her brow.

'I would say mainly not. She's very methodical. With all her outfits and cosmetics and stuff like that.'

Skelgill rather feels this is not the impression Miranda Bullingdon endeavours to convey.

'I take it you knew the jewels were there?'

Karen Williamson looks at him wide-eyed.

'Oh, yes – she showed them to me when I started – asked me if I wanted to try anything on – said I could borrow something if I ever needed to.'

It is Skelgill's turn to look surprised.

'And did you?'

She shakes her head vigorously.

'No – no – I wouldn't dare. Imagine if you lost one of those diamond earrings.'

Skelgill reserves comment. He is wondering if a woman, given the freedom of a dressing table full of jewellery and the opportunity (and the invitation) to try it on, would be able to resist the temptation. The tackle shop he visited earlier – were he to have been accidentally locked in over the lunch hour – how long would it have been before he was swishing handmade bamboo fly rods that he could only dream of owning? But he decides not to challenge her on this hypothesis. He reverts to matters of fact.

'I know you've been asked this – but as I haven't had chance to read the statements – when did you clean Lady Bullingdon's room?'

'Today. I always do her room first thing on a Monday. The missing jewellery wasn't on the dressing table – but it could have been in the drawer.'

'You didn't open it?'

She looks at him and shakes her head.

'It does open by accident sometimes. It's got a mechanism that you have to press – so when you're polishing the dresser you can trigger it. But it didn't open today.'

The sun comes out; Skelgill sighs and shades his eyes with a hand.

'It's giving me a headache – that we don't know when it was taken.'

The woman seems reassured by his reaction. She reaches for the vacuum flask.

'It might be dehydration. Like a refill? Oh – and I've got some chocolate digestives. They'll get your sugar levels up.'

She pours him more tea and pulls an open packet of biscuits from the bag beside her. Skelgill seems to rejuvenate instantly.

'Every first aid kit should have them.'

'Is that what you carry in the mountain rescue?'

'Kendal mint cake, actually.' And now a pause while Skelgill dunks a biscuit and swallows it whole. I try to keep these in the car, or when I'm fishing. It's not a proper mash without them.'

She grins and offers him another.

'My Kieran would eat a whole packet in a sitting if I let him.'

Skelgill has to turn his face away to hide his smile.

'I expect he needs the energy, young lad, getting loads of exercise.'

She nods, and then speaks with sudden eagerness.

'Would you like to see a video of him competing?'

'Aye, sure.'

She carefully balances her own mug on the orange box and, leaning sideways, pulls her mobile phone from her thigh pocket nearest to Skelgill. She shuffles along the bench until she is close beside him, and bends over the handset, her long hair veiling her face but also shading the screen from the overhead brightness while she finds the item. She starts the recording and half turns around to Skelgill. A shaft of sunlight is reflecting off the screen and he automatically shades it with his palm and leans closer to see, so that their heads are more or less touching. They watch, both perfectly still now.

'He's the one with the dark hair.'

Skelgill concentrates upon the action.

'He's good. He's got your natural sense of balance. And your kick, I bet – look at that!'

The woman laughs delightedly.

At this moment there is a sharp crack and Skelgill and Karen Williamson look up simultaneously. It is the distinctive snap of a fragment of glass trodden on; and silhouetted in the vine-festooned doorway, looking a little disconcerted, but quickly composing herself, is DS Jones.

'Sorry to interrupt, Guv – there's been a development. I think you ought to come.'

*

'Guv, look at this – his passport.'

DS Leyton has entered the cramped cottage kitchen carrying an apparently empty black Nike holdall, its white tick logo scuffed and its carry straps frayed and its beading split. He brandishes the passport, held open at the ID pages and steps between his colleagues. He drops the bag onto a small square table as they cluster around.

'That's a corker of a name, "Carol Valentin Stanislav" – no wonder they call him Stan. Age – what would that be – twenty-nine? *Wait a minute* – he's the clown we saw fall off the ladder, remember, Guv?'

Skelgill nods grimly. He takes the travel document from his sergeant and squints at the pixelated image. He turns over to the cover; royal blue embossed with gold lettering, it states: "Republica Moldova".

DS Jones responds to the silence of her colleagues.

'It's landlocked between Romania and Ukraine. The text will be Romanian – it's the official language. It's one of the poorest countries in Europe – they estimate that a quarter of its population is working abroad. By the way, "Carol" is Charles.'

DS Leyton is looking at her somewhat open-mouthed.

'Don't forget – I have relatives from Ukraine.'

For his part, Skelgill stares reflectively at his female colleague. In the poor light, the illumination channelled from a smallish window, her strong physiognomy is cast into sharp contrast, the prominent cheekbones and dark eyes, the sculpted classical features that often turn heads. Skelgill muses that perhaps the Eastern European influence is stronger than he normally allows. But now DS Leyton chips in.

'I keep forgetting you're not as Welsh as you're a Jones, girl.'

She chuckles.

'Heinz 57 – but Cumbrian born and bred.'

She glances rather insouciantly at Skelgill – as if to make some point – but rather than elaborate she reaches for the black holdall.

'This is surely his travel bag.'

There is a crushed airline tracking tag still attached to one of the straps. She flattens it out. It bears the letters 'MAN' – which they all recognise as the IATA airport code for Manchester International.

'Looks like the last flight he took was inbound.'

'Or he wants it to seem like that.'

DS Jones appears momentarily crestfallen; but she quickly collects her wits and nods pensively; her superior is right in principle, if not in management style. She has found him in a capricious mood since her intervention at the walled garden. He had been taciturn during their brisk walk to their present locus, as if he harboured some smouldering resentment. That was unusual – he normally fires from the hip – a preferred trait, in her view. Accordingly, she had not volunteered details of her own interviews, preferring to wait until the subject is raised.

Now, still holding the bag, she seems to detect some irregularity, and weighs it in mid air as if to indicate as such. She puts it on the table and delves inside as her colleagues look on. At one end there is a zipped compartment designed for transporting damp sports kit. From this she produces an envelope, unsealed. Inside is a thick wad of sterling banknotes, in denominations of twenty.

'Cor blimey – there must be a couple of grand there.'

It is DS Leyton that makes this estimate. Skelgill waves a hand at the holdall.

'Leyton, where was the bag?'

'Ah – you see, Guv – there's a little porch at the back door. There's four refuse sacks piled up. It was in the bottom one.'

'What, in with the rubbish?'

'Nah, Guv – it was clean – just the holdall. I do it myself.'

'What are you talking about, Leyton?'

'Well – if we go to a caravan, or a little holiday flat – these places are never very secure, and the local tea-leaves are always on the prowl, knowing you're down the beach for the day. I reckon it's best to hide things in plain sight. Like the nippers' computer games consoles and whatnot. Put 'em in a bin-bag beside the rest of the trash. Maybe stuff in a few of the littlun's disposable nappies – no one wants to stick their hand in one of them!'

Skelgill is glaring somewhat disbelievingly at his colleague – but he can hardly disparage the method when it has apparently just been vindicated. And, frankly, it is smart thinking (discounting the risk of a cleaner visiting unheralded to dispose of the rubbish). He glances at DS Jones, who is looking on admiringly – then he addresses DS Leyton once more.

'What did Daphne Bullingdon have to say?'

'Well – I was about to interview her – before I could start she came straight out with this information – that she'd just been made aware of. Seems the workers have a breakfast meeting with her, early doors Mondays, where she allocates the jobs for the week. The cook brings a tray of bacon rolls and coffee over to the estate office. This Stan geezer wasn't there, but they didn't think too much of it because he's been building an extension at the back of here. It was only when he was needed to help unload a delivery of feedstuffs, about an hour ago – and they couldn't find him – that they notified the office. Now they've realised no one's seen him since Friday. He'd given no indication that he was going away – and wasn't in the habit of doing so.'

'What's his track record like?'

'She reckons he's good as gold, Guv. Been here since October, hard working, bit of an all-round handyman, not a peep of trouble out of him. Seems he found a hoard of old coins when he knocked the wall down, here – and took 'em straight up to her.'

Skelgill is scowling; it is not a reflection upon his sergeant – merely that he is inwardly troubled. He steps across to the sink and runs the hot tap, feeling the water. He places a palm against the kettle. Then he opens a small refrigerator, and moves aside.

'What do you reckon to this?'

DS Jones seems to work out that this is a question aimed at her qualifications; she does not object, and stoops to examine the interior. After a moment she pulls out a shelf on which is a large dish, its contents covered in cling-film, and remarks, using what sounds like a foreign language, half speaking to herself. She reprises, not entirely in English.

'Pierogi – *coltunaşi* in Romanian – homemade dumplings – probably filled with cheese or cabbage or potato. They look quite fresh. I'd say a few days, at most.'

Skelgill bends to inspect the items, his expression that of a teenager being offered some vegetable or other.

'What do you do with them?'

'Boil them in water.'

Skelgill makes a disapproving face and suppresses a groan; but he does not press the case for frying over boiling. Instead he makes a far more strategic move. He digs into his jacket pocket and produces his car keys, which he hands to DS Leyton.

'You pair go back up to the office so you can use their landline. Put into motion whatever background and movement checks are possible. One of you bring Daphne Bullingdon here, maybe with a workmate who knows him best – see if they can identify what he might be wearing – what's missing. Then get a photograph and a description circulated. Leyton – pick me up on the road in an hour. Turn right out of the bottom of the drive, and then first right up the lane signposted to Overthwaite – it'll bring you past here. Just carry on until you find me.'

DS Leyton makes a somewhat doubting face, but otherwise does not question his superior's rather vague idea of a rendezvous.

'What are you thinking, Guv?'

Skelgill glances out of the window.

'I'll just have a bit of a mooch round. You never know.'

He doesn't know, either – but he does know he might absorb something that later will prove to be a small but significant piece in an as-yet-undefined jigsaw – a catalyst, of sorts; there is always the hope. But right now what began as a seemingly straightforward burglary has taken a couple of most definitely unconventional twists, possibly sinister. He drifts into the living room as his colleagues leave. Cursorily, he casts about. The overall impression is of tidiness. There is a worn sofa, a rather threadbare rug, and an out-of-date television set (though there cannot be much of a signal). The restored timber floor and open hearth, however, endow the room with a homely feel, despite the lack of domestic paraphernalia. There are part-burned church candles on the oak mantelpiece. There is an aura of calm, enhanced by the impression of the enfolding woods, green-tinted light and muted afternoon birdsong. He'd feel happy living here, though it is isolated.

He lingers a while longer, allowing his thoughts to settle, much like he would wait for the ripples around his boat, rowed to a promising spot and anchored, to die away; for any fish disturbed to get used to the renewed stillness, and maybe return. It is a meditative mode, not trying too hard. He leaves the living room and follows the dogleg of the hallway to the back door. It opens into a little lean-to porch, covered on all sides. There are the three remaining bin-liners described by his colleague – the 'plain-sight' hiding place. There is a nylon waterproof jacket, the only item on a row of coat hooks, and beneath on the stone floor a pair of cheap wellingtons, of a considerably smaller size than he would take. As he opens the outer door and half turns back, a fishing rod propped up in the corner catches his eye. He almost missed it! It is a seven-foot spinning rod, rigged with a large brightly coloured plastic plug, a lure that puzzles him, not being one that he would employ hereabouts. And – a cardinal sin in his book – it has been left with a tangle of line and a strand of still-green pondweed attached to the treble hooks. He might not be the most fastidious person in the world, but his fishing tackle is always cleaned after use and sprayed with WD40 – you don't want your gear going rusty; you want it ready for next time. This inconsistency has him staring pensively for a few moments. But without straining himself on the matter he exits and closes the door behind him.

The modest, rather run-down property is situated at the western margin of the estate, where the perimeter wall, beyond which runs a quiet public lane, hems in Bullmire Wood. The cottage was evidently at one time a gatehouse, for there are substantial iron gates, rusted and chained and fallen into disuse, heavily overgrown with nettles and docks and brambles, like the environs of the cottage itself. It strikes him that at one time this may have been the main entrance to the estate. What was the avenue leading to Shuteham Hall is now a ride crowded by woodland, though wheel ruts in the leaf litter reveal some signs of vehicular activity. Several pallets of building materials, concrete blocks, shrink-wrapped timber and plastic sacks of sand and cement, may explain the latter. The renovation work in progress appears to be the addition of an extension to the bedroom – in time an en suite bathroom perhaps. A rudimentary doorway has been knocked through, but sealed up again, perhaps until the newbuild is watertight.

It is a warm day, though still pleasantly cool in the wood. The moist air is resonant with birdsong; blackbirds in particular seem to specialise in these conditions; a tide of sound, their fluty melodies flood even the tiniest interstices between trunk and branch and leaf. At ground level the herb layer appears to pulsate, so vigorous is growth at this time of year. The refracted electric sapphire of bluebell swards dazzles the eye, and stippled with pink campion and white stitchwort, nature seems to be making its own abstract version of the British flag – or is it the Stars and Stripes?

Though Skelgill's first love is for the open fells, the oak woods of Lakeland are an intrinsic part of the landscape, always a pleasure after a day out on the high tops, the cream on an upside-down cake. As such, they are second home to Skelgill, and accordingly he divines the difference between two paths that run into the thicket from the clearing at the rear of the cottage. One, well trodden down to bare earth, but barely six inches wide, curving away and passing after about twenty feet beneath a suspended fallen bough, is a badger track. A second, less distinct, where herbaceous vegetation is bruised and shrubs may have been brushed aside, has the hallmarks of human passage. Skelgill has with him the estate brochure. He unfolds it to display the map. He is immediately impressed by the accuracy of its draughtsmanship. Often these things are stylised, almost cartoonish in their representation of an area, but whoever drew this up must have started with a trace from the Ordnance Survey, and there is a helpful imperial scale. Even the compass mark is calibrated to the national grid, and Skelgill uses the sun to rotate slightly on his heel and achieve the correct orientation.

His present location is marked as West Gate House. Bullmire Wood extends north, south and east from where he stands. Over Water lies a good three-quarters of a mile away, in an easterly direction. There are three properties with which he is unfamiliar: Grouse Lodge, well towards the northeast, in a separate wooded area marked Cushat Copse, after which moorland begins to take over; The Bield, its name suggestive of a shepherd's hut on open fellside to the northwest; and – of most interest to Skelgill – Keeper's Cottage. The latter is deep inside Bullmire Wood, beside a ride marked Crow Road that leads via an intersecting diagonal, Long Shoot, to Shuteham Hall, bisecting the walled garden and Garden Cottage and the small artificial lake, rather presumptuously called Troutmere; Boat House is more prosaically labelled.

A 'safe walking route' – if there can ever be such a thing on a shooting estate – a green dotted line, according to the key, links up the various properties and topographical features, and it is obviously the recommended way of getting about. From the gatehouse, the advice would be either to take the avenue back to the hall, or, from the occluded gates, a perimeter path alongside the boundary wall, eventually to pick up the so-called Crow Road. But, curiosity being the better part of valour, Skelgill plunges instead into the undergrowth, the faint path that has its bearing towards Keeper's Cottage.

He knows from experience that quite quickly a route can be forged. Whenever he has tried to keep a good fishing spot secret, for instance beside Bass Lake's wooded shores, it is a devil of a job not disturbing the bankside vegetation and flagging to others the way. In the past he has resorted to wading along the shoreline to cover his tracks. So he reads this as not a regular thoroughfare, a daily route that in time would be established like a wider, less discrete version of the badger path. But it has seen some recent use.

Ten minutes tramping finds him reaching the edge of a clearing. He has been moving rapidly, though ruing that he did not switch to better gripping footwear when he last passed his car, and now he braces against the trunk of a hefty oak to avoid exposing himself. Ahead is Keeper's Cottage, the rear of the building. Crow Road, here a turf greenway, passes the other side. There is a separate shelter fashioned of roughhewn timber with a corrugated iron roof, an open-sided log store stacked at one end with seasoning firewood. The little construction looks new, and beneath it stands the quad bike he saw Lawrence Melling ride previously. The man probably has no need of a car – he will no doubt have use of the Defender referred to by Miranda Bullingdon; probably it will be part of his job to move guests around the off-road tracks of the estate. A long-handled axe has its head embedded in a tree stump, and there are fresh chippings in the grass. Of the keeper's regular dog, the working cocker, there is no sign, and Skelgill would have expected it to have detected his presence – certainly if the animal has free rein about the property.

He stands in the shadow of the oak as if he is expecting something to happen. He does not really know why he is here; he has followed his nose, as the saying goes, easily done in the

Skelgill family, as another saying goes. He feels inexplicably reluctant to progress further, though there are no signs of life inside the cottage, no movement at the windows, no plume of smoke from the chimney, no excited yelping of the hyperactive hound. Yet he has the distinct feeling that he is being watched. He knows this is illogical – he would have heard someone following – and who would be waiting? He wonders if in fact there is something in the air – a scent that subconsciously has triggered some alarm. He is reminded of the keeper's intrusive aftershave when he arrived at the estate office to collect Miranda Bullingdon. Just as he ponders, from the edge of the wood across the ride emerge five roe deer, a buck and two does and two diminutive fawns. They are unhurried, unperturbed; he keeps perfectly still. They drift out of picture, behind the cottage to reappear on the other side; only now do they show a little more urgency, and break into a trot, flashing their white hindquarters as they cross into the woods to his left. Perhaps they too have got wind of something – although they tell him there is neither man nor dog at the front of the building. And then he spies what might have spurred them along – approaching briskly along the ride to his right is a human figure – to his surprise, it is Karen Williamson.

Skelgill edges around the tree, better to conceal his presence, watching with one eye – but she pays little attention to her surroundings; she looks straight ahead and her expression is distracted by thought. He notices she is carrying the hessian bag that contained the flask and mugs and biscuits; two mugs – a fact that had not escaped his attention; she could not have known he was coming to the walled garden. The small irregularity begs further questions – she must have passed close by her own cottage, why is she bringing the bag here?

The young woman disappears from view. He does not hear whether she opens the door, but he presumes she enters the property, for it is two or three minutes before she re-emerges and retraces her steps, perhaps less purposefully than on her approach; she still carries the bag. At this point Skelgill finds his interest sufficiently piqued to overcome his inertia – but in the nick of time he glimpses a movement in the dense undergrowth beyond the ride – Lawrence Melling's dog, foraging like any good cocker; indeed it puts up an indignant hen pheasant that comes barrelling in Skelgill's direction and causes him to duck behind the tree. Perhaps this is just as well, for a second later the gamekeeper himself steps out onto the ride, toting a shotgun and casually glancing right and then left. In this second action he must see the diminishing figure of Karen Williamson, for as Skelgill looks on the man watches, his eyes narrowed, for a good fifteen seconds. But, when he might hail her – since surely she had sought him – he opts not to, and strides out of Skelgill's sight towards the front of the cottage.

Though he is comfortably downwind, Skelgill knows the dog could find him in a trice should it come his way, and he backs off cautiously until there is sufficient foliage between him and the property to enable him to move unseen. Treading carefully he skirts the clearing with the intention of using Crow Road in parallel, to guide his passage to the boundary wall and his ill-defined appointment with his colleagues. But his progress is suddenly arrested – *ach,* the stench! And now he recognises it, intense, pungent, musky: rotting carrion. He catches his breath, so sharp is its bite. And, sure enough, where the clearing merges with the ride there is a section of what looks like fencing, three strands of wire strung between half a dozen posts. Maybe fifteen feet long, as a barrier it serves no apparent function – but its purpose is unequivocal, for it is strung with crows, magpies, stoats, moles and miscellaneous rodents, their corpses distorted, dangling like the crochets and quavers on the score of a manic death metal dirge. A gamekeeper's larder. His intuition was right; he had smelt a rat.

5. RECAP

Monday, late afternoon – Cockermouth

'Never compete with the tea lady, Leyton.'

'What's that, Guv?'

Skelgill has rudely silenced his partner with a raised palm. Now he looks at him in a rather disdainful manner.

'I thought you'd done the presentation skills course? It's the only thing I remember. When the lunch trolley comes in, everyone stops listening.'

DS Leyton regards his superior with some suspicion. He has no such recall and would not put it past Skelgill to have invented this maxim for his own purposes. But, there is some substance to his claim, in that DS Jones approaches bearing a tray laden with frothy coffees and slices of Cumberland sand cake. Moreover, Skelgill has resisted all attempts at conversation during the journey via back lanes to his "private parking space" – an obscure spot requiring extreme local knowledge, reached by literally bisecting Cockermouth's Jennings Brewery to arrive at the confluence of the rivers Derwent and Cocker. Naturally he spent a minute surveying the waters before leading his team to an inconspicuous coffee shop in a narrow terraced street on the upper floor of a bakery. While his logic for delay might have been guessed at along the lines that they have plenty to discuss and that someone should take proper notes for a report and action plan, his colleagues know him well enough to recognise when he needs his own thoughts and feelings to macerate. Indeed, he had endured in surprisingly indifferent silence DS Leyton's somewhat cavalier performance at the wheel of his cherished shooting brake, other than to grunt the odd instruction at unmarked junctions. Now, furnished with energy-giving victuals – the 'tea lady' likewise settled – he gives the go-ahead.

'Start again, Leyton. What do we know about Stan the Man?'

'Ooh – er, in that case we probably want to begin with the passport.'

DS Leyton glances apprehensively at his fellow sergeant, who is evidently almost as hungry as Skelgill – indeed she skipped lunch in order to accommodate his timings – and so has not stood on ceremony in tucking into her cake. She raises an apologetic hand as her colleagues wait, Skelgill decidedly impatiently. Catlike, she licks sticky drizzle topping from her upper lip and narrows her eyes at Skelgill; it is rather by way of "touché".

'Okay – firstly, Immigration have provided us with a digital photo from the passport database, which has been circulated to all ports and forces together with a description. Obviously, since we possess his passport, it won't trigger an alert. Secondly, however, I've been advised that about one-third of Moldovans also have Romanian citizenship through family connections – this allows them to travel and work freely in the Schengen Area.' She pauses to let her colleagues absorb the significance of this fact. 'So, there is the possibility he has another passport. However, no Romanian passport in his name has been used to exit – or indeed enter – the UK. That does not preclude a separate identity.'

Skelgill remains pensive, giving little away. He picks on a more prosaic aspect.

'What's he wearing?'

'That's me, Guv.' DS Leyton raises an index finger. 'Like you asked, I took Daphne Bullingdon and one of the workers back to the gatehouse. A Polish geezer by the name of Artur – that's Arthur in our money – er, now – what's this – can't read me own flamin' writing!'

He squints hopelessly at his notebook and DS Jones leans closer to provide assistance with the taxing surname.

'Czernecka.'

'Just as well I got him to spell it.' He grins at DS Jones – and is about to say something that might be a digression – for he checks himself, seeing Skelgill looking irked. 'Cut a long story short, Stan's not exactly got an extensive wardrobe – his regular leather jacket was on a hook on the back of the front door and his good shoes on the floor. The outer garments apparently missing are a green fleecy with the Shuteham Hall emblem on it, trail shoes, and black denim jeans.'

'His work gear, aye?'

'Seems that way, Guv. Makes sense I suppose. I mean – let's say he's dodged into the castle and half-inched those diamonds – he'd look less suspicious going about in his everyday workwear.' DS Leyton glances at DS Jones as if for corroboration, as though they might have discussed this theory. 'Say he's got connections – we know all about these Romanian crime gangs operating in the Home Counties – he'd just have to leg it back down to his cottage, hop over the wall, next thing he's been spirited away in a motor.'

Skelgill is looking decidedly uncomfortable. Though it is a reasonable line of inquiry in the absence of an actual lead, why would the man make a getaway in distinctive branded work clothes? Why not take a change of outfit? And why leave the cash and passport and why leave the remaining jewels? There could be another half-a-million's worth in the dressing table drawer for all they know. But he does not voice these objections.

'What about his family?'

DS Jones replies.

'We're trying to make contact through the Moldovan authorities. I've not had anything back, yet. Obviously that process will at least confirm his identity – or otherwise.'

And now DS Leyton adds a rider.

'It's believed he last went home to Moldova in December, for a week in the run-up to Christmas. That's what he told Daphne Bullingdon. The estate needed all the staff back on duty to work as beaters for the Boxing Day shoot. His workmates are saying he's not married and there's no kids. But I reckon there might be a girlfriend.' As the sergeant speaks he produces his mobile phone and thumbs through a series of screens. 'I did a more thorough search of the cottage. Look, this photograph was in a bedside drawer, underneath some t-shirts. I took a snap of it.'

Skelgill regards DS Leyton quite piercingly – and yet shows no inclination to scrutinise the picture.

'Was it framed?'

DS Leyton appears perplexed.

'Er, yeah – it was, Guv. She's a pretty girl, look.'

Skelgill now does look. The photograph is of a young woman, maybe mid-twenties, a head and shoulders shot taken in front of a fountain with a circle of jets against a background of trees and a clear blue sky. She has her head tilted to one side and her long dark hair falls across one eye, while the other glints mischievously and she seems to blow a kiss without the obligatory selfie-trout-pout. As his colleague has observed, she possesses a certain natural allure. However, Skelgill makes no remark and instead cuts a forkful of cake. DS Jones picks up the narrative.

'We have his mobile number. It's an active pay-as-you-go account but it appears to be switched off. We've put in a request for information regarding recent use and location. Apparently it's just a basic handset, so there won't be precise GPS data.'

Skelgill has bitten off more cake than he can chew, and his colleagues are obliged to wait patiently for his next question.

'Have we got a definitive last sighting?'

DS Leyton has this information.

'He was spotted a number of times on Friday morning. Then they've got a kind of workshop and materials store in one of the old stables – the Artur geezer runs it, and he says he issued him with a box of anchor bolts for his renovation work – that was around two p.m.'

'Nowt after that?'

'No, Guv. Daphne reckons she's now spoken with everyone.' DS Leyton absently pulls at a handful of the thick dark hair on the crown of his head. 'By the way – she reiterated that she don't think he'd do it – steal the jewellery.'

'So what *does* she think?'

Skelgill's question is terse, and his sergeant seems a little demoralised.

'She don't know, Guv. I caught up with her after we'd been back down to the gatehouse. She says she has no reason to suspect anybody else, nor any knowledge of intruders or strangers – and we've had that from multiple sources. She reckons it would be difficult for someone to get in and out unnoticed during working hours, while there's folk dotting about. She mentioned that Lawrence Melling has been talking about poachers in the grounds at night – and wouldn't that be the most likely explanation?'

DS Leyton again glances at DS Jones – presumably because she has interviewed Lawrence Melling. For his part, Skelgill would be inclined to point out there were no signs of a break-in, but Karen Williamson's comments in regard to erratic locking up temper that position. He turns to DS Jones.

'What do you reckon?'

'Miranda Bullingdon was flashing her jewellery at the Hunt Ball. It was heavily covered in social media. It's a striking coincidence – a trusted worker with sufficient inside knowledge and probably the opportunity disappearing at the same time as the valuables. And an organised crime connection is feasible – especially when it comes to fencing such distinctive items.'

Skelgill is nodding, though reluctantly. This is the logical conclusion, hardly the pinnacle of Holmesian deduction. In his mind all the evidence points to this outcome. But in his gut, none of the feelings do. The affable clown who fell off the stepladder does not fit the bill for a cynical jewel thief. DS Jones seems to read her superior's troubled expression.

'Of course, it could be attention-seeking behaviour by Miranda Bullingdon. It could be an insurance fraud by Lord Bullingdon. It could be an act of revenge or spite by Daphne or Julian Bullingdon. Or it could be a real theft by a different insider, and Carol Stanislav's disappearance is a genuine coincidence. The housekeeper clearly had the best opportunity.'

Both Skelgill and DS Leyton regard their colleague in a rather wide-eyed fashion, as she rattles through these like bullet points in a slide presentation. But, while she assuages his doubts over the Moldovan handyman, her closing observation shifts the onus back onto Skelgill, perhaps calculatingly so. His brow creases. Karen Williamson is the only person along with Edward Bullingdon who has admitted to entering the bedroom. She is obviously struggling to make ends meet. And, as she volunteered, she has a spare key. However, he represses what feels like an heroic yet irrational reflex to leap to her defence – and instead he gives some credence to DS Jones's opening hypothesis, albeit the most fanciful.

'Apparently Miranda Bullingdon told her husband she didn't want to report the loss.'

DS Jones homes in upon the imprecision in his statement.

'Where's that come from, Guv?'

Skelgill takes a drink of his coffee. The foam as always frustrates his thirst and he smears his upper lip with the back of his hand and grimaces as though the concoction were bitter.

'This is relying on Chinese whispers, mind. He was overheard telling Daphne Bullingdon.'

'Daphne never mentioned that to me.' DS Leyton is peeved.

'Happen she didn't take it seriously. It sounds like the sort of thing Miranda Bullingdon would come out with.'

Skelgill's tone is such that he seems to regard the issue as insignificant. DS Jones, however, is more emphatic.

'Particularly if she knows the jewels aren't stolen.'

After some consideration DS Leyton embellishes the notion.

'Or to protect someone she suspects has taken them.'

Skelgill is regretting having stirred this particular little pot, indeed is alarmed that it is all too quickly coming to the boil. He doubts that such altruism would rank highly on Miranda Bullingdon's list of personality traits; and also that despite her apparent indifference to the theft she could not seriously overlook its value. But she is a woman of smoke and mirrors, at once overacting and underacting. To downplay the theft could have a purpose; or it could be her honest sentiment – but it is impossible to tell. And he is disturbed – confused, even – by the resurfacing of feelings that he experienced during their encounter and does not wish to acknowledge; she is double the distraction of Eve with her rosy apple. He is nodding, which can only be misleading for his colleagues, for he responds on a different tack.

'Have we got anything on the estate's finances, yet?'

DS Leyton has snatched the opportunity of a bite of his snack; he shakes his head, swallowing hurriedly – too hurriedly, for he begins to choke and wheeze – and it takes a sharp blow between the shoulder blades from a prompt acting DS Jones to remedy the complaint. Eyes watering, he coughs and splutters, waving his hands contritely as he recovers his breath.

'Flippin' heck – and I'm always telling the nippers not to speak and eat at the same time.' He gestures to his plate. 'It's these massive slices, Guv – they ought to rename this the Cake District!'

For Skelgill, a factor in his choice of café is its reputation for generous portion size, with its handmade local specialities. Unsympathetic to his colleague's plight, he eyes his remaining cake a little wolfishly. However, DS Leyton's close encounter with suffocation has not dimmed his appetite, and the sand cake is incredibly moreish, so to Skelgill's dismay he resumes where he left off. Then he remembers he is supposed to be answering a question. This time he is more fastidious when it comes to ingestion.

'Fraid not, Guv – we're still waiting on the financial analysis. I did manage to get Daphne talking on the subject. She seems to have a half-decent business head on her. She basically reckons the place is washing its face – but they need a big investment to bring it up to scratch. She mentioned that she'd like to do weddings in summer to complement the winter shooting – makes sense while they've got the properties standing empty – like that boathouse as a quirky bridal suite – but Lord Bullingdon won't hear of it – he's old school gentry.'

It strikes Skelgill that fly-casting tuition and trout angling would be an obvious addition, and sufficiently pukka – *huntin', shootin' and fishin'* and all that. They have the artificial lake, well stocked, it seems. However, he is prompted to inquire about the landowner himself.

'So what did his Lordship have to say?'

Now DS Leyton makes a face that suggests his interview was not a success.

'You'd think we'd come to hinder rather than help, Guv. He'd hardly give me the time of day – said he'd already told everything he knew – which was nothing – to our constable this morning. Said he didn't expect we're going to be able to do anything about it – and he'd have to pick up the pieces as usual, whatever that meant. I asked him about locking up and he said of course the castle is locked at night – he does it himself. Then he started ranting about how he's going to sit up with his shotgun and start armed patrols, himself, the gamekeeper and Daphne Bullingdon, and he was moaning about how Julian's a waste of space and doesn't know one end of a gun from another. Then he was talking about setting traps like they used to for poachers in Victorian times! I pointed out the inadvisability of taking matters into his own hands – but he just repeated his mantra about what use have we been so far? This is what happens when the police waste their time investigating false reports of birds being shot when they should be catching actual criminals.'

This somewhat verbose account from DS Leyton nonetheless gives an idea of the difficulty he must have experienced in trying to wrestle information from a more-than-usually bombastic Edward Bullingdon. There are resignedly raised eyebrows from his colleagues, most notably at the last familiar platitude. Skelgill allows a moment for this to pass before he queries a more definite issue.

'What's the score with insurance?'

'He said he's not had time to contact his insurers yet – but anyway he's still waiting for a crime number from us before he can make a claim. I asked him if the jewellery was covered – as specified items, like – and he fobbed me off, saying it's some kind of complex policy they've got with an estate like this. That he didn't expect me to understand it. Probably I wouldn't.'

Skelgill regards his subordinate perplexedly.

'How did he seem?'

'You've met him, Guv – his default mode's set to bad temper.'

Skelgill leans back in his seat and waves a hand casually in the air.

'Leyton – what I mean is – for instance, did he mention Miranda Bullingdon – that she's mithered about it – that there's been a burglar in her bedroom – that irreplaceable possessions have been stolen?'

DS Leyton shakes his head rather ruefully.

'Now you mention it, Guv, he didn't have anything to say about her. He's preoccupied with it being a personal affront – invasion of his property, I suppose. Englishman's home is his castle, and all that – *hah!* – which it is, in this case.'

He looks with some amusement at his colleagues, but though DS Jones reacts amenably, Skelgill merely seems frustrated. He is thinking that if it were an insurance fraud – which he somehow feels is unlikely – then Edward Bullingdon would have to be involved in the process. The bluff and bluster could be the man kicking up dust to impede their progress – but, as DS Leyton says, this is pretty much his normal behaviour. Moreover, there is the absence of one tangible factor that makes him doubt that a scam is afoot. In his experience false claims normally come hand in glove with an amateurish attempt to stage a break-in; and no such tactic has been deployed.

DS Jones, meanwhile, offers an alternative slant.

'I shouldn't be surprised if Julian Bullingdon has had solvency issues.'

Skelgill regards her sharply.

'What makes you say that?'

She ladles froth from the surface of her cappuccino and clamps her lips around the long-handled spoon, slowly pulling it out like the stick of a lollipop.

'Nothing specific that he told me – but reading between the lines I get the feeling he's under a kind of tacit house arrest – confined to the castle and its grounds.'

Skelgill recalls his eccentric appearance on their former visit, in full flight with his flailing butterfly net and trailing hair.

'Is he all there?'

Skelgill's rather cruel inquiry elicits the hint of a frown from his female colleague.

'Oh, yes – he's bright alright – he's got a degree in some branch of botany – from Cambridge, no less.' She sees that Skelgill continues to glower cynically. 'I had no reason to disbelieve him – he sounds well informed – but he's clearly shy and sensitive. Remember – his mother was Lord Bullingdon's second wife – the artistic one – I think he takes after her. I guess that hasn't gone down too well with his father. He has no job – not externally, anyway – and he doesn't seem to have any commercial role in the running of the estate. He says he's working on a project to classify all of the flora and fauna, and is focusing on invertebrates at the moment. He started talking about how he'd like to rewild the fellsides – turn them back into native woodlands.'

'Bang go the grouse.'

DS Jones grins wryly.

'Bang go the pheasants, as well, Guv – he said his vision is for a vegan community that manages the entire estate for the benefit of nature.'

'He's in cloud cuckoo land, ain't he?'

Now it is DS Leyton who supplies a colourful image. But DS Jones does not automatically agree. Evidently she needs a moment to reconsider her encounter.

'I'm not so sure it's as clear-cut as that. He seemed quite determined about it.' She brushes absently at a strand of bronzed hair that has strayed across one cheek. 'I mean – on the one hand he was quite frank about Lord Bullingdon keeping a tight grip on the purse strings – for instance that he wouldn't fund a bat box initiative – but on the other, when you think about it practically, his father's seventy-four, fifty years his senior. Time will take its toll.'

Skelgill makes a rather scornful growl in his throat.

'Lord Bullingdon's going to leave Daphne in charge – never mind that he's giving her a hard time. At least he can see she's committed to running a shooting estate.'

DS Jones, however, seems determined to stick to her point of view.

'Afterwards, I got one of the team to look up Burke's Peerage. Lord Bullingdon's title is governed by primogeniture – despite being the younger sibling and child of the second marriage, Julian will inherit the barony, not Daphne. And, as far as we can determine, the estate as well.'

The trio sit in silence as they mull over this point. It would seem that Julian Bullingdon could afford to play a long hand, though he might in the short term be frustrated financially. Skelgill now picks up a point that had jarred with him earlier.

'So you've got him and Daphne down as no fans of their stepmother.'

DS Jones realises that he refers to her comment about vindictiveness as a possible motive.

'Oh – I was perhaps being overzealous when I said that, Guv.' She grins obligingly. 'When I asked if he had any idea of what might have happened to the jewellery, he said, "Oh, she's probably stripped them off somewhere" – I had this sudden flash, an image of him coming across them and tipping them rebelliously into the nearest bin. Mad, really.'

Skelgill is frowning – as much as anything because she admits to a style of judgement that chimes with his own habit, though some would call it laziness. Notwithstanding, he challenges her statement.

'Were those his actual words – "stripped them off"?'

DS Jones looks puzzled.

'Er, yes – as far as I can remember.'

Skelgill does not elucidate, and she does not ask why he wants to know. In the hiatus that ensues it is DS Leyton that picks up the thread of their discussion.

'So, young Julian – he's got no suggestions as to the theft?'

Rather pensively DS Jones presses her right ear lobe between thumb and forefinger. She is wearing discreet diamond studs, two in each side; she lets go and shakes her head.

'No – like I say – other than he didn't think they were stolen – mislaid, more likely. He wasn't particularly sympathetic –

probably he regards her as profligate – though he didn't criticise her explicitly. I get the feeling the younger generation are circumspect in what they say, in case Miranda brings the wrath of Daddy down upon them. It looks like she calls the shots.'

DS Jones's inflection turns this final observation into half a question, and she looks inquisitively at Skelgill. It seems she has exhausted what she has to say about Julian Bullingdon. Though it remains for her to update her colleagues on her interview with Lawrence Melling, it strikes Skelgill that she is reluctant spontaneously to speak of the gamekeeper; yet he can summon up no enthusiasm to prompt her. Indeed it takes DS Leyton to raise the subject, by harking back to his earlier assessment.

'How did it go with Lady Miranda's fancy man?'

DS Jones reacts with rather uncharacteristic sharpness.

'Why do you say that?'

But DS Leyton, as ever, is accommodating.

'Remember, Emma – last time, he was like a cat with the cream – and that was in front of Daphne and Lord Bullingdon.'

Pensively, DS Jones bites her bottom lip.

'I think he just knows he's good looking – and he does have a certain charisma – there's an aura of self-assurance to go with the handling of firearms.'

Skelgill folds his arms; he glares censoriously, as though DS Jones ought to mirror his sentiment. DS Leyton continues.

'I hope he didn't bring a six-shooter along to his interview!'

DS Jones looks up, a little surprised.

'Actually, it was at the gunroom where I caught up with him. He was oiling and polishing some expensive-looking shotguns. Lawrence was saying they can accommodate up to thirty clients.'

'That must bring in a pretty penny.' DS Leyton makes the hand gesture of filthy lucre. 'Last time I heard what suckers pay for a day's shooting – not to mention when it's grouse – the Glorious Twelfth. You're talking the price of a presentable second-hand motor.'

Skelgill is plainly put out – though it cannot be because he disapproves of the cost of the sport; more likely it relates to DS

Jones's attitude of familiarity with the gamekeeper. He interjects somewhat bluntly.

'So what about his poacher-turned-burglar theory?'

His sergeant seems to start – as if shaken by Skelgill's harsh tone. However, she regards him evenly.

'Funnily enough he dismissed it.'

Skelgill hesitates for a moment, as though he might dispute her statement – but then he moves on, his tone becoming decidedly sarcastic.

'And did you ask him about his saboteurs?'

There is a slight narrowing of DS Jones's eyes, as though she is discomfited by the tension underlying this exchange, but her voice remains calm.

'I did, as a matter of fact. He said he was anticipating a "spectacular" any time now.'

'What's that supposed to mean?'

'He wasn't specific – just something that would make the news – blacken the name of the estate. Along the lines of his conversation with Daphne Bullingdon when we came about the birds.'

Now DS Leyton interrupts.

'Those chicken harriers.'

'Hen, Leyton.'

'Righto, Guv.' DS Leyton affects a grin, evidently not wishing to fall foul of Skelgill's recalcitrance. 'Maybe they're for the chop.'

Skelgill does not reply to this point; but DS Jones expounds.

'Actually, I did mention the hen harriers – and it's obviously a source of irritation. He complained that the conservationists' twenty-four-hour watch on the nest is interfering with his own breeding programmes.'

Skelgill is still scowling; now, rather uncharacteristically, he throws in a piece of hearsay, even borrowing a phrase.

'For what it's worth, Miranda Bullingdon seemed to think it suits Melling to have bogeymen lurking. Justifies his existence. Lets him play soldiers.'

Reflected in DS Jones's insightful gaze there might just be the suspicion that her superior's proprietorial instincts are bruised. However, when neither she nor DS Leyton responds, Skelgill continues.

'So what's his theory on her Ladyship's Crown Jewels?'

DS Jones inhales and shifts back a little in her seat as though conscious of the gravity of what she is about to say.

'Without naming names he suggested we should be looking among the foreign employees.'

In fact DS Jones is here being a little economical with information. Lawrence Melling's response had been more multifaceted. That poachers and saboteurs tend to stick to what they're good at. That he is a good gamekeeper, and not a detective. That how well do the estate really know their staff? On the latter point, a brazen double-edged remark, she had challenged him. In that case – what about him? His response had been that she was welcome to find out for herself – indeed that Shuteham Hall estate maybe wasn't the best place to do it. DS Jones had responded with cool neutrality – but she had mentally noted, it *was* neutrality and not the professional distancing that would be expected of her. But hadn't her strategy in suggesting the choice of interviews been to prise the most information from their subjects? No more would Miranda Bullingdon have lowered her guard before a perceptive female detective than would Lawrence Melling have given the slightest ground to Skelgill. And this remains her rational explanation to herself about her motivation. As for the handsome gamekeeper's motivation – she is yet unsure if his approach was some attempt to deceive her – or if he merely wishes to seduce her.

'Hah – does he include himself, as a Jock?'

DS Leyton's quip snaps his associate out of her momentary reverie. She grins, a little wanly, and shakes her head.

'He just said in his opinion Miranda was too trusting for her own good.'

When no one offers anything further DS Leyton again takes it upon himself to keep the conversation on track.

'How did it go with Lady Bullingdon, Guv?'

Skelgill looks pained; rather ironically he mirrors his sergeant's reaction when asked about the woman's husband.

'I'm just a daft country copper, Leyton. She's from another world – might as well be another planet. You saw her last time. She likes to be in charge and she doesn't give owt away.'

DS Leyton looks rather unconvinced. Skelgill's "daft country copper routine" is something he has had them all participate in at times, when it is judged that affected bucolic ignorance will slip beneath the radar of smugness. So he is surprised to hear his boss self-reference in this way.

'That suggests you think she's got something to give away.'

Skelgill shrugs.

'She reeled off a list of international brand names – where the jewellery came from – then acted like she's lost a pair of cheap earrings. No histrionics, no subtle hints about relatives, no finger-pointing at staff or tradespeople who may or may not have visited Shuteham Hall. Just pretty laid back.'

As he uses this phrase the image of the scantily clad woman reclining on the chaise longue comes to mind; automatically he glances at DS Jones, to see she is watching him closely.

'I'll probably need to speak to her again – depending how these inquiries into Stanislav pan out.'

Skelgill notices he has prepared the ground for this future interview – even though it is stating the obvious – and he detects a wry smile form briefly at the corners of DS Jones's mouth. Accordingly, he adds a caveat.

'And the housekeeper. In fact we'll need to revisit the lot of them.'

There is a silence before DS Jones raises a question, rather offhandedly.

'I get the feeling you don't suspect Karen Williamson, Guv?'

It is perhaps a slightly impertinent inquiry, but Skelgill is conscious he has fallen into something of a trap – and one that he does not fully understand – in having agreed to the schedule proposed by his younger female colleague. Her logic about the productivity of interviews is unarguable – it is no different in principle to his "daft country coppers" tactic. But he was troubled at the time and the same undercurrent of disquiet has risen to the surface anew – a feeling not helped by the contradictory circumstances of her 'catching' him in an inappropriate if not exactly compromising situation with the housekeeper. As is often the case at such times, he resorts to a glowering belligerence.

'You know me, Jones – I suspect everyone. Don't be fooled by appearances.'

Abruptly he rises, tossing off the last dregs of his coffee. He bangs the mug down close to DS Leyton.

'Your round I reckon, Leyton – make mine a tea this time.'

Skelgill heads off towards a pair of timber doors respectively marked with female and male icons. Exiting two minutes later he hears the adjacent cubicle being locked, and he sees that their table is empty, although his colleagues' jackets are in place. On reaching his seat, outward facing at the elbow of the L-shaped cafeteria, he spies DS Leyton waiting at the service counter near the head of the staircase. Casting about for something to occupy his attention, he stretches for a discarded copy of the local Cockermouth newspaper, and begins to work his way in from the back page, scanning for fishing headlines. He has just found an item entitled "Vendace Search Flounders" when a female laugh draws his attention.

A young couple – in their mid-twenties he would guess – are casually strolling towards him, acting like they know the place and indeed as they pass and wheel to their left they seem pleased to find that a comfortable-looking sofa with a broad low coffee table before it is free. They either do not notice or are not perturbed that Skelgill has followed their progress over the top of his newspaper. This may be that they are accustomed to being stared at – in fact a good-looking pair despite their slightly shabby outfits, which might have been purchased from an army surplus store, giving them the paramilitary look of militant New Age types. The young man is a little above average height, with short fair hair and an unshaven weatherbeaten countenance; the girl has long thin dark hair which, though combed, looks like it might benefit from a dose of shampoo; her complexion is tanned, with blue eyes set wide apart amidst pleasing if undistinguished features; she is almost as tall as her companion, and naturally so, for she wears similar army boots; her fatigues are a better fit than his, and she wears only a camouflage vest tank top and no bra, when clearly one might have been helpful – and Skelgill, in the moments it has taken him to absorb this information, is conscious that his gaze is attracted inappropriately. He ducks back into his newspaper, and when he looks again a minute later the couple have settled down facing him and have opened up a laptop before them. The man digs into the breast pocket of his shirt and picks out some small items that he juggles in the palm of a hand before selecting and inserting one into a port on the side of the device. He manipulates the track pad and the pair observe closely for a moment. Seemingly satisfied, they exchange a few hushed words and the young man rises while the girl fishes a small woven purse from a shoulder bag of similar artisan provenance and hands it to him and he sets off back towards the counter.

At this juncture Skelgill's colleagues return more or less simultaneously. As DS Jones slides easily into her seat Skelgill surveys the tray to see that DS Leyton has procured a large mug of tea with milk already added and the teabag floating, a sugar bowl and a single slice of sand cake, and two modest coffees.

'Got some more nosh in case you're still hungry, Guv. Emma and me, we're all done. It's bangers and mash tonight – the missus'll scream blue murder if I don't show appreciation for her efforts.'

Skelgill, having warned of the futility of trying to hold someone's attention when food arrives is in fact waging a not entirely successful battle against the competing instinct stimulated by the young woman's low-cut top. But DS Jones follows his gaze and self-consciously he turns side-saddle his seat. He notices the girl's partner returning; casually he shifts his attention to him: the man carries two cold drinks in recycled jam jars with paper straws protruding – unappetising green concoctions, new fangled smoothies, Skelgill supposes – in his view a triumph of advertising over common sense. If you want to eat some veg what's wrong with chips and mushy peas? The man deposits the drinks carefully and hands back the purse. The girl points out something on the screen and they lean in close together, their expressions intense, their eyes seemingly tracking the same movements. After a few seconds they react simultaneously to something that amuses them. The man slides his arm around the girl's waist; she does not demur, as though she is accustomed to the contact.

'Er, Guv – what we thought, if it's okay with you – I'll email my notes to Emma tonight and she's going to pull together the report for first thing tomorrow? Then we can ping it off to the Chief once we've been through it with you.'

Skelgill rather absently starts spooning sugar into the tea. He nods as though he is not really listening. His colleagues have learned not to expect written contributions from himself – but whether they have appreciated he has largely avoided commenting upon his own interviews is another matter. This is not to say he would withhold some essential fact. It is more the case that, though he has 'findings', he would presently consider it impossible to put these into meaningful words. Take his encounter with Miranda Bullingdon. He was not really interested in small detail. She had already been questioned once, and he skimmed over the surface. His objective, not even explicit in his own mind, had been to gauge her manner. On the face of it, he is none the wiser. (Except he is, of course.) And Karen Williamson, what is he to make of her? Yes, slightly more in the way of facts to toy with – the two mugs in her bag (was she expecting company?), the brief visit with the bag to the cottage (was she moving the jewellery?) – but realistically only unfounded fancies that have no actual substance; they are potentially dangerous distractions. More informative, but just not yet, is how she behaved towards him – again, he knows what he feels but he has no clear sense of what it means. However, he is certainly convinced that he should recast his entire experience through the prism of Carol Stanislav's disappearance. They all should. And thus he responds.

'Aye. There's not a lot we can do until we get something back from the feelers you pair have put out. Reckon we'll have to sleep on it.'

Skelgill, of course, has no intention of doing any such thing.

6. EVENING CALL

'*D*anny?'
'You what?'
'Danny Skelgill?'
'Aye.'

'Don't you recognise us?'

'I recognise your accent – Pereth.'

The man on the other side of the bar, without turning away, points behind and above himself to a plaque fixed on an oak beam. It states: "Graham Bush – licensed to sell all intoxicating liquor for consumption on these premises."

For Skelgill, the penny drops.

'Basil?'

'The one and only – *hah-ha!* – *boom-boom!* Put it there, marra.'

Skelgill stares as if not quite convinced, but automatically shakes the hand that is offered. The man perceives his indecision and adds a further prompt.

'We sat next to one another in the bottom maths set. That old git Doc Birch who used to scop the board rubber at you, or twat you round the lug for no reason!'

Now Skelgill nods. After a moment he speaks reflectively.

'You were in the Air Cadets. You wanted to be a pilot.'

The man guffaws, self-effacingly.

'I were too thick to fly, me. But I still joined the RAF – they took me on as apprentice ground crew. I was posted to Gib, Ascension, Akrotiri, Falklands. Rose to master aircrew rank. Did my twenty years. Retired last spring – I'll be able to claim a pension in three years. Age forty!' He makes a triumphant double click with his tongue. 'Met Nikki, the missus – she were a chef in the NAAFI – she looks after the food. Bought this place with our ill-gotten gains.' He indicates to a blackboard listing the day's specials. 'She cooks the meals, I cook the books!'

Skelgill nods and tries to force himself to look with suitable interest at the menu. It is coming back to him that Graham 'Basil' Bush was something of a liability as a classmate. He had a knack of attracting trouble and sidestepping the repercussions. Before he can answer, the man continues, seemingly unperturbed that Skelgill has not joined in his banter.

'Are you eating with us? You liked your school dinners, as I recall. I could recommend the pheasant hotpot – or the jugged hare – all locally sourced game.'

This sparks a slightly panicked reaction from Skelgill. He looks over his shoulder, although the pub is empty and the door has not opened since he arrived as the only patron.

'Er – I'm meeting a contact to discuss some ideas. I'd better see what he wants to do – he might be having his tea at home after.'

The landlord shows no sign of taking offence.

'As you like. Tell you what – why don't you bring the missus along – have a bar meal – you could meet Nik and be our guests – on the house.'

'That's – er – very kind of you, Basil.'

The man reads the poorly disguised awkwardness with which Skelgill receives this offer. However, perhaps incorrectly, he deduces a reason for his old schoolmate's reluctance. He makes a casual hand gesture.

'Plus one, then – you know what I'm saying – just rock up, any time – it's not like we'll be away – *hah!*'

Skelgill grins agreeably.

'Perk of the job – no need to commute.'

'Aye, that's right. So, what's your line these days, Danny? Surprise me – professor of mathematics!'

Skelgill was hoping to get away without being quizzed about his occupation. Given the references to ill-gotten gains and cooking the books, he casts about in momentary desperation for a diplomatic exit strategy. His gaze alights on a stuffed pike in a glass case fixed to the wall on the right of the bar. Relief.

'I'm working on a project for the Centre for Ecology and Hydrology. Preservation of rare species. The chap I'm meeting's a gamekeeper.'

Basil, who is clearly of an easy-going nature, suddenly seems a fraction more alert.

'What – the gadgee from the big posh place down the road – Shuteham Hall? Now you mention it, he's not been in lately.'

Skelgill hesitates. He scents a lead.

'No – my pal keeps for the Chase-Downes estate over by Bassenthwaite. You know this other bloke, then?'

'Aye – the Scotsman – thinks he's Sean Connery?'

Skelgill frowns affectedly.

'I don't know. Could be.'

'I can't pretend to be on familiar terms with him – but one of our barmaids was, on the quiet, like. Nudge, nudge – know what I mean, squire?'

Skelgill shrugs casually.

'Happen it's the way of the world.'

Basil seems keen to elaborate. Skelgill wonders if he is gaining the benefit of being the first customer of the day, there being a gossip quotient to be fulfilled.

'Foreign girl – Romanian. Gabriela. She didn't stay with us for all that long, had to go home for something – pity – she was good – and a looker – customers liked her – the Scotsman obviously did – *hah!*'

Skelgill is trying to act no more than politely interested.

'So – how did that come out?'

'She were kaylied on her last night here – that were fine, it were a little leaving do – the missus baked her a cake, and the regulars were all standing her drinks. But she spilled the beans to Jen our other barmaid – she's not on tonight, we're quiet Mondays, as you can see. Anyway, Jen reckoned Gabriela was warning her off – rather than boasting, like. Went on about how he's got a secret love nest up on the estate somewhere – and that he's not quite the gentleman he likes to pretend he is.'

Skelgill is reflecting upon the laws of serendipity. But there is a certain equivalence to angling; the more he casts, the more catches. He selects an innocuous cliché from his repertoire.

'It takes all sorts, Basil.'

'We certainly get all sorts of stories coming across this bar – stranger than fiction. I'm just getting the hang of it, Danny. They say to be a successful publican you've got to be a good listener. Not easy when you're stone deaf from mending jet engines – *boom-boom!*'

But at this juncture Skelgill is released from the conversation, for his awaited acquaintance, a middle-aged man, sturdily built in distinctive outdoor garb with a ruddy complexion beneath a tweed cap pushes open the door of the Overthwaite Arms and stands squinting into the relative gloom of the old inn. Basil seems to have a keen sense of duty in such circumstances. He drapes an arm over a Jennings handpump and assumes the affable pose of mine host.

'Hey up – looks like here's your marra. Get theesens sat down by the hearth – I'll bring your ale over. Two of pints of bitter, aye? Tell you what, Danny – they're on the house – auld lang syne and all that.'

Skelgill gives a genuinely meant thumbs-up sign.

'Nice one, Basil. Couldn't chuck in a couple of bags of salted nuts, could you?'

The man points an accusative finger, but grins widely to offset any accidentally implied aggression.

'You always were a bit of a chancer, Danny – although copying my maths homework weren't your smartest move!'

'I still struggle to make two plus two add up to five.'

Skelgill smiles ruefully, waves a hand in admission, and then turns to direct the newcomer towards the said fireside table.

'Alreet, Eric.'

'Alreet, Dan.'

Skelgill feels a curious wave of comfort wash over him in being able to bask amidst the undemanding vernacular of his locality – even these greetings, with their implied questions as to the other's health need no elaboration, merely reciprocation.

Easy. He moves so much in formal circles that his reformed pronunciation bears little resemblance to the Cumberland twang that he actually hears inside his head – the little voice that ticks him off and makes him feel like a fraud, for instance when he refers to "a householder", enunciating the letters "h" which he knows intrinsically are not really there. It must be the encounter with Basil that has brought this thought to bear – his high school contemporary retains his Penrith brogue – yet his talk of twenty years in the armed forces has highlighted for Skelgill that he, too, has spent roughly half his life serving the public. Small wonder that societal mores have chafed the rough edges off his accent. Then again, whenever did he hear his Cockney oppo DS Leyton pronounce the letter "h"?

At this juncture the beers (and peanuts) arrive; Basil is an efficient operator, Skelgill can see, as he brings the two brim-full pints in straight glasses on a small round tray, which he places on the table before moving the ales to fresh beermats in front of each of his customers, spilling not a drop. He even seems to have remembered that Skelgill is left-handed. There is a small exchange of introductions, and the landlord, understanding the private nature of the meeting, makes a diplomatic exit, backing away and bowing, before turning. He makes no mention that the drinks are free. Accordingly, Eric Hepplethwaite raises his glass to Skelgill.

'Cheers, Dan. Sorry I can't hang about, the missus'll have me guts for garters if I'm late for me tea.'

'You sound like one of my sergeants. He was just saying the same thing.' Skelgill grins, though he cannot suppress an unheralded sigh. 'It must beat ready meals and takeaways.'

The other makes a face – if it were put into words it might be along the lines of, "you haven't tasted my wife's cooking" – of course, these are not sentiments that could *ever* be voiced, indeed he glances instinctively over his shoulder, in all seriousness. But the action seems to inform his response.

'Decent little boozer, this. It's changed a lot – it's yonks since I were last in.'

Skelgill looks vaguely apologetic.

'Aye – sorry to drag you out of your way – it's just I've got a couple of bits of business nearby, later.'

'It's hardly a detour, Dan – I'll be gannin' yam by Ruthwaite – tek us ten minutes. Just that I drive reet past the door of The Star every night – so it's a no-brainer under normal circumstances. Any road – how can I help thee?'

Skelgill, supping from his pint, nods and swallows and wipes froth from the tip of his nose and upper lip with his forearm.

'Know anything about this new gamekeeper at Shuteham Hall?'

'The Terminator, you mean?''

Skelgill, enjoying the well-kept ale and taking another swift gulp, lifts an eyebrow in response.

'What's that? We're talking the Melling bloke, aye?'

'Aye – but that's what they're calling him – the Terminator – his reputation precedes him. Vermin beware. Apparently there wasn't a weasel within ten miles of his last place – big estate in the Borders – Duke of Hawickshire's lands. Bit of a coup, him dropping down a division to a mere barony.'

Skelgill ponders for a moment.

'Why would he do that, then? He's from the Borders himself, by the sound of it. Why come south?'

Now Eric Hepplethwaite is taking a drink. Skelgill meanwhile reaches for his peanuts, bites open the packet and tips about half of the contents into the palm of his hand. The gamekeeper lowers his glass and taps the side of his bulbous nose while he swallows.

'Could be he got a golden handshake – signing on fee, aye?' (Skelgill is nodding and munching on the nuts.) 'But if the jungle drums have it right, I reckon he might have jumped before he were pushed.'

'Aye?'

It is sufficient of a question from Skelgill.

'Seems there were a little dalliance with the lady of the house.' The gamekeeper makes a disapproving tutting sound. 'Never a good idea – biting the hand that feeds you.'

Skelgill is staring at the far wall, though not seeing the saturnine landscapes with their bloodthirsty hunting scenes. Into his mind's eye, curiously, has sprung an image of his dog, Cleopatra, the fearsome-looking bullboxer. Despite her generally placid ways – provided she is not provoked – he is still not quite accustomed to the gusto with which she takes a treat out of his fingers.

'Some dogs can't help themselves, Eric.'

Eric Hepplethwaite nods sagely.

'Aye, well – has he been cocking his leg already?'

For Skelgill, this is a bit closer to the mark than he intends to go; he rows back.

'What? Er – no, no – it's nothing like that. Don't get me wrong – just it's my job to turn all stones. You'll probably see it in tomorrow's papers. There's been a big jewel theft from Shuteham Hall – we're talking well into six figures. Quarter of a million, in fact. I'm just trying to get as much background information as I can.'

The man gives a low whistle.

'Inside job?'

Skelgill grins wryly. He takes a drink, puts down his pint, and then presses both palms on the table.

'Look – it could be a complete coincidence – but one of the estate workers has disappeared into thin air.'

'But not the Melling character.'

Skelgill shakes his head.

'So – if you hear owt on the grapevine.'

The man nods.

'Aye – I'll keep me ear to the ground. There's a number of us Allerdale keepers – not your Scotsman – we've set up a WhatsApp group. I'm not aware of any other break-ins hereabouts. The odd bit of kit gets nicked from a shed or a barn. But most estates have got good security these days – what with the attention your boys pay to us lot that keeps guns.'

'I'm glad to hear it, Eric.'

They exchange ironic smiles.

'They've got hen harriers on Over Moor, aye?'

The statement causes Skelgill to start.

'Is that common knowledge, then?'

Eric Hepplethwaite grins.

'I think there's plenty of keepers happy to hear it. Puts the spotlight somewhere else.'

Skelgill makes a sardonic growl in his throat. Much as this man is a trusted ally, their contrasting vocations have them dancing on the knife-edge of conflict.

'There's plenty of legal ways to control predators.'

'Aye – but else what's the point of a gamekeeper? Dan – you know as well as I do – when it's your job, your livelihood – putting food on the table. What would you do?'

Skelgill attempts to make light of the matter.

'Try not to get caught.'

This raises a smile of approval from his friend.

'I never said I do owt wrong, Dan.'

'But you called Lawrence Melling the Terminator – that's not exactly a Blue Peter Badge for services to conservation.'

The man simply laughs and has another pull at his pint, and Skelgill realises he is not going to get any more of an admission.

'Reckon there's much poaching going on at the moment?'

The gamekeeper turns out his bottom lip and shakes his head.

'Nowt you'd call organised. I wouldn't expect much until t' pheasants are released in August – and bear in mind they're not mature until October. I reckon sheep in-bye are more at risk about now.'

Skelgill nods.

'Aye – there's some of that going on. Jud and Arthur Hope caught a couple of lads with a van and dogs the other night, right up beside Stonethwaite. Took our uniform boys a while to get there.'

'That's not so good.'

'It weren't for the two reivers.'

The man nods in quiet satisfaction. Skelgill has another question.

'Would you shoot crows this time of year?'

'Aye – I'd shoot the buggers at any time of year. But right now I wouldn't fart about chasing after them – find the bird ont' nest and put both barrels through it. You know what the Jocks say, *twa birds wi' oan stane.*'

The man sees something approaching a look of alarm on Skelgill's face.

'Yon harriers – surely nowt to worry about there, Dan? There'll be a camera on the breeding site – and they'll have the adults satellite-tagged. That's how they do it nowadays.'

Skelgill is uncertain about such technological detail, though he has no reason to doubt his friend's knowledge in this department. And he can agree in principle.

'Aye – there's twenty-four hour surveillance. The Allerdale naturalists – the Nats, they call themselves.'

'You mek 'em sound like storm troopers.'

Skelgill attempts to tone down the impression he has given.

'Sticklers, more like – but I reckon they're a mild-mannered bunch.'

His companion raises his eyebrows as if unconvinced; probably he has an alternative experience. He dips again into his pint and Skelgill can see he is hurrying through it and will shortly have to leave.

'Had any bother from the animal rights squad, Eric?'

The man looks surprised.

'You don't reckon there's a connection there?'

Skelgill grimaces, as though to confirm he agrees it is a long shot.

'I'm just thinking along the lines of who might be skulking about a shooting estate. Your regular hikers tend to give it a wide berth. Melling's spoken about saboteurs – like he's expecting dirty tricks – queer his pitch.'

'Sounds to me like he's getting his excuses in first, Dan. Double bluff.'

Skelgill nods pensively. It has not escaped him that some of the more extreme tactics employed by so-called environmentalists are liable to backfire. Unless it can be proved – on film, say, or by the unearthing of a stash of illegal chemicals

– a poisoned bird of prey can hand a rogue keeper the pretext that it was planted as an act of mischief.

Eric Hepplethwaite drains the last of his ale and checks his watch.

'Hey up – I'd better get me skates on, Dan. Will that do thee?'

'Aye – I appreciate your time.'

'Like I say – I'll keep me ear to the ground.' He taps a knuckle against the empty glass. 'My shout next time.'

Skelgill grins a little sheepishly. He glances to see if Basil the barman is eavesdropping – but an elderly couple have entered and he is regaling them with some tale of airborne exploits, by the look of his arm movements. Eric Hepplethwaite is just moving away when it seems he is taken by a sudden thought.

'I meant to say – I mean – don't take this too literally – but the keeper yon Melling chap edged out – arl Jack Carlops, he'd been there donkey's years.'

'Edged out? I thought he retired?'

'Early retirement.' The man makes a show of mid-air apostrophes with his index fingers. 'As I heard it, he'd reet got his dander up. Had a few too many in The Star one night, and he were cursing and swearing and threatening bloody revenge.'

Skelgill's ears are pricked.

'What – against the new keeper – or the estate?'

'Both maybe?' He shrugs. 'But if anyone kens their way about t' place, it's him.'

'Know where I'll find him?'

'Those labourers' cottages at Scawthwaite Mire. Moved in wi' his sister – she's a widow.' He grins ruefully. 'And I'd better get a shift on else my missus might decide she'd rather join t' club!'

Without further ado, Eric Hepplethwaite departs. Skelgill drains the last of his own drink. He sees that Basil is still occupied, now expounding over the menu with the older couple. He rises and makes his customary scan of the table for personal possessions – he sees that his friend has left his peanuts unopened. Skelgill pockets the bag and slips away.

Despite what can be seen in the movies, it is not easy to creep about in a car, so when Skelgill bumps his shooting brake and trailer loaded with his boat into the small parking area set aside for Over Water birdwatching hide, he is not in the least surprised when an inquisitive head pokes meerkat-like out of the door of the wooden structure, despite its position some thirty yards distant along the shielded boardwalk through the reeds. The head belongs to Christine Vholes. With her distinctive straight brown hair and long visage with its narrow set eyes she remains staring at him, in the vexed manner of a possessive householder watching a stranger park outside her property, but unable to do anything about it. Only when, through his open window, Skelgill waves a casual hand in her direction is the head withdrawn – to report back to Neil Vholes, no doubt. Skelgill's assumption is bolstered by the presence of the same two vehicles as he saw on his early morning fishing trip. There is the smart Volvo with the personalised plate, VH0 L35 – not a lot of detective work required there – and the dilapidated but rather more intriguing Ford Consul estate, the throwback to the 1970s that on his last visit had been steamed up as though inhabited by an overnight camper. Skelgill backs his trailer down into the shallows, but he leaves the car and instead saunters across to inspect the parked vehicles. The Volvo has tinted windows and just an Ordnance Survey map and a bird guide on the dashboard – nothing to tempt the average thief. The Ford Consul, however, is a case of chalk and cheese. Its contents have Skelgill grinning wryly – it is a car after his own heart, packed with gear and jumbled belongings, more likely to send a potential robber away with a migraine, his limited brain confused by the sheer disorder. What is plain, however, is that someone is living in this car, for the flatbed has been extended by the removal of the rear seat to accommodate a double mattress.

'Evening all.'

Occupying the hide are two couples, and upon them Skelgill's salutation has a disparate effect. Christine Vholes has retreated to huddle beside her brother on one of the narrow benches that line the two long sides; they regard him with a mixture of apprehension and irascibility. Beneath an electric bulb at the far end, facing him over a camping table that has their laptop computer on it – a not-dissimilar pose to that in which he last saw them – and looking entirely relaxed, are none other than the New Agers from the Cockermouth coffee shop. Too young to appreciate the melodramatic irony in his salutation, perhaps they simply take him at face value: a local fisherman, by the look of his instrument-spangled gilet. Certainly, if they recognise him from earlier, they give no such indication.

His boots clump noisily upon the elevated timber floor, attracting librarian-like looks of disapproval from Christine Vholes. There is the impression of a secret bunker, the war room of some underground resistance movement. The Vholes, though not up to the paramilitary standards of the New Agers, are nevertheless clad in their olive-hued birdwatchers' outfits; strung around their necks they have expensive Leica binoculars. A green rubber-armoured Optolyth telescope on a tripod is set up to point through the narrow observation flap across Over Moor. The young couple are seated on what appears to be a fold-down bunk. In one corner a bank of car batteries is connected in series by crocodile clips and wires that come in through a hole in the timber gable, and there is a second table on which there is a gas burner and cooking equipment, a kettle, mugs, packets of tea, powdered milk, biscuits and jars of instant coffee and cocoa powder. On the floor stands a large plastic jerry can of water.

The atmosphere is oppressive; the heat of the day seems to have accumulated in the hide, and it is mingled with assorted smells that would take a more discerning though not necessarily larger nose than Skelgill's to untangle; but there are impressions of cooking oil, unwashed laundry, and what he suspects to be Christine Vholes' cloying perfume. Neil Vholes rather awkwardly extracts his legs from the confinement of the viewing bench and swivels to face Skelgill.

'We're hoping you've come with news of a prosecution, at last, Inspector.'

Skelgill is immediately irked by the man's tone of condescension.

'Unless you want me to issue you with a ticket for your rear offside tyre that's contravening the legal limit – I'm afraid you're going to have to be patient, Mr Vholes.' Skelgill affects a grin and pats his chest, indicating his angling credentials. 'As you can see, I've got my conservation hat on tonight. But I can assure you the gravity of the situation has been made plain to those that need to know.'

The Vholes look at one another but do not speak and again Skelgill suspects them of having some special sibling powers of silent communication. He regards them sternly for a moment, and then looks more inquiringly at the young couple. 'Are you not going to introduce me?'

Neil Vholes responds stiffly. 'Ah – yes – Inspector Skelgill, these are two of our most dedicated volunteers, Cian and Ciara – they have been performing sterling work on the night watches.'

Skelgill makes friendly eye contact with each of the couple in turn, but he does not deem it necessary to stretch to handshakes – they look of a generation and a type for whom it would be alien – but in the exchange of greetings it is immediately apparent that both have accents to go with their Irish names.

'Where are you from?'

It is the girl that responds, assuming charge without looking to check with her companion, or partner or whatever he is.

'I'm from County Louth. Mooretown, originally. Cian's from Galway, for his sins. We're on a structured gap year as part of our ecology Masters at Trinity. We were working at RSPB Leyton Moss – studying the marsh harriers – until we heard about this hen harrier project. They're far more endangered. It was too good an opportunity to miss, so it was.'

Her voice is pleasant and lilting and her enunciation polished. Skelgill, who can just about tell a northern from a southern Irish accent, if pressed would guess she has perhaps been the beneficiary of a private education. He senses that the Vholes are regarding him rather disparagingly, and it prompts him to show off his newly acquired knowledge.

'I believe you've got them satellite-tagged – and a webcam on the nest.'

He detects twitches of annoyance from the Vholes. But the girl responds brightly.

'Sure we have, Inspector – come and see for yourself.' She nudges her companion with an elbow. 'Cian Fogarty – now, let the man in, will you?'

The young man rises obediently and vacates his position on the bunk. When Skelgill sits, the girl slides the laptop a little closer to him, and shifts her position until her hip touches his. He has his shirtsleeves rolled up and her bare forearm brushes against his. She smells unwashed, and yet it is not something he finds unpleasant – if anything, the reverse, perhaps complicated by the faint but unmistakable spicy overture of marijuana. He has to blink to concentrate, lulled by her occasional touch as she manipulates the trackpad, and some hypnotic quality in her soft voice.

'So – here's the female on the nest. She's called Hetty, originally from the Forest of Bowland, where she was tagged as a nestling. She's nearly eight – that's old for a breeding female. There are five eggs, which is marvellous.'

Skelgill stares at the screen – the close-up image is remarkably sharp, the bird sitting in the heather, motionless but for its head with its beady yellow eyes constantly scanning the sky above – and the occasional ripple of a feather in the light moorland breeze.

Then the girl clicks on another icon and brings up a map – Skelgill immediately recognises the lie of the land – Over Moor running up towards Great Cockup, and Skiddaw with its tightening contours, the blue oval that is Over Water, the policies and buildings of Shuteham Hall estate, and even the little stretched triangle of Troutmere. She points with an index finger – the nail rather disappointingly bitten down to the quick, and perhaps the brown stain of smoke on the inside – and she highlights first one and then a second flashing icon.

'There's Hetty on the nest – and that's Galahad – he's still out hunting – look – the blinking frequency tells you he's on the wing. He's only four – a Scottish bird from Dumfriesshire. But he's doing a good job so far – she'll rely on him for her meals for up to five weeks.'

She clicks back to the hen on the nest.

'She's watching for her supper. If we keep an eye on them – if you've got time, Inspector – we can show you a food pass – normally she rises up to take it from him in mid air.'

A frown creases Skelgill's brow.

'I'm surprised he gives it up so easily.'

The girl laughs, her voice suddenly throaty.

'Well, for a start the female's fifty per cent heavier – and, besides, would you fight a woman when she knows what she wants? I think we're secretly the dominant sex, Inspector.'

Skelgill inhales to speak but perhaps does not find a suitable rejoinder, and instead he looks away from the screen and follows the trajectory of the telescope to the outdoors.

'How far's the nest?'

'About half a kilometre. The scope is on it – but the bird's down in the heather, obviously.'

'Looks quite isolated.'

Skelgill says this as though he means it is a good thing.

'There's a beaters' path leading to the grouse butts. It goes within about thirty metres. So far she's sat tight whenever anyone's passed by. We have an inconspicuous side-path for maintenance of the webcam. The keeper makes a patrol most nights at dusk, sometimes after dark – like he's beating the bounds. Taunting us.' She looks at Skelgill with significance. 'He knows we have our eye on him. He just doesn't know how closely! But I think he realises the law is on our side.'

Skelgill has already demonstrated to Neil Vholes his reluctance to get drawn into a discussion along these lines, and now the girl's conspiratorial intonation clearly invites his patronage. He makes a show of looking at his watch and then squinting to assess the twilight.

'Happen I'd better get my act together. It's a sight easier to set up while there's still light.'

He begins to rise, conscious of the warmth of the girl's thigh against his.

'What is it you're conserving, Inspector?'

He is tempted to resume his seat, but he makes a show of flexing his spine and steps away to give himself more space.

'Ach – I'm trying to prove there's vendace in Over Water.' He grins, wryly. 'Given the powers that be can't disprove it.'

She smiles.

'Just like a leprechaun.'

Skelgill meets her gaze, the green-tinted eyes seem curiously familiar – she is endearingly taking the mickey, and he wonders if she suspects a more nefarious motive underlies his mission.

'Keep up the good work, folks.' He turns his attention to the Vholes, who have maintained a disgruntled silence during the demonstration by the Irish girl, observing through their binoculars through the open shutter on the moorland side. Now they grace him with grudging nods. Viewing in the opposite direction they will be able to watch him – at least until nightfall. In fact the young man, Cian, sitting on the bench close to the door, is doing just that, meticulously scanning the lake, perhaps for the resident great crested grebes. As Skelgill reaches him a thought strikes him. 'How do you manage in the dark?'

Neil Vholes takes it upon himself to reply, as though he might be keen to re-establish some position of authority.

'The camera is fitted with infrared night-vision capability. The birds can't see it, but we can see them.'

Skelgill nods.

'Can you view it remotely? Like – when you go home?'

'The satellite tracking data, yes. But the camera is powered by a combination of solar and wind and is self-contained on this site. That is one reason for our round-the-clock presence. Besides – if, heaven forbid, there were an intruder – someone needs to be on the scene.'

Neil Vholes looks meaningfully at the young Irishman, as though he has been delegated the task of rushing to the rescue should the harriers' nest be threatened. Skelgill pats the lad on the shoulder.

'Don't nod off, whatever you do, marra.'

*

Skelgill rows restrainedly, watching the three parked cars diminish in size, testing his eyesight for how far he can retreat before he can no longer read the number plates. He wonders if he should be remotely suspicious that the young Irish couple's Ford Consul has a British registration. If the time comes to cast the net wider, this itinerant pair would have to be included. Quite likely they were here, in the vicinity of Shuteham Hall during the time of the theft, with good reason to be up and about during the hours of darkness; and he guesses they are competent in moving surreptitiously through wild terrain. But they are improbable jewel thieves. More likely they have picked up the old banger at an auction in England, to see them through their gap year. He could easily enough get it checked out. In order to memorise the registration, ARS 10P, he conjures up a mind picture: his colleague DI Smart flipping a silver coin – that should do it. Smiling with some small satisfaction, he parks the notion and turns his mind to the matter in hand.

Just over halfway across the lake, he boats his oars and allows the craft to drift. All is calm, and the steely surface of Over Water extends like the floor of a great ice rink, on which he could step out and glide wherever he so desires. But the illusion of solidity is belied by a myriad of delicate mayflies, laying females that dip their ovipositors through the silvery meniscus, the catalyst for a burgeoning rise of trout.

These brownies would be easy meat. But Skelgill is troubled by the vendace – so little is known about the species. After his first abortive attempt he had consulted fellow angler Jim Hartley. The elderly academic had become consumed by Skelgill's task, and the prospect of discovering in Over Water what is arguably Britain's rarest endemic wild animal.

124

"This is our kakapo, Daniel – our Javan rhino, our mountain gorilla. We can't let it become our dodo. You must find it! There have been more documented sightings of Nessie than of vendace!"

For his part, Skelgill had expressed his frustration: it is the mark of a successful hunter that he knows the habits of his prey. Just what is the killer bait? Employing his research skills the professor had ascertained that the diet of the vendace mainly consists of planktonic crustaceans – 'copepods', well known to aquarium owners who add them live to feed captive fish. But, as Skelgill had pointed out, at sixteen to the inch these are not creatures that can be put on a hook! A more obscure literary source, an ancient tome of fishing lore unearthed by the professor in the local library had mentioned the 'Cumberland vendace' – but unfortunately did not reveal any practical tips, other than the more esoteric suggestion of fishing at midnight beneath the full moon.

There is a small parallel here, however, and Skelgill tunes in to his surroundings. Against the deeper blue sky to the southeast rises a waxing gibbous moon. In the lighter northwest, above the black shoulder of Skiddaw, Venus is the first 'star' to materialise, though there remains a pink flush of daylight reflecting from vestiges of high cloud. The cooling air is redolent with the invigorating night scents of water; the resonant atmosphere pierced by the sporadic calls of crepuscular birds. What a sublime time to be fishing. If only that were his plan.

*

Skelgill is hungry. Since a snatched lunch of patties on the hoof in Penrith all he has eaten are two slices of sand cake and two bags of peanuts. Back ashore in his car, with his Kelly kettle and the rest of his kit there are chocolate digestive biscuits – which reminds him of Karen Williamson and the thought crosses his mind that he could pay her a visit. Surely she would offer him supper. But would she appreciate a tap on her door at this late hour? And what would be his reason for disturbing her? He ponders. True, he could say he is worried about Stan, and ask if she could shed any light on his habits – and there is her curious visit to Keeper's Cottage, though that might be something on which he wishes to keep his powder dry. Then he remembers there is food in the gatehouse – what was it DS Jones called those unappetising-looking dumplings in the fridge – she said *coltunasi,* if he recalls correctly. As things stand, they'll only go to waste – and even boiled they would be better than an empty stomach. The place is not locked, as far as he is aware.

His boat has drifted very gently to within a few yards of the western shoreline of Over Water, and now in the shadow of Bullmire Wood he is satisfied that he has merged into the gloom. He can see a tiny light in the hide – so they must still have the flap open on the lake side – but a minute ago a car left – presumably the Vholes calling it a night, leaving the young Irish pair to their own devices. A cosy little set up, with their gas burner and bunk bed; no boss on their case, and doing something they're plainly into. Without feeling actually jealous – thankfully envy is not one of the cardinal vices to afflict Skelgill (though his colleagues might argue he makes up for it with a couple of the others) – he can't help thinking he wouldn't mind being in young Cian's shoes; nodding off would be the least of his problems.

He winds in frenetically. There is method in this, for he does not want the hassle of returning yet another perch; already he has a throbbing palm from one carelessly unhooked that jagged him with its spiny dorsal fin. The trouble is, perch do love maggots. All fish love maggots – that's why he is persisting with them. And Jim Hartley had concurred: "Daniel, every single freshwater fish in the British Isles has been taken on a maggot." And it was with a maggot that he inadvertently succeeded in Bass Lake. Now he unhooks the flaccid larva from his line and flicks it into the water – and then he is struck by a thought – when will he fish again? Not until the weekend, at best. He picks up his bait box from the bottom boards and squints rather hopelessly in the darkness at the seething contents – even in his fridge these wrigglers will surely pupate in the next couple of days, and he is no fan of casters, let alone bluebottles. He tosses the lot over the side, and mutters ironically.

'Enjoy your dinner.'

He can just make out a fallen alder, the trunk of which protrudes perpendicular to the shore – it serves as an ideal mooring spot, and one he can reliably find again, should he so need. But now Skelgill is handicapped. His powerful pocket torch is a weapon of final resort – the last thing he wants to do is betray his presence. Besides, it won't help him find his way; one direction looks much the same as any other. To avoid the risk of descent into ever decreasing circles he falls back upon method, and his mental map of the estate. Following moon shadows he makes unspectacular westerly progress, weaving a route of least resistance through the shrub layer, holding out in front a branch he has wrenched from a coppiced hazel. In ten minutes he comes up against the boundary wall bordered by the lane to Overthwaite. Now he turns northwards to reach West Gate House. It could easily be missed in the murk of the wood. Dismissing his fantasy of fried *coltunasi* he presses on, hugging the dry stone wall. His next landmark is Crow Road, the broad woodland ride that terminates at a functioning five-barred gate; though it is padlocked, he imagines this provides a convenient means of shipping shooting parties by Land Rover to the more northerly reaches of the estate, avoiding a lengthy loop via the main entrance and public highway.

The turf track makes for easier going than the spongy forest loam. In the ankle-deep grass Skelgill can feel the cool dew soaking his boots, though so far they hold firm, despite that the much-vaunted proprietary linings rarely last more than a couple of years, making his well overdue to spring a leak. The sky has cleared entirely and darkened to a midnight blue; overhead is the Plough and, a little to the left, Polaris and north. From the woods comes the periodic hoot of a tawny owl, like a distant steam train. And every so often he detects a Natterer's bat as a fleeting disturbance in the air upon his face, though its calls are beyond his range.

When he gets to within fifty yards of Keeper's Cottage Skelgill veers from the centre to the edge of the ride – and promptly cracks a twig that precipitates a great squawking commotion. From the canopy half a dozen crows break cover – vaguely he discerns their silhouettes bend and bank away. Crow Road, of course. Maybe not such a wise choice, so near to the Terminator. Indeed he can smell the keeper's larder – but perhaps this is no deterrent to a bird more properly called the carrion crow. He waits for the melancholic complaints to fade, and in time silence returns. He stoops and feels around for a pebble. Stepping out from the shadow of the trees he hurls it in the direction of the property – and scores a direct hit, drawing a reverberating twang from the sheet iron roof of the wood store. He takes cover. But there are no repercussions – and, in particular, there is no barking dog. He waits another minute and then, sticking to the treeline works his way around the back of the cottage. In common with West Gate House it is in darkness – he wonders if there are security lights, and for this reason keeps his distance. And then, once again, like this morning, he suffers the same distinct sensation that he is being watched. Is he hearing something? Are there barely audible footsteps that cease each time he stops to listen? But it cannot be – no one hangs around in woods on the off chance that someone will come by. And not only does the property appear deserted, as far as he can discern the quad bike is not there. Beneath the shelter there is only velvet shadow, when surely something of it would glint in the moonlight.

Much as he itches to search Keeper's Cottage he gives the idea only scant consideration. He might just about be able to talk his way out of being in the grounds after dark, but to be caught inside one of the properties would take some explaining, not least to the Chief. And never mind the present danger: the violent retribution that Lord Bullingdon has threatened to exact upon prowlers; it sounds like his arsenal could equip a small private army. So he moves on, and perhaps only now acknowledges that his coming here at all is a little puzzling, even to himself. To some extent this 'plan' (no plan, really) has unfolded as an extension of his comparatively rudderless progress through the day, like a leaf carried by rainwater finding its course after a long drought. True, a semblance of logic can be ascribed to his evening's itinerary: first, picking the brains of Eric Hepplethwaite about the new keeper, and learning the beat of the local jungle drums; second, paying a surprise visit to the ornithologists to understand their setup and conduct; third, venturing forth on his boat to gain a different perspective of the locality – these are all justifiable as acts of fact-finding. In addition there is his formal mandate to catch a vendace – he has license to be on Over Water and, as per his last visit, is entitled to investigate a potential crime. Yet he might easily have skipped these steps, or put them on tomorrow's agenda.

But there was his unexpected encounter with former classmate Basil – and his remark about Lawrence Melling. *"He's not quite the gentleman he likes to pretend he is."* While Skelgill will not admit to himself why he is troubled quite so severely, and despite its irrelevance to a jewel theft and a disappearing employee, nevertheless the casual revelation has proved to be the tipping point.

Marching doggedly along Crow Road Skelgill curses under his breath as he puts up another flock of roosting birds – woodpigeons that go off with an explosive clatter of wings. He rues that he is blazing a trail through the wildlife – but at least these watchful sentries tell him there is no one in the immediate vicinity, else they would already have flown. At the intersection of Crow Road and Long Shoot he turns right onto the latter and strikes uphill towards the castle. The woods on his left thin out as he reaches the track that leads down to Garden Cottage. Beside the building a small car, a white five-year-old Mini with an *"I Love Karate"* bumper sticker is parked on a patch of hardstanding. In the still air hangs the faint reek of wood smoke. Beneath an open porch there is a single light over the front door, and a window on either side. The curtains are drawn and only a very faint nightlight glows from within that on the left, which has a row of trophies on the sill. He makes a circuit, but the one window uncurtained is the kitchen, also unlit apart from a couple of tiny red neon switches. His impression is that the occupants, presumably Karen Williamson and her kickboxing kid Kieran, are sleeping. In darkness at the rear there is a picnic table close to the back door, while a trampoline dominates a patch of lawn; all around are shrubs, dense laurels or rhododendrons by the look of it, and on one side the towering brickwork of the walled garden.

Skelgill retraces his steps to Long Shoot and continues northeast. Presently, on his right, the topiary lawn unfolds, its sculpted yews frozen like a marauding band of mountain trolls turned to stone by the moonlight. Ahead the old castle looms, a great slab, its pitted face an ancient memorial to the bloody battles that must have been fought out before its blind eyes. But in one of these – a window on the top floor that he calculates must be Miranda Bullingdon's bedroom – there winks a light, indeed it flickers, and he recalls the lime-scented ornamental candle on the deep sill. The room beside it – with which it interconnects – Lord Bullingdon's, is in darkness. Skelgill presumes that Daphne and Julian Bullingdon also sleep somewhere in the old keep, but he knows not where. He checks his watch; the time is approaching eleven-thirty. He wonders if he should have expected more signs of the occupants still being awake. Then again Lord Bullingdon insists that he locks up around ten, and retires. It is often the way of these country places, particularly those that have livestock, early to bed and early to rise. Skelgill considers testing out the man's claim – but it seems too risky; surely any attempt on the main door would resound through the stone halls. Instead he skirts the building and reaches the rear entrance that gives on to the kitchen garden. Now he sees a light in what must be the cook's quarters above the scullery, and stays close to the building. He tries the back door. It is unlocked.

Even with his limited knowledge of the layout, he could be in and out and considerably richer within two minutes. Especially if he knew that everyone else was asleep and that Miranda Bullingdon does not lock her bedroom. Then there is the business of sleeping like an angel. Contemplating this scenario, he quickly retreats, before devilment gets the better of him. He follows the path along which Daphne Bullingdon led him. Passing between the herbaceous beds he dislodges wafts of lavender from wayward stems. He continues past the gunroom and its associated VIP entertainment suite – another place he would like to inspect – and on further to the rearing sheds. He can hear the peeping of the young birds – more subdued than during daytime – and he treads carefully, so as not to cause alarm. A sharp metallic click from the side of the main shed makes him start – he draws his torch to reveal the incinerator, of which Daphne Bullingdon is so proud. For Skelgill it is a sombre reminder of what is going on here: despite the cute chirpings of the poults, they are quite literally cannon fodder in a cold-hearted enterprise. Those that perish in the crowded melee before they mature will end up in here; those that make it to the battlefield will later be decapitated, trimmed and plucked, their blind heads and severed feet to be turned to cinders. He wonders what they do with all the ash; he is aware there are regulations about correct disposal. He approaches the sinister device; it is an imposing piece of kit, the chimney some twelve feet high and the cylindrical body nine or ten in girth. It is imprinted with danger triangles and the warning, "Caution Hot Surface". It also states, "Max capacity 50kgs per hour". Skelgill prefers imperial, and a quick conversion tells him it is the best part of a hundredweight; a lot of pheasant, even at a couple of pounds a bird; more like an emu. Again there comes the ticking sound and he realises it is the contraction of the metal shell. He steps closer and tentatively puts out a hand. It is still warm from operation earlier.

Now Skelgill heads for the 'railway station' arrangement of the covered game preparation area, the estate office and, beyond, part of the same continuous building, the stables. There is a light over the office door and he feels deterred – there is no easy cover – if someone suddenly emerged he would be exposed – and instantly recognisable. He decides on a brazen tactic. He leans his hazel staff against the wall. He extracts his warrant card from his back pocket and has it ready in one hand, the torch – switched on – in the other. If challenged he will simply say he has followed an intruder from the lake. It is a matter of brass neck, and loosely accurate, if he counts his own shadow. Of course, when you are a policeman with reasonable cause, trespassing is a grey area. Thus armed he advances upon the office – but inside it is in darkness, the door locked. He continues; there is a rank of stable doors, from within the odd muted clump of a hoof and the murmur of a beast; he creeps past, he does not want to spook one of them into a betraying whinny. The last door is marked 'Stores'. And, finally, at the end of the building is an open entry – his flashlight illuminates a passage leading to a ladder-like stair. These would be the old grooms' quarters; today the lodgings of the other estate workers. He steps back and realises there is low lighting in a series of small windows on the upper floor, and – now that he listens carefully – subdued voices, laughter and the occasional exclamation; late-night socialising.

Skelgill retraces his steps. Collecting his hazel staff he is glad of the cover of darkness away from the office. Walking briskly he passes the rearing sheds, the gunroom and then the castle itself. He sticks to the lawn edges, off the gravel, so to walk in silence. Passing the walled garden he again nears the turn for Garden Cottage, now on his right.

But his peripheral night-vision is attracted by a darker shadow in the trees to his left, a black cleft in the vegetation. He realises there is a diagonal path descending into the woods – judging by the lie of the land it must lead down to Troutmere, the artificial lake. Across the little valley, on the other side, will be the main driveway.

He approaches the opening and flashes his torch. To his surprise, there is the quad bike, pushed into the cover of the bushes. Skelgill stands and stares, ruminating. The owner of a Triumph motorcycle himself, he is no stranger to this genre of machine. He leans across and carefully puts out a hand to the engine. It is not hot – but neither is it anything like the ambient temperature of under fifty Fahrenheit. The bike has been ridden in the past hour. He feels a quickening of his pulse. And now he commits his first illicit act of the night – trespassing aside. He feels beneath the seat for the fuel tap, turns it to the 'on' position, and wrenches off the rubber outlet hose. Immediately there is a pungent reek of petrol, as the tank begins to drain. He suppresses the sudden hysterical laugh that comes upon him along with the notion of setting the quad on fire. Instead, he sets off.

The path is more of a tunnel through overarching rhododendrons; it is pitch black, winding and steep with treacherous exposed roots. He uses his staff like a blind man feeling for obstacles underfoot; his other hand guards his face from unwelcome projections.

He emerges into the moonlight some twenty feet from the shore of the lake. A strip of mown grass for ease of perambulation rings the perimeter, but the water itself is fringed by vegetation. In daylight Skelgill had noted that it looked surprisingly natural, with well-established reeds, blooming yellow flag and shrubs of sallow. At irregular intervals there are little sandy bays that he had eyed up as angling pegs. A grassed-over dam at the south end, to his right, maintains the water level, and in the angle of the near bank and the dam is the two-storey boathouse. Immediately he sees there is a light showing in the glass frontage beyond the slatted wooden balcony.

He waits.

As far as he can tell there is no one out on the balcony, but behind the pale curtains, which are little more than opaque veils, he thinks he sees movements, certainly changes in hue as though figures cross in front of a light.

In admiring the structure earlier he had calculated that the upper floor, the 'guest accommodation' is reached by the door on the dam side; within there must be a stair. The interior can only be the equivalent of a decent-sized hotel room, probably just a bedroom – Daphne Bullingdon's intended bridal suite. The sliding windows and balcony face over the lake – literally they are *over* the water, since below is the actual boathouse, the miniature enclosed harbour which has been extended by a pontoon that in turn is covered by a roof that slopes down from the foot of the balcony. Skelgill cannot get much closer on land than his present position. For want of optical aids such as the Vholes' Leica, the alternative is to climb from the pontoon onto the pitched roof.

He circles the lake and cautiously approaches the boathouse. To reach the pontoon he takes a walkway around the side. At its lowest point he swings himself onto the sloping roof and begins to inch up towards the balcony. The gradient is a good thirty degrees and gravity is seeking to dump him into the water, but he tells himself it is no steeper than Hardknott Pass – one in three, so it must be doable. Thankfully it is dry, and the gritty roofing felt gives good purchase. He splays his fingers to maximise the traction.

The tops of the French windows begin to come into view through the rustic palings of the balcony. Now he can hear the muted pulse of soft music and the occasional murmur of voices – definitely a male and surely also a female. Then he sees indistinct shapes again moving – could it be a couple coming together in an embrace? Is there a moan – of pleasure – or protest? He stretches, the better to see.

And then the dog barks.

A short, sharp, warning yap.

The black working cocker is on the balcony.

Skelgill ducks his head. He flattens himself, his face pressed against the sandpaper-like surface.

A door slides open, the music suddenly louder.

He hears a female voice – but cannot make out what it says, nor identify its owner.

But of Lawrence Melling's reply, there is no doubt.

'She disnae bark like that without reason.'

The man is listening.

If he comes out and looks over the rail, Skelgill is a sitting duck.

It will only take the dog to approach and 'point'. (Skelgill is thinking: it's a spaniel, it might not).

But does he hold his nerve – or roll into the water and strike for the far bank?

Then the man's voice, sharp, cold.

134

'Come!'

There is an excited skittering of claws; the dog obeys. As the door begins to slide shut the man issues a second command, the tone moderated, suggesting that it is aimed at his companion.

'Stay out of sight.'

The instant the door closes Skelgill springs into action. He slides down the roof and flip-flops onto the pontoon. He snatches up his hazel staff and smears along its length congealed blood from the wound on his palm inflicted by the indignant perch. Two handed like a hammer thrower he hurls the branch across the water. He hears the swish of the reeds as it makes landfall upon the bank along which he came. And now there is no time to waste – boots are thumping down the interior wooden stair. And the outside door bangs open.

'Seek!'

Lawrence Melling sends the dog about its business. But, while the creature disappears into the night, purposeful footsteps advance along the walkway and onto the pontoon. The boots come to a halt.

Directly beneath, up to his chin in water, craning his neck, Skelgill can just make out through the gaps in the boards the soles of the boots, unlaced, and the form of the man.

And the shotgun he holds.

A torch beam is played cursorily across the lake. Skelgill remains absolutely still so as not to create giveaway ripples.

The man stands listening. Skelgill can hear his breathing. He knows he cannot dare to breathe himself. The man stoops and begins to tie his laces – their faces can only be three feet apart. He can smell his aftershave. But just when Skelgill thinks his lungs will burst, the dog suddenly starts up barking frantically. It has got wind of the hazel staff. The man rises and hurries away. He leaves, hanging in the air like a putrid stench, a chilling utterance.

'Wait 'til I catch you, ****.'

Skelgill raises an eyebrow at the expletive – at its vehemence as much as its inherent offensiveness.

He pants silently to restore his breath. He realises he is beginning to shiver. He detects faint movements from the accommodation above. He would dearly love to know who is up there. But getting away is the priority. The last thing he wants is the humiliation of being caught and driven at gunpoint like a pathetic peeping Tom to beg before the feudal lord. Or, perhaps a worse fate. Dripping abundantly, he hauls himself onto the pontoon and pauses, on his haunches. Now he can see the torchlight flickering along the bank where he hurled the stick. With any luck the dog will follow his scent back up through the rhododendrons. He creeps around to the back of the boathouse and sets off at a run along the dam in the opposite direction, instinctively ducking down as though it would make a difference (it might if he is fired at). Within about fifty yards he finds the outfall; it pours over the top of a sluice, splashing onto a rocky bed. He clambers into the shallow water and begins to wade downstream. The beck is a tributary of Over Water; from its mouth his boat can be reached by striking south along the wooded bank. It is a sure route to safety, with the added advantage of leaving few traces for a dog to track.

A minute has passed when a sound arrests him. It is the quad bike starting up. But just as quickly the engine splutters and dies. Then, several times, there are futile attempts to restart it. The starter motor protests like some tortured creature of the night, the engine turns over but does not fire. A second chilling threat, loaded with oaths, filters down through the trees.

*

Skelgill checks his watch; it is twenty to one. It was at midnight, the showdown at the boathouse, and now, his teeth chattering and his breath coming in urgent gasps, he hauls his craft onto his trailer at the Over Water slipway. His hands are numb and his body is not far behind, despite the flat-out row across the lake. He has donned his gilet, left behind for his foray – and thankfully so, for it contains his mobile and keys. But, as yet, it is making scant difference to his core temperature; he recognises that the ducking in Troutmere has prompted a cold shock response.

He needs a piping hot cup of tea. The best option is just yards away – the Irish pair on watch in the birdwatching hide will surely oblige. He can explain his appearance by saying he slipped while he was beaching the boat. But his boots are full of water; he pulls them off and slings them into the hull. And now he hesitates, and climbs into the driver's seat. He turns on the ignition and cranks the heater and the fan to maximum. From the back seat he grabs an army blanket and wraps it over his thighs. He could brew up a Kelly himself, but it would mean crouching outside; it might be mid May, but the clear sky portends of a frost in the mountains tonight. He begins to feel the first welcome waves of warm air percolating around his legs. From the radio emanates the comforting tones of the late-night announcer and the shipping forecast. Dogger; Fisher; German Bight. He reaches across to the glove box and pulls out a half-eaten packet of biscuits – he is cheered: half *not* eaten, yet.

Fifteen minutes later, and still thoroughly damp but now tolerably warm, he leaves the car and walks gingerly in stockinged feet across the stony parking area until he reaches the more forgiving surface of the boardwalk. Silently, although not intentionally so, he approaches the door of the hide. He is about to jerk it open when some instinct warns him. He puts an ear to the flimsy wood and listens. His expression becomes philosophical; this would not be a good moment to enter. It sounds like they *are* a couple. Smiling ruefully he retraces his steps.

Thinking he is still hungry he restarts the shooting brake and gently pulls away, not wishing to cause unnecessary disturbance. Besides, the stretch of track leading to the metalled lane is severely pot-holed, and he does not want to throw the trailer off the tow bar. The beam from his headlamps leaps about wildly in response to the rutted terrain, illuminating the lush green hedgerows and moths confused by the light – and a little owl swoops down upon one such disoriented insect that has fluttered onto the dried mud surface. Instinctively Skelgill switches off his lights – and, just as he does so, at the end of the track a small yellow hatchback crosses from left to right.

He accelerates – he wants to check the registration. But immediately he realises the futility of what he has in mind; towing his boat is like running a three-legged race; the narrow winding lanes will thwart him. And when, in hamstrung pursuit he passes first the deserted right turn to Overthwaite, and then reaches the crossroads signposted left to Keswick and right to Cockermouth, and all is quiet, his pessimism is confirmed as mere pragmatism.

He waits at the junction, pondering his next move. The clock on the dashboard reads five past one. He grimaces – not because of the time, and the realisation that the takeaways will all be closed – but because he knows someone who owns a small yellow hatchback: his colleague, DS Jones.

7. OVER MOOR

Tuesday morning

'Cheers.'

'You're welcome.'

DS Jones sounds surprised – perhaps it is the tone of her superior's word of thanks, as much as that he even uttered it at all. She takes her regular seat before his office window; he has the blind down and tilted to deflect the harsh morning sun. Though the window itself is open and an invigorating potpourri of birdsong carried on the cool morning air infiltrates between the slats. Skelgill takes a couple of thirsty pulls at the mug of tea she has supplied; she does not have one for herself; instead she is provisioned with notes and an electronic tablet.

After a few moments, during which it is evident to DS Jones that Skelgill has something to get off his chest – and for which reason she waits in silence rather than introduce her own subject – he seems to regard her with a mixture of frustration and regret. Or is she reading too much into his reticence? She smiles demurely and crosses her legs and looks away. When his question comes it is rather prosaic.

'How did you go on last night?'

Yet DS Jones glances up sharply – perhaps she is sensitive to his precise phraseology, which might be considered indiscreet to the acute ear.

'Oh – er – I finished the report. I emailed it – about midnight?'

She appends a question mark to her statement, suitably inflecting the final word.

Skelgill frowns; he casts a defensive hand towards his creaking in-tray.

'I've not had chance to log on.'

Unfazed, that when he might have commended her efforts but instead has self-referenced, DS Jones switches into a businesslike mode. She pats the pile of admin on her lap.

'It's okay – I've got printouts.' She hesitates for a moment. 'But, to be honest, Guv – it's only what you already know. I think the feedback that has come through first thing this morning is more pertinent.'

Skelgill appears to give up on whatever is troubling him and resigns himself to following her line.

'Aye?'

DS Jones glances at the vacant seat beside the tall grey filing cabinet.

'Should we wait for DS Leyton? He just took an urgent call as I left. I don't suppose he'll be long.'

Now Skelgill flaps his hand carelessly.

'He can catch up after.'

DS Jones looks momentarily doubtful, as though she knows her colleague might be disappointed.

'Sure, Guv.'

Briefly, to refresh her memory she interrogates the tablet. Then she lays it down again.

'Taking things in a logical sequence, Stan – Carol Valentin Stanislav – *is* who he purports to be. The Moldovan authorities have confirmed the passport is genuine and the family have identified him from the photograph. No criminal record. He's from the capital, Chisinau. He is not known to hold a Romanian passport. The family say he has been working abroad for several years, mainly in the agricultural line. He is unmarried but had a long-term girlfriend in Chisinau whom he used to return to visit, but they believe she moved to work in Germany about a year ago. They say they last saw him in December – the dates correspond to what Daphne Bullingdon told us. They didn't know he was in the UK – but Immigration have confirmed his visa is valid.'

Skelgill looks like questions are occurring to him, but he holds his peace. His sergeant is not to be underestimated, and he is immediately proved correct.

'A work visa isn't easy to obtain for non-EU nationals – especially in a kind of general handyman role. It's possible that the Shuteham Hall estate is his sponsor – but normally it would be for a more highly technical position. We might want to look into that, Guv? Also I wonder why he didn't tell his relatives he was here in England.'

Skelgill nods, politely but without great enthusiasm.

'As for the more immediate situation – no sightings, obviously.' Now Skelgill adds a single more decisive bow of the head – he has automatically assumed that any such news would have been broken first and immediately. 'We've got some basic mobile data. His phone was last active – in other words last switched on – until just after one a.m. on Saturday. At that point it was somewhere in the approximate vicinity of the estate, but not necessarily on the property itself. It could have been intentionally switched off – it could have run out of battery. It has not been on the network since – which might be a matter for concern. We're waiting for details of any recent calls and texts. It would appear to have had very low usage generally – of course, they have two-way radios for contacting staff around the estate, although Stan wasn't issued with one over the weekend.'

Skelgill, thinking, and drinking, puts down his mug.

'He could have another phone – or SIM card.'

'I agree, Guv – we're just going by the number that he provided to Daphne Bullingdon. I've requested an analysis of all mobiles used in the vicinity of the estate in the last month. It could be a bit of a tortuous process, but by elimination we might be able to narrow it down – see if there is a number that has been regularly active and is now suddenly elsewhere.'

Having reached the extent of her update, DS Jones lays her palms upon her pile of materials and leans forward, as though she is soliciting her superior's opinion – but she decides he might respond more candidly to an assertion.

'This information points to him still being in Britain. That would fit with the theory that he took the jewellery and has either hooked up with criminal associates, or has realised it would be too risky to attempt to try to leave the UK and has simply gone to ground.'

Accordingly this triggers a rejoinder, though Skelgill's tone is rather unfairly dismissive.

'Underground. Underwater. I'd say drag the lake – the little one, Troutmere – except his rod and his wellies are back in the gatehouse.'

But DS Jones knows her boss well enough to appreciate that he is a man who uses the maxim "many a true word is spoken in jest" as an actual technique – to provoke those around him, and no doubt to provoke himself.

'But, Guv – we don't have anything to indicate that he came to some harm.'

'Since when did lack of evidence blind us from the blindingly obvious?'

Now DS Jones cannot suppress a wry smile. Here is another classic Skelgillism: oxymoronic, and attributing his own questionable habits to his colleagues.

She persists with her efforts to encourage him to reveal what he really thinks.

'Then again most mispers turn out to be false alarms.'

But Skelgill will not be drawn; his tone remains dry.

'Aye, he could have gone native for all we know. He might be living wild in the woods. Having a crack at the Bob Graham. Then got injured. Fell walking, as Leyton would say.'

As if by some clever intuition on Skelgill's part, his mention of his sergeant brings the sudden appearance of DS Leyton in the doorway of the office. Indeed, as if summoned like a dutiful genie, he skids to a halt, necessitating his grabbing onto the door's jambs. His mop of dark hair is more than usually tousled, and his complexion flushed. A corner of his shirt has escaped from the belt that restrains his somewhat out-of-condition midriff. He takes a gasp of air and yanks at his tie to loosen it.

'Guv – just reported – on Over Moor – *a body.*'

Skelgill glares as though he is actually annoyed – as if this news is unwelcome in the sense that it spoils everything he knows. He glances to see that DS Jones is regarding their colleague with considerable trepidation.

Skelgill utters just one word, his intonation flat.

'Stan.'

DS Leyton opens his mouth to speak, but having sprinted from his desk and evidently having used the stairs rather than the lift, is still in oxygen debt.

'No, Guv – not Stan.' Now he wheezes out the words. 'It's that cocky geezer – the gamekeeper, Melling.'

*

'Who found him?'

'A twitcher chap, sir. Mr Neil Vholes.' PC Dodd, the first officer on the scene, cocks his head in the direction of Over Water. 'He's ower at yon bird hide – I've asked him to wait. He weren't keen on bringing me out here. Reckoned there's some rare buzzards nesting – and he don't want 'em mithered by us.'

Skelgill regards the young constable pensively.

'Aye, hen harriers they're called.' He casts about, calculating his bearings from the roof and angle of orientation of the hide. 'The nest's a good way off. We should be alright.'

Notwithstanding Skelgill's reassuring words, the constable appears to be consumed by self-reproach.

'I thought he were winding me up, sir. Happen I might have upset him.'

Skelgill does not look particularly concerned – questions are queuing up in his mind and he turns to DS Leyton to delegate those most pressing.

'Leyton – get over to Shuteham Hall – I'm assuming they don't know. Don't let anyone leave before we speak to them. Call the SOCO team – make sure they put up a tent – and bring as many screens as they've got – to cover the approach from the lane.'

His sergeant is looking a little pale faced.

'Righto, Guv – I'll get that sorted. I reckon I've seen enough here.'

DS Leyton nods to his trio of colleagues and lumbers away. Skelgill watches him for a moment; it is not like the phlegmatic Londoner to be squeamish. He pulls from his pocket his map of Shuteham Hall estate and beckons to PC Dodds.

'For the time being, you mount a guard at the stile beside the bridleway – where you came in.' Now he jabs a finger at a spot on the map. 'And we'll need an officer here. That's where this beaters' path is accessed from the grounds. Just to stop folk from the hall coming along. Otherwise, no one's likely to approach the scene from any other direction; it's private shooting land for miles around.'

PC Dodds nods, perhaps a little apprehensively.

'Yes, sir. I'll radio that in while I take up position.'

He looks like he feels he ought to salute to Skelgill in order to excuse himself, but Skelgill saves him the trouble by turning away and gazing broodingly across Over Moor towards the site of the harriers' nest. The constable grins rather inanely at DS Jones; she smiles and helpfully tilts her head to indicate he should feel free to depart. As former schoolmates their career paths have been parallel if not line abreast. DS Jones walks across to stand beside Skelgill, though she does not speak, and simply looks the same way. After a few moments they are diverted by a bellicose grunt from behind them. It is the sound of the hefty and none-too-spritely pathologist, Dr Herdwick, rising from a kneeling position held overlong. He puts away a notebook and pencil, and peels off a pair of nitrile gloves. Knowing he has the full attention of his audience, he brushes down his unsuitably heavy tweed outfit before declaiming in a tone that to an outsider would sound decidedly lacking in solicitude.

'It appears your man shot himself in the foot.'

The two detectives cross to stand facing their medical colleague. Skelgill, for the first time in the ten or so minutes that they have been at the scene, finds himself looking analytically at the reason for their presence. Why, he cannot say, but his senses have been attuned to the surroundings, innocuous though they might seem, rather than the dramatic sight at their epicentre. But now he focuses. And his eyes immediately narrow.

The body of Lawrence Melling lies contorted and stiff on the hard baked earth of the beaters' path, a pose reminiscent of a 'fouled' footballer frozen in the throes of faked agony. But any pain felt was surely real, for the left leg is clamped at the shin and calf by the jaws of a cast iron mantrap. The archaic apparatus bears a striking resemblance to that which Skelgill saw displayed in the fortified entrance to the castle. By the dead man's right side is a shotgun. On his face and hands there are smears of blood. The ragged trouser leg, shredded by the pathologist in the fashion of Robinson Crusoe, is even more heavily bloodstained.

But it is not the barbaric medieval spectacle that now arrests Skelgill – indeed he assimilated all this within the first few seconds of his arrival upon the scene. That he feels suddenly detached, and that the voice of Dr Herdwick fades to a distant drone, has a more mundane cause: a varnished staff capped by an antler that protrudes from the heather bordering the beaters' path; a waxed-cotton hat that lies close by; and a cape, crumpled beneath the dead man.

"The teeth of the trap alone would not have resulted in such catastrophic hypovolemia. However, what remains of his lower leg is full of lead pellets. The fibular artery has suffered acute trauma. Exsanguination would have occurred within a few minutes." The voice halts, as though the speaker is expecting a question, but when none is forthcoming he adds a clarification. "That's death by loss of blood – is that plain English enough for you?"

Skelgill exits his trance.

'He's got Bullingdon's gear.'

This statement means nothing to Dr Herdwick; his great bushy brows become knitted – but DS Jones at least reads the gravity in her superior's tone.

'Pardon, Guv?'

'Remember – when he came flapping into the estate office, looking for his wife? He'd put on that cape and hat, and was carrying the thumbstick – like he was on a mission to search the grounds.'

DS Jones looks searchingly at each item in turn. She suspects that if Skelgill were asked to describe what Miranda Bullingdon had been wearing, quite likely he would just say, "white". But outdoor paraphernalia is right up his street. She makes a quiet observation.

'It didn't rain last night.'

Skelgill jerks his head around to look at her. But, when he might comment, he holds back, as though a second thought has outranked the first. It is a little while before he does have something to add. Tentatively with the tip of his boot he taps the shotgun.

'I don't reckon that's the gun he had the day the buzzard was shot.'

DS Jones frowns, her normally smooth brow creased; during her interview with Lawrence Melling he demonstrated several of the firearms, trying to impress her with their value, especially Lord Bullingdon's prized possession; but they were so similar in appearance. She realises this is her own 'white' moment.

'Why would that be?'

Yet Skelgill regards her question as rhetorical – for it can only be speculative – and he demonstrates no inclination to reply. But mention of the weapon has prompted the pathologist, who is always glad to stick in his two penn'orth when it is not his department.

'If it was an unfamiliar gun it might explain why it went off when he walked into the trap. Snap. Boom. Goodnight Vienna.'

For a second Skelgill glares angrily at his medical colleague; but he knows the man well enough to contrive a way to put him in his place. He adopts a sardonic tone.

'You mean he didn't try to blow off his own foot to escape from the trap?'

Dr Herdwick affects the taking of offence.

'Now, now, Inspector – I'm just trying to help. It looks plain enough that you've got an unfortunate accident on your hands.'

Skelgill decides there is no need to argue. Besides, Herdwick can be a cankerous old devil and he doesn't want him taking his

146

bat home. He notes already he has used 'you' and 'your' when 'we' and 'our' might be more collaborative. So he nods slowly, thoughtfully – even ostentatiously. Then, when the man appears placated, he speaks.

'But I'd like to know what time of accident.'

It is a curious phrase, but it suffices; indeed it would bear semantic scrutiny, especially when uttered as it is by a detective. And the doctor, having found the ball returned to his specialist court, now grimaces with a good degree of reluctance.

'We'll know more when the cavalry arrives. And more still when we get him back to the lab. There's factors such as the temperature profile last night. His physical condition. The rate of blood loss. There's computer programmes for this sort of thing nowadays.' He stares rather ruefully at the corpse, his lined face seemingly regretful of these modern advances. And, when eventually compelled to speak – perhaps to fill the expectant silence, unaware that the detectives are biting their tongues – his words perhaps echo such sentiments. He begins with an exclamation of frustration, best not printed. 'But from a good old-fashioned perspective: the condition of the dried blood, the advancement of rigor mortis – not least, gut feel,' he checks his wristwatch as the detectives look on, 'I'd say you wouldn't be far wrong with midnight.'

'Midnight!'

Skelgill cannot help his reflex reaction, and a tone that implies he thinks this is impossible. But the doctor responds stoically.

'Give or take. You know your darts, aye? Midnight's your bullseye – between ten p.m. and two a.m. is your twenty-five. Name your odds.'

Skelgill looks a little more relieved upon hearing the wider range. But his thoughts are racing. It places his own presence very close to the probable time of the gamekeeper's demise. The implications of this are yet to be appreciated and acted upon. For the present, he pushes them to the back of his mind. He turns to DS Jones.

'We'd better speak to Vholes. In case he tries to clear off.'

'Surely I don't have to go over this once again, Inspector – I have a heads of departments' meeting at midday. I related everything I know to your constable.'

Skelgill wishes he had a fiver for every time he'd heard a version of this protest. He shrugs stolidly and casts about the interior of the hide. He and DS Jones have entered to find Neil and Christine Vholes seemingly birdwatching as normal, although it strikes him that the pair had their Leicas fixed zealously on the point on Over Moor where a white scenes-of-crime tent is hurriedly being pitched.

'We'd like to hear it from yourself, sir – the horse's mouth as they say.' This draws a disapproving expression. 'For accuracy, sir – I'm sure you'll understand the importance of that.' The rider seems to mollify him a little.

However, Neil Vholes sighs excessively and glances at his sister who evidently consents to his acting as spokesperson – and he begins without further prompting.

'At approximately eight o'clock this morning we noticed that Galahad the male hen harrier was behaving oddly. The bird had brought prey for the female; he was circling, and calling agitatedly – but she wasn't coming off the nest. I imagined there might be a predator nearby – and that Hetty did not want to risk revealing the whereabouts of their clutch. I was scanning with my binoculars and that was when I noticed the dog.'

He stops as though this is sufficient – but to Skelgill mention of the hitherto unseen canine is something of a curved ball.

'The dog, sir?'

The man regards him wearily.

'A black cocker spaniel. It was moving about in the vicinity of the – er – *accident*. I was just seeing occasional glimpses of its head. At first I thought it must have been a raven, until I got a clear view.'

Skelgill is looking perplexed. He is obliged to digress.

'And where is the dog, now, sir?'

Neil Vholes' tone becomes increasingly indignant.

'In our car, Inspector – I didn't see what else I could do with it – I certainly didn't want to leave it to rampage about the moor.'

Skelgill parks the practical aspect and refocuses his thoughts; but the man does not voluntarily restart his narrative.

'So you went from here to – what – to catch the dog? That's what you thought you were doing?'

'Precisely, Inspector. I had no idea what I was going to find. The – er – the gamekeeper was not visible from this angle.'

Skelgill looks at Christine Vholes.

'And did you both go?'

'Christine remained here.' Neil Vholes' interjection is swift and decisive, as if he means to suppress a possible contradiction. But, for her part, she nods implacably. 'I drove back onto the lane and followed it, and took the bridleway until I reached the nearest point. You have no doubt been using the stile and the footpath to gain access yourselves.'

Skelgill nods, but does not otherwise answer. After a moment Neil Vholes continues.

'The footpath meets up with the beaters' path. I turned onto that and in fact the dog came running towards me. I had one of our own dog's leads but I couldn't get hold of the infernal creature – it kept darting away each time I got close. And then I realised it seemed to be trying to draw my attention to something. Which of course it was.'

He swallows now and grimaces with distaste, as though what happened next was offensive to his sensibilities.

'You have no doubt witnessed what I found. I could see immediately that the man was dead. Naturally I knew not to touch anything. I managed to collar the dog and came back here as quickly as I could. Christine had our mobile phones in the rucksack.' He gestures to a new-looking green daypack balanced on the bench seat.

Skelgill has listened reflectively. It is a few moments before he breaks the silence that has ensued.

'Did you touch anything at the scene, sir – the dog apart?'

'Of course not, Inspector – credit me with some intelligence.'

Skelgill remains patient.

'At what time did you arrive here, sir?'

Skelgill notices that Christine Vholes begins to nod almost before her brother answers.

'Just before seven.'

'Did you see anyone else?'

'Not out on the moor.'

Skelgill waits but the man is unforthcoming.

'The Irish couple – Cian and Ciara. What about them?'

'They were asleep in their car when we arrived. Christine went out to speak with them a few minutes later, and they had driven off.'

'Is that normal, sir?'

Neil Vholes looks strangely embarrassed; he glances a little uncomfortably at DS Jones before turning back to Skelgill.

'You may have noticed we have no formal washing and toilet facilities here, Inspector. They use the transport café on the A66, at the Lamplugh roundabout. I believe they may also eat their breakfast there.'

Skelgill inhales through clenched teeth; he senses that DS Jones is watching him.

'When will they be back?'

Neil Vholes looks surprised.

'I have no idea. I would need to look at the rota. It is on the Nats website. Not until this evening, at the earliest, I should think. In the meantime I imagine they will be sleeping somewhere in their car.'

'Have you got a mobile number for them?'

Skelgill's question is curt and Neil Vholes frowns and glances briefly at his sister.

'I don't believe their budget extended to mobile telephones. As far as I am aware they conducted all of their communications via their laptop using free Wi-Fi.'

Skelgill looks momentarily stymied – but it is clear that another thought suddenly occurs to him. He steps away from Neil Vholes towards the table at the end of the hut. Connected up is the expensive laptop with the distinctive customised case that the man had produced at police headquarters.

'The webcam – is it recording?'

Neil Vholes immediately replies.

'It can record. But it is directed only upon the nest. That would be no use to you.'

Skelgill rotates on his heel and stares at the couple.

'But it's got sound – I heard the birdsong when Ciara demonstrated it. Any sound would have been captured.'

Neil Vholes looks to his sister. She rises from the bench and walks somewhat reluctantly to the table. She turns the laptop around to save her from squeezing onto the bunk on the other side. She bends at the waist to interrogate the machine. After a few moments she speaks without looking up.

'The server has the capacity to record up to twenty-four hours. But, to prevent the memory from becoming overwhelmed, the default setting is on an hourly loop – since we always have a presence. I can confirm that is the current position, I am afraid, Inspector Skelgill.'

She stands upright and holds out an open palm towards the screen, as though inviting him to see for himself. He senses that DS Jones wishes to check, but he manages to convey through a glance that they should not bother. He addresses Christine Vholes.

'Do you have anything to add to Mr Vholes' account, madam?'

He watches closely to see if she makes any reference to her brother, but she regards him evenly.

'No.'

'What time did you leave, last night?'

Skelgill assumes that they know that he knows the answer to this question. Christine Vholes holds his gaze.

'It must have been ten-thirty-five. I noticed it was ten-fifty when we arrived home, and the journey always takes almost exactly fifteen minutes when there is no traffic. We live just this side of Stanthwaite, Inspector.'

She continues to look at Skelgill, now more quizzically. After a moment he shrugs and indicates with a toss of his head to his colleague.

'We'll return the dog.'

He detects from the body language of the Vholes that they are little irked by his presumptive manner. He starts towards the door but suddenly swings around to face them. His voice, however, carries a casual drawl.

'How did you know he was the gamekeeper?'

There is a distinct hesitation in Neil Vholes' reaction.

'Inspector – I – *we* – have met him.' He exchanges glances with his sister; this time she more overtly nods to demonstrate her accord. 'A week or so ago we participated in a group tour of Shuteham Hall estate – it had been organised through the Nats. The gamekeeper was one of the employees to whom we were introduced – he gave a short talk about the pheasant rearing and release process.'

Christine Vholes is smiling self-assuredly.

Skelgill nods once but does not pursue the matter. Instead he leads the way from the hide across to his car, which is parked beside the Vholes' Volvo. He throws up the tailgate, and defiantly stares down their disparaging glances at its dishevelled contents.

The Vholes have a travel crate and the spaniel looks pleased that it is about to be freed from what must be an unfamiliar confinement. They make no offer of their leash – and so Skelgill opens the cage and reaches in, letting the dog first sniff his hand. He moves to stroke it around the ears and then gently but firmly grips it by the scruff of the neck and lifts it out. Christine Vholes makes an involuntary squawk of protest but Skelgill ignores her and transfers the animal to his own vehicle, where it immediately finds something of an unspecified nature to eat. He closes the tailgate and rounds to the driver's door. When it is apparent that he is not about to grace them with departing formalities, Neil Vholes blurts out a protest.

'Inspector – your people can't hang around here – near the nest, I mean. The hen harrier is a red-listed species. It is technically a wildlife crime to disturb a breeding site. The offence carries a jail sentence.'

DS Jones watches Skelgill with consternation. Such insubordination from a civilian, coupled with Neil Vholes' condescension is likely to provoke an unfavourable reaction. So he surprises her when he smiles affably.

'I've ordered screens to cover the last part of the approach from the track. The team are all briefed about the significance of the birds. They won't take any longer than is necessary, sir. However it is our statutory duty to examine a crime scene.'

The Vholes are looking at Skelgill with considerable dismay, despite his conciliatory speech. Neil Vholes, in particular, remains most vexed.

'Why is it a crime scene, Inspector?'

Skelgill returns their gaze, his expression uncharacteristically bland, and his demeanour inquisitive, polite even.

'Did you see him lay the trap, sir?'

The man frowns confoundedly.

'Of course not, Inspector. But what else could it be but an accident?'

'It might have been an accident, sir. But at this stage, I reckon if I tried to convince the coroner that a fatal incident involving an illegal Victorian mantrap needs no investigation, then I might just find myself looking for a new career.'

Neil Vholes is plainly riled; no doubt he considers himself a far more important personage than the rather unkempt country detective. And, thus infuriated, he is unable to keep a note of schadenfreude from his voice.

'Surely it is quite obvious the man has become hoist by his own petard.'

Skelgill shrugs and nods across the car for DS Jones to get in and he does the same. He reverses out and accelerates abruptly, leaving the Vholes to stew amidst a cloud of slowly settling dust. Meanwhile the cocker spaniel has finished exploring the rear compartment and now scrambles over to forage amongst the debris that clutters the back seat. Skelgill cranes to observe it in his rear-view mirror. He wonders if Lawrence Melling brought it with him from the Scottish Borders, or inherited it on the Shuteham Hall estate; it does not seem to have absorbed anything of the unbiddable personality of its erstwhile master. DS Jones notices his interest.

'You're not thinking of adopting, Guv?'

Skelgill starts from his reverie.

'You're kidding – I've got my hands full already. Plus there's the cost. Besides – these things are crackers – especially working dogs like this. Doggy day care's no place for them. They want to be tearing up the undergrowth for woodcock.'

DS Jones nods reflectively, but before she can add anything Skelgill issues an instruction.

'Just while we're driving round – call in the search on the Irish couple. Mid-twenties, slim build, both a bit above medium height – especially the girl – she's dark, he's blonde, they usually wear combat gear, he's Cian Fogarty, she's Ciara – don't know her surname – they drive a 1970s Ford Consul estate, ARS 10P, white with a black roof.'

'That's impressive, Guv.'

Skelgill makes a face that reluctantly acknowledges his talent. However, when ordinarily he might share how he remembered the registration number, he seems not to be in the mood.

'You saw them yourself – they were in the café yesterday afternoon.'

DS Jones experiences a sudden flash of recognition.

'Ah – the good-looking guy and his girlfriend with no bra.'

Skelgill acts like this is something he did not notice. He makes a meal of manoeuvring around a series of potholes. DS Jones continues.

'They had a laptop – they were engrossed in that. Come to think of it, I didn't see any mobiles.'

Still Skelgill does not answer. DS Jones calls in to headquarters, specifically mentioning the transport café – but also that the local patrol ought to check public parking places and eateries in Cockermouth. It is running through Skelgill's mind that they should more widely circulate the description of the couple and their distinctive old jalopy. If they did leave at seven a.m. they could be the thick end of two hundred miles away by now. However, his attention is diverted as they arrive back at the point from which the incident is being accessed. Already there are more vehicles; the rest of the SOCO team has arrived. Across the moor he can see they are erecting screens as he has requested.

At the rear of his car he pats his pockets without success, and instead delves into a crate and fishes out a length of baler twine. He fashions a makeshift leash; he ties a bowline; it is not ideal, but perhaps the dog will behave itself, and at least it will not choke.

'What are you thinking, Guv?'

'We'll walk it back to the castle. I want to retrace Melling's route. Can you text Leyton and tell him we'll meet him there.'

Skelgill feeds the dog through the stile and clambers over onto the narrow moorland path. While he waits for DS Jones to transmit the message a meadow pipit rises up from nearby in the heather, making the best of its limited vocal repertoire, its notes gathering speed before the crescendo is released as it comes parachuting down over its territory. For Skelgill it is the archetypal sound of the fells – and from somewhere across the moor floats the haunting call of the cuckoo. They go hand in glove – almost literally for those pipits that fall victim to the guileful African usurper. As if it is not enough to run the gauntlet of the harriers. Mother Nature's game – fascinating for the spectator – red in tooth and claw for the participant.

'They're a strange couple, Guv – the Vholes?'

DS Jones's remark breaks into his contemplation – it is a question really, and prompts him to consider the pair.

'Aye – they're a bit up themselves, as the saying goes. Did I tell you they were brother and sister?'

'Er – no, actually. But I can see the resemblance, now you mention it. There's an odd vibe between them – I wonder if they're twins?'

'They work together, an' all. Jim Hartley reckons they're at Caldbeck – environmental science or something.'

'At the college?'

'Aye. So he said. No doubt we'll get chapter and verse in good time.'

DS Jones nods reflectively.

'They're not going to like it when we call them in for formal statements.'

Skelgill pulls a face that seems intentionally bereft of sympathy. However, they are approaching the SOCO tent and the dog, which has thus far kept largely to heel, begins to strain on the twine and lets out a short yap. The side of the tent is open and the sound attracts the attention of a powder-blue-suited female whom Skelgill identifies as the Crime Scene Manager; the recognition is mutual and the woman picks up something and comes out to meet them. She raises to eye level a clear polythene evidence bag. It contains a small black torch, similar to that Skelgill himself uses – in fact so similar that for a second he feels a surge of anxiety – but didn't he leave his in the boat when he hauled it ashore?

'It was in his thigh pocket. It's in working order.'

Skelgill appears slow to process the woman's words – but DS Jones makes a little intake of breath that suggests she appreciates their significance. The woman watches Skelgill with a look of curiosity – she knows his reputation as something of an eccentric. Abruptly, he smiles broadly – whether the penny has dropped or he is just acting out the stereotype is evidently not clear, and she remains perplexed.

'Nice job. Helen, aye?'

Skelgill has sneaked a look at her badge – "H. Back – CSM" – but it appears he gets her given name correct. She seems to relax. She nods and smiles behind her mask, if the crinkling of her eyes is anything to go by, but she begins to move away, keeping the item and returning to her pressing work. Skelgill grins. 'And if you find a watch smashed at the time of the incident, that would be ideal.'

The woman flashes a frown of the order that *he should be so lucky* – but then she halts and turns to face him.

'If it's of any interest – he's not wearing underpants.'

Skelgill waves away the remark, as though she makes it in jest – despite that it must have struck her as being of some merit. He wonders if he detects in DS Jones a trace of unease – but as they turn and walk on she addresses the issue at a broader level.

'What do you think he was up to, Guv?'

'Apparently he did a regular nightly patrol – letting the birders know who was boss.'

'But if he was walking in darkness – not using his torch – they wouldn't have seen him.'

Skelgill merely inhales more heavily, but declines to offer an opinion just when it seems he might speak. But the extent of the conundrum has not escaped his colleague.

'And wearing Lord Bullingdon's gear – for no apparent reason.'

Skelgill decides he ought to join up some of the dots. Prominent in his thoughts is Eric Hepplethwaite's offhand remark concerning the eradication of crows, two birds with one stone; putting both barrels through the nest.

'The camera that's trained on the sitting bird – it's got night vision – infrared. I reckon Melling would have known that. This sort of thing seems to be common knowledge among the keepers.'

DS Jones skips nimbly ahead of Skelgill and turns to face him, stopping him in his tracks. Her expression is animated.

'Remember – what he said about the nest? There's no guarantee it would be successful. What if he were going to impersonate Lord Bullingdon and destroy it?'

Skelgill shrugs in a way that does not entirely dismiss her suggestion; it is not difficult to imagine the enraged Lawrence Melling doing the very thing – a fit of pique. However, he sidesteps his colleague and walks on; she catches up and pushes for an answer.

'Guv?'

'It's crossed my mind.'

Enthusiastically, in quick succession DS Jones nods and then shakes her head.

'What I don't understand, though, is the couple on watch in the hide – the Irish – why didn't they hear the shot?'

Skelgill can think of a reason – but he provides a more prim explanation than that which springs to mind.

'Who's to say they stayed awake.' He rakes back his hair with the fingers of his free hand. 'Or maybe they did hear it – it's a shooting estate – there's poaching going on. There's a trigger-happy keeper controlling the vermin. It can't be the first time a shotgun's been fired at night. Think about it – say they hear a bang – they'll check the camera. The bird's okay – so they let it pass.'

DS Jones seems to be racking her brains. In a studenty outfit of a lightweight mauve sweatshirt, black stretch jeans and black-and-white trainers with mauve trim she sometimes makes Skelgill think the decade between them is wider than he finds comfortable. Without breaking stride she reaches down and deftly picks up a short stick. As she waggles it absently before her eyes it attracts the dog – she notices and lets it leap up – it seems pleased with its acquisition.

'But the trap, Guv – where does that come in? Much as I dislike the idea of Neil Vholes being right – what he said about Lawrence Melling being hoist by his own petard – it's plausible.'

There is a curious note in his sergeant's voice, perhaps even of pathos – Skelgill glances at her sharply; she is plainly conflicted.

'Did he strike you as the kind of bloke that'd lay a trap and then forget about it?'

DS Jones does not answer immediately. It might be that she recognises that there are two questions in one, with potentially conflicting combinations of answers.

'No, Guv. Far from it.'

Skelgill makes a frustrated growl in his throat, and falters momentarily in his stride, as though he has suffered a spasm of cramp in a calf.

'It's like the first time you climb Scafell Pike.'

DS Jones senses that he requires her to show some interest in his cryptic pronouncement.

'How do you mean, Guv?'

'It started with a buzzard, unsolved – then the jewels, unsolved – then Stan goes missing, unsolved – and now this. It's one false summit after another.'

*

'How long was that, Guv?'

Skelgill checks his watch.

'Just coming up for twenty minutes. We could have gone faster – but maybe not in the dark.'

The pair have climbed a stone step stile to discover Lawrence Melling's quad bike beside the track that leads down through the policies of Shuteham Hall. The spaniel seemed ready to leap into the dog box, and Skelgill has tethered it to a post while he examines the machine. DS Jones approaches.

'The keys are still in it.'

'That's not so uncommon on private land.'

'Maybe suggests he was in a hurry?'

Skelgill regards her with a look of amusement. He indicates with a sweep of an arm slewed tyre marks in the turf.

'I reckon we can agree on that.'

Now he throws one leg over the saddle and grips the handlebars as though he is trying the machine out for size. Casually he leans down to the near side. DS Jones watches as he fiddles with a small tap and with a jerk pulls off a rubber hose that connects it. Then he turns the tap again and a stream of clear liquid runs out. As the stench of petrol fills the air he turns it off.

DS Jones looks a little alarmed.

'Guv – you'll leave prints.'

Skelgill reacts fiercely; but it is hard to tell if his expression is one of guilt or annoyance.

'Jones – it's hardly a murder weapon. Besides – I've got you as a witness.'

DS Jones regards him rather suspiciously. But then in a more considered tone she asks a question.'

'What were you doing?'

'Checking there's fuel.'

She nods. But as usual she is quickly thinking through the scenarios.

'He couldn't have got beyond here. He would have had to go on foot.'

Skelgill does not seem bothered that her logic defeats the purpose of his actions. He rubs both hands on his thighs and checks his palms. DS Jones notices the wound. It is obviously new since she saw him yesterday.

'You've cut yourself, Guv.'

'I was attacked by a perch.' He grins sheepishly. 'The fish kind.'

He does not offer further explanation, which DS Jones might consider unusual when there is an opportunity for an angling lecture, and sympathy to be garnered – instead he crosses to untie the working cocker. DS Jones regards him pensively but does not press.

Skelgill is thinking he could drive the three of them back up to the castle. As they stand, the track curves away in both directions into woodland, offering seemingly identical options, but the dog starts forward and gives its sharp warning bark. Its superior hearing alerts them to a vehicle that is approaching, the crunch of tyres on loose stones now becoming audible – and a few seconds later DS Leyton's car appears rather ponderously around a bend. They can see that their colleague has a female passenger. The vehicle grinds to a halt. DS Leyton clambers out along with a uniformed WPC. She is in shirtsleeves beneath a stab vest with its many accoutrements (a garment Skelgill quite fancies for himself). She has a reel of police barrier tape in one hand.

'Leyton – what's going on?'

'PC Dixon's been assigned to control this access point – your instruction, I believe, Guv. Then when I got Emma's text I figured you'd be coming this way – thought I'd save everyone the walk. Kill two birds with one stone.'

Skelgill seems a little indignant – it might be that his plans have been stymied – or perhaps just that his sergeant by coincidence has used the phrase that has been preying on his mind. His brusqueness transmits itself to the new arrivals; DS Leyton steps alongside the young WPC, rather as though he has taken her under his wing. Skelgill notes she is small and slim and would certainly be considered quite attractive. Rather demurely she makes eye contact with each of him and DS Jones. DS Leyton clears his throat.

'I've got a couple of bits of information that could be important, an' all, Guv – didn't want to hang about in letting you know.'

Skelgill looks hesitant. He does want to know – but he is torn by the presence of the unfamiliar female officer. He addresses her and gestures towards the stile. Now he sounds surprisingly apologetic.

'It'll just be for a couple of hours, while SOCO clear out.'

The girl steps forward.

'It's no problem, sir. It's a nice day.'

Skelgill frowns, his expression doubtful.

'You'll be alright, on your own, lass?'

The girl smiles and to his dismay reveals a missing front tooth.

'It's fine, sir – I'm a black belt in karate, if that's what you're thinking. I shan't let any folk past.'

Skelgill has an urge to recoil, but he tries not to show it and instead to look impressed by her prowess. He raises a hand to signal his acceptance – but just as he begins to turn away he hesitates.

'Do you know of Karen Williamson – in the karate line?'

The girl nods.

'Aye – she's on the district coaching staff – her bairn's a national age-group champion.'

When Skelgill does not immediately respond the constable regards him inquiringly.

'Is there some problem with her, sir?'

Skelgill seems momentarily distracted.

'What? No – she works here, that's all. Just a coincidence.'

'Right, sir.'

Skelgill nods and now bids PC Dixon farewell and the three detectives climb into DS Leyton's car. Skelgill automatically takes the front passenger seat; the dog seems to understand its place is in the footwell. Skelgill has pulled out the estate map and holds it against the windscreen.

'You'll need to birl, Leyton. This track's a dead end.'

'Wilco, Guv.'

DS Leyton jams the car into reverse and then pulls away rather more flamboyantly than he arrived, but as soon as he has completed the manoeuvre Skelgill is onto him.

'What's the story?'

DS Leyton snatches a quick sideways glance at his boss; but his expression is hard to read.

'At first I thought the place was deserted – couldn't get any answer at the castle. PC Dixon had been dropped off and she was wandering round near those chicken sheds. We went along to the estate office – there was Daphne holding the fort.'

'How did she react?'

'As you'd expect, Guv. Disbelief – but I reckon she's a tough cookie – she soon pulled herself together and started issuing instructions, and she helped me with contact details. I did question her about last night – she reckons she was doing admin in the library until about eleven – went to bed – slept through – got up at seven. She says Melling wasn't in the habit of checking in with her, so she had no reason to think anything untoward had happened to him.'

'Did you see Lord Bullingdon?'

'No – like I say, Guv – it's just Daphne. In fact – until I found her I was beginning to think the whole lot of 'em had gone and done one. Seems Lord Bullingdon's up at the north end of the estate meeting the Forestry Commission – his phone was diverting to voicemail – like he had no signal. Lady Bullingdon's skipped off to Whitehaven – to a beautician – left about half eight this morning. Daphne didn't think she ought to contact her until she'd spoken to her father. I've got her number if you want to call her – but she's due back at lunchtime, in any event.' Again he glances across, to see Skelgill is now staring

162

anxiously ahead; there being no response, he continues. 'Julian Bullingdon's gone AWOL – but she reckons he's out chasing bugs and will turn up when he's hungry. He doesn't have a phone or walkie-talkie. He objects to the radiation.'

Skelgill makes a groaning sound that might be scathing or possibly despairing.

But DS Leyton is undaunted; he still has a shot in his locker.

'Perhaps more importantly, Guv – a titbit on Lawrence Melling.'

'Aye?'

'I got Daphne Bullingdon to contact the estate workers – and the geezer Artur – who looks after the stores – he reckons last night Melling came looking for fuel.'

At this juncture DS Leyton breaks off to negotiate a veritable crater of a pothole. As they are all flung about the car Skelgill senses that DS Jones has transferred her scrutiny to him. He endeavours to play down any reaction to this news – and now DS Leyton picks up his monologue.

'Artur and his crew have a nightly card school in their digs – Melling came hammering on the door. They've got a red diesel pump at the back of the stables – but his quad runs on petrol, and they keep a supply of gallon cans locked up in the storeroom. Obviously, Artur's one of the keyholders.'

'What time was this?'

'Ten past midnight. I double checked – he reckons one of the other geezers actually picked up his phone and read out the time – as if to say who the flippin' heck's knocking at this ungodly hour.'

There is now a pause before Skelgill speaks.

'Twelve-ten.'

It is neither a question nor really a reiteration of what his sergeant has said; rather more as though the phrase has escaped from Skelgill's thoughts. Still he is conscious of DS Jones's gaze upon him, and he swivels in his seat to face her. She must surely notice some smouldering embers in his grey-green eyes. Certainly she regards him with an enigmatic smile. For his part, Skelgill grins somewhat manically.

'I should have taken Herdwick's bet. Bang goes his bullseye! Melling couldn't have reached that trap much before a quarter to one.'

DS Jones regards her superior thoughtfully. Of course, she might point out that the pathologist's offered wager allowed for two hours leeway, each way. However, another point, more salient, exercises her analytical mind.

'But, Guv – surely that depends on where he had run out petrol?'

Skelgill raises his hands in a conciliatory manner, as though it is not a point worth fighting over. But then he makes a rather half-hearted defence of his position.

'Aye – but if he turned up on foot at the stables, it couldn't have been that far.'

DS Jones nods, though she has more to add.

'Also, he may not have driven directly to the start of the beaters' path. So it could have been later.'

'Aye – I've got no problem with that.'

She might wonder from these words why he did have had such a problem with midnight, but, for now, she does not raise the query.

Skelgill is battling to contain a strong sensation of relief. Now categorically *not* the last witness to see Lawrence Melling alive, suddenly he is unshackled. For the time being, at least, he can keep under his hat his more clandestine movements of last night.

'Leyton – did he say owt else to Artur – like what he was up to?'

'No, Guv – just made it clear that he was in a hurry. Seems Melling wasn't pally with the workers – he considered himself above them – wouldn't pass the time of day. Besides, I suppose Artur just assumed he wanted to go home to kip. And he wanted to get back to his three-card brag.'

Without warning Skelgill slumps back in the seat and lets his hands fall limp on his lap. He closes his eyes, and his whole body seems to relax, and he rolls with the pitching of the car as though he were instantly consumed by sleep. He certainly does not look like he is thinking; and it would be a correct assessment; he is not employing his grey cells in the hope of some eureka moment. But he is beginning to feel his way around the problem; his instincts are freed to rise to the challenge. In the analogy of false summits that he made to DS Jones, the mountain is taking shape. And every mountain has its top; even in the worst conditions persistence and a helping of common sense are all it takes to reach the true summit. Once there, with a clear view all around, the mountaineer can pick out a route, a strategy to guide him home.

'Reckon these incidents are all connected, Guv?'

Skelgill opens one eye – but he resists the urge to trot out the platitude, "your guess is as good as mine". Instead, he catches his subordinate completely off guard.

'Stop the car, Leyton.'

DS Leyton knows Skelgill well enough not to question his authority, and the vehicle slides to a halt on the gravelly surface. Skelgill immediately opens the door and hauls himself out by the grab handle. Then he ducks back in to address his bemused colleagues.

'I'll meet you in the coffee shop – same as yesterday. Say – an hour and a half.'

The two sergeants exchange glances and DS Leyton as the more senior in service takes upon himself the risk of reprimand.

'What about the interviews, Guv?'

Skelgill seems quite blasé about the matter.

'Leyton – you said it yourself – there's no one here apart from Daphne Bullingdon – and the staff, maybe. We'll come back.'

DS Leyton nods confoundedly.

'What are you going to do, Guv?'

'I'll walk back to my car. You pair head straight for Cockermouth. See if you can beat the local bobbies and find the Ford Consul and its occupants. If you do – get chapter and verse.' He regards DS Jones. 'You know what we're looking for.'

They both nod dutifully. Skelgill withdraws. But just as he is about to slam shut the door he hesitates.

'And no nicking my parking spot.'
As they pull away they realise Skelgill still has the dog.

8. COCKERMOUTH

Tuesday afternoon

S kelgill has reached his summit.

There is the added bonus that his parking spot is unoccupied. That he has not heard from his team, however, suggests their quest has been less successful. Not that his was a 'quest' as such, for the word implies a tangible goal.

Also vacant upon his arrival is the bench seat overlooking the convening rivers. Early for his rendezvous he settles to watch the spaniel. Having promptly chased away four grazing mallards and a moorhen, it drinks thirstily in the shallows. The weather has been dry for a couple of weeks; the Derwent before him is tamed; at his back the Cocker slides past silent and meek. Both run clear, when at times their differing silted hues delineate their reluctance to meld, for a good distance downstream. But such placidity can be deceptive; a cloudburst over the fells, and Skelgill's bench could disappear beneath two fathoms of deadly rushing floodwater.

For the time being, however, sitting comfortably, he reprises the last hour or so.

He had first struck off through the woods, crossing the main driveway and following his nose down to the environs of Troutmere. He had tried the door of the boathouse, but found it locked, and had decided against another tilt at the pitched roof. With a small degree of difficulty, he had recovered his hazel rod from the reeds, initially underestimating how far he had managed to hurl it. He had deemed that with a bit of tidying up it would make a half-decent fell-walking staff.

From the lake he had climbed the twilit tunnel through the rhododendrons. Where last night the quad bike had been parked there now lay discarded a red one-gallon petrol can. He had contemplated taking it with him to preserve it as evidence, but in the end had settled on prodding it by means of his stick into the safe cover of a thick clump of stinging nettles.

Retracing his steps he had traversed the dam and headed up into the surrounding trees, re-crossing the drive into woodland of a more ornamental nature; in due course he had reached the track that took him back to the stile, now strung with barrier tape. In the lee of the wall the grassy area was a veritable suntrap, and he was not surprised to see that PC Dixon had removed her heavy stab vest and was reclining with her back to the stones. She had leapt to attention, until he had reassured her that, in her shoes, he would be doing the same thing – indeed, that he would probably be spark out on the turf – truer than she could know, given his abridged and fitful sleep last night. Certainly the notion had been appealing, as was the prospect of chatting to the girl – until she flashed him a smile. He found it horrifying and compelling in equal measure that the disfigurement transformed such an attractive countenance into a grotesque mask – and though wanting to he failed to contrive a way to ask about her missing incisor. Presumably a karate incident – and he had recalled his first encounter with Karen Williamson, and her black eye. What was it with these good-looking women that put their looks on the line for sport? Though he was then reminded that sport is the exceptional reason, and there is usually a more sinister explanation. It had occurred to him to ask what she knew of Karen Williamson's domestic situation, but he had concluded it would keep. Instead, cutting a length of tape for PC Dodds to cordon off the stile at the other side of the moor, he had departed with a commitment to instruct the latter to radio the all-clear as soon as the SOCO team departed.

The walk back across the moor he had covered in quicker time than with DS Jones, again keeping the dog on the leash; to all intents and purposes the private land is an unofficial nature reserve, so designated by its controversial avian squatters. He had not intended to disturb the forensic officers at work in the tent. But since it straddled the beaters' path his noisy detour

168

through the deep surrounding heather gave away his presence, and from the partially zipped flap had popped the head of the Crime Scene Manager. His first impression – that there had been an expectant look in her eyes, that she was hoping it was him – was borne out immediately that she had pulled down her mask and stepped out of the tent.

"Inspector – you ought to hear this."

That she did not just think of her role as gathering evidence, but saw the bigger picture, she had already demonstrated – in relation to the torch, that it was unused. Now she was about to doubly prove her worth.

"You've found the watch."

Skelgill had grinned cheekily, but she was on a mission and sidestepped his humour.

"Possibly better than that."

Skelgill had waded out of the heather to meet her on the path.

"It must be good."

She had looked like she might not disappoint him.

"We've been taking some measurements and photographs, and we've got a metal detector. The angle of the entry wounds and the spread of the shot, including pellets in the surrounding earth suggest the gun was discharged from about thirty inches from his shin at an angle to the tibia of at least thirty degrees."

Skelgill correctly reads the implications of her diagnosis.

"Is that doable?"

"Would you like to try with your stick? It's about the same length as his gun."

Skelgill had regarded her approvingly. Why wasn't Herdwick this proactive? He had tethered the dog to a guy of the tent and wielded his staff like a shotgun; he had seen enough of Lawrence Melling to know he was right-handed.

"It was the left leg, aye?"

The woman had nodded. Holding the stick at the point where the trigger would be approximately, Skelgill had tried various positions. Thirty inches away was just possible – albeit involved holding what would be the stock up above his right ear. And thirty degrees was also just possible – though the stance seemed unnaturally cramped over. But thirty inches *and* thirty degrees – as he had remarked, it was like trying to lick his elbow! Despite that he and Lawrence Melling were men of roughly similar stature, no matter how much Skelgill contorted he could not do it. They had discussed the implications of the trap – what the sudden shock might have done to the man's posture, but still it would have required a spasm of such an order as to defy the laws of human trigonometry. Skelgill had even acted out a couple of charades, imagining what would become of both himself and a loaded shotgun, safety off, wielded at the ready, walking into the jaws of the trap. But in none of these scenarios could he meet the conditions. In the end he had lain prone, his left leg bent a little, and Helen Back had held the staff in the position from which she calculated the gun had been discharged. It required her to stand at his head and reach over him lengthways. The 'gun' was close, but tantalisingly out of reach.

"So you're telling me someone else pulled the trigger."

His synopsis had been delivered in the manner of a statement. But at this point she had retreated into her shell. It had been one thing to state and demonstrate the facts as she had discovered them – but clearly quite another to deal with the bald implications. Perhaps it was above her pay grade – not least since the recalcitrant Chief Pathologist had summoned her on the premise of an accidental death.

"I'm just advising you of my preliminary findings. They're subject to final confirmation. We'll run a 3-D computer simulation to get the exact measurements."

Skelgill had scrambled to his feet and taken back control of the dog.

"Have you phoned this in?"

"We've only just finished the outline calculations – we wanted to check that it was something we ought to pay close attention to. Besides – we're having a problem getting a mobile signal."

Skelgill had nodded sympathetically.

"I'll call old Herdwick from my car. Get him used to the idea."

Skelgill had departed the scene with the venerable pathologist's earlier words brought to mind. *Snap. Bang. Goodnight Vienna.* In a sense, Dr Herdwick had inadvertently demarcated these three stages. And he had triggered Skelgill's odd phrase: "what time of accident?" Not what time Lawrence Melling walked into the trap. Not what time he died. The crux of the matter is the bang, and the question, when did it occur?

A glance at his wristwatch tells him it is time to meet his colleagues. He stretches – and the spaniel, detecting a change is occurring, immediately comes running. Rather than lock it in the car Skelgill takes a chance on the café being dog friendly and puts it on the string leash.

'We'll have to think about giving you a name, lass.' Its gender, at least, he has worked out – but he only ever heard Lawrence Melling issuing terse orders; such is the fate of a working dog. 'I quite like Hetty, but it's taken.'

Skelgill's colleagues are occupying what could become their regular corner table, should this investigation be strung out. They see their superior intercepted by a female member of staff, who is evidently informing him that dogs are not permitted; he produces his warrant card and they hear him tell the girl it is a drugs dog. They have tea and sand cake ready for him. He contrives a face of greeting-cum-thanks, though the expression of neither is his strongpoint with those close to him. But his colleagues know him well enough not to take offence – and, indeed, they see that his whipped countenance conceals something of import. He, in turn, reads their anticipation, and so he does not beat about the bush.

'Happen he were shot.'

Skelgill says no more, but gently shifts the dog out of sight with his left boot and ties a half hitch around his chair leg (from bitter experience with the 'canine cannonball' he knows never again to tether a dog to a table). He proceeds to pour tea and ladle sugar into his mug, and then takes a bite of cake – which plainly impedes his ability to relate more; his colleagues look at one another and DS Leyton speaks.

'You talking murdered, Guv?'

171

Skelgill, chewing, too much to attempt to answer, nods in an exaggerated fashion. He washes down his mouthful and wipes his mouth on his sleeve.

'I stopped by the SOCO tent. It's a fine margin – but the angle and spread of the shot couldn't have been achieved if Melling were holding the gun.'

Both sergeants are more than a little wide-eyed – but it DS Jones that has paid closest attention to his words.

'A fine margin?' (Skelgill nods – and his eyes narrow as though he suspects she is about to challenge this as too close to call. But he need not have feared.) 'Guv – you mean someone did their best to make it *seem* that he was holding it?'

Skelgill cocks his head to one side, a gesture of accord.

'Otherwise why bother? Why not just let him have both barrels between the eyes?'

Skelgill is revisited by the spectre of lying prone looking up at Helen Back and thinking he was glad she was wearing trousers. Of all the stances she might have adopted were she brandishing a real shotgun and wishing to shoot him – even in the lower leg – it was by far the most improbable. Unless, as DS Jones has astutely concluded, it was to make the injury appear self-inflicted.

Now DS Leyton asks a less ambitious but nonetheless pragmatic question.

'What about prints on the gun?'

Skelgill absently breaks off a small hunk of cake and reaches between his legs. His hand comes up empty.

'It's gone to the lab. Obviously for DNA swabs as well. And they need to confirm a match with the lead shot and the empty cartridge – various ballistic tests.'

DS Jones looks like her mind is racing.

'That gun – the more I think about it, the more I'm sure it was the one that Lawrence Melling was servicing at the time I interviewed him. I think it's Lord Bullingdon's favourite – some kind of heirloom. I know that no prints don't prove non-use – but I doubt if there'll be any prints on it that precede it being cleaned yesterday.'

Her colleagues nod in silence – Skelgill because he has resumed eating. But DS Jones has plenty to say.

'Guv – it only took us five minutes to drive back up to where the track meets the main driveway, quite close to the office and stables. If we assume like you suggested that Lawrence Melling had not had to walk far to get the petrol – say five minutes, then a couple of minutes to refuel the quad bike – he could have reached the spot where he died in as little as half an hour – based on our walk.'

Skelgill holds up a hand to prevent further unnecessary speculation while he drinks some more tea.

'I found what must be the petrol can – in bushes above the lake, close to the walled garden – not even five minutes from the stables.'

DS Jones eyes her superior with a hint of suspicion – that he could pull such a seemingly obscure rabbit from the hat. Skelgill raises his mug to his lips but keeps it there, as if by way of saving him from elaborating. But in fact his thoughts have taken a leap away – in two directions at once. Away to Over Moor, where Lawrence Melling could have walked into the trap and been shot pretty much straightaway, at – say – forty, maybe forty-five minutes after midnight. And away to Over Water – where simultaneously Skelgill himself was ... but wait ... where was he *exactly* at that time? It was midnight at the boathouse and twelve-forty when he beached the boat. He heard no shot as he rowed across the lake. In the still of night despite the frantic pulling of his oars, the rasping of his breath, and the thumping of his heart, it would have reached his ears. But then he had got into his car, turned on the rumbling engine, cranked up the rattling heater – and listened to the shipping forecast. In such circumstances – would he have heard a shot? Unlikely. What about the couple in the hide? They were not exactly dead to the world (as he had suggested to DS Jones) but they were certainly deaf to it. Dr Herdwick's so-called 'bullseye' was midnight – twelve-forty-five was comfortably within range of his 'twenty-five' – truth be told, it would be a skilful prediction. Skelgill doubted if the computer would get much closer.

And then there was the yellow car that sped past at one o'clock.

Skelgill emerges from his daydream to find he has finished his tea and is staring at DS Jones, who regards him a little uneasily but reaches for the pot and offers to top him up, which he accepts. She seems to understand that he is wrangling with some issue; for her part she looks to be searching for the right question to crystallise his thoughts – but DS Leyton makes an intervention.

'Who would most want to kill Melling?'

It is a poignant question – not least for the subtle insertion of the word 'most' – and the underlying hint of fatalism in DS Leyton's tone. As such, Skelgill considers his sergeant deserves first go at providing the answer.

'What do you reckon?'

'Cor blimey, Guvnor – I should say his fan club wasn't the biggest in the world – maybe with one notable exception. *Hah!*'

The detectives do not need to run through the list of persons connected with the estate who may not be paid-up members, as DS Leyton puts it, of Lawrence Melling's fan club – nor do his colleagues have any doubt that he refers to Lady Bullingdon as the purported exception; however it is to this latter suggestion that DS Jones offers a caveat.

'How many murders are committed by the person most closely involved with the victim.'

It is a statement rather than a question – and Skelgill is nodding – it would be naivety in the extreme to cross Miranda Bullingdon off their list of possible suspects. Moreover, he is troubled by the overarching conundrum – are they trying to solve several crimes, or just one? Yet again, alarm bells warn of a descent into unproductive theorising when there is still a plethora of evidence to be gathered. He gestures with his mug to the empty seating arrangement opposite, the comfy sofa and the low coffee table.

'What about our Irish friends?'

His colleagues sit to attention – this issue has been overshadowed since Skelgill dropped his bombshell. DS Jones takes it upon herself to answer.

'They didn't go to the transport café. The washrooms are reached through the diner and the two women serving say they would have seen them – they know them by sight. A local foot patrol has checked all the other coffee shops and the town centre car parks. Of course, they could have driven elsewhere – Keswick, maybe. We've put out an all-cars alert – but nothing back so far. Most likely they've parked up somewhere quiet.'

Skelgill is scowling broodingly.

'We need to speak to them. One thing's for sure – they were in the same neck of the woods as Melling when he was shot.'

DS Jones is nodding. She places a palm on her mobile phone.

'I checked the rota on the Nats website. It's the same shift pattern all week. The Vholes are on from seven p.m. until ten – and they also do a slot in the mornings, before work, presumably – seven a.m. until nine. The Irish are due back for the nightshift at ten p.m. tonight. I suppose it's not the end of the world if we have to wait until then.' Skelgill, however, is looking like he disagrees – but DS Jones continues quickly. 'The girl – Ciara – her surname is Ahearne, by the way. I've put a DC onto tracking down their connections in Ireland – relatives, and college – just in case they do have mobile numbers. Failing that to get their email addresses and send them a request to contact us urgently.'

Skelgill looks vaguely chastised – he is reminded they don't call DS Jones 'fast-track' back at headquarters without reason. He glances at DS Leyton, who has detected his embarrassment and who now winks surreptitiously at him.

'When we head back, Guvnor – I reckon we'll be wanting to see Lord Bullingdon first?'

Skelgill nods, his expression rather grim. Just where will they begin the questioning?

9. THE BULLINGDONS

Tuesday, mid afternoon

'**S**teady on, Leyton – if Julian Bullingdon's still prancing about with his butterfly net – you could flatten our prime suspect.'

Skelgill has left his own vehicle at the confluence, with half a mind to a takeaway later. He refers to his sergeant's enthusiastic driving along the wooded approach to Shuteham Hall; now that he is becoming familiar with the twists and turns he is putting his car through its paces. But when DS Leyton might take umbrage – after all it was Skelgill who almost did the very thing on their first visit – it is the latter part of the remark that rouses him.

'*Prime* suspect, Guv – I thought young Julian's not supposed to know one end of a gun from the other? And he sounds like a pacifist, to me.'

To the consternation of his passengers, DS Leyton cranes around to look at DS Jones for confirmation. She nods urgently – she would agree to anything – and makes a face that evidently conveys sufficient of what he seeks for him to return his attention to the task in hand, although another interpretation might be terror. Skelgill, having instinctively taken up a brace position, gradually relaxes.

'They're all prime suspects as far as I'm concerned – and I include Stan in that.'

Delivered in flat tones, this rejoinder proves to be a conversation stopper – that Skelgill is not discounting even the missing Moldovan from his calculations. As they bump along in silence, Skelgill turns to watch as glimpses of Troutmere become available; and then the grassy plateau with its artistic belvedere

176

and incongruous telephone kiosk. As they near the castle and the topiary lawn unfolds, Skelgill suddenly cries out.

'What's that?'

'Come again, Guv?'

'The car, Leyton – you donnat!'

DS Leyton can have no idea why he should be such an idiot for not immediately understanding that the cause of his superior's agitation is surely the most mundane aspect of the view: a small yellow hatchback that is being driven slowly along the track known as Long Shoot that comes up on the far side of the topiary lawn and passes in front of the hall to merge with their own trajectory.

'It's a VW Golf, Guv.'

'Head him off!'

Stung by one insult DS Leyton does not wait for another, despite that Skelgill's order must seem entirely disproportionate to the circumstances. He puts his foot down and within fifteen seconds skids to an untidy halt blocking the junction of the side track with the main driveway – although the yellow car, if it were wishing to escape, could simply veer onto the lawn. However, it stops and Skelgill in short order is out of DS Leyton's car and has wrenched open the driver's door of the Golf.

Perhaps it is the terrified expression on the gaunt, equine face of Julian Bullingdon – who looks like he thinks he is the victim of a kidnap attempt – that brings Skelgill to his senses – and he contrives to row back from his overly assertive approach.

'Would you mind getting out, sir?'

Julian Bullingdon, however, looks no less disconcerted – until, glancing in trepidation at the stranger's accomplices as they emerge from the supposed getaway car, he recognises DS Jones. Taking hold of a lock of his long sun-bleached hair, rather falteringly he appeals directly to her.

'Are these your – I mean – are you all detectives?'

Skelgill might feel a tad guilty but he is still in a hurry. As the young man climbs from the driver's seat, and straightens the peculiar rustic smock-frock that he evidently favours wearing over his baggy cotton trousers and sockless sandals, Skelgill comes straight to the point.

'I need to ask you, sir – where were you last night between the hours of eleven p.m. and two a.m.?'

'Cushat Copse.' Julian Bullingdon blinks several times and gives a nervous laugh that might be interpreted as a knowingly futile attempt at defiance. 'I'm – er – just heading up there to collect my trap. See what I've caught.'

'Your trap?'

'I set it last night and left it in place – it's the standard procedure.'

Skelgill swallows. He can feel the gaze of his subordinates upon him.

'Could you describe this trap, sir?'

Julian Bullingdon makes a hoop with his arms held out in front of him.

'To be honest it's rather primitive – the catching area has a diameter of about three feet – it has a suspended mercury vapour bulb powered by a small portable generator. The interior is filled with egg boxes for the Lepidoptera.'

Skelgill is looking confounded. DS Jones steps forward.

'A moth trap?'

Julian Bullingdon's pale blue eyes seem to light up, that she is showing interest.

'That is correct, sergeant. Cushat Copse is a fragment of ancient woodland – entirely sessile oaks – formerly coppiced, of course, hence the name – it adjoins the northwest side of Over Moor. By day we have Cumbria's only colony of high brown fritillary – and by night emblematic moths such as oak eggar – although it is a moorland species, despite its descriptor.'

Skelgill is just recovering his bearings.

'Wait a minute. So you're saying you were out catching moths.'

'Quite. I set up at dusk and remained until about one o'clock. There ought to have been sufficient fuel in the generator for it to run until just before dawn. The insects become inactive during

178

daylight, so they should be fine. I simply need to identify and count them.'

Skelgill can't help stepping away and turning in a circle, gazing to the heavens as he does so, as if for divine inspiration. In the little hiatus, Julian Bullingdon seems to steel himself.

'Look – what's all this about? Is this something to do with tracking down our jewel thief?'

The detectives regard the young man with stony-faced unanimity. Yet he returns their stares with blank ingenuousness. It would seem that news of Lawrence Melling's death has not reached this itinerant member of the household. Skelgill makes an executive decision.

'Mr Bullingdon, there has been a serious incident involving your gamekeeper, Mr Melling. It means we need to establish the whereabouts of everyone who was on the estate last night. Sergeant Jones will accompany you to collect your trap. She'll explain the position and take some details from you.'

Skelgill speaks with uncharacteristic tact – but his manner is firm and Julian Bullingdon shows no sign of objecting. He glances a little apprehensively at DS Jones and she nods to him reassuringly. He climbs into the car and closes the door. As DS Jones circles to enter on the passenger side Skelgill beckons her to the rear of the vehicle.

'Last night – I was fishing on Over Water.'

He flashes a stern look that is plainly intended to curb cross-examination.

'Ah – the perch.'

'I spoke to the Irish and the Vholes before I went out on the lake. They were all in the hide. The Irish must have got there early for their shift. I saw the Vholes go home just after ten-thirty. When I came back in – just as I was leaving – a car crossed ahead of me in the lane. It could have been coming from the moor. That was dead on one o'clock. Be aware of this – but don't tell him we know. A yellow car.'

DS Jones does a little double take, as though something that has been niggling her has just made sense. She looks at Skelgill with an expression that is at once quizzical, wry and possibly even amused.

'Yellow car.'

She says no more but neither does Skelgill – she nods and steps away and breaks off eye contact to open the passenger door; she slides in with a friendly "Hiya" directed at Julian Bullingdon. As the vehicle pulls away – indeed driving onto the lawn to pass DS Leyton's car – Skelgill looks askance at his sergeant.

'You can make a better job of parking than that, Leyton – you'll be getting us a bad name. Stick it in the shade and leave the windows down by a couple of inches.'

DS Leyton looks irked but then decides his superior is ribbing him – and there is the cocker spaniel to consider.

'Two ticks, Guv.'

While DS Leyton manoeuvres into the shadow of the castle Skelgill approaches the main entrance. He tries the blackened iron handle. Perhaps to his surprise it turns and the great oak door gives way against his shoulder. He enters – the darkness defeats him for a moment – but as his eyes become accustomed to the gloom, he sees that the mantrap is gone.

'Leyton – come and see this! Oi – Leyton!'

'What's all this shouting? We'll have no trouble here!'

Skelgill spins on his heel to see the misshapen form of Lord Bullingdon suddenly appear in the stone archway that leads from the gate keep into the main body of the castle. It immediately strikes him that to impersonate the old man would take a lot more than to don his hat and cape. His distinctive crooked posture and shambling gait would not be easily to replicate. Though the other cloak, that of night, might offset some degree of inadequacy.

'Oh – it's you, Inspector.'

There is displeasure in the man's voice, but before Skelgill can reply DS Leyton lumbers in behind him, apparently unseeing in the dimly lit hallway.

'Struth, Guv – it's like the Black Hole of Calcutta in here!'

Edward Bullingdon looks a little aghast. Skelgill opts to dispense with any formalities. In the fashion of getting in the first punch, he reaches out a hand towards an iron hook where the trap was hung.

'Lord Bullingdon. Your trap – it's gone.'

The man shuffles closer and squints with his already narrowed leading eye. But now his response wrongfoots Skelgill.

'That's correct. I expect Melling took it. I noticed its absence when I locked up last night.'

Skelgill looks to DS Leyton – questioningly, so. His sergeant seems to know what he means and nods in confirmation.

'Sir – I understand you've been made aware of the circumstances of Lawrence Melling's death.'

Edward Bullingdon gives a scoffing exclamation.

'*Pah* – Daphne said something about him becoming caught in a trap – bled to death – am I correct?'

Skelgill nods, his expression severe. The man does not seem in any way affected.

'We'll need you, sir – or someone who knows reliably – to identify the device. But it seems too much of a coincidence to think it isn't the trap that was here. Can you recall when you last saw it?'

At this the man seems to assume a deliberate air of indecision. He casts about – and loosely indicates towards the suit of armour and various of the mounted weapons.

'These things have been here for decades – one becomes blind to them.'

'But you noticed the trap was gone last night.'

'That was because I was specifically thinking about it.'

'In what way, sir?'

Now Edward Bullingdon shifts a little uncomfortably on his feet.

'I was thinking we could get it photographed – put up some signs, to deter intruders – "Beware Traps" – that kind of thing.'

'But not actually to use the trap itself?'

'Good grief, no – what are you thinking, man?'

Skelgill remains grim faced.

'It seems somebody had that idea, sir.'

'I can only assume it was Melling, Inspector – and that he had some kind of foolish mishap while trying to set it. It's probably a two-man job.'

'But you didn't discuss it with him?'

'Certainly not.'

Skelgill pauses.

'Can you explain why Lawrence Melling was wearing your cape and hat, and was carrying your thumbstick, sir?'

'What!'

The man appears dumbstruck. Skelgill is obliged to elaborate.

'The items were found with his body on Over Moor, not far from the hen harriers' nest site. The staff and hat were lying nearby – the cape he still had fastened around his shoulders.'

'Good heavens – this is ridiculous, Inspector.'

Skelgill shrugs noncommittally.

'Where do you normally keep them, sir?'

'In the scullery beside the back door.'

'And when did you last use any of the items?'

Now the man's tone becomes impatient, as though he is rallying from the shock.

'I couldn't say – not in the last week, certainly.'

'You didn't notice if they were there last night, sir – when you locked up?'

'What – no, of course not – one doesn't go around checking the inventory every minute of the day and night.'

Skelgill turns to DS Leyton.

'The gun?'

His sergeant produces his mobile phone and opens a photograph taken at the scene. He holds it out and Lord Bullingdon reluctantly peers at the screen. Skelgill continues.

'Is this your gun, sir?'

'Inspector – they are all my guns.'

'Put it another way, sir – is this the gun that Lawrence Melling regularly used?'

Lord Bullingdon seems discomfited, but after a moment he answers, his voice even.

'No – it is not. It is a Beretta – made bespoke in Italy for my grandfather.'

Skelgill senses that DS Leyton is shuffling his feet in a way that conveys some excitement; but he responds stolidly.

'And what time did you lock up, sir?'

'Two minutes to ten.'

'That's very precise.'

'I always listen to The World Tonight on my bedside wireless – it starts at ten o'clock.'

Skelgill nods, his manner accepting.

'Did you see anyone, sir – from the time you were locking up – until, say two a.m.?'

The man scowls, exaggerating his one-eyed dominance as though it is a rather preposterous question – but then he obviously has a thought.

'As I locked the back door I called goodnight to Cook – she was banging pots about in the kitchen. After that – I went directly to bed – so, no, of course – I did not see a soul.'

Skelgill detects a certain awkwardness underlying his response.

'You didn't hear any noises – or happen to get up and look out of a window?'

'Not until I woke at just before six.'

'What about Lady Bullingdon, sir?'

Skelgill decides to leave the question at that, free of parameters. Lord Bullingdon growls indignantly – but perhaps, Skelgill suspects, not so much at his inquiry as the subject itself.

'My wife went up to her room immediately after dinner – she said she had a headache.'

'What time was that, sir?'

'Around nine-fifteen.'

'And – er – you didn't see her when you went to bed?'

'When I passed her door I could hear water running – the cast-iron Victorian bath – so I did not disturb her.'

'Who else was in Shuteham Hall last night, sir?'

'Just my wife and two children – and Cook, as I said.'

'And they were all indoors when you locked up?'

'Look – I don't know what the devil you're getting at, Inspector – I can assure you that whatever Melling was up to, none of my family were in cahoots with the man.'

Skelgill remains outwardly forbearing.

'I'm sure you appreciate, sir – we have to establish the whereabouts of those folk who might have been in the vicinity.'

Edward Bullingdon glowers pugnaciously.

'You seem to be treating us as suspects, Inspector – and here we are, victims of a theft and a member of staff gone missing. Yet we are persecuted for the dubious shooting of a buzzard. I should have you know that I am on first name terms with the Chief Constable of the county.'

Skelgill is becoming irked, but doing his best to conceal it. He detects unease in his sergeant, who seems to be wheezing a little.

'Sir – as things stand, the forensic team has been unable to confirm that Mr Melling's death was an accident. Given that it involves an illegal mantrap, your friend the Chief Constable would expect his officers to follow the correct protocol. If we mess up, happen he'll be the one hauled in front of the media – or, worse, the Police and Crime Commissioner. I'm sure he wouldn't thank anyone for that.'

'Yes – of course – I see that.' Lord Bullingdon blusters incoherently for a moment or two. 'Daphne was in the library when I retired. As for Julian – he was probably around the place somewhere.'

'But you didn't see him – at dinner for instance?'

'He's got peculiar tastes – calls himself a lacto-ovo-pescatarian or something like that – sounds like some blasted religious order.'

Having digressed, the man offers no further elaboration – but despite such blatant obfuscation, Skelgill decides he won't press the point. The old man's stance seems clear enough. He might be quick to denounce his son's incongruous habits, but he has not shopped him as far as his whereabouts are concerned. No matter – Julian Bullingdon seems to be perfectly obliging about his movements, provided he is telling the truth. Skelgill moves on to the gamekeeper.

'How would you describe your relationship with Mr Melling, sir?'

'What? I don't have a relationship, as you put it, Inspector – these people are hired hands. I expect them to do their jobs. Daphne deals with their contracts – government red tape – all that confounded human resources nonsense.'

'In that case, sir – how was Mr Melling doing – he was quite new, I gather?'

Edward Bullingdon scowls.

'He'd not been in place for a season – it was too early to judge.'

'Was he popular?'

'Since when is being popular part of the job description? As far as I'm concerned it's the last thing one looks for in a gamekeeper. And now I have to find a darned replacement. *Pah!*'

'Maybe you could bring Mr Carlops out of retirement?'

Edward Bullingdon glares severely at Skelgill.

'Are you connected with the man?'

'Never met him, sir. But word gets around these parts.'

*

That Daphne Bullingdon resembles the proverbial rabbit in the headlights is amplified by her congenital facial disfigurement – and doubly disconcerting to Skelgill in that when someone looks half-terrified he finds it difficult to believe they are guilty. Rather more comfortably ensconced than their standing interview with her father in the dank gloom of the gate keep, he and DS Leyton have seats in the estate office at the clients' coffee table, and to go with it frothy cappuccinos from a machine, and inadequate Italian biscuits. It is not difficult to notice Daphne Bullingdon's hands shaking as she dispenses the refreshments. It seems that the efficient façade met by DS Leyton earlier in the day has somewhat crumbled. It prompts

Skelgill to recalibrate his intended approach. He is reminded – by the location – of the tension he observed between the woman and the late Lawrence Melling. Even in that short exposure it was evident that she regarded the man as undermining both her authority and her guiding ethos. So it is along such lines that Skelgill phrases his opening gambit; perhaps it will put her a little more at ease.

'I gather you've been doing a spot of PR with the naturalists.'

Daphne Bullingdon seems not to understand the question.

'I'm sorry, Inspector?'

'You organised some sort of open day – for Allerdale Natural History Society.'

'Oh – yes – I see what you mean.' She casts about rather absently, and makes a hand gesture that might be vaguely indicating out of doors. 'Yes – it was following your suggestion, in fact. I looked on their website and saw that they have weekly field trips to various sites of local interest. I contacted their programme secretary and she was most interested – and it happened that a walk scheduled for the following week had been postponed because the designated leader had gone unexpectedly into hospital – so we were able to offer an alternative. In view of the immediacy of the situation with the hen harriers, it seemed to make sense.'

'What did you do?'

'Well – I acted as guide.' She reaches and extracts a brochure from the dispenser on the table and unfolds the map and lays it flat. 'Basically, I took them around a loop on part of the safe walking route –' She hesitates and glances suspiciously at Skelgill, as though she wonders if there is some trick in his question. But after a moment she continues. 'We met Lawrence at the main release pen where he was doing some refurbishment and he explained how the birds are brought in and begin to range freely – and then we gave the visitors afternoon tea in the library. We have our own heather honey – it is one of Julian's projects.'

Skelgill smiles inoffensively.

'How did it go down?'

She seems to understand he does not mean the honey.

'Well – the first thing I should say is that they commented favourably upon the variety and density of our populations of woodland birds – we have breeding nuthatch, tree pipit, green woodpecker.' Again she pauses, but now she appears to be absorbed by the memory of the event; her tone becomes introspective. 'And I honestly think – when people understand that the rearing of pheasants is a commercial operation more akin to the husbandry of sheep or cattle – and a net contributor to the local economy – they see the likes of Shuteham Hall in a different light.'

Skelgill takes a drink and manages to get froth on his nose – but it probably serves to conceal a grimace as he smears it away. This is surely wishful thinking on her part – and he doubts she showed them the gamekeeper's larder, hung with a dozen wind-dried birds, the mangy brush of a fox and the atrophied corpses of stoats and weasels.

'What about the moorland – the grouse?'

Daphne Bullingdon frowns; it is an act that seems to crease her entire face, like a currant. She is clearly aware that, as a so-called "rich man's sport" the shooting of grouse has no such straightforward defence.

'Because of the present sensitivity – the risk of disturbing the harriers – we did not attempt to cross Over Moor – besides, I understand the hide at Over Water is the best place from which to observe them.'

'I was thinking of the politics.'

Daphne Bullingdon seems to rally.

'Inspector, as one of the party pointed out, the red grouse is Britain's only endemic bird species. They rely for food on young heather shoots – and it takes a systematic programme of selective burning to create the right conditions. The mature heather would simply blanket the moor over the course of several years. We also provide medicated grit under veterinary supervision to combat strongylosis, which can wipe out an entire population. So if it were not for grouse moor management, the red grouse would decline and disappear.'

Skelgill is listening pensively; given his local provenance he is no stranger to the dilemma, that many grey areas occupy the porous boundary between country sports and conservation; both are fallible human constructs. But the drift of the conversation enables him to close in on his own priorities.

'Notwithstanding – you're actively managing Over Moor?'

'Er – yes – of course – although with due diligence as regards the harriers.'

'I understand Mr Melling made regular circuits of the moor – using the beaters' paths.'

She regards him a little apprehensively; it is plain he is working up to something.

'Naturally – they are the least intrusive means of getting about. It is important to monitor the wildlife populations – and keep a general eye on the estate property.'

'Who else would use these paths?'

'Well – at this time of year – nobody – at least, not on a regular basis. We might send a team out to repair the butts – or to conduct some controlled burning – but that would be an ad hoc exercise – and it's too late now for burning, the birds are breeding.'

Skelgill rubs his eyes with the fingers of both hands; is a gesture of tiredness, or possibly exasperation.

'You see, madam – what I'm wondering is if Mr Melling took the trap, what did he have in mind – was it off his own bat or was anyone else involved – had he consulted with you, for instance?'

Daphne Bullingdon looks horrified at the prospect.

'We would never have condoned the notion, Inspector – it is inconceivable that any of the family could have been involved.'

Skelgill notes that she has embraced the collective 'we' with her reply; it is a line consistent with that of her father. He holds out a hand to indicate DS Leyton.

'Yet Lord Bullingdon did previously mention to Sergeant Leyton the idea of taking exactly such precautions – in relation to the theft of Lady Bullingdon's jewellery.'

Now she looks doubly aghast.

'But, Inspector – you can't take literally what Daddy says – especially in a moment of stress. He may give the impression of being a *hang 'em and flog 'em* type – but I can assure you that given the time to consider matters properly he is far more law-abiding than you might imagine.'

Skelgill further notes that she has left some latitude for indiscretion; and he is reminded of the man's blustering admission to the accidental potting of protected species, an attitude of shoot first and identify the remains later.

'As regards the incident itself, we're waiting for various forensic reports – but we have to consider the possibility that this was not an accident.' That he is being blatantly disingenuous is only apparent to the implacable DS Leyton at his side. He allows a few moments for the gravity of his words to sink in. 'Lord Bullingdon thinks Mr Melling alone took the device – but he didn't seem the sort to walk into his own trap – unless it had been moved to somewhere he wasn't expecting it.'

Daphne Bullingdon gasps.

'But – that – that would be *murder*, Inspector.'

Skelgill tilts his head to one side.

'Aye – well, manslaughter – possibly.'

The woman appears dumbstruck, but Skelgill waits for a reply.

'But who would do that?'

'If you're asking me from a point of view of opportunity – it would be a person who was aware of his movements. That's a list we could make a good stab at ourselves. From a point of view of motive, madam – then that's what I'm asking you. To put it bluntly – had he made an enemy of someone?'

She seems entirely shocked by the prospect. She stares fixedly at the map on the table.

'There's nothing that I could speak of – not to the extent that you suggest. But –'

But, what, madam?'

'Well – I just mean – that one wouldn't know if there were a skeleton in his closet – an enemy from the past.' Again her features contract. She looks up intensely at Skelgill. 'But the trap

'– surely that suggests foreknowledge – how could an outsider be sufficiently aware to contrive the incident?'

Skelgill regards her evenly. She is making a good fist of playing detective.

'What about Mr Stanislav?'

Daphne Bullingdon shrinks at this suggestion.

'Stan? But he wouldn't say boo to a goose – he's our resident comedian – not even – '

She cuts short her rejoinder, though Skelgill suspects she was about to cite Lawrence Melling. He continues without pressing for clarification.

'They could have had a set-to.' He leans back in his seat and turns up his palms in a gesture of enquiry. 'There has to be something behind Mr Stanislav's disappearance. And now Mr Melling's accident.'

But Daphne Bullingdon is resolutely shaking her head.

'It's just a coincidence I'm sure, Inspector. At least in the sense of whatever has become of Stan.' She glances urgently at DS Leyton and then again at Skelgill. 'You don't have any news?'

Skelgill seems a little surprised that she has asked. Now he looks at DS Leyton, as though he himself does not want to get sidetracked by replying. Accordingly, DS Leyton steps into the breach.

'We've got various feelers out, madam – with the Moldovan authorities and the British ports and so on.'

DS Leyton perhaps says this to make it sound like they are taking the disappearance seriously – but Daphne Bullingdon appears puzzled.

'I'm sure it's more likely he's remained in the vicinity.' She turns questioningly to Skelgill. 'Don't you think you ought to be conducting a search?'

Skelgill regards her pensively. If she is trying to divert the course of the discussion, then with his response he calls her bluff.

190

'Madam – I'm fully expecting that we'll have to bring in a search team – with dogs – in relation to Mr Melling's death. So you might say we'll be able to kill two birds with one stone.'

He scowls, unhappy at falling victim to what is becoming the cliché of the hour. And now he hauls the conversation back around to the gamekeeper.

'How did you come to recruit Mr Melling?'

Daphne Bullingdon shifts a little uncomfortably in her chair.

'He became available – at a time I was beginning to undertake succession planning.'

'Was he recommended?'

'Her – er – he submitted his CV – speculatively, to a number of estates, I believe.'

Skelgill is quick to recognise the utility of such a document.

'Do you still have that?'

'Yes, of course – I keep confidential HR files for all the staff – some are more detailed than others.'

She glances at DS Leyton – they have had a similar discussion in relation to the Moldovan, Stan, for whom relatively scant detail was on file. When she makes no offer, Skelgill prompts her.

'Could we see it, madam?'

She rises stiffly and moves somewhat ponderously around behind the service counter. Bending out of sight, from what must be a low cabinet she retrieves a clear plastic wallet file, which she hands to Skelgill upon her return. His immediate reaction is the raising of an eyebrow. The front page comprises a full-length colour photograph of Lawrence Melling, posed with gun and dog like a male model in an outdoor clothing catalogue. Indeed the image has a professional quality about it in all respects – clever lighting that highlights his chiselled features; and perhaps retouching that smooths the tones of his skin and hair and carefully groomed beard. His county outfit is notable for its too-tight moleskin breeks and tattersall shirt casually unbuttoned to reveal hints of a sculpted musculature.

Skelgill looks sharply at Daphne Bullingdon; she is clearly blushing. Suddenly he is reminded of a certain unease that has troubled him, and which still leaves its lingering traces. Glowering, he flicks brusquely through the couple of pages of appended type and hands the document to DS Leyton.

'Mind if we borrow this?'

'Er – of course not, Inspector – although I'm afraid it has no details of next of kin.' She again glances at DS Leyton. 'I explained earlier to your sergeant – that is something we don't have.'

DS Leyton taps the pages with the knuckles of his free hand.

'We've got someone working on that, madam. We believe there might be connections up in the far north of Scotland.'

Daphne Bullingdon regards DS Leyton somewhat blankly, and not surprisingly does not respond. Skelgill leans back in his seat and folds his arms.

'I gather bags have been falling in recent years – especially the grouse.'

'Well – yes, that is undeniable – and we are always looking to adopt modern methods.' She suddenly frowns as though she immediately regrets her answer. 'But – that, er – is a nationwide phenomenon – indeed a global issue affecting many strands of wildlife – look at the Atlantic salmon, Inspector.'

Skelgill is the last person who needs a lecture on the king of fish – but he resists any temptation to digress; besides, more salient is that she was initially stung by his remark.

'Your former keeper, Jack Carlops – when was he actually due to retire?'

Now she looks sharply at Skelgill, seemingly surprised that he has this knowledge.

'Oh, er – it would be this coming autumn – we reached an amicable agreement as regards compensation – and we are maintaining his National Insurance contributions until he becomes eligible for his pension.'

Skelgill notes that she makes an excuse for an issue he has not raised.

'If you were still paying him – why not have the two of them – get the old dog to teach the young pup some tricks of the trade?'

Daphne Bullingdon continues to look discomfited.

'Well, you see, Inspector – Lawrence, when I interviewed him, he laid out a very clear practical methodology of how he would run the operation. I think it was only fair to give him a clean slate to work from.'

Skelgill gets the feeling that he knows just where the balance of power lay when it came to Lawrence Melling negotiating his new terms of employment; and that plain spinster Daphne Bullingdon's emotions if not her judgement were clouded by matters extraneous to the eradication of vermin. He waits a moment before he speaks again.

'Have you heard or seen anything of Mr Carlops since he left?'

The woman looks alarmed – as though there is something that springs to mind – and Skelgill pictures an altercation, a scene reminiscent of when he met Lawrence Melling in the woods – the young pretender seeing off the deposed forerunner, drawn back to his old stamping ground.

'Er, no – he has moved in with his sister – over at Scawthwaite Mire.'

It is not a particularly convincing point – Scawthwaite Mire is probably only ten minutes' drive from the gates of Shuteham Hall, and no great challenge on foot for a countryman. However, Skelgill merely waits for her to continue.

'You see, Inspector – keepers of Lawrence Melling's calibre do not become available very often – at the time it was important to take the opportunity.'

He feels she is overselling her case. But he sees no merit in arguing.

'I'm sure you made the correct commercial decision, madam.' He sees her visibly relax. 'Do you know why he wanted to move from Scotland?'

It is a relatively innocuous version of the question. He could have asked why did Lawrence Melling "drop down a division", as Eric Hepplethwaite had suggested. Or he might have inquired whether some controversy drove him away from his prestigious position in Hawickshire. These are stones that surely any recruiter worth their salt would not have left unturned.

'Well – I appreciate we may not be the biggest – but Shuteham Hall has a longstanding tradition – and a reputation as one of the finest shooting estates in the north of England. We have a good mix of sport – it provides a year-round challenge for the keeper. You can imagine those estates that primarily depend on grouse – the mountain habitat is monotonous and the season lasts fewer than four months.'

Skelgill nods.

'Did you sign off on his recruitment – or was anyone else involved in that?'

'Oh, well – naturally, as part of the interview process he got to meet the other members of the household – one wouldn't undertake such an important commitment without their endorsement – but I dealt with all the technical aspects.'

Skelgill makes a face that seems to suggest he thinks this was a reasonable state of affairs. He reaches for his drink and drains off the last from the cup.

'Would you like another, Inspector?'

'Er, no – thanks all the same, madam.'

Skelgill does not speak for a moment – and Daphne Bullingdon begins to look fearful once more. Skelgill gives the impression of there being something of import, and yet uncharacteristically for a moment or two he hems and haws.

'There is one matter, however – on the subject of dogs – we've rescued Mr Melling's working cocker from the moor.' He jerks a thumb over his shoulder. 'She's in the car.'

'Oh, right.' Daphne Bullingdon sits up – and then begins to rise. 'I had better come and take her off your hands.'

DS Leyton glances with some alarm at Skelgill – his superior's expression is impassive. But Daphne Bullingdon abruptly sits.

'If we have finished, that is, Inspector?'

Skelgill seems distracted. 'Aye – I suppose so, for now.'

They move in unison. DS Leyton holds open the door of the estate office – which Skelgill marches through. As Daphne

Bullingdon acknowledges DS Leyton's chivalry, Skelgill abruptly turns on his heel.

'Do you shoot, yourself, madam?'

10. MORE LADIES

Tuesday, late afternoon

'I shan't detain you long, Lady Bullingdon.'

'Oh – I don't mind, Inspector – be my guest.'

Miranda Bullingdon sweeps an arm towards the cushioned leather stool beside her dressing table, as she sinks down upon the chaise longue at the window. Skelgill notes that the scented candle is still on the sill; he wonders, was the wick burned yesterday afternoon? He accepts her offer, though he feels rather uncomfortable, the seat being low and his legs reasonably lanky. For her part, Miranda Bullingdon is looking stunning – there are no two ways about it, and Skelgill is a little in awe, that such perfection is possible in a human being, from the gloss of her newly reconstructed toenails to the halo around her reconfigured hair, and all points in between. She wears a simple short dress of fine teal silk that clings to her shapely form; her tanned legs are bare and she wears open-toed stiletto-heeled sandals in a paler shade of aquamarine. Her wide mouth with its full lips carries a relaxed smile and she regards him languidly from within the depths of the almost black pools of her large eyes.

'I suppose it would be indiscreet to ask if there were any news of my trinkets?'

Skelgill looks unruffled – although in doing so he senses he probably conveys some surprise. Yet he half expected the question. If it is a tactic, it is a clever one. Or maybe she is simply being straight about her priorities. A woman that looks like this really has no need to resort to diplomacy. Though he notices she wears no jewellery, and wonders if this is deliberate.

'There's no rule about what to talk about first.'

She smiles.

For his part, he could explain they have feelers out among their underworld contacts; that they have a computer specialist monitoring black market jewellery channels; that they have intimated a reward – all things true; wheels that DS Jones has put in motion.

'There's nothing so far, I'm afraid.'

She nods coolly. Having parried her first thrust, Skelgill thinks about making a little probing riposte. Then suddenly he finds himself throwing caution to the wind.

'Lawrence Melling was intentionally shot.'

'Good grief.'

The woman does not physically respond in any way – not a muscle moves, not a flinch nor a recoil, she does not even blink – but beneath her customarily husky tone there is undoubtedly a note of, well – what is it? – Skelgill thinks possibly *revulsion*.

He waits a moment, to see if there is any other reaction, delayed – but she simply waits, too – as far as she is concerned, it is his call. That he has played his ace, and she has raised him, so to speak, leaves him a little short of ammunition – but, there it is, he has seen her reaction, for what it is worth. He fumbles for what might be his next-strongest card.

'How do you feel about it?'

'Lawrence?' She regards him earnestly – but there is a subtle inflection that suggests she is surprised that he would ask such a question, with its implication of some special relationship. 'I am just getting used to the idea, Inspector – I only heard from Teddy half an hour ago. Aren't there supposed to be five stages of grief – the first being denial, into which one should not read too much?'

Skelgill appears a little contrite.

'You seemed to get on quite well with him.'

'I had no reason not to.'

Her answer is a challenge to Skelgill to say what he might really mean. He understands this and makes a not-wholly-convincing sally.

'Exactly, that's what I'm saying. You weren't burdened with the working relationship that Lord and Daphne Bullingdon had with him.' He senses that she eyes him with a degree of amusement, as though his valiant floundering were deserving of sympathy. 'I thought you might know something about him that could shed light on the matter.'

She is unflustered. She readjusts a lock of her fine black hair. She answers calmly.

'If anything, it strikes me as a working matter, Inspector – a mantrap out on the grouse moor? It is hardly my department.'

Skelgill makes a face of reluctant acceptance.

'Are you aware of him having a recent dispute or conflict – anything that he might have mentioned?'

She narrows her eyes reproachfully, as if to signal her disapproval of the continued suggestion that she might be a confidante; but a rueful smile curves her lips.

'Wasn't Lawrence in a permanent state of conflict with all those around him?'

Skelgill's eyes widen a little.

'You tell me, madam.'

'Oh, it's not for me to say – but there are some people for whom it is second nature to ruffle feathers whichever way they turn. To test limits. To break the boundaries.' She stares pointedly at Skelgill. 'I'm sure you know what I mean.' Then she sighs and settles deeper into the chaise, momentarily closing her eyes.

There can be little doubt – that she means him – and probably herself. Skelgill feels the first tingling of a flush on his cheeks. Involuntarily he runs a hand up over his forehead and rakes his hair, like a jousting knight hauling back his visor to reveal beneath the implacable mask a countenance that petitions for a truce. She watches him with undisguised interest, her eyes appraising his whole form. When she does not speak he finds himself reverting to country copper pragmatism.

'Did you hear or see anything unusual last night? In particular – around midnight.'

She remains composed.

'I came up here directly after dinner.' She crosses one leg over the other and runs her fingers lightly across the exposed flesh above her knee. 'I think I caught too much of the sun yesterday – and I had an early start this morning. I was in bed by eleven – it seemed before I knew it my alarm was waking me.'

'You didn't get up at all – look out of the window – hear anyone, any disturbance?'

She casts a languorous gaze over the sumptuously appointed four-poster bed.

'I sleep like an angel, Inspector. How about you?'

Certainly Skelgill cannot imagine that this serene creature slumbers like the proverbial log – but he is not sure exactly how an angel sleeps – there is some suggestion of ethereal wandering. The idea sends a shiver down his spine; not least that her question sounds like an enticement.

He applies will power.

'So you didn't leave the room.'

Though it is at best a fairly meek statement, Miranda Bullingdon meets him halfway.

'What did Teddy tell you?'

She smiles knowingly and her tone is conspiratorial – as though she is quite openly disposed to protect her husband, to supply him with an alibi as required.

'That you had a headache – that he didn't disturb you.'

She seems unfazed, though she gives the hint of a shrug, an expression of 'so be it'.

'I don't envy you this part of your job, Inspector.'

'Aye?'

Skelgill is not expecting this.

'You must investigate. You must pry. You must ... *suspect.*' With sudden feline ease she shifts into a more upright position, pulling up her knees and encircling them with her arms, her left hand gripping her right wrist. She gazes rather wistfully ahead, at nothing in particular. 'Some years ago, there was a man with whom I was having a – a liaison, shall we say. Given his position it would have been inconvenient were it to be made public. He was very careful – however, one can never really be careful enough. His philosophy was that while a fool may fall under suspicion, it is a bigger fool that confesses to it.'

Skelgill senses that he is willingly falling under her spell, the siren music of her husky voice; that he finds himself agreeing; that this is a perfectly reasonable stance to take – besides, for him of all people to decry it would be an outright case of the pot calling the kettle black (although he might argue that his own taciturnity is only ever employed in the cause of justice). As has been his constant experience with this skilled sorceress, he is torn between whether to attempt to decipher her incantations, or simply read what is written between the widely spaced lines, and accept stalemate.

From somewhere he unearths a self-deprecating rejoinder.

'Like you say, madam – someone has to go round rifling through the bins.'

'I quite understand.'

But he is running out of options. She *does* understand – that he might lead the inquiry but that does not equal the agenda. If it suits her she will answer; otherwise she will respond with her own question. Now, rather woodenly, Skelgill falls back on a stock question; it feels like going through the motions.

'How long have you lived here?'

'Oh, it is almost five years. Prior to that I was a resident of the Royal Borough of Kensington and Chelsea.'

'That was before you were married?'

'Which marriage?'

He raises his hands in contrition.

'A modelling career is like naked skydiving, Inspector.'

He must look sufficiently perplexed; she enlightens him.

'Exhilarating – but a severe anti-climax without a parachute.'

He realises she is spotlighting the question he has skirted around. Though ostensibly a mismatch, in fact it is not difficult to see what marriage to an elderly peer of the realm provides. That elusive grade above A-list status on the social circuit. Respectability and a shield from undesirable suitors. And – quite likely under the circumstances – the freedom to lead the life she so desires.

But he is not convinced that a deeper understanding of her background – nor of Lord Bullingdon's, come to that – will offer anything other than padding for a report. Gut feel tells him so. The events that he is investigating seem very much rooted in local soil, and in the present day.

'Occasionally, fellow skydivers must come to one's rescue.'

She is looking at him how? Alluringly? His mind labours as though time is slowing down; he has a sensation of drowning in jasmine-scented honey, a hapless drone summoned to the queen's private cell. She seems in no rush whatsoever, certainly not to get rid of him. He starts – realising he has begun to drift. And he recognises the law of diminishing marginal utility – as each minute lengthens it becomes less productive; and he has another lady with whom to tangle.

*

'This could become a habit.'

'We can go inside if you prefer.'

'I'm always glad of fresh air.'

'Well – help yourself.' Karen Williamson hesitates just as she is about to swing her legs over the rustic picnic bench. She indicates the platter of sandwiches she has uncovered before Skelgill.

'I was wondering – about your colleagues?'

'They've got their adult teeth.'

Despite his terse rejoinder she seems mollified – but perhaps his terminology prompts her.

'You okay with Kieran? He won't pay attention to us. And it means I can keep an eye on him.'

'Good to see it.' Skelgill observes with approval the boy in his karate suit bouncing energetically on the trampoline. 'Bairns spend too much time goggling at screens.'

'It's a great thing about living out here – he can take his bike round the tracks.' Though her expression becomes a little sombre. 'So long as it's not the shooting season.'

Skelgill inhales reproachfully between clenched teeth.

'When there's guns to hand it's always the shooting season.'

'You disapprove?'

Now he shrugs resignedly.

'In my job, it's hard to feel comfortable in the presence of a shotgun.' He gazes vacantly across the cottage lawn, to where there is a planked door set in the tall brickwork of the walled garden – it would have been the head gardener's access from his modest home to his horticultural domain. 'Once you've had a close shave – you never quite trust them not to have a life of their own.'

'I suppose in your job you see them where they're not meant to be – in the hands of armed robbers and drug dealers.'

Skelgill scoffs, though in a manner that does not intend offence.

'You'd be surprised. In Cumbria we've got double the national average of legally held guns.'

She nods slowly, but then she returns to her point.

'When I say disapprove – I was thinking of political correctness – shooting wildlife and all that.'

Now Skelgill looks more conflicted.

'There's a dozen arguments each way. I'm a fisherman myself. But I don't like to see animals mistreated.'

Again Karen Williamson nods in accord.

'It was a bit of an eye-opener for me when we came here. I'm a townie born and bred. Jam eater.' She grins self-mockingly. 'All those pheasants they rear like battery hens and then release to be shot.' She pulls reflectively at a strand of hair that has escaped from her band and which is curling down one chiselled cheek. 'I suppose it doesn't help – having to cater for some of the clients that come up from London – treat you like the feudal system was never abolished. Think you're their property for the weekend.'

Skelgill glances up from his mug of tea.

'Oh – don't worry – I can look after myself.' She chuckles, and he senses that she subtly flexes her limbs and torso. The early evening air is balmy and she wears a lycra vest top; he becomes aware of the toned muscles of her bare arms. He detects a waft of body odour. It is a moment before he responds.

'What about Lawrence Melling?'

Skelgill is sure he catches a flash of alarm in her dark eyes. She stares at her son on the trampoline. It seems there is a flush of colour in her face.

'It's a shock.'

Her apparent interpretation – that he has changed the subject from the gamekeeper's behaviour to his fate – is not unreasonable, but it seems to Skelgill that she is avoiding the crux of his question. However, he is unperturbed. For the second time in two days following a session of heady free fall with Miranda Bullingdon he feels like he has landed in familiar territory; that occupied by the grounded housekeeper.

'Have you told the bairn?'

She looks sharply at Skelgill – as if this question is unexpected.

'Aye. But I didn't mention a trap – I didn't want to terrify him. Scare him from wandering around. I just told him there's been a shooting accident. He seemed alright with it.'

Skelgill is watching the boy – he performs impressive backflips, like some cartoon kung fu character. But his thoughts are with Karen Williamson's being inadvertently so close to the mark. While the cause of Lawrence Melling's death will emerge in due course, Skelgill and his colleagues had decided to refer only to the trap and the outside possibility of it being moved by a malicious party. Of course he broke this rule in a moment of madness – but it served his purpose. Now he refrains from repeating the experiment.

'How did you get on with him?'

He sees that she bites her cheek at the corner of her mouth.

'I'd say he had a cruel streak.'

It is a candid answer. Under such circumstances – even when there is only the smallest possibility that someone fears they might incriminate themselves – Skelgill is accustomed to responses that range from bland platitudes to crocodile tears; the question is rendered meaningless. Instead Karen Williamson's rejoinder opens up such a broad panoply of options that he is spoilt for choice. It is like those moments on the water when half a dozen trout rise in synchrony, as if to confound the angler. He reaches a swift decision.

'I heard on the grapevine that he were a bit of a ladies' man.'

She is clearly conscious of Skelgill's close attention. But she turns to look him straight in the eye. He sees a fighter.

'Aye – well, he fancied himself, alright.' However, she suddenly relents and holds up her hands in contrition. 'But you shouldn't speak ill of the dead, as they say.'

She reaches for the teapot and tops up Skelgill's mug. He shrugs as if to show he does not exactly feel bound by the adage.

'How well did you know him?'

His question is posed as casually as he can contrive. With good reason he might have asked directly – *did you ever sleep with him?* – but his intuition spares her an awkward denial.

'I wouldn't say he were the sort you could get to know.' She looks again at Skelgill and he wonders if he now sees in her lanceolate eyes an appeal for leniency – indeed she transfers her gaze concernedly back to her son. He is half expecting her to say, "We all make mistakes." Instead her response is more prosaic. 'I've not had a lot to do with him lately.'

Skelgill uses the excuse of eating a sandwich to work out what he feels he ought to say next. In the event he also opts for the practical.

'Last night – what time did you go to bed?'

To his surprise she looks uneasy.

'Er – it were about eleven – no – maybe earlier, ten-thirty?'

'You didn't watch a TV programme that finished at a particular time?'

'No – I just had stuff to do – washing up, hanging laundry – ironing Kieran's uniform and packing sports kit that he needed for today – and putting up his bait. Then the place were a midden.'

Skelgill is struck by this list of alien chores. He turns and regards the cottage rather pensively. It is effectively single storey; though there are a couple of small skylights flush with the slate roof that must illuminate a loft; he had not noticed them when he skirted around close to the building in the dark. It is not a big place – it must be two bedrooms and a sitting room – but all the same it cannot be easy after a hard day's domestic labour to come home to more of the same.

'Did you hear anything in the night – any disturbance?'

She shakes her head quite quickly, as though she has been expecting the question. But then she hesitates and looks at him quizzically.

'I might have heard the quad bike?' But she does not sound convinced.

'What time?'

Now she inhales, and sighs in turn. She shakes her head.

'I'm only thinking I may have heard it. I couldn't say any more than that. It was after I went to bed – but it could have been Kieran that shouted out in his sleep. Or it could have been the night before.'

Skelgill nods reflectively. The property is only fifty yards or so from the main track, Long Shoot, and the quad bike had initially been concealed just a short distance further, in the undergrowth. The cottage retains its original inefficient sash windows; something as raucous as the machine's engine would surely have carried indoors. But he opts not to enlighten her about the quad bike's movements. Instead he revisits a theme unsuccessfully explored with Miranda Bullingdon.

'Did Lawrence Melling's cruel streak stretch to the making of enemies?'

Karen Williamson does not answer immediately, and her steady unfocused gaze, eyes narrowed, shows her to be deliberating – but certainly not trying to hide that she is so doing. If Skelgill were pressed he would say there is something she wants to tell him, but is weighing up the pros and cons. Finally, she poses a question, the nature of which interests him.

'Are you saying that what happened to him wasn't an accident?'

Skelgill regards her dispassionately, as though this is no big deal, just standard procedure.

'We don't like to jump to conclusions.' However, his tone becomes more purposeful. 'But a gamekeeper stepping in a trap

205

that belongs to the estate – it's not the way round that you'd expect things to be.'

'It was the barbaric-looking contraption – from the collection of weapons and armour at the entrance?'

'As far as we can tell.'

She frowns self-reprovingly.

'I didn't even notice it were missing.'

'When were you last in there?'

'Yesterday – I came out that way, I often do – about a quarter to five – I like to get Kieran's tea on for five – he's always starving, ravenous if he's done sport.'

'If the trap wasn't there – wouldn't you have noticed? You must know the household contents better than their insurers.'

She grins ruefully.

'Aye – I know what you mean. Happen I would have noticed. But I couldn't swear – it's always quite dark.'

'Who uses the front door – evening times?'

Now she shakes her head.

'I'm not often around after five. But I don't think there's much foot traffic at night. During the day the family mainly uses the scullery door at the back – that's the quickest way to the office and most of the estate buildings – plus the stables, and the cars are garaged beyond there. Regular deliveries and whatnot – they know to continue past to the estate office. It's probably only if a visitor comes that someone would go to the front.'

Skelgill nods pensively. But he decides not to speculate. Instead, abruptly, and perhaps too bluntly he changes the subject.

'Does the pocket rocket miss his dad?'

'Well – he's got –' Her response is something of a reflex – in part the maternal protectiveness that he might have anticipated – but also there is perhaps a revision of something she was about to utter. 'Me – I do my best – and there's young guys in the karate club – and a couple of the coaches – they're good role models and they spend time with him – and one of his best pals, his dad is big into sport – they sometimes travel together – we split the lifts where we can.'

Skelgill does not say anything in response. If he dangled bait she was not interested. In his judgement she has turned tail and muddied the waters. But he is always alert to what folk *don't* say.

He looks on admiringly at the Duracell boy, now performing competent backflips. But he glances at his watch. His phone is off and his sergeants probably won't know where to look for him. He finishes his drink and puts down the mug with an air of finality. He pre-empts her actions.

'Don't get up – keep your eye on the bairn. Thanks for tea – that filled a gap. I'll know where to come next time.'

She rewards him with the same enigmatic smile as on their first encounter a couple of weeks ago; strangely, he feels a little guilty.

As soon as Skelgill has disappeared around the side of the building, the boy vaults from the trampoline and runs across to his mother.

'Well done, Kieran – now you carry on – practise your Gedan Mawashi Geri on the grass.'

She rises and hurries inside without taking the plates.

Meanwhile, maybe fifteen yards from the front of the cottage, Skelgill has turned and is surveying the property, hands on hips.

11. THE BELVEDERE

Tuesday, early evening

'Leyton – where are you?'

'We're waiting in my motor, Guv – where I left it.'

There is a moment's hesitation, as though, unseen by Skelgill, he refers to his fellow sergeant. 'We thought you might want to go for something to eat?'

'Nay, I'm not hungry, Leyton – I'm at the viewpoint by the red phone box – under the pagoda thing. There's seats here and no one earwigging. You pair come over here so we can catch up.'

Skelgill hears a sigh of resignation.

'Roger, Guv – I'll drive us round to the nearest point. Just be two ticks.'

Though it is approaching eight p.m. rich sunshine still filters through the trees; there remain a couple of hours of daylight, and the avian evensong is just getting going; blackbird and robin melodies, tenor and treble respectively; the saxophonic coo of a cushat; and the erratic timekeeping of a chiffchaff.

From the belvedere Skelgill has a clear view over the waterfall that supplies Troutmere; the lake surface simultaneously flat and contoured, as it reflects its surroundings. The rustic boathouse basks in the rosy glow of the sun, the balcony half in shadow.

As he contemplates the unmoving scene – the colours are vivid like an acrylic painting – his thoughts drift back to last night – to midnight – a contrast in monochrome – when the French windows were fleetingly ajar and he caught a snatch of a female voice – distinctly female – but otherwise indeterminate. He tries to replay the tone, the timbre – and he listens for the echoes of those other voices he has heard in the past twenty-four hours.

One of them is not coming clean.

'Wow!'

Skelgill is jolted from his brown study – he jerks around.

'What a vista – imagine having this in your garden, Guv.'

It is DS Jones – she approaches energetically across the short turf, in which she seems to leave no impression – whereas coming behind her, labouring to catch up, Skelgill can see that DS Leyton makes bruised footprints.

But her bright ebullience becomes tarnished – it can only be that he regards her with such a strange intensity. DS Leyton, oblivious, chimes in with an apologetic complaint.

'We tried calling you, Guv – seemed like your mobile was off.'

Skelgill transfers his gaze from DS Jones.

'Aye – I've had no signal.' He cocks his head briefly to one side. 'I had to ring you from that box.'

DS Leyton looks flabbergasted.

'What – is it working?'

'And I reversed the charges.'

Skelgill waves a dismissive hand and makes a scoffing exclamation. It is sufficient for his sergeant to realise it is a kind of wind up.

'Ha-hah – you had me going there, Guv. Mind you – this place is bonkers – I wouldn't put it past the Bullingdons to have had it connected up.'

Skelgill is seated in a timber chair fashioned in the Adirondack style, and there are four others, two either side, ranged in a crescent beneath the roof of the belvedere, around a woodstove and all giving views of the lake. His subordinates seem unsure for a moment of where to settle, but DS Jones grasps the nettle and sits right beside him – she makes a little cry of surprise as the unanticipated declination throws up her knees. But, as DS Leyton, with a groan, and in a more circumspect fashion lowers himself into the seat next to her, she shifts into work mode.

'The yellow car, Guv.' (Skelgill's attention is immediately won.) 'The Volkswagen Golf – it's a pool car – they all use it, including members of staff. It's just left parked in a big open-sided barn behind the stables, unlocked, with the keys in. First come first served. Julian Bullingdon says he didn't drive it at all yesterday. His moth trap has been set up since Friday – and last night he walked there and back – it takes about twenty-five minutes each way. He was on site from about nine-thirty until around one a.m. When he got back he went into the library to look up a moth in a textbook – he noticed the clock chime the half hour, one-thirty.'

'How did he get in?'

'He says he left the back door on the latch – and it was still unlocked when he returned. He wakes Cook if necessary by throwing gravel at her bedroom window.'

Skelgill realises he has omitted to ask the sixty-four thousand dollar question.

'What about the gunshot?'

DS Jones inhales sharply, as if to acknowledge the significance of this point.

'He didn't hear anything.' She glances sideways at Skelgill in time to catch a suppressed grimace. She is ready for this. 'But, actually, Guv – that might tell us something. I got him to refuel the generator that runs the moth trap. When you're beside it, it's noisy. I doubt if you'd hear a gun until you were some distance away. If he left the moth trap at one a.m. – that suggests the shot had already been fired. Otherwise, walking back, he probably would have heard it. Plus it fits – with your sighting – of the car.'

She is reticent with these last few words – it seems an awkward moment – she glances a little guiltily at DS Leyton. He comes to her rescue.

'I managed to winkle that bit out of her, Guv. Neat bit of surveillance on your part.'

Skelgill scowls – but lets it pass over. Plainly they need to share this information – he just hadn't got round to it, the car still troubling him. Meanwhile DS Jones draws the conclusion from her narrative.

'If Julian Bullingdon is telling the truth – then it potentially narrows down the time of the shooting to between twelve-forty and one a.m.'

Skelgill, however, is looking discomfited. It feels to him like they are hunting a wraith across the open moor – their torches flashing here and there – but when they close on their quarry and their beams converge, a disembodied shadow rises and flees into the night.

After a while he folds his arms and intones somewhat monotonously.

'What did he say about the Golf – who might have been using it?'

'That he had no idea, Guv.'

'And did he look like he had no idea?'

'He seemed plausible, but –' She looks earnestly – first at DS Leyton and then back to Skelgill. 'But – who *should* we believe at present?'

This is the very sentiment that has been dogging Skelgill for some time, probably since his very first brush with anything to do with Shuteham Hall – Lawrence Melling, after the shooting of the buzzard in Bullmire Wood. It is as if the very nature of the place – its isolation, its privacy, its lack of security – is engineered to inhibit tangible evidence, and its inhabitants on a spectrum between the guilelessly obtuse and the downright evasive. It fosters conjecture, and DS Leyton duly obliges.

'If that motor was sitting with its keys in the ignition – behind the stables – it could just as easy have been one or more of the estate workers took it – Artur, included. We've only got their word that they resumed their card school. If Melling put their backs up they might have decided to give him a taste of his own medicine. Especially seeing as they'd been caning the vodka.'

Skelgill can immediately think of a welter of objections – such as knowing where Melling was going, getting ahead of him, placing the trap – but he does not even want to get drawn into this journey; without map or compass; the terrain crisscrossed by unmarked lanes, where each wrong turn compounds the disorientation; eventually to encounter the inevitable straw-chewing yokel. "You can't get there from here." He exhales and pushes his hands into the air as if he is trying to beat away an onslaught of midges.

'Leyton – leave it alone.'

DS Leyton, however, is only marginally deterred; perhaps a hankering for his deferred dinner galvanises his resolve.

'Are you sure it was a yellow motor, Guv? White can look like yellow in the dark – and white's much more common. Must be fifty to one against.'

Skelgill glowers. It was a fleeting glance in the moonlight – and it would be easy now for doubt to creep in. But he trusts his instincts – he knows from fishing that first impressions are invariably right. A bite has a dynamic quality that is lacking in a snag on rock or weed. But when he does not answer DS Leyton persists.

'Did you get a butcher's at the driver, Guv – any passengers?'

Skelgill objects less to this question. He shakes his head.

'I'd just switched off my beam so I didn't blind an owl and run it over.' He sees that his colleagues are looking at him with some distrust. 'Straight up – it went after a big moth that was thrown by my lights. There was a three-quarter moon and I saw a yellow hatchback flash across the end of the track. But I didn't get the make.'

There ensues a silence. Clearly, Skelgill has not yet updated his subordinates – regarding Miranda Bullingdon and Karen Williamson. Likewise DS Leyton – who to his chagrin was despatched by Skelgill to see Cook and the estate workers. Skelgill seems in no hurry to hear about the latter. DS Jones, on the other hand, is itching to progress. She fashions a question that tackles her dilemma in a suitably roundabout way.

'Given what we've all learned – can we eliminate anyone?'

But Skelgill does not answer. He gazes out over the lake – perhaps he gives a slight shake of his head – most likely it is frustration.

DS Leyton holds up an index finger.

212

'Cook.'

Skelgill swings round as if to challenge his pronouncement.

'She's in her late seventies, Guv – she's waiting for a new hip – she moves at a snail's pace. She could barely lift a ladle – let alone that there cast-iron mantrap.'

DS Leyton looks like he could come up with more reasons – but Skelgill makes a face of acquiescence. And he poses a constructive question.

'Did she hear Lord Bullingdon locking up – like he reckoned, he called out to her just before ten?'

DS Leyton shakes his head.

'She's a bit mutton, Guv.'

'What?'

'Mutt and Jeff – *deaf*, Guv.'

Skelgill scowls and DS Leyton grins sheepishly. But he has something to add.

'Funnily enough she said she was cooking a lamb hotpot – leaving it on overnight. She nipped out to the kitchen garden for rosemary – about twenty past ten. She swears she locked the door when she came back in.'

DS Jones homes in on this.

'That's two people who claim they locked the back door *after* Julian Bullingdon left it open – at maybe nine-thirty. Yet he maintains it was unlocked when he got home at just before one-thirty.'

Skelgill, who has his own slant on this, finds himself making a suggestion. 'Happen Cook forgot. She would have put it on the sneck so she didn't lock herself out.' It is not the only explanation that he can think of, but perhaps it suits him since it sounds the most logical.

DS Leyton looks like this is a distinct possibility; he makes a hand gesture that suggests he will not defend the elderly retainer's waning faculties.

Following another period of silence DS Jones picks up her point about elimination.

'What about the Irish pair, Guv – if they were in the birdwatching hide as you were leaving – they couldn't have been in two places at one time?'

Skelgill instinctively glances at his watch – perhaps it is the prospect of shortly being able to interview the couple. But a frown reveals some unease. He did not actually look in the hide. He only went by the noises that were emanating from within. And it was almost one a.m. If Lawrence Melling was shot as early as twelve-forty – then, it would be tight, but "two places at one time" would no longer apply. His words come out somewhat hoarsely.

'We'll see what they've got to say for themselves at ten.'

Yet suddenly he rises and looks like he is ready to go – despite that it could be at least two hours before the Irish couple turn up for their shift. His colleagues regard him questioningly. DS Leyton rattles his car keys.

'What do you want to do, Guv?'

'Reckon I'd better check on old Mary Ann.'

'Come again?'

'She's me Ma's eldest sister, one of the mad Grahams – she lives just along from the brewery. I drop in every so often.'

His subordinates might not think this to be such an act of altruism if they knew that the 'mad aunt' can be relied upon to have some local dish or other simmering on the hob.

'I'll see the Irish. You pair can knock off. If you could just drop us back, first.' Skelgill sees that DS Leyton is looking a little relieved, despite the detour – though DS Jones is plainly less enthusiastic about the prospect. However, before she can object, he issues further instructions, addressing her directly. 'See if you can put some wheels in motion tonight – submit a request for a search tomorrow – including a blood dog – not just the crime scene, but the various properties that Melling or his assailant might have used – the gatehouse, the boathouse, Melling's cottage, the stables area, the rearing sheds, the VW Golf – think it through.'

DS Jones is at least engaged by this prospect; her eyes narrow; clearly she *is* thinking it through.

'You know, really, Guv – we'd want to check the footwear and clothing of – well – everyone we can think of – for possible blood spatter?'

DS Leyton is looking a bit wide-eyed. Skelgill is looking grim. But he nods.

'It's not going to happen – not just yet – turning the place upside down and going through their wardrobes?' He makes a frustrated growl. 'Besides – if Helen Back's right about the way he was shot, we'll be lucky if we get any blood spatter. But what you can do is put pressure on Forensics. Email them tonight and get on to them first thing. If there's anything on the gun or the trap, we need to know. Tell them it's a matter of life and death.'

Now his colleagues look shocked. It is not a phrase he will use glibly; moreover, he says it with such unusual resolve that DS Leyton is prompted to ask for clarification.

'What are you saying, Guv – you reckon someone else is at risk?'

Skelgill glares at his subordinate.

'Leyton – we've got a killer on the loose – who may be in hiding – and if he's not, we may have a double killer on the loose. Until we understand why Melling was shot, it's like blind man's buff. All these folk playing the game – and we're half in the dark. But one of them might be a witness and not realise it. One of them might be next.' He holds out his upturned palms in a more conciliatory gesture. 'Look – if Melling had been shot, the jewels had been nicked and Stan had disappeared – in that order – I might be thinking, no problem – we know who's done it and he's flown the coop. But, right now, we can't take any chances.'

He beckons with his head and sets off towards the driveway, following the line of his colleagues' arrival. As his sergeants catch up, DS Jones has a point to convey.

'Guv, I was thinking – the crime scene, while we're searching that area tomorrow – maybe we should get an expert along from English Nature – just to advise on minimum disruption to the hen harriers.'

Skelgill nods, though rather grudgingly.

215

'There's no cause to go near the nest – Melling obviously never made it that far. I'd say it's just the stretch between the trap and where we've been parking. Although our lot have probably obliterated any tyre marks by now. But you're right – we don't want to hand the media an open goal.'

He can see the headline, "Ham-fisted Cops Scare Off Rare Harriers".

Rather portentously, DS Leyton contributes his two penn'orth.

'It ain't gonna be easy to keep it under wraps, Guv. Those Vholes characters – they'll be watching us like flippin' hawks – *hah!*'

*

A coalition of the mind prompts Skelgill to pass the turn-off for Over Water birdwatching hide. He rounds a sharp bend before bumping up carefully onto a rocky verge to tuck his car against the dry stone wall. The logical aspect of his motive is that if he parks near the hide the Vholes and anyone else inside will hear him, and he would rather retain the element of surprise. He would also rather not meet the Vholes. Undoubtedly, as DS Leyton had prophesised, they would complain about disturbance of the harriers – as they had already begun to do earlier – and, if Skelgill personally interviews them again (not managing to delegate to one of his sergeants) he wants to do it as far away from Over Moor as possible.

The other driver of Skelgill's behaviour is purely instinctive. He has sailed close to the wind a couple of times – into promising waters, yes, but with disappointing results. Allowing his sixth sense to get a firmer hand on the tiller feels like a good option from now on.

Accordingly he scales the wall and trots back to the turn-off, whence in the cover of the tall hedgerow that borders the track he makes his way down close to the parking area. His wristwatch tells him it is nine-fifty p.m. – the clear sky suggests earlier; there is still an element of half-light, though the daytime birds have fallen silent. He can just make out the Vholes' Volvo through a gap in the foliage. He waits a couple of minutes; the stillness is punctuated by tantalising plops that emanate from Over Water – sounds that keep him on edge, so conditioned is he to respond to the stimulus. He begins to wonder – out of every hundred rises, how many of them would be a vendace – or does the vendace *never* rise to feed? Another mystery yet to be fathomed.

There is the sound of a car approaching. It must be the Irish couple arriving for their shift. Given their mobile disconnectedness and that no news has yet been released by the police he is working on the principle that they are unaware of the incident involving Lawrence Melling (not dismissing the outside possibility that they were involved in it, of course). As such, he intends to intercept them before the Vholes do. He wants their version of events, untainted by hearsay.

To his frustration, there is the click of the hide door. The Vholes miss nothing. He begins to barge through the hawthorn; it is unforgiving – but just as he is about to emerge the incoming vehicle performs a smart pirouette on the gravel close by. It is not the Ford Consul. Far too nimble, instead it is a small green Fiat, an old model, hand-painted with explosive sunflowers that could just be mistaken for the impact holes of armour-piercing rounds. Skelgill draws back into cover. The hedge is heavy with may blossom and he is drenched in its sweet musky aroma; though it is hardly Chanel Nº5, it conjures an image of Miranda Bullingdon.

Two young women, aged about twenty, he would guess, both with long straight dark hair and dressed like birdwatchers, in bulky sweaters with binoculars prominent on their chests, get out of the car and begin to walk in the direction of the hide. One of them has a small rucksack. Coming along the planks of the boardwalk he can hear rapid footsteps. Then the strident voice of Christine Vholes.

'Oh – it's *you?*'

As well as perplexed she sounds distinctly disappointed – to the extent that Skelgill wonders what reaction her tone will engender. However, one girl at least remains phlegmatic.

'We've swapped shifts – Ciara phoned me – they're on a twitch.'

'I beg your pardon?'

'There's an eastern kingbird on the Isle of Mull.'

'Well – this is – this is not like them.'

'It's a life tick for them both.'

The girl seems accepting that this is more than enough justification – but Christine Vholes tuts indignantly.

'They have always given priority to the harriers.'

'Ah, well – me and Mel – we'll do our best to stay awake. We've brought a bottle of rhubarb gin to keep us going.'

The new arrivals snigger conspiratorially; Christine Vholes merely gives a headmistress-like shake of the head and turns and leads them out of Skelgill's sight and into the hide. He is pondering his next move when there are more footsteps – and he sees that the Vholes are apparently leaving. From his concealed position he watches as they trudge to their car in silence – unless they are again using their telepathy – and enter, and drive away. Now he extricates himself from the thorn hedge and strides along the boardwalk. He decides to tread heavily.

A head turns as he enters the dimly lit hut.

'Mr Vholes – did you forget – *oh?*'

'DI Skelgill – Cumbria Police. There's nothing to worry about, ladies.'

Skelgill, conscious of the circumstances, walks directly up to the girl he knows to be not-Mel and takes the unusual precaution of actually handing her his warrant card. To read it she sways a little towards the naked light bulb that inadequately illuminates the hut from above the bunk. The girl that *is* Mel is already seated and is connecting up a laptop – presumably to resume viewing the harriers via the webcam. There is a sticker on the back of the screen – in curling script it seems to spell the word 'raptor' in the shape of a soaring bird of prey. Not-Mel nods to her companion and returns the card to Skelgill – at the same time offering a hand to shake.

'I'm Claire – this is Mel.'

Skelgill bows his head appropriately.

'Sorry to intrude – but we need urgently to speak to Cian Fogarty and Ciara Ahearne. They may be important witnesses to a serious incident.'

The girl Claire looks alarmed – but not in any way that makes Skelgill think she will withhold information. Indeed, she is immediately forthcoming.

'They went to Scotland this morning. Cian's a massive twitcher – and there's an eastern kingbird on Mull – it's an American vagrant – a mega.'

'A mega?'

She nods.

'It's what twitchers call a really, really rare bird – a once-in-a-lifetime occurrence. A megatick.'

Skelgill decides not to reveal he was eavesdropping.

'How do you know this?'

'Ciara phoned me this morning – they were still on their way.'

'We've not been able to get mobile numbers for either of them.'

'Oh – well, it was a payphone – I know because the money ran out. She said they'd stopped at the motorway services.'

Skelgill is juggling multiple questions in his mind.

'Did you delete the call record?'

'Er – no – but it might have been withheld – I can't remember.' With a wiggle of her torso she pulls her mobile from the back pocket of her jeans. 'Let's see – er – yes, look – this must be it – eleven-forty-three.'

Skelgill squints at the handset. The number is displayed. He types it into his own phone and sends it as a text message to DS Jones.

'Thanks – that might be handy.'

'You're welcome.'

'Did Ciara Ahearne say when they were coming back?'

Claire shakes her head.

'Like I say – the money ran out – but she only asked if we'd stand in for them tonight – I assumed they'd try to get back tomorrow. They might be driving already – if they saw it this evening. It only takes a couple of seconds to twitch a new species.'

Two ticks, as Leyton would say.

'This kingbird – it's genuine, is it?'

'Yes – it's on Birdline.'

Skelgill grins wryly.

'You weren't tempted, yourselves?'

The girls exchange a brief glance. Now Mel chirps up.

'We're trainee nurses, at West Cumberland Infirmary – plus, well – we're not twitchers.'

Skelgill has received lectures before now from his friend Professor Jim Hartley – a proficient amateur ornithologist as well as an expert angler. It seems that to be a 'twitcher' is to belong to an elite cohort, a particular kind of birder (or 'birdwatcher' as the professor prefers). The former type is obsessive, stressed-out and not always popular with the more easy-going latter. And probably vice-versa. He nods.

'How well do you know them?'

It is Claire that answers.

'Oh, well – we've seen them and chatted at a couple of meetings of the Nats – that's our society – ' (Skelgill is nodding) 'and I suppose all the people on the harrier rota are aware of one another.'

'How would she have got your number?'

Claire ponders for a moment.

'You know – I'm on the committee – they have our contact details on the website. It must have been that. Maybe that's why they rang from the services – where they could get Wi-Fi and look me up.'

She regards Skelgill a little anxiously, as if he ought to be suspicious over this point – but he does not appear concerned. Indeed, he flips open his wallet and extracts a calling card.

'If she should ring you again – could you ask her to hang up and call me?'

The girl takes the card and holds it rather reverently.

'Sure, I will – definitely.'

She smiles engagingly – and there ensues a moment's silence before Skelgill responds.

'I'll leave you to your harriers and your –' He almost says "gin" but in the nick of time realises there is no evidence of such – and indeed he wonders if it were merely an insouciant response to the overbearing Christine Vholes. But now that he has hesitated he feels he ought to say something and he decides in any event it will make sense to enlighten the young women. He indicates in the direction of the nest site. 'As dawn breaks you'll see there's a scenes-of-crime tent out on the moor. The incident involved the death of a gamekeeper. There'll be an official from English Nature to make sure the forensic team doesn't disturb the birds. I reckon they'll be done by noon.' He steps towards the door and opens it to leave. 'You could do me a favour – and mention that to the Vholes – I gather they'll be back at seven a.m.?'

The girl Claire nods – she does not appear surprised that he is aware of this.

'No problem.'

Then the girl Mel spontaneously calls out; there is something knowing in her tone.

'Stay for a drink, if you like.'

12. SCAWTHWAITE MIRE

Wednesday morning

'**G**uv – that number – it's a payphone at a motorway service station on the M74 just south of Glasgow – on the northbound carriageway.'

'Hold your horses, Jones.'

Skelgill has answered the call on hands-free but now he pulls into a passing place and takes up his handset.

'Carry on.'

DS Jones does as requested.

'Otherwise the car's not been detected by any cameras. I've checked with Caledonian MacBrayne. The ferry for Mull sails from Oban, roughly every hour. Yesterday and on the dawn sailing this morning – no record of the Ford Consul – and you have to provide your registration number when you buy the ticket and each vehicle is scanned as it drives on. But they could have gone over to the island as foot passengers – if they'd hooked up with other twitchers it would make sense to split the cost and share a lift. Apparently there were three hundred people trying to see the bird yesterday. I've made a request through Police Scotland for a local patrol to look for the car parked in the town. And I'm just waiting for the duty officer at the Tobermory station to call me back – I thought they might be able to get their island patrol out to wherever all the twitchers are gathering.'

Skelgill makes a curious face – perhaps a brief appreciation of having a subordinate he does not need to instruct; instead the luxury of being able to think about what she tells him.

'At least Glasgow's in the right direction. If they were on the run, I reckon they'd be heading for Ireland. They would have turned off at Gretna – the A75 for Stranraer.'

DS Jones does not respond immediately – it is as if she is assimilating something new in his statement.

'On the run, Guv? I thought they were in the hide?'

Skelgill makes an exasperated groan and clambers out of his car. He stares across the open moorland that rises gently before him to a line of grouse butts on the horizon – they are like deserted battlements of some ancient conflict.

'Jones – I'm ninety-nine per cent certain they *were* in the hide – but that was one o'clock, near as dammit.'

She understands he has just sufficient reason for doubt.

'But they didn't leave until the end of their shift – at seven in the morning. If they were involved in some way, wouldn't they have just cleared out in the middle of the night?'

Skelgill recognises that his sergeant's logic is sound – but it does not entirely trump his gut feel. That said, he does not try too hard to imagine other reasons why they made such a prompt exit yesterday morning. The story of the eastern kingbird is becoming fairly convincing. Absently he stoops to retrieve a fragment of slate and slings it left-handed into the heather – to his horror a brace of red grouse explode from the point of impact, flying low and fast, their calls resounding across the moor: *go-back go-back go-back*. He checks around guiltily – but to his relief he is unobserved.

Rather abruptly he changes the subject.

'I suppose it's too early to have anything from Forensics?'

'There's nothing in my inbox, Guv – I'll start ringing round at eight-thirty.' When Skelgill does not comment she continues, more tentatively. 'I can hear a skylark.'

He understands it to be a question.

'I'm about to have a word with Jack Carlops – the keeper before Melling.'

'Oh?' Her tone is inquisitive, tempered by the knowledge not to expect more.

Scawthwaite Mire sounds as though it ought to have its own demonic black dog, like Dartmoor's 'Hound of the Baskervilles', but these days it is an area of tamed pasture south of the hamlet of Uldale, with drainage ditches emptying into the nascent River Ellen, a watercourse that numbers among its many mountain beck and spring sources Over Water itself. The river enters the sea more fully formed at the coastal town of Maryport, and notwithstanding its limited proportions has runs of salmon and sea trout. Skelgill, despite sniffing the air like a wolf that detects quarry on the wind, resists the temptation of an inspection, the shallow stream here being the realm of minnow and bullhead and stone loach – barely bait-sized fish, though his stock in trade as a lad.

On such a note a small boy who is evidently waiting for the school bus saves him from chapping the door of each of the row of farm labourers' cottages. Clearly well briefed in the matter of stranger danger, he backs away from Skelgill's car, but provides him with the necessary information; the Carlops residence is the furthest in the terrace.

An abundance of semi-native flora throng the modest walled front garden; stately purple foxgloves, robust comfrey with its drooping clusters of two-tone flowers, and contrasting yellow dotted loosestrife. There is the impression of a gardener who is both relaxed, yet knows what he or she is doing. There is a front door, but it being the end house Skelgill takes the opportunity to slip around to the back – in any event the rear is surely the regular thoroughfare.

A scene of more obviously organised horticulture greets him. Apart from a square of paving slabs with a timber table and two seats for leisure purposes, the remainder of the long, narrow garden has the look of a well-managed allotment: raised beds of finely tilled loam and rows of sprouting onion sets; deep furrows concealing seed potatoes; stands of canes ready to accommodate ambitious runner beans. Further down there are blossom-covered apple trees clustered around a new looking shed.

Skelgill is conscious of a presence at the kitchen window – at the sink; he heard the clink of crockery as he rounded the corner and there lingers on the air a hint of fried bacon. He is about to rap on the door when a sudden commotion has him spinning on his heel.

His first fleeting apprehension is of an armed assault – two figures, one standing with a gun raised, and the other lurching from the hut. This impression is quickly replaced by a more realistic assessment: that of a scarecrow pointing a broom handle skywards, and an elderly man in a green boiler suit and work boots, a Dutch hoe under his right arm, who staggers to a halt but remains bent double. Frantically he rubs at his crown with his free hand, all the time working his way through the alphabet of expletives. Reaching the letter 'g' he runs out of steam, and somewhat painfully straightens up to his full height, inspecting his palm for traces of blood. Skelgill, approaching, his expression a mixture of concern and poorly concealed amusement, half-heartedly waves his warrant card.

'Mr Carlops – DI Skelgill, Cumbria Police. Are thee alreet, sir?'

Skelgill has instinctively lapsed into his Buttermere brogue.

'Where's t' ambulance when thou needs it?'

Skelgill, raising himself on tiptoes – for the man is well over six feet, maybe six-four – surveys the damage.

'Happen there'll be a bit of a bruise, that's all.'

'I should've kept yon arl shed. T'were much bigger.' He indicates to a compost heap, beside which there is a pile of ashes; presumably the cremated remains of the late lamented hut.

Skelgill casts about the garden admiringly.

'Looks like you've got this place well sorted.'

His observation carries an implied knowledge of Jack Carlops not having been here all that long; the man seems to get this.

'Aye, well – oor Doris's Fred – he'd let it go – but he were a gardener in his time – I just had to whip it back into shape.'

As the man casts his own reflective eye across his handiwork, Skelgill steals a glance at him. A gaunt weathered figure, maybe a little hunched and not moving with complete ease, as though he suffers a bad back; but he does not look like a candidate for retirement, early or otherwise. His brown eyes are bright, set astride a hooked nose beneath curved brows; a weak chin and small mouth; a seemingly intact head of grey hair but cropped very short, matching what might be a week's silvery facial growth; features that combine to give him an alert hawkish countenance. He is probably Skelgill's epitome of a keeper.

He is wondering about his next line when a harsh cry comes from the cottage.

'Jack!'

Skelgill turns to see a woman – he would judge considerably older than Jack Carlops – standing in the open doorway. The man leans his hoe against a water butt and steps past Skelgill.

'Howay up, have a mash.'

Skelgill begins to follow. He does not try to keep pace; instead he reflects on events. What should he read into Jack Carlops not immediately inquiring as to his business? The man seems to know he wants to talk with him; possibly so does his sister. Indeed, neither of them appears particularly surprised by his presence – but neither do they seem put out. It is as though they know something is afoot and are unquestioningly accepting of a degree of omniscience on behalf of the police.

Jack Carlops enters the kitchen without removing his boots; it frees Skelgill from uncertainty.

'Oor Doris.'

Skelgill nods at the introduction and gives his name and title. The woman, like her brother, is of above average height – and (in accordance with his first impression) he would guess ten years older, seventy-five, maybe. She seems in good fettle and moves easily, and – long grey hair aside – is facially something of a double for her younger sibling. However, the familial looks do not extend to mannerisms – she is edgy, and jerky in her movements – birdlike, yes, but more fowl than hawk. She is dressed in an apron-type overall that covers most of her outfit, and looks like she intends to be busy about the place. Skelgill wonders if he detects some anxiety, or whether he is simply looking too hard – best to leave it to his intuition to decide whether these are people behaving normally, or people *trying* to behave normally. He accepts the chair pointed out to him at a small kitchen table at which two mugs of tea have been placed on a calico cloth and where Jack Carlops is already settled.

Skelgill feels there is a danger of his taking advantage of their hospitality; a semblance of guilt gets the better of him and he moves swiftly to the point.

'Have you heard about Lawrence Melling – at Shuteham Hall?'

There is a moment's hesitation as the pair exchange glances. Jack Carlops answers.

'Nay – what's that about, then?'

Skelgill, by ladling sugar into his tea, is trying not to make too much of a drama of the announcement. Now he looks up, not at Jack Carlops but at Doris, standing by the sink.

'Monday night – early hours of Tuesday – he died in an accident out on the moor.'

The woman stares as if this statement cannot be true – but not at Skelgill; instead she seems to regard her brother as the sole arbiter of its veracity. Skelgill turns back to the man; he is glaring disbelievingly.

'An accident? What kind of accident?'

Skelgill is interested that Jack Carlops questions the news as though it were an improbable event. He seems calm enough – though Skelgill senses that his sister is itching to speak; she shifts on her feet and begins to move items pointlessly about the drainer.

'He stepped in a mantrap and his gun went off. He bled to death from a leg wound.'

Jack Carlops' frown deepens.

'A mantrap, you say?'

Skelgill nods earnestly.

'Do you recall – it's usually hung just inside the main door of the castle?'

Now the man seems a little outraged.

'What's that doing ower ont' moor?'

Skelgill hesitates long enough to make the moment potentially uncomfortable – but, just as he begins to yield the high ground, to relent and make a face of honest helplessness, Doris suddenly blurts out what has been on the tip of her tongue.

'We were watching *T' Birds*.'

Not surprisingly, his mind conjuring an image of the hen harriers, Skelgill raises an eyebrow.

'Pardon, madam?'

But Jack Carlops intervenes.

'She means t' film – Alfred Hitchcock – ont' telly. We watched it after Newsnight and t' weather forecast were finished.'

A shade disoriented, Skelgill finds himself responding conversationally.

'I didn't realise it were on.'

'It's a new series. Late night horror and suspense. Canna be doing wi' yon detective mysteries.'

'Right.'

Skelgill raises both hands off the table – it is a tacit acknowledgement that they are providing him with an alibi, unasked for – but – yes, that he probably would have posed the question in due course. Shrewd country folk such as this are not the kind of company to patronise.

'Actually – what I wanted to ask – can you tell me anything about Lawrence Melling?'

He detects an easing in the body language of the woman. But now, perhaps for the first time, her brother appears discomfited.

'What kind of thing?'

Skelgill looks like he might be short of suggestions.

'Did you meet him?'

'Never set eyes on him.'

He glances apprehensively at his sister, and it prompts a response. She steps towards Skelgill brandishing a wooden spoon.

'Oor Jack – he knew when he weren't wanted. Those Bullingdons – couldn't look him in the eye – after all them years of service. Then they couldn't get him out fast enough.'

Skelgill is uncertain if she is slating her brother's former employers or blowing her own trumpet for providing a roof over his head, for she waves the wooden spoon in a proprietorial manner. Or is it just a smokescreen? For his part, Jack Carlops looks rather like he wishes she would hold her tongue. He makes a weak effort at regaining the initiative.

'Happen they wanted to bring in some modern methods.'

Skelgill decides he ought to be more direct.

'Word is he was known as the Terminator.'

The man regards him rather shiftily.

'There's plenty of folk as would say that about any keeper.'

Skelgill grins.

'Some might say it's a badge of honour, eh?'

'Aye, prince among thieves.'

Skelgill sits back in his seat and relaxes his arms; the little exchange seems to have defused the tension.

'Marra of mine, Eric Hepplethwaite – keeper at Todd Hall beside Bassenthwaite?' Skelgill pauses to allow for recognition.

'Oh, aye? I ken Eric.'

'He reckons Lawrence Melling were a bit of a ladies' man – ran into a spot of trouble at his last place, up in the Borders.'

Jack Carlops lifts a hand to the swelling on his crown and presses it tentatively. It is developing into a decent sized egg and Skelgill has to admit that it probably merited the greater part of the colourful outburst.

'Aye – there were some crack about that. That he were of law unto hissen wi' t' birds.' The man makes a wry face at the double entendre.

'Who would know?'

Jack Carlops grimaces.

'Who starts a rumour? It wouldn't be a rumour if you kent that. Besides – can you mind next morn a quarter of what's been said int' pub of a night?'

Skelgill nods philosophically. The man, too, remains taciturn. The silence provides another opportunity for the sister to stick her oar in.

'Jack – thou told me it were that Rapture thingamajig.'

Whatever this means, it strikes Skelgill that she is following the same line, protective of her brother. Jack Carlops does not respond, and Skelgill is obliged to reprise the question.

'Rapture?'

The man waves a hand as though he does not know how to explain – or perhaps even that he has doubts over the validity of the statement.

'They say it's some online animal rights faction – guerrilla, like – hackers and whatnot.'

Skelgill regards him quizzically.

'I've not heard of them.'

'They target estates where birds of prey have been disappearing – raptors – reckon that's the reason for their name, aye?' (Skelgill shrugs. Raptor – Rapture – he supposes so.) 'The regular sabs plant hidden cameras to catch keepers using pole traps and suchlike – this lot, they hack your phones and your emails. Get some dirt on you.'

At first hearing this sounds innocuous – but it quickly dawns on Skelgill that, as Professor Jim Hartley is fond of saying, there are more ways than one to skin a cat. Get hold of someone's private communications and you can do a lot of damage. To be privy to a peccadillo is as powerful as proof of poisoning by paraquat. Skelgill suddenly feels an irrational compulsion to get out of the cramped kitchen and the claustrophobia of the loitering sister. Any other questions that he might have – as yet only partially formed – can wait for another time.

He knocks back his drink with an air of finality and rises. He suspects he reads some relief in the expression of Jack Carlops; but sister Doris seems more uneasy at his brusque departure. He makes his excuses and backs out of the kitchen, closing the door behind him.

He eschews his car and walks as gravity takes him. He joins the lane and turns downhill towards Uldale. The bordering pastures are wire fenced, bolstered by patchy hedges of shrubs inedible to sheep: blackthorn, dog rose and gorse, the latter mightily abloom – indeed a copious hatch of coal black St Mark's flies, drunk on its coconut nectar swirls in ungainly aerial courtship; the stretch is like one long invertebrate pick-up joint, and Skelgill absently spits out several unfortunate specimens as he moves through. That these are the *Bibio* – the hawthorn fly – much prized and imitated by the trout fisherman does not seem to distract him, when ordinarily the combination of a hatch, a nearby trout stream, and his rod in the car would have him twitching like an ornithologist on the trail of an eastern kingbird; it is a sign of his detachment from consciousness. Indeed, before he knows it he is leaning over Stanthwaite bridge, gazing down into what meagre water winds through the Ellen, here just a stride wide, crowded by thirsty alders rooted in its shingle. He comes around without any great sense of revelation; if anything there is an anti-climax that is echoed in the cascading song of a willow warbler, a descending scale that in the birdsong game of snakes and ladders lands on a snake time and again.

When he gets back to his car his phone is ringing – it is DS Jones's ringtone and the display tells she has tried several times, as have others.

'I was about to call you.'

'Morning, Guv –' She pauses, perhaps optimistically, and then continues. 'It's just that I have some news on Cian Fogarty and Ciara Ahearne.'

'Aye?'

'They were definitely on Mull – as we thought, they hitched across to the island. The local police tracked down the two guys that gave them a lift. But they left last night – apparently they were talking about driving cross-country to see some Slavonian grebes south of Loch Ness. So they may have done that overnight – or they might be travelling now. We've had no reports of their car since, but the Oban police can't find it in the town.'

Skelgill ponders this information.

'It's a heck of a cover story.'

DS Jones hears the sarcasm in his voice.

'I know, Guv.' She takes on his ironic tone. 'Although I suppose we might think otherwise if they don't come back tonight.'

Skelgill makes an indistinct murmur of agreement – but before he can comment more pointedly DS Jones moves to the next pressing item on her agenda.

'Also, some information from Forensics. They found Lawrence Melling's fingerprints on the shotgun and his bloody handprints on the trap – but no one else's prints on either item.' There is something in her voice that makes Skelgill think she is about to revisit the idea that Lawrence Melling shot himself – but, after a pause, she corrects the impression. 'From analysis of the trousers the lab has concluded that there were two successive bleeds. Probably only a few minutes apart – but blood begins to coagulate almost immediately.' She pauses briefly. 'It supports the theory that Lawrence Melling tried to prise open the trap – hence the blood on his hands – and then the shot was fired.'

Skelgill is nodding grimly. It is as he has been picturing since Helen Back's instructive lesson.

'Suggests gloves were worn.'

They both know that gloves have extra significance when it is not the weather for them.

DS Jones continues.

'The lab are running more detailed tests – for alien DNA – but that's going to take longer.'

'Don't hold your breath.'

It is a little harsh of Skelgill. But DS Jones does not take it personally.

'Nothing more on Carol Stanislav, Guv – or the jewellery, come to that. You'd think we'd have had something by now.'

Skelgill inhales audibly – as if he disagrees.

'Happen nothing *is* something.'

Despite the cryptic phrase his tone is grave, and DS Jones seems reluctant to probe; such caprice can make him an uncomfortable person with whom to have a discussion. But she knows he would not say it without reason. She soldiers on.

'Guv – I've been trying to find out what I can about Lawrence Melling – prior to his arrival at Shuteham Hall. I came across an interesting article online, cached from the Selkirk

Chronicle. It's just ... here ... hold on a second – I bookmarked the page.'

While she locates the website Skelgill puts his phone on hands-free and starts the car and pulls away. Now she finds it.

'Okay. So – it's from last December. I'll read it verbatim. "Local Selkirk man Kenneth Scott, 47, has been recruited to the prestigious position of head keeper on the Borders estate of the Duke of Hawickshire. The employment of Mr Scott ends a period during which the estate was without a head keeper, following the resignation in September of Mr Lawrence Melling. Chronicle readers may recall that in June Mr Melling was tried at Jedburgh Sheriff Court on a charge of the wanton destruction of a golden eagles' nest, the only breeding pair in the Borders. Mr Melling was acquitted on the grounds of insufficient evidence. When approached for a quote, the Duke of Hawickshire declined to respond in person, although the press release issued by his estate office announcing the new appointment stated that Mr Scott comes with an excellent reputation for conservation and resource management, in an industry that is an important contributor to the Borders economy." That's it, Guv. What do you think?'

Skelgill finds there are moments in every case when serendipity trips him up, leaving him knowing he has stumbled upon something, but often still too disoriented from the mental somersault to understand exactly what.

'Guv? Can you hear me okay?'

DS Jones must just be wondering if she has been reciting the article to a dead line – when Skelgill abruptly cuts in.

'Can you look up an organisation called Rapture.'

She hesitates.

'Rapture – as in ecstasy? Well – I mean, you know – the emotion?'

Skelgill gives a half laugh.

'Probably not – I reckon it's meant to be a play on words. From *raptor* – as in bird of prey.'

'Oh – okay, that should help – will I do it now?'

'Nay – hold on – wait till we're through – do it properly. Jack Carlops just mentioned it to me. It's supposed to be cyber vigilantes – hackers that target gamekeepers and the like – probably all field sports – maybe even livestock farmers.' He scoffs derisively. 'Anglers, for all I know.'

To DS Jones he must sound as though he harbours doubts – yet there is an undertone of urgency.

'Okay. Is there something else?'

'Come again?'

'I just wondered, Guv.'

Skelgill seems distracted – it must seem to his colleague that he is listening to another conversation at the same time – which, in a sense, he is.

'What's Leyton up to?'

'He's at Shuteham Hall – overseeing the search. Obviously we've got limited time and resources and he's making sure they prioritise what they look at.'

'Right. What else?'

It might sound odd that he is now asking the same question as she has just posed – yet it seems he has detected something. And he is right, but DS Jones is a little reticent.

'Oh – just that the Chief was looking to get hold of you.'

'Aye?'

'It's nothing new, as such.' She realises there is no point in procrastination. 'Apparently Neil Vholes has complained to the regional director of the RSPB – and he's got the ear of the Chief. But I imagine she's just paying lip service in wanting to speak to you.'

'Jones – she doesn't know the meaning of the expression.'

DS Jones is forced to agree.

'What will you do?'

'These things are best snuffed out at source.'

'The Vholes?'

'Aye.' He forces a laugh. 'Kill two birds with one stone, eh?'

234

13. CALDBECK

Wednesday, late morning

Cumberland born and bred, Skelgill had found himself humming the old county's unofficial anthem, *"D'ye ken John Peel"* as he passed through the village of Caldbeck, birthplace and burial site of the infamous huntsman; there would be no doubt which side of the fence he would be found, with his hounds and his horn in the morning. But Skelgill was soon distracted from the ditty as the road crossed the eponymous river – Cald Beck, that is, a vigorous brook that eventually wrestles its way into the Eden at Carlisle. To be an angler moving around England's most watery county is not a prescription for concentration; unless actually fishing, when Skelgill can stare for hours at a float.

Caldbeck Agricultural College sits amidst a once landed estate a couple of miles from the village. Though modern buildings have been added, the nerve centre is still housed in the original Georgian mansion. Skelgill now broods in the grand entrance hallway, following a rather unsatisfactory encounter with a snooty receptionist, a middle-aged woman in a tweed suit who, despite being seated had contrived to look down her nose at him, perhaps for the lack of letters after his name. And maybe he cut off his own nose to spite his face, but her reluctance to smile and instead to regard him with suspicion verging on disdain, had raised his hackles – and so he had been rather abrupt in his request (more of a demand) to see Neil and Christine Vholes, in no particular order. Becoming increasingly obdurate the starched gatekeeper had responded with, "One cannot just walk in off the street and expect to interrupt senior members of the college". Skelgill's retort was a belligerent, "I'll wait", and he had stomped across to occupy the visitors' sitting area.

Now, he faces the woman, so that she cannot overlook his presence – and also so that he might see anyone who may pass by. He knows the Vholes are here because he has located their distinctive Volvo in the staff car park. He suspects that the receptionist – who uses a headset for telephone communications, and is adept in lowering her voice so as to become almost inaudible – reaches one or both of them, for she glances furtively at him whilst speaking. But she makes no effort to convey any news of such to Skelgill. He forms the distinct impression that even if the Vholes are free, the woman is making him pay. So be it.

In the absence of any decent magazines (there is often a Trout & Salmon in these sort of waiting areas) and not being a man that looks at his phone other than for practical purposes, Skelgill casts about for mental stimulation. There is an array of freestanding display boards, such as would be used at a conference or exhibition to promote the college, with photographic images representing the range of courses – the likes of Animal Management, Forestry and Horticulture. It seems these days it is part of a greater conglomeration of establishments scattered around the north of England, each of which offers regional specialities. For example, he learns that in Yorkshire there is the National Beef Training Centre; and there is the opportunity for practical study at four twinned colleges in Eastern Europe. But it is a qualification unique to Caldbeck that catches his eye: Gamekeeping.

Skelgill is confounded. A diploma in gamekeeping? It is like when he jokes in the pub that he has a degree in beer tasting. To the best of his knowledge being a keeper is something handed down from father to son, an arcane craft painstakingly assimilated and laboriously honed; from dawn until dusk and beyond, long hours tramping the woods and fells at the coattails of the gnarled elder. How would you learn in a lecture theatre to recognise the smell of a fox or the bark of a roe deer or where to find a crow's nest?

Rather intrigued by this conundrum, he reaches for one of the bound prospectuses laid in a neat fan on the coffee table before him. The design style corresponds to that of the display boards. Squinting rather uneasily he finds his way to the relevant section. It informs him that the college's Cumbrian farms comprise over four thousand acres, providing ample training opportunities; there is a gunroom and a game larder and student gundog kennels, along with a hatching and rearing programme; a driven grouse moor and a deer management forest. The college boasts "unrivalled careers guidance", with its comprehensive UK database of game management estates, and longstanding often-personal contacts with estate managers and head keepers that enable bespoke opportunities to be identified for internships, apprenticeships, and temporary and full-time employment.

Getting his head round the polysyllables, Skelgill begins to feel what he must admit is a slight pang of – well, if not discontent, then certainly regret. Twenty years ago something like this with an angling slant could have been right up his street. But he reminds himself of his regular reasoning when this notion crops up – that any vocation that involved fishing would surely have turned out to be a busman's holiday (or, rather, some peculiar inverse form of such). He is nodding sagely to himself when a sharp voice penetrates his thoughts.

'Yes? Yes?'

Is someone calling a dog? Skelgill looks up. It is the receptionist.

'Dr Vholes will see you now.'

The woman is indicating with a pen, officiously, as if it were a sergeant major's baton.

'Left at the top of the main staircase and it is the first office on the right.'

Rising, Skelgill thinks about keeping a copy of the prospectus – but in the event he replaces it; empty-handed he cannot fling anything at the woman.

The instructions are plain enough and via a traditional broad staircase with curving bannisters and thence through contemporary reinforced glass fire doors Skelgill reaches an imposing panelled door in polished oak with a brass nameplate that simply states, "Dr Vholes".

He knocks. After a couple of seconds there is no answer. Should he knock again more forcefully or simply enter? Thus in two minds, he is caught on his heels when the door opens and before him stands a beaming Christine Vholes.

It must be the first time he has seen her smile; no longer the default stern countenance – and the transformation is amplified by other details: that her hair is swept rather stylishly beneath and around a navy blue Alice band; that she wears a moderate amount of make up; that she is dressed in a rather Prime Ministerial tailored navy suit worn over a relatively low cut white blouse, in the 'v' of which nestles a silver bird-shaped pendant, and there are complementary earrings. Even her pale eyes – hitherto cold and suspicious – appear to be welcoming. It dawns upon him that she is actually a handsome woman.

Skelgill evidently does not hide his bewilderment – not least that she has obviously got up from behind her desk to cross the carpeted floor of what is a sizeable office overlooking the grounds to admit him. But it seems she reads an alternative misapprehension into his surprised expression.

'Ah, yes – it is *I* that am Dr Vholes – Neil is a mere Master of Science – he was rather too impatient to labour through a Ph.D. – though he insists he has not yet abandoned the idea.'

Skelgill realises that, yes – he did assume he was entering the office of Neil Vholes, and that this is not the sister acting in some quasi-secretarial role; it is her domain. This spacious, bright and airy space is hers and hers alone, and seems to be a mark of considerable seniority. With a sweep of an arm she indicates towards a fireplace where a pair of slipper chairs sit either side of a coffee table, upon which a gleaming china tea service is set out, along with a full plate of expensive-looking chocolate biscuits. This must be for his benefit.

'Make yourself comfortable, Inspector. A little early for elevenses – but let us throw caution to the wind. I shall be mother.'

Skelgill is conscious that he has not yet spoken, other than perhaps a muttered greeting. Having girded his loins for a duel with the Vholes twins at their most antagonistic, this is not what he expected. Still playing catch up, he finds the woman continues to make the running.

'Sorry to keep you waiting, Inspector – I believe Neil is lecturing wall-to-wall this morning – and I was taking part in a videoconference. I am a non-executive director of the Chartered Institute of Human Resources Management – we hold every other board meeting by virtual means – doing our bit to save the planet, you know?'

Skelgill nods a little blankly, accepting in turn the tea she has poured and then a biscuit, before adding his own milk and sugar – he goes easy on the sugar, sensing there is a lack of decorum in more than two teaspoonfuls. He feels he ought to make some comment to show that he is paying attention.

'You're on the personnel management side of things then, Dr Vholes?'

She leans back in her chair and rather reflectively glances up at a traditional oil landscape hung above the mantelpiece. It is a somewhat clichéd Scottish highland scene, not particularly expert, a too-gold eagle soaring out from its eyrie set upon jagged cliffs against a lowering sky. If a bird can look determined, this one does; perhaps she identifies with it.

'Yes – one would assume, given my interest in ornithology, that I am – like Neil – a biologist.' She chuckles, introspectively. 'But one might say from a professional perspective it is human behaviour that has always fascinated me. As Head of HR here at Caldbeck, my remit covers both staff and students, across all of our sites and facilities in the UK and beyond. From conditions of employment and careers, to welfare and counselling, animal husbandry and bio-security policies. One never really knows what might turn up next – we even have contingency plans should some alien disease leap from animals to people, heaven forbid.'

Skelgill looks momentarily alarmed – but he contrives to take her final point as a link to the purpose of his visit.

'I wanted to reassure you that our work on the moor will be completed this morning – under the supervision of an officer from Natural England. And should we need to return for any reason we'll adopt the same procedure – with screens and suchlike.'

Christine Vholes appears flattered.

'Inspector, it was not necessary for you to come in person – besides, we were encouraged when we saw that the hen harriers were behaving perfectly normally last night.' She lifts her cup and saucer but pauses the cup in mid air, level with her chin. She seems to be deciding whether or not to relate some confidence. 'I am afraid Neil can be rather hot-headed at times – but, you see, the persecution of wild animals is a highly emotive matter.'

Now she takes a sip and raises her pencilled eyebrows in what might be a brief sign of apology – for her brother's complaint to the Chief and perhaps her understanding that Skelgill has been despatched to make a grovelling apology.

'Moreover we received your message from young Claire and Melanie this morning.'

Skelgill seems to feel obliged to particularise.

'I reckoned they'd see you before our folk got on site – you start your early shift at seven, I think you said?'

She nods, but now a little distractedly.

'You were hoping, of course to speak with Cian and Ciara about the unfortunate incident.'

Skelgill makes a face of resignation. He drinks some tea, his long fingers struggling with the handle of the delicate china cup. The Vholes, of course, know that he was there – but not that he was hiding in the hedge. They will assume that he has obtained the same explanation as they did from the stand-in nightshift girls about the absence of the Irish couple. He responds accordingly.

'They seem to be on a birdwatching jaunt in Scotland. We've not managed to make contact with them. Apparently they gave the impression they're coming back today.'

Christine Vholes regards him rather in the manner of a medical practitioner who is intrigued that her patient is unaware of their ailment.

'Oh – I can give you an update on that, Inspector – I took a call from them whilst I was on videoconference.'

Skelgill looks hopeful – but for a moment the woman's expression seems to darken.

'They expect to arrive back – but not until the early hours of the morning.'

Skelgill leans forward, resting his forearms on his thighs.

'Do you know where they rang from?'

She shakes her head.

'It came through the switchboard – there was considerable background noise – traffic – and the call was necessarily brief – in fact it was cut off and I suspect they ran out of change. It must have taken them a while to convince Margery at reception to put the call through – since she knew I was engaged in the board meeting.'

Skelgill mentally notes that he will not be asking 'Margery' about the call.

Meanwhile Christine Vholes makes a sound of disapproval.

'We shall need to organise replacements.'

Skelgill leans back and folds his arms. He tries to appear sympathetic to her plight.

'Happen these things can't be predicted – when a rare bird's going to fly in. And they've kept in touch, in a fashion.'

'Well – it isn't exactly that.'

Now she looks at Skelgill as though there is something more distasteful that she would rather not tell him but considers it her duty to do so. However, she waits for him to offer a prompt.

'No?'

'No, Inspector. There has been considerable erratic and unreliable behaviour lately. And some rather peculiar mood swings. I am not sure they are altogether stable.' She regards him conspiratorially. 'I strongly suspect they are taking drugs. More than once we have arrived at the hide in the morning to find them dead to the world in that awful car of theirs.'

Skelgill inhales like a smoker trying to get the last from a depleted reefer; an act, it seems, intended to convey that he shares her disapproval but that his in-tray already creaks under the weight of his worries. He is, however, reminded of the spicy body odour of Ciara Ahearne; undoubtedly she exuded the cloying reek of marijuana. He opts to mollify Christine Vholes as best he can.

'I suppose beggars can't be choosers – there's not so many folk prepared to camp out and watch a birds' nest for no pay.' (She looks dissatisfied; he continues.) 'And I should think the risk to the harriers is quite low at the moment – given the recent attention – access to the site's taped off – plus I would imagine most folk would know you've got a camera trained on the nest.'

This latter remark is perhaps a suggestion that the prime menace – the gamekeeper – is no longer part of the equation, and that any residual threat from Shuteham Hall is surely diminished. But she remains unconvinced.

'One would rather not count one's chickens. At this critical stage one can never be too vigilant.' But now she smiles gracefully. 'Maybe if you were on watch, Inspector? Perhaps we could tempt you away – to put down the fishing rod? We have a vacancy tonight.'

Skelgill simpers unconvincingly. He can feel his phone vibrating in his jacket pocket – it has been doing so sporadically during the meeting – but now he pulls it out to demonstrate that someone is trying to reach him. He frowns when he sees the caller display, and delivers an expression of apology to Christine Vholes.

'I'm going to have to return this call.' The implication is that he means in private, since he has not immediately answered. 'Keep the powers-that-be happy.'

The woman looks rather self-satisfied – perhaps that this might be Skelgill having to report back in relation to her brother's complaint. But she does not make any attempt to rub it in. She merely rises as Skelgill does so.

'Thanks for the refreshments, madam.'

'You are welcome.' She begins to chaperone him to the door. 'And how is your own conservation project progressing – the rare vendace, if I recall correctly?'

Skelgill's instinct is of mistrust – but then why wouldn't she approve of the principle? He makes an exclamation of resignation and holds up his handset – the illuminated display shows it is ringing again.

'That's on hold at the moment, as you can imagine.'

'Perhaps we will see you at the weekend?'

'Aye – if I'm lucky. But I couldn't tell you which weekend.'

'Well – drop into the hide if you see our car. Tea is always available.'

*

'Sorry to pester you, Guv.'

'Nay – I was in with Christine Vholes – I was looking for an excuse to get out.'

Skelgill, from his stationary position, squints through the windscreen at the grand frontage of Caldbeck College; he is half wondering which are the windows of the Head of HR's office.

'Oh, okay. How did it go?'

This is potentially a clever question from DS Jones, since Skelgill has not really provided an indication of his motive for the visit; she knows it would not be like him meekly to apologise, nor aimlessly go through the motions without fresh intelligence. The difficulty, however, is that while in her experience Skelgill has a knack of walking the tightrope that wobbles between futility and salience, he doesn't always appreciate it himself – thus to expect onward communication can be a forlorn hope. She is right. He feels unnerved without understanding why.

'Ask me later. When I know.'

'Sure.'

But now he surprises her.

'She's heard from the Irish pair. They've phoned her from the roadside.'

'Really?'

'They're supposed to be arriving back tonight – early hours.'

'So – tomorrow, morning – for practical purposes?'

'Aye.'

'Oh well, that's good.' DS Jones seems to consider this for a moment, before she continues. 'Guv, about Rapture. There's no website – but I've found what might be them on Twitter. I'll send you a screenshot of the profile.'

'What about in relation to Lawrence Melling?'

'I can't locate anything. To be honest, there's no indication of who's behind Rapture, or even what it's about – perhaps other than their logo – you'll see what I mean. If it's what you were told, they don't appear to be seeking publicity – instead they're operating under the radar. They might just be using Twitter for recruitment. If you're happy, I could try to sign up from my personal account?'

'But there's photos of you on that, aye?'

'Yes.'

Skelgill makes a grumbling noise.

'Or how about if I contact one of my old university friends? There's a girl I shared with in London who is now working for a biotech company – she'd have a convincing profile.'

But Skelgill finds himself disinclined to go along with this. To embroil a random member of the public even very peripherally in a murder investigation is fraught with risk; and one close encounter with the Chief's stinging tentacles in a day is sufficient. But perhaps DS Jones, too, realises it is unwise.

'I guess I could set up a fake profile – the only problem might be that they were suspicious that I have no history.'

Skelgill does not seem very enthusiastic.

'Look – you can give that a go. But gamekeepers seem to know about Rapture. Try that angle. Otherwise we might need to call in the spooks.'

'Sure.' She seems a little crestfallen. 'What will you do, Guv?'

Skelgill sighs somewhat wearily.

'Reckon I'll head over to see how Leyton's getting on. While we've got a search in progress it's a good excuse to poke about a bit.'

'Okay – I'll hang up and text you this screenshot, Guv.'

'Aye.'

Skelgill makes as though he is about to set off, but within a few seconds the message arrives. He opens the image – and instantly his expression hardens. He stares at the screen of the phone in its holder on the dashboard. Now he shakes his head slowly. Of course – it said Rapture – not Raptor! He sits back and gazes ahead, his eyes unfocused. Then he leans across and rather laboriously jabs an instruction into his handset, finishing with the selection of a telephone number. He puts the call on speaker, though does not yet drive off.

'Good morning. West Cumberland Infirmary. How may I help you?'

Skelgill is about to speak when a realisation grips him.

'Er – sorry – wrong number.'

He ends the call with a muttered curse. No surname! Now he types again. The signal is poor, and his request seems painfully slow to execute – but when another telephone number is displayed, he repeats his actions. Eventually a connection is established – and, after about a dozen rings – an answer.

It is a rather breathless voice, a young female.

'Hello?'

'Claire?'

'Er – yes?'

'It's DI Skelgill – I got your number off the Nats website.'

'Oh – er – hi – sorry – you've come up as withheld – and I'm on the ward.' She speaks apprehensively, in hushed tones. 'I've not heard anything – from Ciara, I mean – although I've had my phone switched off most of the morning.'

'What?' Skelgill seems momentarily disoriented. 'No – what it is – that laptop your friend connected to the webcam in the hide – who does it belong to?'

'Er – well, it's Mel's – is there a problem? She's in theatre – observing a caesarean.'

Skelgill ponders for a second.

'It's got a sticker on it – the laptop. It spells the word Rapture – in a fancy script, like a soaring bird of prey. What's that all about?'

'Oh – actually – *I* found that.'

'Found it?'

'Yes – in the hide. I don't know if you've noticed – there's a kind of brochure holder just inside the door, next to the sightings board. There are information leaflets – like for the Over Water SSSI – and other local reserves. There were two or three of those stickers in one of the slots.'

'Is this recently?'

'Maybe a month ago?'

'Any idea who put them there?'

'No, sorry. Unseen people randomly drop off leaflets. A couple of weeks ago a whole stack appeared advertising a new garden centre, which I thought was a bit cheeky.'

'And what about this Rapture – what is it?'

Now she sounds a little bemused.

'Actually – I've no idea. I mean – I just thought – we both did – that it looked quite cool – kind of a slogan if you support birds of prey. Like a dove for peace – or a rainbow for the NHS.' She pauses reflectively. 'To be honest – I don't know if it *is* anything more than that.'

Her inflection almost turns her response into a question, and Skelgill concludes that, however tantalising an avenue this is, he has probably turned off into an unproductive cul-de-sac.

'Aye – happen you're right. Well – sorry to interrupt you at work.'

'I'm getting daggers from the charge nurse – she probably thinks it's a personal call. Can I say that it was a detective?'

'Aye – or put her on, if you like.'

She chuckles.

'She'll probably suspect you're my boyfriend impersonating a police officer.'

'There's plenty of folk think I do that already.'

*

Skelgill, now parked outside the main entrance, the ancient iron-studded oak door of Shuteham Hall, is on the phone again. He is waiting on hold. He sees DS Leyton appear around the corner of the building; he is moving at a much faster pace than is customary, and has an expression of some alarm written across his malleable features. Huffing and puffing he approaches the open driver's window – but, just as he is about to utter, a voice comes on the line over the loudspeaker – and Skelgill holds a finger to his lips to silence his colleague – and he indicates with further gesticulation that he should get in the passenger side and do so quietly.

'Hello? Are you still there?'

The voice is clear and the accent pukka. A male, he sounds like he is perhaps in his mid-forties.

'Sir – yes. This is DI Skelgill from Cumbria police.'

'Yes – I was informed. How may I help? I am rather busy.'

'I won't beat about the bush, sir. I'm investigating the death of a Mr Lawrence Melling. I believe he used to work for you.'

Skelgill now pauses – and exchanges a knowing glance with DS Leyton. He sees that his colleague is perspiring – he wipes his brow. The man responds.

'What happened to him?'

There is no discernible emotion in the voice. No alarm, concern or interest even.

'It was a shooting accident on the grouse moor adjacent to Shuteham Hall. On the face of it he appears to have been alone and was injured by his own gun. He bled to death.'

There ensues a longer pause. The man gives the impression of one thinking through his next move at chess.

'Why are you calling me?'

Though the voice is unwavering there is a distinct elevation in pitch, a semitone of trepidation – as if he neither wants to ask this nor hear the response. Skelgill contrives to make his own voice sound casual.

'It's just routine, sir. Mr Melling seems to have been a bit of a loner. We're trying to piece together any background information that might help to explain what happened.'

'Are you saying he committed suicide, Inspector?'

The voice sounds distinctly suspicious now.

'Would you reckon he'd be the sort to do that, sir?'

The man tuts, annoyed to find the question turned back on him.

'I have no idea about these things.'

Skelgill waits – but plainly the man will be no more forthcoming. Skelgill knows he has limited time.

'I was wondering why he ceased to be in your employment, sir? To leave such a prestigious estate – to leave Scotland – there doesn't seem to be much logic in that.'

Skelgill leaves the question hanging.

'I am afraid I cannot help you there, Inspector. Mr Melling departed of his own accord and with satisfactory references for his work. Now I must bid you good day. Cheerio.'

The call ends without mutual consent.

DS Leyton makes a face of consolation.

'Duke of Hawickshire, Guv?'

'Aye.'

'Cor blimey – he's a tartar. He didn't tell you much.'

'He told me all I needed to know, Leyton.'

DS Leyton looks puzzled – and for a moment as though he could be sidetracked – but his own pressing news returns to the fore.

'Something else you need to know, Guv – we've found blood – and it belongs to Stan!'

Skelgill is clearly caught off guard – but his only response is a curt nod that means DS Leyton should elaborate.

'I got here early doors – met the dog handler at the estate office – stone the crows, if the dog's not gone and found something before the geezer had even started – traces of blood around that chopping block! Daphne Bullingdon – she was there – she was trying to say it would be animal blood, rabbit probably – they use the area for processing game before it's packaged – cut off the heads and feet.' He makes an unintelligible gurgle, indicative of distaste. 'Meantime, the dog's gone after a trail – it led to that incinerator by the chicken sheds.' (Skelgill does not interrupt to correct his sergeant.) 'Round the back, there's a shovel – more blood on that, mixed in with sawdust.'

Skelgill is now scowling grimly.

'How do you know it's Stan's blood?'

'I got one of the forensic officers to drive the swabs straight over to the lab – they'd already got Stan's profile from samples they'd taken from the gatehouse, off've his personal possessions. They put the new swabs through as a priority test and – *bingo* – a match. I just got it phoned through – that's why I came looking for you.'

Skelgill is silent for a moment; then he begins to push open the driver's door.

'Come on.'

He leads the way, striding out at a pace that requires DS Leyton to break into the occasional lurching trot to maintain. They leave the old keep and follow the main driveway towards the estate office. Skelgill can hear and smell the pheasant poults even as they pass the gunroom – but only when they approach the rearing sheds does he relent. More cautiously he rounds the corner as if there might be a wild animal that he does not want to spook; but he is merely absorbing the scene, his eyes are alert, his features strained. He stands off, six feet short. DS Leyton comes up beside him. They might be visitors to a cemetery, respectfully perusing the epitaph on a gravestone they have sought out. After a minute, Skelgill speaks.

'I've seen these things around and about. Farms these days – they have to have them by law – you can't just dig a pit and bury diseased livestock or butchery waste any more. There's even rules about disposal of the ash.'

DS Leyton is nodding, his own expression now alarmed.

'There's different specifications – depending upon what size and volume of carcasses you've got.' Skelgill inclines his head towards the shed. 'These pheasant poults – they're not very big but there's a high attrition rate. This model of incinerator – it would take a sheep or a pig.'

DS Leyton swallows. He looks on a little disbelievingly, but he manages to speak.

'What – whole, Guv?'

Skelgill glances sharply at his colleague – as if his partner's foreboding tone has suddenly registered its meaning.

'You'd dismember it, Leyton.'

There is a further silence. Skelgill is recalling that on Monday night – close to midnight – the machine was still warm; it had been operated earlier in the day. Now he steps forward and checks the heat with an open palm. The metal is cold and he stoops and jerks up the hinged door of the ash pit at the base of the unit. It is empty.

'We need to find out what they do with their ash.'

The corollary of this discussion being thus far unspoken (though no doubt both detectives share a common notion), DS Leyton reads from a panel affixed on the chimney.

'It says max temp 1,100°C, Guv – would there be anything left?'

'There might be a gold tooth.'

DS Leyton exhales heavily and is about to speak when he receives a text notification. He seems relieved at the distraction. He pulls his handset from his jacket pocket. He frowns as he reads the message.

'They've found something in the lake, Guv.'

'What – Over Water?'

'Nah, Guv – the ornamental one in the grounds.'

Automatically Skelgill turns and begins to walk back in the direction of the castle; he knows the quickest way to Troutmere is the tunnel down through the rhododendrons opposite the walled garden. He calls out without looking back.

'Does it say what?'

DS Leyton is once again part-jogging to keep up.

'Just says "items" – that's all.'

Skelgill does not reply, but as they pass the gunroom he cocks his head to one side.

'Anything in there?'

'Not really, Guv – so far the rest of the search has drawn a bit of a blank. I managed to get Lord Bullingdon to agree to let the dog have a quick run through the downstairs of the main house. First off he was objecting, saying he can't have us accusing one of his family just because they've stood in something by accident.'

'Stood in what?'

'Yeah – good point, Guv. But I suppose word's getting about that we're treating this more seriously than if Lawrence Melling had just tripped himself up. It don't take Einstein to put two and two together. And Daphne's seen that we've found traces of blood.'

Skelgill inhales, hesitates.

'Aye, well – I did hint to Miranda Bullingdon that it could be foul play – just to see what her reaction would be.'

DS Leyton does not seem put out that Skelgill has broken their agreed rule; it is what he does best.

'What did she say, Guv?'

'Something along the lines of have you found my jewellery, yet?'

'Cor blimey, she's got some brass neck, ain't she?'

Skelgill is nodding slowly. They are passing the hall again and he returns to DS Leyton's account.

'How did you convince Lord Bullingdon to let you in?'

'I just said there may come a time when we need to search the entire place – but that we might be able to circumvent that – at least if we can give the all-clear to the public areas, the entrances. I figured that if anyone came back with blood on their boots or trousers, that's where there'd be a trace. Plus they leave most of their outdoor gear along by the back door.'

The pair by now are skirting the topiary lawn and heading on the beginning of Long Shoot towards the walled garden.

'But the dog didn't find owt.'

'That's right, Guv. I left the handler to start working his way round the various properties – outbuildings and cottages.'

As they approach the turn off for Garden Cottage – home to housekeeper Karen Williamson – Skelgill is prompted to comment.

'Trouble is, Leyton, they've got a demon cleaner – if she polished fingerprints off the furniture after the jewel theft, what's to stop her mopping up blood from the floor after a murder?'

'Whoa – what's this, Guv?'

It is not Skelgill's devil's advocacy that draws DS Leyton's alarm – but that his superior has plunged off the track into the shrubbery.

'Short cut to the lake. Mind your napper.'

Despite that the ground is dry and that at least some daylight penetrates the rhododendrons, DS Leyton still appears relieved as they emerge just above the shoreline of Troutmere. They are met by the sight of a forensic officer kneeling on the grassy bank of the dam; she appears to be sealing a large clear plastic evidence bag. The young woman glances up at their approach and gets to her feet; she holds a similar bag in each hand. Skelgill recognises her as the assistant who had been with Helen Back on Over Moor yesterday.

'These were trapped against the grating that covers the outfall, sir. Neither item looks like it's been in the water very long.'

'What are they?' It is DS Leyton's inquiry.

'A kind of all-purpose boot. Size eight – so it's most likely a man's.' She raises first one then the other bag. 'And a pair of black Armani boxer shorts – thirty-four inch waist – also probably a man's.'

'That would be – like – a twelve in women's, wouldn't it?'

Skelgill turns a bemused look upon his subordinate, clearly wondering why he is showing off such peculiar knowledge. The girl, however, is nodding.

'They'd hardly be boxers if they were a woman's, Leyton.'

'I don't know, Guv – this girl I used to –' But now DS Leyton realises his digression has quickly run its course. He makes an effort to dig himself out of the predicament. He points simultaneously to the items. 'Those sort of sizes – they could belong to the same geezer.'

Skelgill can at least nod in principle – but he does not look wholly convinced. He turns to stare out over the water, his features grim. The natural inclination of a policeman in these circumstances – knowing that a person is missing – is to order the dragging of the lake; and this is not the first time the thought has occurred to him. But there is the conversation he has just had with DS Leyton beside the incinerator. Why would a boot and a pair of boxers be floating in the lake when there is a far more effective means of disposal? Moreover, a body in a lake – could a boot become detached? Possibly. But boxer shorts? And there is another contradictory reason he can think of. He suddenly turns and without asking he takes the two plastic bags from the officer.

'We'll borrow these.' She looks alarmed. 'Won't open them – don't fret.'

And he marches off, leaving DS Leyton to make their apologies. Skelgill heads back up the overgrown path and crosses Long Shoot onto the short track that leads to Garden Cottage. It is lunchtime, and he is thinking that Karen Williamson may be in. He leads DS Leyton around to the back – and he sees immediately that the woman is in the kitchen. She catches sight of the detectives and lifts a hand in acknowledgement.

Perhaps she has a boiling pan or kettle to attend to, for it takes her a few seconds to reach the back door – and then it is locked, delaying her a moment more as she locates the key. Finally she reveals herself; she is wearing an apron and her hair is loose, and she wipes her hands on her midriff and sweeps back her wayward locks.

'Inspector.'

'You know DS Leyton?'

Skelgill is not sure himself – though she must have set eyes upon his colleague – but he does not delay any longer with formalities.

'I'd like to pick your brains.'

She looks anxious – and glances at the plastic bags that he holds at his side, correctly assuming it is something to do with them.

'Sure – yes – but would you like tea and a roll – I was just doing some – to take up to the office in case anyone was hungry?'

Skelgill senses DS Leyton is looking at him disapprovingly, along the lines that they do not have time for this.

'Aye – why not – I'm parched – and I could eat a horse.'

'Do you want to sit at the bench and I'll bring them out?'

The detectives do as bidden. Skelgill makes a strange sign to his colleague, tapping his temple with a knuckle – as if this is sufficient to justify the diversion when they might be at a critical point in a murder hunt. DS Leyton grins resignedly; however, he secretly has to acknowledge that, working with Skelgill, one rarely goes underfed. They settle, and take in the surroundings – it is another pleasant day, with barely a breeze and just a drift of diffuse cloud here and there, but overwhelmingly powder blue sky. The afternoon sun packs a punch, its warmth amplified in the enclosed rear garden. There is the temptation to relax, to succumb; Skelgill especially is tired; he has not been sleeping soundly. Karen Williamson appears a minute later bearing a tray. There are half a dozen filled rolls and two mugs of tea with milk already added. She seems unsure of what to do, but when Skelgill does not speak she passes out the mugs and side plates and offers round the platter of rolls. Then she slides into the bench opposite the detectives. She still wears the apron and just a vest top – which makes it look like the apron is all she has on. Skelgill again notices the sculpted musculature of her arms, a condition that in a more delicate form seems to continue into her facial characteristics. Under his scrutiny she seems to feel obliged to comment. She looks pointedly at the two bags Skelgill has laid on the end of the picnic table.

'You've found something important?'

For his part, it is for good reason that Skelgill has given her plenty of time. If she had recognised either of the items she might spontaneously have said so – or, perhaps, more importantly, reacted but tried to cover up such. But he has detected neither response.

He swallows, and takes a thirsty gulp of tea.

'Aye.' He holds up his bitten roll. 'Thanks for these, by the way – spot on.'

DS Leyton, eating, makes a noise indicating similar thanks and approval.

'You're welcome – like I said.'

She smiles a little coyly – and again Skelgill senses DS Leyton is watching, more surreptitiously. He reaches and lifts the bag with the boot in it.

'Do you recognise this?'

'It's the sort of boot I've seen the guys wear around the place – the estate workers – not exactly a walking boot – more of a trail shoe – a bit more practical and not so heavy.'

Her reaction is interesting – almost as if she is trying to avoid telling a lie.

'Any idea who it might have belonged to? Obviously, I'm thinking of Stan.'

Karen Williamson hesitates.

'It's a popular make – I really couldn't say, for sure. But – I suppose it's possible.'

'Did you clean for him – at the gatehouse – and what about at Keeper's Cottage?'

She looks sharply at Skelgill, but only briefly, and then shakes her head.

'No – the estate employees all clean for themselves. I'd only do a place if it were to be temporarily occupied by guests or clients.'

Skelgill looks a little disappointed.

'The reason I ask –' He stops mid-sentence and holds up the bag containing the boxer shorts – he is watching her reaction carefully – she seems to look at them with interest, but certainly not recognition. 'I was thinking, you see – if you cleaned you'd probably have a good idea of folk's possessions.'

She nods, understanding his point.

'I do the laundry for the Bullingdons. But no one else.'

'Any suggestions on these?'

She looks closer.

'It's an expensive brand.'

Skelgill again notes the nature of her reply. He lays the bag down.

'Thirty-four inch waist – covers a lot of folks.'

'Rules me out, obviously!'

Both Skelgill and Karen Williamson look at DS Leyton with surprise – and he suddenly colours, realising he has spoken out of turn – and perhaps that it seems he has not been tuned in to Skelgill's casual but thoughtful questioning. However, Skelgill wrong-foots him with his rejoinder.

'In that case you'd better not have a second roll – and we'd better make tracks.'

He downs the last of his tea and rises. He gestures to the remaining food and is seemingly about to thank Karen Williamson when she interjects.

'Where were they – these things?'

Skelgill does not reply immediately, extricating his long legs from the picnic bench.

'In the lake.' He gives a toss of his head to indicate roughly behind him. 'Troutmere. Hard to tell if they'd been flung in or fallen off.'

He does not wait for her reaction, but just gives a vague wave of thanks and turns away, leaving DS Leyton to gather up the polythene evidence bags. He catches up with his superior at the front of Garden Cottage. Skelgill is staring rather broodingly at the bumper sticker on the white Mini.

'Couldn't have been that one you saw, Guv?'

Skelgill responds tersely.

'Leyton, it was yellow.'

Skelgill turns and moves off. He leads his colleague back to the junction with Long Shoot. They swing right and continue, mainly in silence as Bullmire Wood and subdued afternoon birdsong and columns of gnats rise up around them. In due course they reach the intersection. Now Skelgill takes the left-hand option and announces the name of the track, Crow Road. His sergeant responds, melodramatically hunching his broad shoulders and pulling in his head.

'Sounds like something from Alfred Hitchcock, Guv.'

Skelgill does a little double take.

'You're the second person to mention him, today.'

'It was on the telly the other night, Guv – *The Birds*. Too late for me – but the missus stayed up and watched it. She's a bit of a night owl. I reckon I'd be having nightmares if I watched that sort of thing before I went to kip. Worse than cheese.'

Skelgill grins wryly. He regularly eats a cheese sandwich before he turns in; although it is a choice determined as much by availability as preference.

After a few minutes more they approach Keeper's Cottage. The open front porch has police tape strung across its uprights. As Skelgill ducks underneath he speaks out.

'Those boxers, Leyton – pound to a penny they belonged to Melling.'

'What makes you so sure, Guv?'

Skelgill opens the front door and enters and calls over his shoulder.

'Helen Back – she mentioned to me and Jones – Melling was going commando on the night he died.'

Following behind him, his sergeant emits a groan of sorts, but it might be the action of bending beneath the tape. Skelgill does not wait, and quickly finds the bedroom where he begins pulling open the drawers of a chest. At the third he stops and waits for his colleague.

'There you go, Leyton.'

DS Leyton arrives at his shoulder and peers into the drawer.

'Same make, Guv.'

Skelgill is nodding. There must be about a dozen pairs, several identical, and all new-looking and carrying various designer brand names. DS Leyton is prompted to comment further.

'Fancy pants.'

Skelgill does not answer; he closes the drawer with a knee and turns to look around the bedroom. It is neat and tidy but has the feel of temporary occupation – like a room that would be found in a rented holiday cottage, neutral and ready for the visitor to deposit their valise on the bed. DS Leyton is still musing over the underwear.

'So what's a pair of boxers doing in the lake, Guv? Was he up to a spot of skinny dipping?'

Skelgill could formulate a theory – this is one aspect of his ill-gotten gains in the information department that he has not shared with his colleagues; but for the time being he remains ambiguous.

'You might not be all that wide of the mark, Leyton.'

'It takes two to skinny dip, Guv.'

Skelgill is staring at a reproduction painting on the wall at the foot of the double bed. It is a traditional hunting scene, men on foot with a pack of dogs in open fell country; more likely something from the time of Jack Carlops than Lawrence Melling.

'There's word among the keepers hereabouts that Melling was a bit of a playboy.'

'That don't surprise me, Guv – look how he behaved that first time with Lady Bullingdon.'

'Jack Carlops – the old keeper he replaced here – reckons there's some shadowy animal rights group called Rapture. They operate online and get compromising information on their targets.'

'Hah – sounds more like the Russians, Guv – *kompromat*, they call it, don't they?'

Skelgill is nodding pensively.

'Jones is looking into it. According to reports, Melling survived a court action for destroying a golden eagles' nest in the Borders. But he didn't leave his job until months after that. There's a rumour that he made himself unpopular with the Duke of Hawickshire.'

'What – like – to do with the Duchess of Hawickshire?'

'Aye.'

'So that explains your call, Guv?'

'And the Duke clearly didn't want to discuss it.'

DS Leyton places the evidence bags on the chest top and pulls open the drawer again, as though its contents might be a source of inspiration.

'You reckon these cyber sabs were stalking Melling, Guv?'

'If you've found someone's weak spot – why not? And once you've hacked his devices he's got nowhere he can hide.'

But DS Leyton's face becomes creased with doubt. He closes the drawer and turns towards Skelgill.

'Mind you, Guv – it's one thing trolling someone – exposing or blackmailing them – but murdering them? And then there's the practicality – the flamin' trap an' all that.'

Skelgill is nodding.

'Aye, I know, Leyton. The death – the murder, if it were – has all the hallmarks of village justice.'

Skelgill steps past his colleague and leaves the room. He has half an inclination to look around the property – but it does not feel to be his most pressing need.

'Come on – let's go and see if we can find a match for that boot.'

For purposes of expediency, his colleague wearing unsuitable footwear and being unpractised in picking his way through tangled woodland, Skelgill leads them to the locked gate where Crow Road joins the lane to Overthwaite; thence they follow the estate boundary as it curves gently around to West Gate House.

Again there is a festooning of police tape to deter intruders, or accidental encroachment by estate workers; Skelgill heads around to the rear enclosed porch. There is no sign of forensic officers.

'I take it you would have heard by now if the dog had found anything more.'

Skelgill's remark is really a statement of the obvious.

'Reckon so, Guv. They've probably finished for the time being. There's an urgent job up in Carlisle waiting for them.'

Skelgill pushes open the outer door and immediately directs his colleague's attention to the wellingtons.

'I reckon they'll be the same size, Leyton.'

DS Leyton picks up one boot and turns it over.

'Size eight, Guv. Spot on.'

'There's no way Melling was an eight – he'd be a ten or eleven.'

DS Leyton nods. While this is not something he would have noticed, he accepts that Skelgill – with all his mad capers – is an authority when it comes to outdoor footwear. But he does notice the fishing rod.

'Like you said before, Guv – it don't look like Stan fell in while he was fishing.'

Skelgill murmurs agreement, though his features show some concern; but perhaps it is the inappropriately oversized and garish lure that again offends his angler's sense of propriety. He moves on.

'Show us that photo, Leyton – the one of the lass.'

DS Leyton understands and leads the way through into the bedroom. The space is cramped and it is with difficulty that he edges down one side of the bed and reaches to pull open the top drawer of a slim nightstand. From beneath some layers of clothing he extracts the framed photograph.

'Stick it on the top.'

'Come again, Guv?'

'Set it up – like it would be on display.'

The frame has a fold-out fin and DS Leyton places the picture at an angle and reverses his movements to stand beside Skelgill.

'He must have had it there, Leyton – else why's it in the drawer?'

'I suppose so, Guv.' He sounds doubtful. 'Although why would he tuck it away under his t-shirts?'

'You tell me, Leyton.'

Skelgill's rejoinder makes it sound like the answer is blindingly obvious; yet there is something in the nature of it that causes DS Leyton to realise his superior is looking for affirmation. He clears his throat in the manner of a 'man of the world'.

'Well – I suppose – if you had a different lady coming round – it's not exactly going to thrill her to see that sitting there – pretty as the girl is.' He clicks his tongue against the roof of his mouth. 'In fact, that might make it worse.'

Skelgill is nodding.

'Aye, happen it would.'

They remain in silence for a few moments; DS Leyton senses that he should not offer up any theories on this matter – the chances are, whatever Skelgill is thinking, he will be wide of the mark. But he is reminded of a technical point that he knows to be accurate.

'By the way, Guv – that picture was taken in Moldova.'

'Aye?'

'The DC who's been dealing with Immigration and looking into Stan's background – he sent a copy of the digital photo I took. Apparently it's a park in the capital, Chisinau – it's where Stan was from, of course.'

Skelgill seems to react to this – he looks fleetingly pained – indeed as though a jab of discomfort has struck above his brow. But it may be unconnected – perhaps the effects of the heat and the sunshine and that he is probably dehydrated by his normal standards. But he quickly shrugs off the reaction and he turns to leave the room.

'Come on – let's show these exhibits to the Bullingdons before Forensics get their knickers in a twist.'

'In this case, their boxers, Guv.'

While DS Leyton might have expected his superior to join in the small joke, he emerges from the bedroom to find him standing facing the exit holding up a warning hand.

'Leyton, did you leave the door open?'

Skelgill's voice is lowered. DS Leyton steps alongside to see that the external door of the porch is ajar by about a foot.

'I closed it, Guv – I noticed there's a broken coat hook on the back of it.'

Skelgill moves off – but quickly rather than cautiously, as if he senses a pursuit is imminent, as opposed to a threat. His ears pricked he skirts around the back of the cottage and stops at the corner. Now he waves on DS Leyton like they are playing a game of cops and robbers, and he makes sudden dash towards the log store that formerly housed the quad bike.

As he rounds the property in his superior's wake, DS Leyton sees Skelgill pull up short – and also that there is a figure standing within the open-sided structure, seemingly examining the underside of the corrugated iron roof. It is Julian Bullingdon.

Confronted, but not challenged verbally, he acts as if it is the most natural thing that the two detectives should materialise and be interested in whatever he is up to.

'Poplar hawk.'

For a moment they share a degree of puzzlement – is he showing them a bird? Skelgill out of curiosity ducks beneath the shelter and sees that he has a compact torch trained upon a sizeable grey-and-blood-red moth, resting in the eaves. Julian Bullingdon continues as though he was interrupted mid-lecture.

'Probably our most widespread hawk moth. We have quite a few white poplars on the estate – especially in the new plantation alongside Troutmere – but there are mature specimens scattered throughout the woods. The adults are just hatching now. It is a particularly fascinating species in that it commonly produces halved gynandromorphs, although I have never yet found one myself.'

He looks at the detectives as if in expectation of a commensurate scientific contribution. But Skelgill responds with a more pragmatic question.

'What made you look here?'

Skelgill backs out of the shed and the young man follows him.

'The estate is generally very dark at night.' He directs a hand towards the cottage. 'So, the vicinity of light sources – the inhabited properties – are good places to hunt for Lepidoptera that have rested up for the day. I'm always hopeful of a new species.'

Skelgill is beginning to look impatient. Accordingly he dispenses with any further preliminaries and nods to DS Leyton.

'Mr Bullingdon – can you tell us if you recognise these items?'

DS Leyton steps forward and holds the two bags up at head height for ease of inspection. The young man peers somewhat myopically at first one bag and then the other. And then, quite uninhibitedly, he makes a sweeping gesture with both hands, from his chest downwards, indicating his person.

'They are hardly my kind of thing.'

He wears the same eccentric outfit as they have seen on previous occasions. The oversized bare feet in sandals preclude the size eight outdoor shoe; conversely, the boxer shorts would drop off his scrawny frame.

His argument needs no further elaboration, but Skelgill is interested that he has responded not as a witness but as if accused.

'You don't know who they might have belonged to, sir?'

He shakes his head; he regards Skelgill with some bemusement, as though he thinks the question is misdirected.

'I really couldn't say.'

Skelgill nods, and turns to move away, but then he hesitates.

'Sir – does Rapture mean anything to you?'

Julian Bullingdon blinks, his expression artless as usual.

'Well – aside from its everyday use – it refers to a meeting with the Lord. I should have thought you would know that, Inspector.'

'Right.' Skelgill glances peevishly at DS Leyton. 'We'll leave you to your hawk moths, sir.'

Julian Bullingdon seems to have no need of further discourse, not even a farewell; he returns to the shadows of the log store and resumes his search for roosting insects.

As they move away DS Leyton falls in more closely alongside his superior. They are following the woodland track – the original driveway – that leads from West Gate House to Shuteham Hall itself.

'Bit of a coincidence, Guv – that he's down here just at the same time as us. And it was convenient – that moth being there.'

'What – you reckon he had it in his pocket?'

'Dunno, Guv – maybe. I wouldn't put it past him. I thought you were thinking he'd been snooping. He could have followed us – out of sight, in the woods.'

Skelgill is irked by the prospect – that, if so, he did not notice – but he has to acknowledge that his sergeant's assessment could be correct.

'Who knows, Leyton.'

'And what were you expecting by asking him about Rapture?'

Skelgill makes a scoffing sound.

'Pretty much exactly what I got.'

They proceed in silence for a minute or two, Skelgill glowering, his head bowed, his eyes on the ground before them. Thus it is DS Leyton who first espies two figures walking in their direction.

'Hey up – we've got more company. Look at this pair, Guv – like flippin' peas in a pod.'

Skelgill glances up to see Lord Edward and Daphne Bullingdon, surprisingly close – they must have emerged from a side path. There would never be any doubt, as DS Leyton alludes, to their being identified as father and daughter – the same gait (the limp more pronounced in the elder); the same lop-sided deportment; the same peculiar facial disfigurement, not exactly ugliness, just a slightly unnerving asymmetry.

But more eye-catching than this is that Lord Bullingdon carries a short one-piece aluminium stepladder, and Daphne a tote tray from which protrudes the hickory handle of a hammer; beneath her other arm she cradles a stack of commercially manufactured plastic signs.

'Saves us a job, Guv.'

DS Leyton speaks quietly out of the side of his mouth. Skelgill nods. His colleague means the need to track them down. The two couples converge and draw to a halt about six feet apart. Skelgill can see that the signs read, "Danger, Trespassers Will Be Prosecuted". He cannot help thinking that, if word gets out about the mantrap, the signs might be superfluous, and poachers a thing of the past. However, when neither of the detectives speaks, Daphne Bullingdon is the first to yield. Her voice is tentative. She addresses Skelgill.

'Any further news, Inspector?'

Skelgill glances at the evidence bags held by his colleague, as though he will ask him to step forward. But instead he poses a question.

'I wanted to ask how you deal with the disposal of ash from your incinerator.'

'Good heavens – and why is that important?' Lord Bullingdon interjects, pre-empting his daughter. 'Are you trying to pin a breach of some minor technicality on us?'

Before Skelgill can explain Daphne Bullingdon turns to remonstrate with her father.

'Daddy – there is no problem – it is a perfectly reasonable question.' She looks back at Skelgill. 'Inspector, we deal with a certified contractor, Greens of Aspatria. Our waste is collected every Tuesday. Most is pre-sorted and goes to recycling; the ash is sent to landfill. It is fully traceable.'

Skelgill somehow doubts this latter aspect; his job gives him an insight into the dark arts of waste management; among the cowboy operators corners are cut at every opportunity. However, more significant at this juncture is that the incinerator was emptied by prior arrangement. So now he indicates to DS Leyton that he should show the exhibits. But just as his sergeant begins to make a move the Bullingdons become distracted – and disconcertedly so, to judge by their expressions. Skelgill glances over his shoulder just as the accompanying sound – the rumble of hooves – reaches his ears. It is Miranda Bullingdon, in full flight on her bay stallion, kicking up great clods of earth in her wake.

'Pah – she's ruining the track!'

The exclamation of disapproval escapes Lord Bullingdon's lips. But as the patently competent horsewoman reins in her mount, seamlessly decelerating through a canter and a trot and into a walk, to approach with graceful ease, her husband seems to lose the will to chastise her.

In any event, she largely ignores her family members, and reserves her attention for Skelgill. Capturing his gaze she nods imperiously. For a moment he half wonders if she is expecting him to come forward to help her dismount, as they had seen Lawrence Melling do on their very first visit. But he stands his ground, and she seems content with her elevated position.

She has come from the direction that could have brought her past Julian Bullingdon, and he speculates whether she is likely to have consulted with him. He sees her eyes shift to the evidence bags that DS Leyton is holding, and he decides to cut to the chase.

'Our search team has fished two items from Troutmere. They may recently have been discarded. A work boot and a pair of boxer shorts.'

'Let me see.'

Before Skelgill can dictate otherwise, he finds his sergeant responding to Miranda Bullingdon's command. But as DS Leyton steps across to the shoulder of the horse and holds up the two items, it is Edward Bullingdon who again interjects.

'Miranda – this is preposterous!' He glares at Skelgill. 'Inspector – I do not intend for my wife to be questioned about some alien male underwear!'

Skelgill inhales to respond, but Miranda Bullingdon has a ready rejoinder.

'Teddy Bear, darling – don't be so sensitive.' She casts a gloved hand towards the bag containing the boxer shorts. 'Besides, these are exactly the style I have been encouraging you to wear instead of those silly old-fangled Y-fronts.'

She smiles coyly – but Lord Bullingdon simply colours – and now he seems lost for words – whether it is because she has blatantly provided him with an alibi of sorts, or perhaps that they find themselves airing their dirty linen in the public eye.

Daphne Bullingdon intervenes; perhaps keen to take the conversation away from the topic of her father's smalls.

'Inspector – that boot – I have seen Stan wearing a pair very similar, if not identical.'

There is a moment's silence – and now DS Leyton turns towards her.

'Madam – you'll recall we established in conjunction with Artur that Stan was likely wearing his work boots when he went missing. Could this be one of them?'

He steps closer and raises the bag and Daphne Bullingdon squints critically at the contents.

'Well – it certainly could be.' She looks inquiringly at DS Leyton and then at Skelgill. 'Can you not determine this sort of thing from DNA?'

Skelgill regards her contemplatively for a moment.

'That's where they're going next.' He glances at his wristwatch. 'In fact Forensics are probably champing at the bit.'

He looks at Miranda Bullingdon, to see that she smiles gracefully at his unintended humour. But he seems to suffer another jab of pain, and she notices.

'Inspector – if you need to get them somewhere in a hurry, climb up – there's room on my horse for two.'

DS Leyton, knowing Skelgill, would not be surprised if he accepted the offer – but then he too realises that Skelgill seems momentarily inconvenienced. Stepping into the breach, he holds up the bag containing the boxer shorts and declaims loudly.

'So – no takers on the underpants?'

He waves them about like an East End costermonger who has reached his rock-bottom price.

'No? Ladies and gentleman – we'll love you and leave you.'

And with a glance at Skelgill, who for once follows his sergeant's lead, DS Leyton nods to the assembly and the pair of them move away. Once they have passed beyond earshot, he addresses his superior with concern in his voice.

'You alright, Guv? You were looking a bit peaky back there.'

Skelgill raises a hand to his right temple.

'To be honest, Leyton – I reckon I'm getting a migraine. Used to suffer them as a bairn.   Not had one for donkey's years. Ma used to blame it on me being a cuddy wifter.'

'You what, Guv?'

'A lefty, Leyton – and not the political sort.'

'Ah, cack-handed.'   DS Leyton ponders this information. 'They say your lot's brains are wired up differently – maybe that's why. Mind you – you're supposed to be more creative, ain't that right?'

Skelgill makes a self-deprecating growl. For once it sounds unaffected.

'I don't know where that comes from, Leyton. I can't draw to save my life. And I wasn't exactly teacher's pet for writing, either.'

As for musical talent, DS Leyton has suffered many tuneless renderings – but though he declines to remind his boss of the

267

fact, he would be the first to admit that there *is* something different about Skelgill – some ineffable quality that enables him to see the world in his own peculiar light.

Now, however, he is definitely showing signs of not being himself.

'Ain't the best thing to have a kip, Guv?' DS Leyton turns to glance up solicitously at the taller Skelgill as they stride along. 'Why don't you call it a day? I'll check these items with Artur and the other estate workers. Then get them into the lab pronto. I reckon we're due a forensic breakthrough – maybe on these – more likely on the gun or the trap – but that's out of our hands and it's gonna be tomorrow at the earliest. I'll contact that Greens crowd and then I'll catch up with DS Jones. We can work out where we are and run through it with you in the morning.'

Skelgill inhales and sighs heavily.

'Aye, maybe that's it.'

'You don't sound convinced, Guv. I'm sure you'll feel better.'

'I don't mean me, Leyton.' Skelgill jerks a thumb back over his shoulder. 'I feel like we should be homing in on one of this lot by now.'

DS Leyton shrugs rather phlegmatically, as though he does not quite take Skelgill entirely seriously.

'It did seem a bit like they were tailing us, Guv.'

14. LAST GASP

Thursday, early hours

Teetering, hovering.
The hinterland where conscious and subconscious intertwine.
A fragile, uneasy coexistence.
Falling, weightless – no, not falling, skydiving.
Lady Godiva, naked – both so.
Fingertips touching, tantalising.
Air rushing; dark mane trailing.
Splashdown – Over Water.
No cold shock; smooth transition.
Still deeper, swimming now.
Breathing unnecessary.
Eye contact – imploring.
Light fading.
A nylon line; Stan's lure, futile.
The bottom; fascination; maggots writhing.
Silver fish flashing; a feeding frenzy.
Vendace!
Embrace.
Enveloping abandon.
Becomes panic.
She is drowning!
Kick for the surface; kick and haul; haul for life.
Air.
Carry her through the shallows; rocks underfoot.
Exhausted, collapse ashore.
Prone, heartbeat pressing upon him.
A cough – water expelled.
The perfume – familiar; spicy.
A voice, at last.
"It is a bigger fool that confesses."

The accent – *Irish?*

The face?

But there are only ashes.

Skelgill knows he is dreaming; but despite its sinister twists it is not a dream he wishes to exit. But the hinterland is behind him; the ebb of the fantasy is inexorable. He is powerless to prevent the last ripples of the crazy narrative from slipping away. He is awake. He turns his head. His digital clock reads 01:59. His migraine is gone.

*

Skelgill realises his hair is still damp. The cold shower has only partially restored a sense of reality. The nightmare has left an undercurrent of veracity. As with a drug, whose residue persists in his arteries, come vivid flashbacks and felt sensations indistinguishable from the day's tsunami of data that finally caused his server to crash.

On arrival home, by then half-blinded by the brainstorm, he had texted his neighbour – would she hang on to the dog? No problem there, Cleopatra is a regular last-minute boarder. He had slumped on the settee. Lights out. Yet he had woken in bed. And on rising this morning there was evidence of a cheese sandwich consumed in the kitchen. Hardly doctor's orders.

The dashboard clock reads a quarter to three. The Irish couple may be back by now. But, if they're sleeping he'll leave them – maybe until six, six-thirty. He's got a rod; he can fish from the bank. No maggots, though. *(Hah* – those maggots – still alive and kicking!) Try some daft spinner like Stan's. It will pass the time. Maybe there's a monster pike in Over Water.

As he steers sedately through the dark winding lanes he wonders – should he call Jones? She'll be disappointed to find he's interviewed the Irish without her being there. But he doesn't want to chance them clearing off – when the Vholes turn up at seven. Though that seems unlikely this morning, if they've travelled through the night. Maybe he should just make sure they don't leave – and then ring Jones at a more civilised time.

He reflects again on the dream – upon dreams – how they are candid windows on the conscience – they reveal your troubles, your secret aches and deepest desires. But aren't they also supposed to unravel your problems, sorting, rearranging, and making new connections? The subconscious to the rescue: diving deep into the psyche, surfacing with pearls of wisdom; while the hapless conscious guddles fruitlessly in the shallows?

When Skelgill undertakes a task – such as the 'eyrie' he has recently built in his loft, or the arbour he constructed in his garden (both projects owing something to his yearning for boyhood dens) – he does not make a plan, a drawing with measurements and lists of materials. Instead, he sits or stands on the spot, maybe for twenty minutes or so. Then he goes away. And he comes back another time, another day. He loiters again, just being there; maybe he stalks or circles, looking slowly about – his demeanour not analytical, merely absorptive. It is the same when he finds a new place to fish. What to do may not be immediately apparent, but it is possible to learn everything he needs to know by osmosis; it will come in its own good time. In a work context, colleagues and superiors – and tutors or trainers – have resigned themselves to his manner; they have given up trying to cajole or marshal him to use their methods. A lone wolf, Skelgill has the mind of a cat.

But now the lupine component must shift into the ascendancy. For as he turns into the opening of the track that leads down to Over Water his headlamps catch the red reflectors of a vehicle. He recognises the pattern: it is the old Ford Consul. The Irish couple have returned. There are no other cars. The chances are, they will be asleep – either on the bunk in the hide or in the big Ford itself. There is no benefit in waking them. He switches off his ignition; the light fades as the headlamp bulb filaments cool, and he knocks the gear lever into neutral and rolls almost noiselessly down the last of the gentle incline. He swings his car onto the slipway, overlooking the lake – merely a black void. He hauls extra hard on the handbrake and, for belt and braces purposes, toggles the shift into reverse.

He sits.

Does he want to fish?

The mere fact that he is asking himself the question tells him the answer. It is just not something he can easily admit to himself. But he wants to fish free of the clouds that keep blotting out his sun, free and easy, with a sense of unlimited time available to unfold before him. On the other hand it is another three hours or so before he can reasonably contact DS Jones. Was this such a good idea after all? Well – at least he knows the Irish are back – he would have been anxious about that. But now what? Try to sleep again? He's had way more than his regular quota – roughly six till two – the thick end of eight hours, apparently minus a ten-minute sandwich break. And the slumber was deep and restful, despite those last few turbulent moments. He cranes to see the sky – there are stars, which mean it will be cold – a grass frost by dawn. Though he is okay now, in twenty minutes he will to start to feel a chill. There are army blankets in the back, in the flatbed, covering his gear. Better to be prepared.

He pushes open the door, but before he has even moved he hears something that alerts him. The engine of the Ford Consul is idling. A flash of alarm comes to him – they are about to leave! He snatches a torch from the console and lurches from his seat – but as he regains his balance he pauses – for now he senses something different is afoot. The car does not give the impression that it is about to be driven off. It stands in stolid stillness, not poised, not straining in gear, no telltale dashboard lights showing. Instead – it must be – they have turned on the engine to keep themselves warm. Skelgill relaxes. He decides to take a chance with his torch.

And then he sees the hosepipe.

*

'That's an amazing contraption, Guv.'

Skelgill glances up at DS Jones. The flames that lick from the chimney of his Kelly kettle as he squats to feed the little fire within illuminate his face, his features stark.

'Aye – so long as you've got a lake or a beck and a spot of driftwood you've got a mash.'

The water comes to a boil with a sudden bubbling gusto and Skelgill yanks the body off its base, simultaneously lifting by its handle and tilt-chain. He crouches over the two tin mugs on the ground at his colleague's feet. She sits resting on the flatbed, beneath the raised tailgate.

'It's just powdered milk – but I put some cold in with it – shouldn't be too hot for you.'

DS Jones chuckles.

Has Skelgill's tea ever *not* been too hot for her?

But she thanks him and makes an effort to drink – she seems appreciative.

'I grabbed my work stuff but I forgot my water bottle – I'm not sure I was even properly awake until I came off the A66 and had to start thinking about which turns to take.'

Skelgill rises and lowers himself beside her, for a moment cradling his mug between his two hands and gazing pensively at the little fire quickly dwindling in the dented aluminium base of the kettle. DS Jones speaks again, her tone now more serious.

'What happened, Guv?'

Skelgill starts – and exhales exhaustedly, as though he might be reluctant to tell – but then he gathers himself and inhales with more purpose.

'I got out of my car and heard theirs was idling – lights off and no sign of activity. I figured they'd turned the engine on to keep warm. I shone my flashlight on the car and saw the hosepipe.' He sighs. 'It's a bit of a blur after that.'

'But you knew what to do.' She encourages him.

But Skelgill grimaces.

'There's only so much you can do. We practise for carbon monoxide poisoning in the mountain rescue – you get idiots who run their stoves inside their sealed tents – unventilated caves.' He pauses, as if reflecting upon some incident. 'I ripped the hose off the exhaust – stopped the source. But the car was locked. I had to get a rock to smash the driver's window so I could release the tailgate. Then I just dragged them clear and phoned 999. They were both alive. Luckily I had the club's first aid kit from an exercise last week in the car – so I was able to start giving them oxygen.'

He jerks a thumb over his shoulder.

'Then the crews arrived and took control. That's when I phoned you.'

They sit sipping in silence; Skelgill's approach more akin to slurping.

After a while DS Jones speaks again.

'It must have been a shock.' Her voice is a little tremulous, as if she is thinking what would she have done, or how would she have felt.

'It's a shock them topping themselves – trying to.'

'How do you mean, Guv?'

'Coming all the way back here. Why not jump off the Oban ferry? Why not smash head on into a forty-ton artic on the M74? Whatever.'

DS Jones ponders.

'Maybe it was a spur-of-the-moment decision.'

Skelgill takes another pull at his mug.

'Christine Vholes reckons they're using drugs – they're smoking weed, that's for sure.'

'I guess they'll conduct blood tests at the hospital, Guv.'

'Aye.'

Now there ensues a longer silence. The blue flashing lights from the ambulances are flooding the damp ether with an insubstantial twilight, tangible but too weak to delineate any of their surroundings.

'What made you come here, Guv – so early I mean?' She gestures in the direction of the shoreline. 'Were you fishing?'

'Skydiving.'

DS Jones cannot help but giggle.

'What?'

Skelgill gives an ironic grumble.

'Leyton told you I had a migraine?' (She nods.) 'I followed it up with a mad dream – I won't bore you with the detail.'

DS Jones shifts position slightly as though she wouldn't mind – and perhaps also that she senses he would rather not tell her. Skelgill continues.

'After that I couldn't sleep. This place was going to be the first port of call this morning anyway.' He gazes out into the darkness where the lake laps not far away. 'I did think about fishing – but –' His voice falters as he recalls the situation. 'Lucky I didn't just nod off – else I wouldn't have heard their engine. I got out to get a blanket.' He reaches behind and touches the coarse cloth. 'Do you want one?'

'Oh – no – thanks, Guv. The tea's warming my toes!'

Now she is being a little ironic.

Footsteps approach across the gravel. The senior paramedic from one of the two ambulances that hem in the Ford Consul appears, her complexion as she faces them a flickering ultraviolet hue. She frowns stoically.

'That's us. Could be a lot worse. They're stable.'

Skelgill makes a face that is both appreciative and hopeful.

'Think they'll pull through?'

'Aye – they'll pull through alright – just a question of what damage has been done. Stroke of luck for them that you had that oxygen.'

Skelgill makes a contrary face.

'They might not agree.'

The woman grins wryly. She holds out a clear polythene bag, which DS Jones accepts.

'Personal possessions – the wallets you can work out – the bag of weed was on the girl and the plastic bits were in the lad's shirt pocket.'

Skelgill is about to respond but an impatient cry reaches them. The drivers are keen to head for the hospital. The woman speaks.

'We'll take them to the WCI – be there in half an hour at this time of night.'

'Cheers.'

The woman leaves them. Skelgill mulls over the thought that trainee nurses Claire and Melanie work at the West Cumberland

Infirmary and whether there is any merit in alerting them to the predicament of their fellow birders – but perhaps it is something that can wait until morning proper. The emergency vehicles depart, the cast of their blue lights fading into oblivion. While he is pondering, DS Jones is delving into the polythene bag. He turns to watch, expecting her to extract the drugs – but in fact she opens her palm to reveal three small flat plastic items, more or less identical.

'What are they?'

They are working by the small interior bulb behind their heads.

'Memory cards – except they're not.'

'What do you mean?'

'They're empty – these are just the cases.'

Skelgill stares distractedly at the items.

'They were looking at them in the café.'

'Sorry, Guv?'

Skelgill's statement seems to have omitted something in the sequence of his train of thought. He backtracks.

'In Cockermouth – the first time we saw them – before we knew who they were. The lad – Cian – he got those out of his pocket – they were viewing something on their laptop, remember?'

DS Jones nods pensively. She weighs the cases in her palm.

'These are actually for micro SD cards, Guv – they're designed for miniaturised cameras – like my dashcam, that sort of thing. The memory cards must be still in the camera – well, *cameras*, I suppose.'

Skelgill feels the hairs on the back of his neck prickling. It might be coincidence – for the air temperature is still dropping and he wears only a shirt himself; moreover, the adrenaline of the dramatic rescue is ebbing in his veins. But his forearms, his whole body would be shivering if he were truly cold. And he recalls the concentration of Cian Fogarty and Ciara Ahearne crowded over the laptop – excited to see what the memory card that the young man had inserted would reveal. There was even the impression that they had come to the café for the prime

276

purpose of doing this – an act rather like the good old days when folk collected photographs from Boots and made a great ceremony of opening the presentation wallet and working their way through its memories.

'They use infrared.'

'Sorry, Guv?'

'These wildlife cameras – motion activated. They have infrared – like the webcam on the harriers' nest – so they work at night, when most animals are on the go.'

'Er, yes – I suppose so – but what are you thinking?'

Skelgill pauses.

'I reckon I know where we might find one – and how.'

He rises and swivels and leans over into the flatbed. The mountain rescue kit is in a large zipped holdall just behind where he has been sitting. He rummages in the bag and produces a soft black leather case that has the dimensions of a hardback novel.

'What is it, Guv?'

'They.' He begins to unzip the case. 'Night-vision glasses. So long as any camera's got some battery left, I reckon we'll see it when its spotlight comes on.'

DS Jones inhales as if to speak but then she checks herself.

'What is it?'

'Well – I was thinking – the Irish will know where they are – but –'

'Exactly.' Skelgill begins to clear away his camping equipment. 'It's down to us to find them before the batteries go flat.'

*

'I need you to be the guinea pig.'

'Provided there are no mousetraps.'

Skelgill stifles a laugh – but despite her irrepressible spirit he asks himself, is he putting his colleague in any danger? Without seeking permission he reaches up and helps her complete the awkward clamber over the five-barred gate; but she seems to accept the contact as reassuring, and allows him to cushion her body weight as she drops down. They have driven in Skelgill's car, from Over Water circling clockwise past the opening of the main driveway of Shuteham Hall, taking the Overthwaite turn, and passing the old gatehouse and on as far as the locked terminus of Crow Road. Now they must proceed on foot. Skelgill had contemplated a route through the grounds, using the driveway, Long Shoot, and Crow Road from the opposite direction, but covertness has prevailed.

'Here, you can use this.' He hands her his flashlight. 'And you can stick to the short grass. I just need you to go far enough ahead so I can watch through this contraption.'

DS Jones chuckles; her tone is nerveless.

'Sure – I was just joking.'

Skelgill cannot think of a suitable retort – other than something along the lines that another unexpected drama would be par for the course – but he does not wish to alarm her; besides, there is no doubt that she is up for the fight, and he is glad of her positive energy. As they stride briskly through the darkness, steering a course by the just-lighter sky above the trees that line the woodland ride, it is DS Jones that speaks again.

'What makes you think Keeper's Cottage might be the place?'

Skelgill's honest belief about this is not the answer he decides to provide. To tell her that he has twice experienced the distinct feeling of being watched while prowling about Lawrence Melling's cottage is hardly the most convincing reason to be trailing her through a dark forest in the early hours of the morning.

'Just logic.' He senses she glances at him. 'If they're recording wildlife – then their cameras could be anywhere – I suppose I'd find a badgers' sett or something like that. But if they're not recording wildlife – but something else – '

'*Protecting* wildlife.' DS Jones completes his argument, for the sake of clarity.

'Aye.'

'Keeping tabs on the gamekeeper – and anyone else they suspected of being a threat.'

Skelgill is nodding in agreement. Although she can't see this response, she perhaps detects his accord. She continues.

'Before I went to bed, Guv – I was looking online, searching various terms – trying to find something about Rapture. I can't say I got anything concrete – no direct references to Rapture as such, but I came across a chat group – some kind of forum – it was a few years since there'd been any activity – but one post did state that there was money to be made in being a "wildlife crime whistleblower" as it was termed. It specifically mentioned sporting estates, and farms where driven shooting takes place. But it was all a bit cryptic. The poster was anonymous, and there was the suggestion that if you were interested you should PM them – personal message, I mean. To do that you had to sign up to the forum and create a profile – but when I tried to click through to that part it came up as inoperative.'

'Happen you're getting warmer.'

DS Jones seems to find an extra spring in her step – perhaps his encouragement. But just as she is about to reply she abruptly changes tack.

'Yuck! What's that awful smell?'

Now it is Skelgill's turn to chuckle.

'Shine the torch – over to the right.'

They are passing the keeper's larder. In the stark beam the corpses strung on the fence against the velvet blackness beyond seem particularly vivid in their petrified death throes. For a moment Skelgill wonders if they should check here for a hidden camera – but then, if you wanted to catch Lawrence Melling in the act of doing anything illicit, this is not the spot, for this is the public face of his occupation, and the trophies are legitimate vermin, according to the law.

'The Terminator's handiwork.'

DS Jones does not respond to his remark – or comment further – but that she keeps the beam trained on the hideous sight as they pass tells him that she is horrifically fascinated. But now they are approaching the cottage, and Skelgill slows his pace.

'I'll stop here. You walk on. Try round the back first – to the right of the building. I'll give you a shout when you go out of sight and we'll approach from the other side.'

'Okay, Guv.'

Skelgill watches as she moves away. Keeper's Cottage is just detectable as a darker shadow in the clearing – and now the torch beam plays on its walls and roof as DS Jones gets her bearings. When she reaches within about twenty yards of the property he raises the night-vision glasses. It takes no more than ten seconds for his 'guinea pig' to trigger the camera.

'Got it!'

Skelgill cannot contain his glee. In the mini-movie on the screen before his eyes he sees his colleague wheel around. She waves the torch beam about, but of course the infrared spotlight on the hidden camera is invisible to her.

'It's on the wall – over the door!'

That Skelgill is excited is not just that his hunch seems to have paid off – but that the camera is located in such an audacious position. He had expected it to be on a tree, or perhaps in the log pile beneath the canopy. He jogs up to find DS Jones shining the torch on a nestbox above the back door.

'Looks like they've got a sense of humour, Guv.'

Skelgill concurs with her sentiment. Tall enough to reach, he stretches up and unhooks the birdbox from the nail that supports it. It is old and the lid partly rotted away, though he notices it has been fixed down with a couple of relatively new-looking brass screws. He kneels and traps the box between his knees, and with the aid of his Swiss pocketknife he removes the screws while DS Jones provides steady illumination. Sure enough, fixed to a bracket by a rubber strap is a small outdoor-style camera, with camouflage livery. Working in silent tandem Skelgill cuts the strap and DS Jones reaches in and removes the camera with an evidence bag. While Skelgill gets to his feet and props the empty nestbox against the wall of the cottage, DS Jones examines their find. She makes a little exclamation.

'Ah – I can see the memory card is fitted.'

'I don't suppose it has a screen.'

DS Jones turns the device over in the torchlight.

'I think that's considered an unnecessary luxury for this kind of gadget.' She inhales, as though it is a prelude to a problem, and her tone becomes somewhat contrite. 'My laptop – it's under the removable seat in my car – back at the bird hide.'

'We might get that far, yet.'

Skelgill sounds unperturbed. He shrugs off the small nylon backpack that he has carried and offers the open mouth for her to deposit the camera. He grins encouragingly.

'One down, two to go.'

They stand silent for a moment, a little breathless, as much from the thrill as the effort – but Skelgill suddenly raises the backpack against his ear.

'What is it, Guv?'

'It's still switched on – it must have an autofocus – I can hear it.'

He holds the bag open and DS Jones retrieves the camera. Sure enough, she locates the power switch and, with a little difficulty through the polythene, manages to turn it off. She replaces it in the bag.

'I don't think we swore, Guv.'

'That's not like me.'

Skelgill is reminded that some of his own movements must be recorded on this device – moreover, is that what alerted him – what unnerved him when he cautiously prowled about? Did he subliminally hear the tiny mechanical movements of the camera? It seems more plausible than sixth sense. He stands pensively for a moment, and perhaps the set of his jaw prompts his colleague to question him.

'Where next, do you think?'

Skelgill turns to stare into the darkness in the direction of Shuteham Hall.

'I reckon if you were going to monitor the keeper you'd put them on a route you know he'd use. There's already an official camera on the harriers' nest – so maybe between here and there.'

DS Jones makes a murmur of agreement.

'This cottage – like you said, Guv, it was a logical bet. The nest – it must be almost two miles. That feels more like a needle in a haystack.'

Skelgill is nodding – despite that she perhaps underplays the achievement to date. But he pats the binoculars that rest on his chest.

'Aye – but at least we've got a needle detector. Come on – let's get a shift on while it's still dark. For once, the night's our friend.'

'Sure, Guv.'

'Meantime – see if you can raise Leyton – try a text first. I reckon we should get him down here.'

'He's probably filling a bottle as we speak.'

'In which case he'll be glad to hear from us.'

*

'What are you thinking, Guv?'

Skelgill has stopped at the turn for Garden Cottage. At a distance there is the lone light above the front door.

'We should check down here. It's where Karen Williamson lives.'

DS Jones hesitates, as though she does not feel this is the best use of their time.

'Will the binoculars work – in the light of that lamp?'

'Aye – they'll be fine. Come on, we'll just do a quick recce.'

He finds himself digging in his heels, despite that he shares her reservations. Somewhere nearer to Over Moor, or perhaps the big release pen in Bullmire Wood will be better prospects; these are the places he would hide a camera.

'Just skip down – I'll follow once you're out of sight.'

DS Jones moves away briskly. He watches through the night-vision glasses until she disappears behind the parked car – but when he reaches the same point he finds her returning. She comes right up close so that he can see the look of urgency on her face – and she raises a finger to her lips. Her voice is lowered to a whisper.

'Guv – come and see – and listen.'

He follows her around the side of the property and sees immediately that there is a pale glow in the roof skylights, one of which is open by several inches. From within, voices emanate. Speaking in turn are a male and a female – the latter, Skelgill is certain, is Karen Williamson – but though there is urgency in their tone they are evidently restraining themselves and keeping the volume down. The young boy, Kieran will be sleeping, of course.

Skelgill is reminded of what Karen Williamson said to him about guests – that sometimes she was obliged to provide B&B for estate visitors. It strikes him that on such occasions she and the boy would need somewhere else to sleep – which might explain the function of the loft. There must be a bedroom of sorts up there. And now, in this context, other aspects of his interactions with her begin to assume a heightened significance – not least that she has perhaps skilfully contrived to entertain him outside the property. Then there is her curious, brief visit that he surreptitiously observed to Keeper's Cottage. And there is even the issue of the two mugs that she had at the ready in the walled garden – a secluded spot that can be reached from the dilapidated door in the wall that separates the latter from the cottage garden in which he and DS Jones stand.

'Stan.'

'Guv?'

DS Jones sounds disbelieving.

'It's Stan – I tell you. She's been hiding him.'

'Guv – how do you know?'

'Never mind – what time did Leyton say he'd get here?'

'Guv – we can manage.'

'Jones – Stan's an unknown quantity – the woman's a black belt at karate.'

DS Jones stares belligerently at Skelgill; he sees she is not in the least bit fazed – but he adds force to his argument.

'Leyton can stop a bus. If he's ten minutes away he can block off the front door while we go in the back.'

DS Jones yields reluctantly. She is already reaching for her phone.

'Tell him to drive in – and all the way round to the tunnel in the rhododendrons – he knows where that is. And tell him to radio for the nearest patrol to come, too.'

DS Jones is nodding. She speaks softly into the handset microphone, conveying the salient details to her colleague. She ends the call.

'He's just turning into the main driveway.'

'Go and meet him at the top of the track. Then when you get back we'll know he's in place.'

DS Jones merges quietly into the deeper shadows beyond the corner of the cottage. Skelgill stands still, straining his ears. The muted conversation continues. Though the words cannot be discerned the tenor seems to be that the female is trying to convince the male of something but he is putting up objections. Skelgill finds his hands coming to rest on the binoculars slung around his neck. He is reminded of the original purpose of their visit – a stroke of luck that intuition brought him this way. But to pass a minute or two he wanders around the perimeter of the cottage garden, holding the binoculars out in front of him so that he can see the screen. But no invisible light is activated.

And now DS Jones returns and gives him the thumbs-up. Skelgill approaches the back door and tries the handle. He is not surprised to find it locked. He is about to hammer on the wood panelling when something stops him. DS Jones looks on in anticipation. Skelgill takes half a dozen backward paces and calls out sharply, but not over-loudly.

'Karen!'

The voices in the loft fall silent.

'Karen – it's DI Skelgill – and colleagues. We have an officer at the front door and a support vehicle about to arrive. I don't want to wake your bairn. Can you come to the back door please?'

There is no reply – nor any sudden sounds of panic or desperate moves that could indicate an escape attempt is imminent. And after about thirty seconds the kitchen light comes on. And then the door is unlocked. Karen Williamson stands facing them in a flimsy nightgown. Behind her, a couple of yards back, barefooted, in perhaps hastily thrown on black jeans and creased t-shirt, his expression defeated and – yes – clearly afraid, is the man Skelgill recognises from his passport photograph as Carol Valentin Stanislav – Stan.

*

'Whatever you think – it weren't Stan – *I swear* – on my son's life!'

'Okay – calm down, lass. I want to hear it.'

For the benefit of Karen Williamson's sleeping son, Skelgill has retreated to the garden. Karen Williamson has pulled on a quilted gilet – rather incongruous with the satiny shift, but her mind is clearly distracted. Now he chaperones her across to the picnic table and encourages her to sit; she complies, though facing outwards, the light from the kitchen window illuminating her drawn features. He and DS Jones stand; perhaps they remain to be convinced she will not make some kind of dash to be reunited with Stan. He has gone quietly – meekly, seemingly resigned to the inevitable – with DS Leyton and a constable from the squad car that turned up soon afterwards. Right now, Skelgill is keen to obtain a succinct account – for he considers time to be against him. Karen Williamson's emotions, however, still hold sway.

'He's terrified – his English isn't brilliant and he'll probably admit to something he's not done. He's a lovely guy – he wouldn't hurt a fly.'

Skelgill can see that she is genuinely distressed. She might have harboured Stan entirely out of altruism, but it is not difficult to guess that there is more to the relationship. Though he reminds himself it is a murder investigation, instinct tells him not to play the bad cop. Besides, does he not have some goodwill of his own in the bank?

'Listen, lass – we're not the KGB. If Stan's not done owt wrong then he's got nowt to worry about.'

He reaches out and touches her bicep; it is an instinctive gesture, the human-to-human stress conductor in play. After a moment she nods reluctantly, but still does not say anything.

'So you could maybe put us on the right track by explaining what it is you think he hasn't done – and what he's been doing here.' He jerks back his head to indicate the cottage.

She inhales deeply a couple of times; perhaps it is a relaxation technique from her martial arts repertoire.

'Lawrence Melling nearly killed him – he thought he *had* killed him – drowned him – Stan pretended – somehow managed to swim away under water. He came here – it was the middle of the night – Saturday night – what else could I do but take him in?'

Skelgill shrugs as though this is fine by him.

'Why did Lawrence Melling try to kill him?'

Karen Williamson sighs tremulously. She looks confused.

'I'm not too sure. Stan doesn't want to talk about it – doesn't want to get me involved. He just said he was monitoring Lawrence's movements – something about the boathouse – that's where it happened. Lawrence caught him – like I say – tried to drown him.'

Skelgill stares, unblinking – he is recalling his own close encounter with the enraged gamekeeper. He glances at DS Jones to see she too is observing the woman with great intensity.

'Why didn't you report it to the police?'

'I wanted to – Stan wasn't sure what to do – that it would land him in trouble. But then before we could agree or decide – the jewellery was stolen and suddenly everyone's trying to pin it on him. He wouldn't have stood a chance.'

Skelgill exhales and folds his arms, as though he begs to differ. But Karen Williamson continues.

'And then Lawrence Melling was killed –' She looks fearfully from one detective to the other. 'That's what the word going round is. Stan's the obvious fall guy for that as well – especially if he tried to explain the attack on him. And you'd just think he'd hidden the jewellery somewhere and was denying it. It was an impossible situation for him. Except I can promise he was here – with me – all night, every night.'

Skelgill seems entirely non-judgemental, when it is plain she expects reproach; indeed his expression is remarkably amenable. But what she cannot appreciate is that he has been wrestling blind with this impossible conundrum these last several days. To have his subliminal suspicions confirmed is like one distant Christmas morning when the postie-delivered package he had been assured was a roll of foil for the turkey turned up in his stocking as a six-piece travel rod in a tube case.

'After we'd chatted – on Monday in the walled garden – why did you go to Keeper's Cottage?'

She looks at him, wide-eyed. And then at DS Jones.

'That boot you brought, with your other sergeant – it was Stan's missing one – he might have needed it. He lost it beside the lake – in the fight.' She smears the fingertips of both hands simultaneously from the bridge of her nose across her cheekbones, as though she imagines there are tear stains. 'Obviously, you found it later – but we thought maybe Lawrence Melling had taken it away – so as not to leave any trace of Stan beside Troutmere.'

Now DS Jones intervenes.

'Madam – just to get this clear. You're saying that Mr Melling thought he'd drowned Mr Stanislav in Troutmere – and that he was expecting that the lake would conceal the body?'

Karen Williamson regards DS Jones forlornly.

'That's right – I mean – I know a body's supposed to float eventually. But I expect he would have been checking regularly and would have had a plan to deal with it.'

Skelgill makes an exasperated growl and performs a pirouette on his heel.

'Meanwhile we're keeping watch on the ports for Stan and a suitcase full of diamonds.'

Skelgill says this as much to himself as anything, and he sees the look of alarm in DS Jones's face. It is true, that to share this sentiment with Karen Williamson is inappropriate – as yet he cannot dismiss the possibility that she is an accessory of sorts, or may have to be charged with obstructing the police. Right now, he cannot fathom where all this will lead. There is much to do, and new questions are stacking up as fast as old ones are being resolved. There will be feedback from DS Leyton – is Stan innocent, or responsible for both of the crimes? There is the hoped-for recuperation of the Irish couple and their story – can they assist with the incident on the moor? And – most pressing of all (if no longer seeming most important) – there is the impending dawn, and their hunt for the cameras, and what they might reveal. Now he glances apprehensively at the sky in the northeast. He pats DS Jones purposefully on the shoulder – in case she might think he would want her to remain; and then contrives to smile to Karen Williamson, though he does so perhaps just a little manically.

'We need to go; we turn to dust at sunup. We'll leave you to mind the bairn. Don't do anything daft, like fly off to Moldova.'

*

'Guv – could Stan know something about Rapture?'

'I'll tell you one thing – he doesn't know owt about fishing.'

'Pardon, Guv?'

They are both a little breathless, having hurried along Skelgill's short-cut across the estate – down the rhododendron tunnel; over the dam at the end of Troutmere; up through the poplar plantation; across the main driveway into ornamental woodland; eventually meeting the track that Lawrence Melling had taken by quad bike en route to his death.

'To answer your question – aye, maybe. Happen he were 'monitoring' Melling, as Karen Williamson just said. And that's my point. His cover – his disguise – was a daft little fishing rod with a lure big enough to catch a shark. Aye – you might get a pike on it in Over Water – if there's any in there – but Troutmere, no chance – just some stockies, couple-of-pounders.'

'I wonder what he'll claim he was doing – that generated such an extreme reaction?'

Skelgill senses that DS Jones is fishing for details that he has been reticent to reveal. He answers somewhat obliquely.

'Interesting thing is, Karen's story stacks up – about Melling clearing up after himself.'

DS Jones hesitates – though it may be the familiar reference to the woman that sidetracks her thoughts.

'He missed the boot, Guv. Although I suppose if it was dislodged in the lake he wouldn't have known about it.'

'It's the fishing rod I'm talking about. I noticed on Monday it had a strand of fresh water crowfoot snagged round the treble hooks. I reckon Melling returned the tackle to make it look like Stan had gone back to his cottage – and disappeared from there.'

DS Jones now falls into line with the hypothesis.

'Presumed by us to have committed the burglary and absconded with the jewellery.'

Skelgill glances at her as they move – they can neither see much of one another, but they seem to be in harmony on this point.

'Looks like Melling had us thinking exactly what he wanted us to believe.'

DS Jones is silent for a moment.

'The implication being that *he* took the jewellery.'

It takes Skelgill a while to respond.

'Aye.'

'But, how?'

Skelgill wonders for a moment if his colleague is being just a little bit disingenuous; that she knows he knows more than he is comfortable to reveal. But, little by little, it is beginning not to matter.

'I reckon I can explain that, as well.' And now he almost goes the whole hog. 'And the boxers.'

'Hey!' She is not expecting him to be so forthcoming. 'Are we talking Miranda Bullingdon?'

However, perhaps Skelgill has reached his limit for the present. He becomes more circumspect.

'I think we'll find – when we speak with her – that she's got a little saying, along the lines of *never admit anything that can't be proved.*'

DS Jones makes another couple of unsuccessful attempts to winkle more detail from her superior, but he will not be moved. Instead, rather like a lizard that forfeits its writhing tail to distract a predator, he tempts her with the greater controversy.

'Who killed Cock Robin?'

DS Jones inhales – but then exhales rather than answer immediately.   She needs a few more seconds to compose her reply.

'Well – we could keep our longlist, as previously discussed – or we could create a radical new shortlist – now we know Stan had a powerful motive.'

It is a salutary answer – a reminder that it is easy to overthink a situation – a trap that it is normally Skelgill's role to be warning against falling into.   However, he instinctively plays devil's advocate.

'Except – you know you meet some people – and they're just – *honest?*' (He prefaces the word 'honest' with a rather colourful adjective to emphasise its gravity.)

'You mean Karen Williamson?'

Actually Skelgill is thinking of Stan – based on what he has heard about him, and even the little comic cameo they witnessed when he fell off the ladder, and his manner just now, compliant and respectful before being carted off rather unceremoniously by DS Leyton.   But – yes – in his mind an equivalent sentiment applies to the housekeeper.

'Aye, well – I reckon so far she's just about managed to avoid telling white lies.'   He looks at his colleague with a grin. 'Whereas I tell them all day long.'

'Grey ones, even – when it's the Chief, Guv.'

Skelgill nudges her playfully.

'Aye, well – we've got this mutually beneficial arrangement.   I say what she wants to hear and she pretends to believe me.'

Their moment of levity, however, comes to an end, for they round the final bend in the track, and ahead of them in the gloom is the just-discernible wall and, beyond it, the shadowy expanse of Over Moor.

'I'll go ahead, Guv.'

DS Jones skips away and Skelgill raises the night-vision glasses. He has got the hang of the device now – holding it out before him, at chest height, so that he has the additional benefit of his own albeit imperfect eyesight.

Just as DS Jones closes in on the stile the hidden camera is triggered.

'There! Six foot to the right of the bottom step – just above the ground – near where that tape's dangling.'

As Skelgill comes up DS Jones exclaims in triumph – she has located the device in a niche in the dry stone wall, with rocks loosely replaced around it. It would be next to invisible to the unsuspecting eye – especially as anyone approaching would be most likely sizing up the stile and planning their route over it.

She bags the camera securely as before – and Skelgill is ready with his rucksack. This time she calls the score.

'Two down, one to go.'

Skelgill tightens the drawstring and slings the pack over his shoulder.

'Here – take these.' He hands her the binoculars.

'But – why?'

'Just in case there is a giant mousetrap.'

Before she can protest he grabs the torch and vaults over the stile.

'Come on – we've got half an hour before the light beats us.'

He raises a hand to guide her down – as if there are no limits to his chivalry! She is probably considerably more agile than he, if not quite possessed of his ingrained schooling in scrambling and clambering and general indestructibility. She comments on their latest finding.

'Guv – if anyone carried the trap from Shuteham Hall they must have come this way – this camera will have recorded them. If Lawrence Melling brought it, we'll find out. Or – if it was Stan.'

Skelgill makes an exaggerated expiration of breath, to demonstrate his reticence about counting chickens. Yes – if these cameras enable them to turn back the clock – they may understand what has taken place. But fresh in his mind are startling contradictions: the unexpected and unopposed 'capture' of Stan; the limp forms of the Irish couple as he dragged them clear of the fume-wreathed Ford. If DS Jones thinks the former has moved to the top of the list of suspects, what about the latter – where do they rank? And, yet – neither idea consumes him with anything like certainty; it feels like the centre of gravity lies elsewhere in his subconscious.

He does not respond to his colleague directly, but instead sets off, employing the torch to light his way along the worn beaters' path that forges an easy route through the heather. He calls back.

'Let me get a cricket pitch ahead. Twenty-two yards.' He adds the rider in case she thinks he means a whole cricket ground and lags too far behind.

It is about a mile and a quarter from the stile across the moor to the boundary wall. At the pace Skelgill is setting he estimates it will take them twenty-five minutes. But is he being optimistic to think that the Irish couple have sited a third camera along this traversing route? Further on it curves northwards and rises towards the first line of grouse butts. It seems DS Jones is having a similar debate with herself. She calls out; her voice as hushed as is practicable.

'Guv – isn't it most likely they'll have hidden it in the stone wall near the other stile – where we've been parking on the track?'

He does not want to make a shouted conversation of it. He gives a wave that she probably cannot see. But her logic is reasonable. If the Irish were trying to monitor encroachments that threatened the harriers' nest, then these two stiles at either side of this narrow section of the moor are the key access points, from west and east, Shuteham Hall and the public bridleway respectively. From the south there is only impenetrable marshy fen that borders Over Water, and from the north energy-sapping heather, almost impossible to walk any distance through.

As he marches steadily his eyes flick continually to the horizon in the northeast – there is no doubt that the familiar skyline of Skiddaw is becoming more sharply delineated from the paler, milky glow in the heavens above. He assumes these night-vision cameras, in order to optimise the battery life, have a sensor that deactivates the infrared beam at a certain level of daylight. Time is running out – and as if he needed reminding a skylark strikes up – but not from overhead, as is the bird's daytime habit; instead the sound emanates from in front of him, at ground level. The creature must be perched, stretching its vocal chords in preparation for the dawn chorus proper, when larks and pipits and chats and other moorland species daily beat the bounds of their territories. But the trilling stops abruptly as he approaches – and then just as suddenly a cry breaks out from behind.

'A flash!'

Skelgill halts.

'What?'

DS Jones breaks into a jog and catches up with him.

'Guv – I saw a brief flash on the screen. Just fleeting.'

'Go back – we'll both go back. And I'll cover this stretch again. Watch more closely.'

'No, Guv – it was ahead of you – maybe about twenty paces.'

Skelgill reassesses the situation.

'Okay – you stop here. I'll walk on.'

They do as agreed. But Skelgill counts fifty paces and still there is no call from his colleague. He turns and begins slowly to walk back. The sky is lightening by the minute and the moor is becoming infused with a vaporous grey-brown twilight. Skelgill finds his eyes adjusting and he begins to comprehend the more detailed lie of the land. He recognises exactly where they are. He stops dead in his tracks. DS Jones is slowly approaching, still monitoring through the screen.

'There's nothing, Guv. It ought to be about here.'

'I'll tell you why, lass.' His stern demeanour cannot hide the undertone of expectancy in his voice. He directs his torch beam, which still has some limited effect. 'That's the little side path that goes towards the harriers' nest. This is where the mantrap was. This is where the SOCO crew have been coming and going. Look at the flattened vegetation. If there's a camera monitoring this spot – and why wouldn't there be? – our lot have probably worn the batteries flat – triggering it every few minutes. The flash you saw was it – on its last legs.'

DS Jones rises up onto the balls of her feet, as though Skelgill's excitement has been transmitted to her through the peaty earth.

'It must be close, Guv – but what set it off?'

They stand and look about, turning slowly in unison. But the conditions do not favour the task – it is too dull still to see clearly, but too light for Skelgill's torch to be of much help. Then he has an idea.

'Happen it were the bird.'

'Sorry, Guv?'

'That skylark that were singing – I bet it triggered it. Look!'

With his faltering torch beam he picks out a short, stout wooden post, barely protruding from the heather, part-decayed and tilted at an angle, the crumbling top flecked white with bird droppings. He has noticed it before – and unthinkingly assumed it acted as a marker to show where the almost invisible access path to the webcam begins. He pockets his torch and strides across – and heaves the post out of the ground. As he does so a fragment of wood flakes away – and there is revealed the third camera. He looks across at DS Jones – she is staring at him open mouthed, and for once he reciprocates.

*

'Don't tell me it's out of charge, as well.'

'No – it's alright, Guv – I think it's just a bit cold – I've got a USB lead, in case.'

But with a little musical flourish the laptop springs into life. DS Jones, wearing protective gloves, inserts the memory card from the last found camera into a slot on the side of her device. For practical purposes she is sitting in the passenger seat of her car, Skelgill leaning over from the driver's side.

'Ah – excellent.'

'What?'

'My photos app – it's reading the card – look – I'll just import all the files – it will only take a minute and then we can interrogate them by their chronology. Also, we get a back-up copy.'

As far as Skelgill can see not a lot seems to be happening on the computer screen. One by one icons are popping up as the individual files load. He sits straight for a moment and takes hold of the steering wheel. He realises he is cramped and fumbles around beneath the seat until he locates the release catch, and slides back to the position of maximum leg extension. Then he starts fiddling with various controls, experimenting as to what they might be. He adjusts the rear-view mirror – but ducks away as the rising sun dazzles him. He tries the electric door-mirrors – she has them angled too low in his book, but then he does not have smart alloys to worry about. When DS Jones does not complain that he is messing up all her settings (he would be agitated), perhaps this point strikes him and he turns to see she is staring at the screen, her fingers splayed in mid-air like a concert pianist waiting for the conductor's cue.

'What is it?'

'Guv – there's a three-minute sequence recorded at twelve-forty a.m. on Tuesday.'

'That's when I got into my car, at the hide.'

'This must be it.'

'Can you play it?'

'Let's see if it works.'

She double-clicks on the highlighted icon and suddenly the whole screen becomes filled by a night scene that opens with instant action.

From along the path a ghostly figure moves towards the camera, now about fifteen feet away, and just entering the limits of the infrared illumination.

There is a sharp mechanical noise.

Then a guttural yell – a male voice.

The man half-rotates and collapses upon his back, head closest to the camera.

He begins to writhe and cry out in agony.

295

He attempts to sit up and reach for his feet.

He falls back groaning.

He tries again, several times, with the same result.

Raised on one elbow, he starts to shout.

"Help! Help!"

The Scots voice is now recognisable.

Perhaps a minute passes.

Then suddenly – a newcomer! Two!

They arrive from off-camera, passing close at waist height, gradually revealed at full length as they approach the prone man.

The image is too grainy to tell at once who they are; they seem to be wearing close-fitting beanie hats, and gloves.

But what is clear is that they simply stand and gaze down at him.

One of them directs a torch into his face.

He jerks into life.

"Thank God – help me out of here!"

They do nothing.

They continue to stand and stare.

The man's appeals become imbued with panic.

The onlooker without the torch moves to the right.

The person picks up the shotgun.

The man on the ground: "What are you doing?"

There is no reply.

The figure with the gun moves back into position at the man's head.

The other with the torch directs the beam onto the man's lower limbs.

The first bends over the prone man, extending the gun.

The man on the ground: "No!"

There is a simultaneous crack and muzzle flash.

The man jolts.

He cries out, consumed by agony.

But his voice subsides; it becomes a low tormented keening.

The figure with the gun steps back to the right and lays it down, out of reach.

Both figures now converge on the left of the man.

They look down at him – their heads bowed rather like mourners at an interment.

They turn away in unison and begin to walk back towards the camera.

Again they are indistinguishable.

As they come close only their midriffs are visible.

But, just as they pass – a voice, female.

"A cold-blooded killing, Neil."

*

'Guv – I hear a car!'

'Aye – it's them. Hold still.'

'I'll start filming now.'

'Alreet.'

Skelgill has the bit between his teeth. His colleague can feel the tension in his body as he crouches close beside her. He is like a coiled spring. For her part, her heart is racing; she hopes she can hold her mobile steady. With her free hand she presses a Bluetooth earbud into place.

'Lima, this is Juliet, are you reading me, over?' She listens for a reply. 'They're here. Wait for the word "go" – we want to give them as long as we can – to see how they behave around the Ford. Stay on the line. If I lose you I'll yell.'

Skelgill glances at his sergeant. She is right at his shoulder, touching him. She seems in control; he can smell a hint of some perfume, and also perhaps perspiration – although that could be his own – and there is the sickly sweet stench of the may – for they are concealed in the hawthorn hedge, close to the parked Ford Consul. They have replaced the hosepipe. There is nothing they can do about the smashed driver-side window – but it will not be immediately apparent from the probable direction of approach.

The time is just before seven a.m. The crunch of tyres on the loose gravel of the track becomes louder; does Skelgill imagine it, or is the driving tentative? The Volvo lumbers into sight and then swings away, to park some thirty or forty feet off.

297

Interesting. There seems quite a long pause, a hiatus, between the switching off of the engine and the opening of a door – doors plural – for the Vholes twins emerge simultaneously.

Skelgill has a good view. He keeps his fingers crossed that the dense foliage and the still-low sun rising behind the hedge will hinder critical scrutiny of their position. The birdwatchers watched. He sees that they are dressed in outdoor gear – but not the spanking brand new outfits in which they appeared at police headquarters to lodge their complaint about the buzzard; this is older attire. The Vholes do not speak but converge at the rear of the Volvo and begin to walk together, steadily, but with a distinct attitude of caution. They make a beeline not in the direction of the hide but diagonally towards the parked Ford Consul.

'Should I check the hide, Christine?'

'There would be a car, Neil.' (Skelgill feels a chill run down his spine at the sound of her voice; though it does not quite carry the incomprehensible malevolence of her sinister phrase, twice uttered.) 'And there would be police if anyone had raised the alarm.'

'The engine has died. What if there wasn't enough fuel?'

'There was a quarter of a tank, Neil – do you think I wouldn't have checked?'

'Of course, Christine.'

'Besides, it only takes ninety minutes to kill.'

The Vholes stop short of the Ford, perhaps nine or ten feet away from the tailgate; not close enough yet to see within.

'Remember what to do, Neil.'

'Yes Christine. We both look in the rear window – put our hands naturally on the glass. You pull the hose away. I use a rock to smash in and get the key. We drag them out.'

Silence.

'And most important, Neil?'

'Oh, yes – of course, Christine. You search the bodies – I put on my gloves and search the car. As soon as we find the memory cards or the empty cases you call 999.'

'THERE'S NO NEED TO CALL 999.'

Skelgill breaks out of the bushes. His voice is authoritative, stentorian and – yes – triumphant. Any such intervention would be a dramatic enough shock for the Vholes – but the sight of the craggy detective, seemingly inured to the thorns, a creamy confetti of fine blossom spangling his unkempt hair must seem like a moment from their own worst nightmare.

They panic and begin to turn towards their car – it seems like in slow motion. In contrast, like a speeded-up scene from the Keystone Cops, the door of the birdwatching hide bursts open and a stream of uniformed officers tumbles out, led by DS Leyton (who is rapidly overtaken by the fitter, more sprightly constables). Simultaneously a large police van rumbles down the track from the lane, effectively blocking the only exit. DS Jones has given the word *go!*

15. SKY DANCING

Friday, late afternoon

S kelgill is engaged in a battle.
Seated at his desk, hands shielding his eyes from his surroundings, he is hunched over a letter printed on the headed paper of a prestigious firm of lawyers. Working around it, in no particular order (as is his wont) he has picked out certain salient phrases.

"... clients deny any involvement in the death of Mr Lawrence Melling ..."

"... entirely inconclusive video evidence ..."

"... defence of alibi ..."

"... CCTV clearly shows ... clients returned home at 10.50pm ... did not leave thereafter ..."

"... immediate release without charge ..."

"... invasion of privacy ... damage to reputation ... public apology ..."

'Here she comes now, Guv.'

DS Leyton stands sentry at the door of Skelgill's office, his head angled so that he can see along the corridor. Skelgill looks up, as though he has forgotten DS Leyton is there.

'Right – just sit down.'

DS Leyton remains resolutely in place, seemingly ignoring the request of his superior. But before Skelgill can complain he steps back to admit DS Jones and close the door behind her. Her tardy approach is now explained for she balances a heavily laden tray on top of her laptop computer and a stack of manila files.

'Never compete with the tea lady, Guv.'

DS Leyton winks at his superior.

DS Jones smiles brightly.

'The canteen were giving away the last of the treacle scones – they've been out of favour today.'

Now DS Leyton quips.

'That's because we've been up to our eyes in it – eh, Guvnor?'

Skelgill grins, but reluctantly. Like all of them, he still looks tired from lack of sleep over the past forty-eight hours. But despite the evident setback he is undoubtedly sidetracked by the contents of the tray. He waits rather grim faced as DS Jones dispenses the refreshments. When she is ready and seated he hands her the letter.

'Leyton just brought this down from the Chief.'

DS Jones looks first inquisitive but her expression quickly changes to one of alarm as she digests the contents of the missive. She stares at the page for a moment – but then she begins defiantly to address her colleagues.

'Wait a minute. If we've had them in custody since yesterday morning – and they weren't expecting to be arrested – how do they know their home security camera recorded their car arriving when they claim?'

There is a silence – perhaps even a stunned silence. Certainly DS Leyton is looking gobsmacked. A light dawns in his eyes.

'They knew they'd need an alibi!'

DS Jones is nodding vehemently.

Skelgill reaches over and puts out a hand, indicating he wants the letter. When DS Jones passes it to him he crumples it in his palm and aims it at the waste bin behind the door. The 'ball', however is imperfectly formed and travels in a curve – but DS Leyton instinctively jerks forward and heads it into the bin.

'*Hah!* Let's hope that's not an own goal, Guv!'

'Leyton – it's all piss and wind. We know it is.'

DS Leyton seems distracted by his moment of glory – but when he recovers he adds a note of sobriety.

'Mind you, the Chief doesn't quite seem to see it like that, Guv.'

Skelgill regards his colleagues sternly.

'But we were there – all through this. Not sitting in an ivory tower watching a wind sock.' Despite his custom-made metaphor his subordinates recognise the belligerence in his tone and they both nod resolutely. Skelgill casts a hand dismissively in the direction of the waste bin. 'We can't let that knock us off our stride.'

Accordingly he tucks into his scone – an oversized bite even by his standards that seems to signify that an army marches on its stomach, and now is the precursor to marching. His troops follow his lead.

'Have we even had lunch?'

Both eating hungrily, his colleagues simultaneously shake their heads – as if to reassure Skelgill that *they* have not, and that surely *he* has not – despite that they must both think it is unlikely that he has failed to cram in a Cumberland sausage sandwich or a bacon roll somewhere along the line.

DS Leyton finishes his scone and considers the remainder on the tray. He seems in two minds, and Skelgill identifies the opportunity.

'Leyton – you kick off.'

DS Leyton licks his fingers and rubs his palms along his thighs. He glances at DS Jones, acknowledging her situation as a latecomer.

'Well – I've just come from interviewing Stan again. The interpreter bothered his backside to turn up this time – but to be honest Stan speaks English well enough – at least, he understands – even if he can't always find the right words.'

'I know the feeling.'

Skelgill's subordinates grin obligingly. DS Leyton continues.

'In a nutshell, it seems quite straightforward. His background is in agricultural engineering – he got a qualification from an institution in Chisinau. His old college is twinned with Caldbeck Agricultural College here in Cumbria. They have this scheme – for *alumni* – they call 'em – right?' He looks a little apprehensively at DS Jones – whom he knows will know this sort of thing. She nods reassuringly. 'That enabled him to apply for an overseas student working visa – and Caldbeck College put him onto the vacancy at Shuteham Hall.'

'Christine Vholes.'

Skelgill is looking penetratingly at his sergeant.

'I reckon so, Guv.'

Skelgill gazes up to the ceiling – in lieu of the heavens being visible. He is reproaching himself for missing the obvious – that Christine Vholes' position gave her access to the 'unrivalled' database of shooting estate contacts he had read about while kicking his heels in reception. But then he reconciles himself to the possibility that the point *had* sunk in – and that it contributed to the unease that took him to the bird hide in the early hours. He nods to DS Leyton – to indicate that he should continue.

'Then he reckons, some time later – out of the blue – he started getting these emails from this Rapture group. He didn't know who they were, and ignored them in the first place. But there were suggestions of easy money to be made for what just seemed like conservation work. Reporting on wildlife sightings. In the end he signed up and started submitting observations – some money was paid into his account. All seemed hunky dory. Then gradually the requests for information began to shift to include examples of wildlife crime. Again – that didn't seem too unreasonable – but next thing he knows they're asking for specific information on Lawrence Melling. Not just his gamekeeping, but also his relationships with the landowners and other employees. Stan was a bit uneasy at this point – but he began to provide some details – nothing too controversial – he wasn't aware of anything particularly unsavoury – but he did report that Melling wasn't popular and bullied the other workers. Then the demands came to find out about his private life.' DS Leyton raises his eyebrows suggestively and glances between his colleagues. 'Stan says he wanted to draw the line here – and he told them so – and it was at this point that he started receiving threats himself.'

Skelgill shifts position, straightening in his chair.

'What kind of threats?'

'Well – we're talking blackmail, really, Guv. It was suggested that if he didn't come up with the goods, the authorities would be informed of what he'd been up to – and his visa would likely be revoked. By now, he's got himself romantically involved with the housekeeper – Karen Williamson – although they were keeping that under wraps. But, of course he didn't want to get sent back home to Moldova. So he felt he had no choice but to carry on. At the end of the day, he wasn't actually doing anything illegal – just dangerous, as it turned out.'

Skelgill is nodding pensively; DS Jones looks more alarmed. DS Leyton seems to be seeking a diplomatic form of words.

'He'd worked out that Lawrence Melling was entertaining ladies – at night, using the boathouse – quite a swanky little love nest designed for guests of the estate – and his brief from Rapture was to find out who the current female was – and if possible to get a compromising photograph. Obviously the suspicion was that it was Miranda Bullingdon – if so, that would be dynamite.'

He pauses and leans forward to take a drink of tea; his colleagues wait.

'You were right, Guv – he got himself a fishing rod – he admits he hasn't got a clue – but he figured it gave him an excuse to knock about by the lake. He says he would wander along each evening just as it was getting dark, keep out of sight, and watch the boathouse for lights coming on. To cut a long story short, on Saturday night – into the early hours of Sunday – there were people in there. He started by working his way round the bank, moving from one spot to another. Then he left his rod and climbed up onto the balcony. He'd got his phone out ready to take a photo – he could see there was a gap in the curtains – but what he didn't know was Melling's dog was on the balcony – and it set up a right racket, barking at him. Before he could get away, Melling came bursting out of the sliding doors and attacked him. There was a fight – more of a wrestle – and Melling being bigger was getting the better of him – trying to strangle him, almost choking him out – telling him in no uncertain terms he was going to kill him. Stan managed to break free and flip over the balcony. But he slipped on the sloping roof and went into the lake. He reckons he's a good swimmer but somehow he had the presence of mind to pretend he was drowning – coming up for gasps of air and calling for help. He reckons Melling got a torch on him and just watched him. He took a massive gulp of air and went down for what he hoped would look like the last time – and then swam underwater for as long as he could hold his breath. He came up under some bushes a good way off, and waited, trying to work out what to do. He heard the outside door of the boathouse open and close quite soon after – as if someone left – but he could see there were still lights on and a person moving about – including on the balcony for a while after that. Then the lights went off and presumably Melling left – and his torch showed he was searching round the bank in the other direction. That must be when he found the fishing rod. At that point Stan crept out and legged it to Karen Williamson's place. After that, his story ties up with what she told us.'

DS Jones has been listening avidly. Now she poses a question.

'Does he know what happened to his mobile phone?'

'He reckons Melling must have found it on the balcony and chucked it in the lake.'

A collective nod and perhaps even a sigh of relief travel around the room. It does all stack up – especially for Skelgill. Indeed, his sergeants see he is distracted. He rises and turns to gaze at the map of the Lake District on the wall behind his desk, though he stands too close to usefully read it. He is gripped by the thought – did Lawrence Melling think *he* was Stan – not dead after all, not giving up, back from the brink to haunt him? Or did he think he was another spy sent by Rapture – another dispensable foot soldier? Is that what prompted him to attempt summary revenge by blasting the harriers off their nest?

Skelgill turns and sits and reaches for another scone; they have an ample supply. After a mouthful and some tea he nods to DS Leyton – in a manner that is as close as he will normally get to acknowledging good work. But before Skelgill can move on, DS Leyton has a point to add.

'The blood, Guv – around the game preparation area and the incinerator?'

'Aye?'

'Innocent explanation, can you believe? Stan had been chopping a load of wood for Karen Williamson's cottage – cut his hand – lost quite a bit of blood – just bandaged it up himself with his neckerchief. He cleared it up with a pile of sawdust and shovelled that into the incinerator when he passed with the wheelbarrow.'

Skelgill nods broodingly, but does not comment.

'And there's us thinking poor geezer's gone up in smoke!'

Now Skelgill frowns more unfavourably, as though he does not share his colleague's view; but he keeps his opinion to himself. DS Leyton looks like he has finished his account, and decides he can manage a second scone. Rather philosophically, he adds a closing remark.

'Hard to see if either of them did too much wrong, Guv. Stan or Karen Williamson.'

Skelgill is asking himself whether events in the long term would have panned out differently had the couple come to the police after the first incident. Indeed, had he himself inadvertently played agent provocateur in round two? But it is the same type of conjecture that usually gets him nowhere (in fact, in the wrong place), and is futile now that history has been written. He turns to DS Jones and indicates with an upturned palm that she should begin.

She opens her laptop and places it on the corner of Skelgill's desk and angles it so that both her colleagues can see.

'I've watched every second of every film clip.' She blinks several times as if her toil has taken its toll on her eyesight. Then she glances wryly at Skelgill. 'That's a lot of badgers and roe deer and even the occasional fox. Despite the best efforts of the Terminator.'

Skelgill raises an eyebrow, and remains attentive.

'Obviously there's the final sequence on Over Moor – and other key points which I'll come back to – but just to join up the dots on Stan and Lawrence Melling. The files from the camera at Keeper's Cottage are the last ones that I've just been through. At around two-thirty a.m. on Sunday – in other words following the events in the account that Stan has given us, someone appeared at the rear of the property, over towards the log store. It's at the very limits of the camera's capability – it's not possible to identify the person. But you can see that they bury an item –

possibly a white polythene bag folded over on itself a few times – beneath a kind of freestanding tree stump.'

She plays the footage – it is as she has described. Skelgill's eyes are burning bright – but it is DS Leyton that utters what must be their common conclusion.

'The jewels!'

They all three exchange glances. DS Jones indicates to the screen.

'Whatever they are, they're probably still there. The camera records no one disturbing the stump.' She looks at Skelgill. 'Obviously – at least until we took away the camera.'

Skelgill is nodding, but he knows she has much to cover, and he indicates she should move on. She glances at the screen as though she is toying with showing another video, but then she has second thoughts and turns to her colleagues.

'Probably most significant are two events. At just after nine-forty p.m. on Monday a figure that I believe is Neil Vholes carried the mantrap and set it on the beaters' path, five or six paces to the west of the little side-path to the harriers' nest. He brought the trap from the easterly direction. They must have had it in their car – then he drove it round to the bridleway during their shift, due to finish at ten p.m. – before the Irish could arrive and see him from the hide in the last of the daylight.'

Skelgill picks up a chewed biro and draws an unintelligible hieroglyph on his desk pad – it might be a shamrock leaf – seemingly a reminder of some sort. DS Jones hesitates in case he intends to speak, but he nods for her to continue.

'Then at twelve-twenty-five a.m. – now Tuesday morning – Lawrence Melling skidded to a halt on the quad bike at the western stile, on the Shuteham Hall side of Over Moor. He had the dog with him, even though it doesn't appear in the subsequent sequence. He put on the cape and the hat, and took the shooting staff and the antique shotgun – all of which belong to Lord Bullingdon – and climbed over the stile. Fifteen minutes later he walked into the trap.'

She pauses, as though some respect is due, though her smooth features remain implacable.

'It seems the killers – we say the Vholes – were waiting quite close by – perhaps just on the other side of the wall, beside the eastern stile. I can show you these clips.'

But DS Leyton has a pressing question. For DS Jones's benefit he employs some moderating London vernacular.

'What the crispy duck was Melling doing dressed as Lord Bullingdon?'

Skelgill plies his colleague with a somewhat reproachful glare.

'He was going to blast the nest, Leyton.' He glances at DS Jones, acknowledging that she had made the very suggestion. 'Make it look like Lord Bullingdon did it. There's the official Nats webcam, remember – and Melling knew about it. You heard what he said that first time in the estate office. Since then we've learned all about the trail of destruction he leaves in his wake. But why take the rap when he could put old Bullingdon in the frame? Power to his elbow in more ways than one.'

DS Leyton nods reflectively.

'Looks like the Vholes saved his Lordship's bacon.'

Skelgill makes a somewhat disparaging harrumph. But it is a fact, albeit an unintended consequence. Now he picks up the narrative.

'I reckon they spotted the mantrap when they went on the Nats field trip organised by Daphne Bullingdon. Then they just drove in and took it on the same evening they used it. Reverse up to the front door – all you'd need is thirty seconds – take a chance on the car being seen – even that's unlikely. Neil Vholes planted the trap.' Skelgill gestures to DS Jones – referring to the video confirmation of this. 'They went back later to see if they'd caught owt. As it was, Melling was on the warpath – Rapture on his back, we're crawling about looking for the jewellery and for Stan – he loses the rag, charges off, not paying attention to where he puts his feet in the dark.'

Skelgill abruptly snaps his fingers, the sudden sharp click causing both of his subordinates to start. After a pause it is DS Jones that speaks.

'How are Ciara Ahearne and Cian Fogarty, Guv?'

It has been Skelgill's self-delegated task to visit them at the hospital. For her part, while DS Jones is itching to hear their account – for they may provide now-vital circumstantial evidence – her natural solicitude puts their welfare first. However, Skelgill deals with this in a somewhat convoluted manner.

'I tell you what.' He looks portentously at his colleagues, first DS Leyton, chewing ruminantly, resting his head against the filing cabinet beside his chair, and then at DS Jones; the afternoon sun slants between the tilted slats of the venetian blind and picks out the golden highlights of her hair. 'I don't reckon it were me that saved them.'

He waits – DS Leyton makes a kind of lurch forward, as though urging him to speak. After a gulp of tea, Skelgill obliges.

'I had a word with the forensic mechanic that's examined the Ford Consul. There's a material crack in the exhaust manifold, and the silencer's maggoty – badly corroded. He reckons most of the exhaust gases would never have made it to the tailpipe, especially if it were constricted. If anything saved them, it was that old rustbucket itself.' Now he turns back to address DS Jones. 'The medical report bears it out. While they suffered a degree of carbon monoxide poisoning, the main reason they were comatose was they'd been given sleeping tablets. I interviewed them both – Ciara – she's right as rain – the lad's still a bit dopey. They arrived back from Scotland just after midnight – so we're talking the early hours of yesterday – and the Vholes were in the hide – they hadn't arranged any cover after all. Christine Vholes made them some cocoa – and Neil Vholes talked them into going to bed – said he and Christine would finish the nightshift. The Irish were knackered from their journey – and feeling drowsier by the minute – so they bunked down in the back of their car. Next thing they woke up in the WCI.'

Skelgill finishes his drink and looks rather dejectedly into his mug. There is an optimum ratio of tea to treacle scones and there are still scones left. But he steels himself.

'Ciara Ahearne reckons she and the lad were operating off their own bat – nothing to do with Rapture – she hasn't heard of it – but that they definitely considered the harriers were facing an imminent threat. What she hadn't realised is that Cian had put the pair of *them* in mortal danger. They didn't clear off to Scotland without a word like the Vholes told us. He'd written them a note on the wipe-clean sightings board in the hide. It was as I'd suspected – they'd noticed a disturbance towards one o'clock – a possible shot fired. His message said the harriers were okay – but they might have recorded some activity. They – the Irish – would check when they got back. Obviously he didn't explain they'd got their own concealed cameras – but it was more than enough. The Vholes realised that there might be footage that would expose them.'

DS Jones is looking relieved.

'Thankfully we were ahead of the game on that score, Guv.'

DS Leyton is more effusive.

'It was a flippin' game-changer – you pair sniffing that out.'

Skelgill grins ruefully – but now he taps the leaf-like scrawl on his pad and looks at DS Jones.

'Your point about Neil Vholes setting the trap – Monday night. We've got corroboration of the timings. Ciara Ahearne reckons she and the lad turned up early for their shift. The Vholes' car wasn't there but Christine Vholes was in the hide. She looked flustered and told them Neil Vholes had needed to make an important phone call and had driven somewhere to get a better signal. They didn't think too much of it, and he came back a few minutes later. Obviously the Vholes were bricking themselves about this as well – because it would come out if we interviewed everyone. They must have pretty quickly realised they needed the Irish out of the picture – along with anything that would make us suspect and start searching for hidden recording devices – which is why they wanted the empty memory card cases. But in the short term the Irish chucked a spanner in the works by clearing off to Scotland.'

DS Jones distractedly brushes away a strand of hair that has fallen across her cheek.

'The Vholes didn't hang around, though, Guv.'

Skelgill looks at her rather intensely, before nodding slowly.

'Christine Vholes was preparing the ground for an apparent suicide when I went to interview her at her office – badmouthing the Irish for being into drugs, their unreliable behaviour – something I'd overheard her directly contradict the day before. She was at pains to make sure we weren't going to turn up on Wednesday night – offering me the chance to come along and help – and asking when I'd next be fishing. And she never so much as mentioned Lawrence Melling.'

Skelgill dunts his forehead with the heel of his hand.

'I'm kicking myself, now – the straws in the wind, little inconsistencies from the Vholes. All I know is the more I saw them the less I trusted them.' He pauses to look at DS Jones. 'You asked why did I go there – to the hide in the middle of the night? Maybe that was it. When I think back to speaking with Neil Vholes on Tuesday morning – he knew Melling was the keeper. He was trying to push the idea of it being an accident – Melling falling into his own trap – and yet he talked about treating it as a crime scene. Then there was the nonsense about the working cocker. For a start – I doubt he could see the dog from the hide – but he knew Melling's body was there – and he knew the way. I reckon Vholes went to check Melling was dead – not to retrieve what he claimed was some random dog disturbing the harriers.'

Skelgill bangs his desk with the side of his closed fist.

'We can't let some gasbag of a lawyer and their high-and-mighty contacts get them out of this.'

He glares fiercely at DS Leyton.

'What's the delay with the forensics on the trap and the gun?'

DS Leyton looks a little dismayed.

'I rang them earlier, Guv – truth be told, they've been having trouble getting anything. Like those videos show, the Vholes – if it was them – they were wearing gloves and looked like they knew what they were doing.'

'*It was the Vholes, Leyton* – don't even doubt it for a second.'

DS Leyton nods a little shamefacedly and takes out his mobile phone – as if in the faint hope that there has been a message.

'Stone me!'

'What is it?'

'I've had the flippin' thing on silent, Guv – didn't feel the text come through – too much padding.' When he might make something of his joke, instead his focus sharpens upon the screen of his handset. 'This is actually from the forensic officer – the girl we met by the lake. They're searching the Vholes' house. The Chief's obviously not pulled them off the job – *and listen to this.*'

He reads aloud:

' "While checking outbuildings – neighbour mentioned separate garage – in block of four in lane accessed by gate at foot of rear garden. Heavy-duty locks breached. Items found include nearly new male and female outdoor clothing with positive traces of blood on footwear and trousers. Reel of hosepipe with missing section, pattern matches hose used on Ford Consul." '

Now DS Leyton's eyes widen and he swallows, as though a lump has risen in his throat – but it is the double fist-pump that tells his colleagues the best is yet to come.

' "Registered in the name of Christine Vholes, two-year-old VW Golf, yellow." '

He stares excitedly at Skelgill.

'Guv – they must have gone home in the Volvo – parked under the security camera – and sneaked out the back and returned in the Golf – you *did* see a flamin' yellow motor!'

He raises his phone and shakes it triumphantly.

'And I bet they used it to steal the trap. Anyone noticing it from a distance would just think it was the estate's pool car.'

A movement to Skelgill's right causes him to turn to see that DS Jones is silently celebrating as though England have scored a last-minute winner against Germany – and he too feels a welling up of emotion that has some equivalence. He senses that his eyes are stinging – but he fights back the elation, deciding that action is the best cure. He rises to his feet and reaches for his keys and steps across towards the door. As he opens it he places a palm on his sergeant's broad shoulder.

'Leyton – have a proper conversation with Forensics. Put into motion whatever you think needs done. Then get yourself an early night.'

DS Leyton looks at once surprised and grateful.

'Actually, Guv – after last night's palaver I promised the missus a takeaway of her choosing – what with it being Friday, an' all. She'll be on cloud nine if I turn up on time.'

'And stick it on your expenses – I'll deal with the Chief.'

DS Leyton grins conspiratorially.

'Where are you off to, Guv?'

'Happen I'd better find out what's buried at Keeper's Cottage – before someone else beats us to it. Just as well Julian Bullingdon's got a moth trap and not a metal detector – I reckon Stan's not the only one who's been keeping an eye on certain persons' nocturnal adventures.' He grins wryly. 'Then I thought I might kill two birds with one stone – I've got a long overdue appointment with a non-existent fish.'

DS Jones springs to her feet.

'I'll come with you, Guv.'

When she might employ a questioning inflection, she does nothing of the sort; assertive would be closer to the mark. She makes brief eye contact with her boss before smiling at DS Leyton and slipping past both him and Skelgill. 'I'll log off and meet you in the car park.'

*

'Ah – your delightful assistant. I somehow imagined you would come alone, Inspector.'

'I need a reliable witness for what I have to do this evening, madam.'

Miranda Bullingdon steps back to admit Skelgill and DS Jones. Skelgill notices her scrutiny is drawn to his colleague – while DS Jones in turn is unable to prevent her gaze from wandering about the expansive, luxurious surroundings.

Miranda Bullingdon looks like she has just emerged from the shower. She is wearing a brilliant white towelling robe that

313

contrasts with her tanned skin and her hair is damp and dishevelled. Skelgill looks around. The boudoir is not entirely suited to what he has in mind. Miranda Bullingdon crosses one foot over the other, and tilts her head to one side, regarding him with her characteristic blend of innocence and amusement. Skelgill is carrying in one hand a somewhat soiled polythene bag.

'Mind if we use your bed, madam?'

Now she smiles casually, as if this were a familiar question.

'It is at your disposal, Inspector.'

The four-poster is a raised divan, mid-thigh-high and Skelgill does not need to bend over to empty, judiciously, the contents of the bag onto the quilted silk counterpane. But despite his best efforts, small fragments of leaf litter fall amongst the glittering ensemble.

'These appear to meet the description of your missing items, madam.'

Whatever reaction he is expecting – and perhaps he has learned not to expect the expected when it comes to Miranda Bullingdon – she still contrives to surprise him.

'Ah – and where had my little darling Teddy Bear hidden them?'

*

'Sure you're up for this? It could be a long boring wait.'

'Then you need me to keep you awake, Guv. Just tell me if I talk too much.'

Skelgill, rowing vigorously, is unable to shrug as he would naturally do – and instead pulls a kind of agonised face, at once indifferent and appreciative. After a short while, DS Jones harks back to the case.

'What do you think prompted the Vholes to go to such extremes, Guv?'

'Aside from insanity?'

She smiles patiently; though they both must feel that there is some truth in his jest. Skelgill feathers his oars and holds them still in mid air. He needs a moment to recover his breath.

'For all we know it's not extreme for them – there might be a catalogue of sporting 'accidents' that need looked into. Christine Vholes' position gave her access to the name and address of just about every keeper in the country. Okay – Melling was obviously a particularly nasty piece of work – and if the Vholes are behind Rapture, they've been on his case for a while. He destroyed the golden eagles' nest in the Borders – so they put paid to his job there. Then he turns up like a bad penny to threaten the rarest birds in Cumbria, right in the Vholes' own back yard. They'd found his Achilles heel – so they put the same plan into motion. But suddenly their mole – Stan – goes missing – presumed dead. So they see red and take matters into their own hands. Meanwhile Melling's up to his old tricks – but he's also feeling the pressure of the persecution – he probably wasn't thinking straight, either. Looks like the two pots came to a boil on the same night.'

DS Jones has listened pensively.

'Do you think they planned to kill him – or, just –?'

'Give him a taste of his own medicine?' Skelgill completes the sentence. 'Here's what it feels like to be caught in a pole trap.'

DS Jones nods reflectively. They both know this is unlikely to be something they will find out. But now a lighter, inquisitive note enters her voice.

'Does Miranda Bullingdon always give interviews in her bedroom, Guv?'

Skelgill grins.

'Happen it's all part of her modus operandi.'

'You mentioned Julian Bullingdon – do you seriously think he knew what was going on – that he was on the trail of the jewellery?'

Skelgill shrugs – as if he is not too worried about this point.

'I reckon he could do with the windfall, for his nature projects – given his old man won't put his hand in his pocket.'

DS Jones nods reflectively. She decides to reserve judgement on Julian Bullingdon.

'What did you think – about what she said – it being her husband? She didn't want to explain why.'

Skelgill chuckles ironically.

'Like I said before, it's her golden rule. Don't tell what you don't need to.'

'Yet she named him. It sounded ridiculous that he would take the jewellery – but, when you think about it, it could have been true. I mean – to take it, knowing they'd been meeting in the boathouse – and to bury it near Keeper's Cottage. When it came to light, it would have looked like Lawrence Melling was the thief – it provided the perfect excuse to dismiss him.'

Skelgill makes a face that expresses some ambivalence.

'On Saturday night they'd got back late from the hunt ball. She'd probably had her fill of champagne. I reckon she lit a candle in her window as a signal when she could meet. That came pretty quick – Melling had probably watched them arrive. She slipped out the scullery door and left it on the sneck. The boathouse is just a couple of minutes across the big lawn. When the you-know-what hit the fan, she made a hasty retreat. Probably forgot she'd even been wearing the stuff. Easy pickings. Perfect cover.'

'Yet it didn't stop her returning – either of them – two nights later?'

But Skelgill turns the question back on her.

'Are you surprised?'

DS Jones briefly closes her eyes as if in contemplation of her answer, her long fair lashes suddenly more noticeable.

'I suppose – when you consider that Presidents have risked their Presidencies for it.'

Skelgill seems to suppress a sigh; it is a moment before he responds.

'But I reckon she's relieved that's him gone.'

'Lawrence Melling?'

'Aye.' He gazes rather pensively across the surface of Over Water. 'The whole lot of them probably are, despite the manner of it. The job done by outsiders – they can get back to playing happy families.'

316

There would be a temptation for Skelgill to imbue these words with sarcasm – but for whatever reason he does not feel the need to do so. After another silence, DS Jones looks at him questioningly. Now Skelgill grins in a rather boyish manner.

'But – coming back to the jewellery – happen it's just as well we can't identify anyone that's on that first camera – apart from my ugly mug when I took that birdbox down!'

DS Jones correctly reads into his change of tenor something of a desire for a relaxing of confidences. She concludes she might just as well push her luck.

'Guv – on the subject of people being in the wrong place at the wrong time – did you happen to think the yellow car you saw was mine?'

Skelgill is caught unawares, and colour rises to his cheeks. But, rather than deny it, he makes an oblique admission.

'I suppose you might have been doing a bit of sleuthing on the side.'

DS Jones gives an affronted gasp – she regards him with mock reproach.

'Now where would I have got the idea that that was a good thing?'

Skelgill responds with a peculiar facial expression, but certainly one that is part sheepish. He indicates with a twist of his head their surroundings generally.

'What detective worth their salt, finding themselves on the spot, isn't going to let their curiosity get the better of them?'

DS Jones chuckles; now she is in full flow.

'I don't suppose you saw Miranda Bullingdon throw Lawrence Melling's boxer shorts into that lake, did you?'

Skelgill splutters.

'I wouldn't quite go that far, lass – I'm just putting two and two together. It would be a quick way of removing any evidence of shenanigans in the boathouse.'

DS Jones smiles knowingly.

'Well, I guess we know she's never going to admit it.'

'Just like no one's going to admit to shooting that buzzard – it's another little unsolved mystery.'

317

'But, Guv – surely that was Lawrence Melling?'

Skelgill looks at her, severely for a moment, and then a rather cryptic grin spreads across his face.

'That's not where my money would be.'

'Well – who, then?'

'I think we're in agreement that a good handful of folk would like to have seen the back of Lawrence Melling.' (DS Jones nods.) 'But if I had to guess who shot the buzzard it's a toss up between Jack Carlops and Daphne Bullingdon. I'd say they both had it in mind to find a way to reverse a bad recruitment decision. While Rapture prefers to catch a keeper with his pants down – the good old fashioned method is to shoot his fox.'

Though the idiom may not be entirely apposite, his colleague understands his meaning – but suddenly she cries out in alarm.

'Guv!'

She is pointing behind him.

'Whoa!'

Skelgill's reaction is due to the fact he has not been concentrating and he suddenly realises they are drifting perilously close to Over Water's wooded western shore, specifically the half-sunken alder he has been using as a mark; he backs the oars furiously to turn and hold the craft. The action seems to bring to an end the business aspect of their conversation. And now DS Jones refers to their present mission.

'What makes you think tonight's the night, Guv? Is it the weather?'

She glances about; it is a sublime evening, the sun has set but twilight is still half an hour away and from a perch at the edge of Bullmire Wood a blackbird serenades them with its liquid melody.

'Ground bait.'

DS Jones frowns perplexedly.

'That sounds like something the rat catcher puts down.'

'It's an angling method. You pre-bait your swim.'

Now she plies him with a look to show she is no less confounded.

'A swim – it's the place you fish – a specific patch of water – maybe an inlet or a shady spot or a deeper section. You go in advance and chuck in some ground bait. It's called that because it sinks to the bottom. The fish find it and like all animals they'll return to a place they've found food.'

'Ah – so you've pre-baited a swim?'

Now Skelgill looks a little conflicted.

'Not exactly.' He indicates with a sweep of his arm towards the protruding alder. 'I scopped a box of maggots overboard on Monday night. They were ready to pupate.'

'So what makes you think it will work for vendace?'

Skelgill opens his mouth to speak – but he realises he is about to say that he dreamt it – and he finds himself having to formulate another explanation.

'It basically comes down to a lack of a Plan B.'

DS Jones giggles – his artless admission is endearing, especially coming from him.

'Maybe I'll bring you luck, Guv – remember that time with the pike?'

While they have been talking Skelgill has dropped anchor and now has nylon line gripped between his lips and cannot answer other than nod. DS Jones watches with a certain fascinated dismay as he deftly hooks a maggot and flicks it overboard. He leans and grabs a handful from the writhing box of larvae and tosses them into the water, creating a little rain-like splatter around his bright orange float.

DS Jones appreciates that the silence that ensues is what is called for – and indeed they both begin to enjoy the tranquillity, and the simple beauty of their surroundings – albeit that Skelgill clearly has a renewed weight of expectation on his shoulders. Several minutes must have passed when DS Jones whispers urgently.

'Guv, your float – it's moving.'

Skelgill curses under his breath.

'I know – don't worry.'

'What's the problem?'

'It's a perch. I can tell from the bite.'

319

'Shouldn't you do something?'

Skelgill does not answer – but she sees that his demeanour subtly changes – he watches intently, not blinking – in fact as though despite his words he is actually seeing something that is now unfamiliar. He sits totally still, except for his right hand, which slowly winds the reel, taking up the slack in the line on the surface. Then without warning he strikes. It is not a hard strike – just a flick of his left wrist – and then he is reeling in more quickly, adjusting the rod to keep pressure on the line. There is no doubt now that he is perplexed – his eyes fixed like green lasers upon the point where the line enters the water – and he reaches without looking for his landing net and adroitly dips it beneath the swirl at the surface. He pulls in the net; his expression is agog.

A small slender silvery fish flaps half-heartedly.

'What is it, Guv?'

'A vendace.'

'Wow!' DS Jones pulls her mobile phone from her hip pocket. 'I'll get a photo.'

Skelgill seems to be speechless – it is a far stronger reaction than when they unearthed the six-figure sum of jewellery at the rear of Keeper's Cottage earlier. But he carefully unhooks the fish and in a practised manner presents it to facilitate the shot, holding a rusty steel ruler alongside for size comparison. DS Jones satisfies herself that she has captured the image – but Skelgill continues to stare at the unremarkable specimen.

'Hadn't you better put it back, Guv?'

Skelgill looks up at her, his expression suddenly alarmed.

'George wants to know what they taste like.'

DS Jones looks shocked.

But now Skelgill grins.

'I'll make something up.'

He lifts the fish and gently dunks it overboard, and relaxes his grip. DS Jones leans to watch. The creature takes a moment to orientate itself, and then, with a parting splash, is gone. Skelgill rinses his hands and wipes them on a rather disreputable-looking square of frayed towel.

'You've done it, Guv!'

Skelgill looks uncharacteristically unassuming. He shakes his head.

'Aye – vendace in Over Water – who'd have thought.'

Rather absently he begins to weigh anchor, hauling in the dripping wet blue nylon rope, a fathom at a time. DS Jones seems surprised.

'Are we going?'

Skelgill gives her a strange look, suddenly severe.

'You don't think I do this for fun, do you?' But again he breaks into a grin. 'There's times when you have to get your priorities right.'

DS Jones smiles, but does not otherwise answer; she settles back against the stern, to the limited extent that comfort is possible in anything to do with Skelgill. He adjusts the position of his fishing rod so that it runs the length of the boat, sticking out over the prow and not obstructing the oars. He turns the craft and sets a course for the slipway. DS Jones, opposite him and thus facing the direction of travel, suddenly exclaims.

'Oh, look – sky dancing!'

'What?'

Skelgill cranes around to see.

'It's the harriers – they're on the wing. The girls in the hide must be getting a fantastic view. I just saw the male pass food to the female in mid-flight. I was reading about it. They call it sky dancing. He does it to impress her!'

'Like I say, lass – get your priorities right.'

Skelgill puts his back into his oars. He has not forgotten his old schoolmate and now landlord Graham Bush's open invitation of dinner for two at the nearby Overthwaite Arms.

***

Next in the series ...

NO BODY

Nobody saw her. Nobody can find her.

When 37-year-old Lisa Jackson sets out for work one Friday morning she is in high spirits. Things are going well with her new boyfriend. But when she does not reach her desk, or answer her mobile phone, her colleagues and family raise the alarm.

Suspicion immediately falls on co-worker Ray Piper. A married man, he and Lisa have recently ended an affair. But steely-eyed Piper denies any knowledge of Lisa's disappearance.

Yet as the police begin to piece together her last movements – and match them to those of her ex-lover – a narrative emerges that leads to only one possible conclusion.

With Skelgill and DS Leyton otherwise engaged, it falls to DS Emma Jones to head the investigation – a chance for the bright young detective to shine. But soon she finds herself engaged in a deadly battle of wits with a cold and calculating adversary.

Will she hold her nerve? Will she succeed alone? And what will happen if she does not find Lisa – for *no body* undermines her case.

As the trial date nears, hopes begin to fade – Lisa is gone without trace. And a scheming killer may walk free.

'Murder Unseen' by Bruce Beckham is available from Amazon

Printed in Great Britain
by Amazon